I0743045

By Sally Brandle

Novels

The Hitman's Mistake

Torn by Vengeance

The Targeted Pawn

Enhanced Memoir

Sapphire Promise

TORN BY VENGEANCE

Love Thrives in Emma Springs, Book 2

SALLY BRANDLE

COPPER HORSE PUBLISHING

SECOND EDITION

SALLY BRANDLE

Cover Design by Syneca Featherstone

Photo by Shannon Mulqueen of Blue Raven Photography

Published in the United States of America by
Copper Horse Publishing

ISBN: 978-1-944232-08-5

To Brian, Mark, and Neil, who

believe in my writing success.

Thank you for your faithful encouragement and

gifts of dark chocolate.

Love, Sally

Acknowledgments

The Hitman's Mistake, my first book, received comments from many beta readers before it landed in the capable hands of my editor. While friends read, I continued to write five more books in the Love Thrives in Emma Springs series. None of them included Kyle and Corrin's story until my dental hygienist finished *Hitman* and demanded to know their happily-ever-after.

Talented authors, editors, and friends have helped craft this story. Many thanks to Jodi Ashland, Susan Wachtman, Christine Lamb, Kent and Lynette Allen, Becky Oosting, and editors Dana Delamar, CJ Obray, Bethany Douglass, and Elisa Page.

Special gratitude to the original publisher, Soul Mate Publishing, and especially editor Sharon Roe, for her continued patience and dedication.

A huge shout out to Cobh Rescue Horses. Our equine cover model's Facebook page is: CRH Peanut and Pixie – Rescue Ponies. Many thanks to Oonagh O'Brien for her great care of these little ponies and Shannon Mulqueen of Blue Raven Photography for wonderful photos.

NOTE: The fictional incident Corrin experienced in a boat is based loosely on a frightening scenario from the author's young teen years, which time never erased.

CHAPTER 1

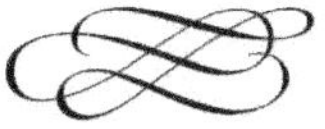

H.P. slid to the edge of the wingback chair, chafing to slip a figurative noose over Corrin Patten's neck. Revenge was so close he could taste it. He glanced at the over-polished expanse of desk separating him from the head crony of the law firm. *Convince or control?* "Is the agreement ready?" he challenged.

"I reviewed it this afternoon." Meyer tilted forward in his old-fart, padded desk chair. "The partners of Meyer, Fitch, and Brine are honored to represent your legal needs, Mr. Piersall."

"Call me H.P. The succession plan for Piersall Enterprises grants me total authority. Board approval is a formality."

Meyer adjusted the framed photo at his elbow of a skinny woman posed beside two kids. "We were saddened to hear of your father's stroke and hope for his full recovery."

His old man would never have considered severing ties from the family's current law firm. "I assumed Chap Brine would be my contact. My projects require someone I know and trust."

"I handle the contracts for all our clients. Is that a problem?"

Damn. He didn't want prying eyes questioning every move he made, unlike scatterbrained Brine. "It shouldn't be a problem."

"Great." Meyer handed him a Montblanc pen. "You're wearing an unusual ring. An heirloom?"

The old coot's vision remained sharp, maybe too sharp. He angled the three-carat ruby to reflect light. Meyer needed a warning. "The dagger represents our family motto to go for the throat in business dealings." He locked eyes with the holier-than-thou senior partner.

"Figuratively speaking." Meyer stared back, then blinked. The geezer's lips tightened, but he hadn't flinched.

"Whatever completes the job," H.P. snapped.

Meyer cleared his throat. "My staff will put in the hours necessary to handle your legal issues."

And each minute billed would be well worth the exorbitant price. "I expect irrefutable results, not promises."

"We take pride in our distinguished list of clients."

Total bull. The old man knew it took money to run alongside the big dogs, nothing more.

The distinct sound of a door shutting echoed from the hall. Steps approached.

H.P. jumped to his feet and clicked the office door closed. Anger rose in his chest. "You assured me by ten on a Wednesday night, we'd be alone," he hissed, stepping back from the half-glass wall of Meyer's office, giving them a one-way view from their side of the mirrored glass to the hallway.

Corrin Patten walked by, the essence of pretty privilege on parade.

H.P.'s heartbeat pounded double time in his tight chest. He took in the aren't-I-the-picture-of-innocence face and big rack.

The elevator bell chimed, and she disappeared into the empty car.

Soon, she'd be begging for mercy. He fought to control the anger gnawing at his gut. "Corrin Patten works late."

"Yes, I noticed you've requested her assistance. Someone recommended her?" Meyer probed.

"Something like that." He squeezed the expensive pen until the imprints of the etched letters pressed into his thumb.

"I see." Meyer slid out typed papers from a file folder. "Your signature on the representation contract moves us forward."

"I'm ready to get started."

Hesitation rimmed Meyer's watery blue eyes. He painstakingly removed the binder clip on the cover sheet. "Do you have questions before signing?" he asked.

"No. I expect your crew to be ready at a moment's notice for any required action."

"We'll promptly employ necessary legal actions," Meyer repeated.

H.P. flipped his thumb toward the elevator. "So, we're clear: your top lawyers and Ms. Patten will represent us?"

Meyer swallowed hard. "Ms. Patten is currently assisting me on a case, limiting her availability."

Conniving old bastard. "Patten's on my team from day one and listed in the contract, or it's no deal," he stated.

"I'll get an addendum typed." Meyer flipped pages to the first tiny yellow flag, then slowly rotated the paperwork. "We can proceed in signing the standard agreement."

"I expect preferential treatment." H.P. scrawled his name and pushed the contract back.

Meyer opened his mouth to speak, closed it, and filed the paperwork in a drawer. "Our experienced staff will begin projects as soon as you present them."

"I'll contact Chap from now on."

Meyer nodded. "Please do."

The Montblanc pen felt light in his fingers. He'd waited in the shadows for the right moment to sign Corrin Patten's death warrant. Next, he'd watch her walk to the gallows.

~ ~ ~

Turbulence dropped the airplane, digging Corrin's seatbelt deeper into her roiling stomach on the Thursday morning flight. The tray table above her knees rattled. She scrunched her eyes shut to block out the memory of being trapped in another rocking, bobbing seat, and dug her fingernails into the armrests.

The plane lurched—pitching and thrusting her like the speedboat ride ten years ago when it jetted through white caps. The horrible trauma surfaced, and with it, an image of the pervert who'd destroyed her innocence.

A hand touched her arm. She raised her fist, ready to break free and fight again. She gasped for air.

"Hey, are you okay?" her seatmate questioned as the shuddering stopped.

No gaudy ring on the stranger's fingers. No vice grip pinned her in a boat's bucket seat. "Yes, thank you," she said. "Nervous flier."

He nodded and returned to his magazine.

The airplane swooped down from the angry sky, bounced twice on the runway, and taxied to the terminal.

A wave of jitters hit. Miranda would be shocked to see her in Montana. The last time they'd talked, they'd planned to meet in Seattle prior to her testimony.

"'Spontaneous' and 'Corrin Patten' never grace the same sentence," her BFF frequently joked. Well, today she'd refute Miranda's statement. She shoved legal files into her bag on the floor and looked through the window.

Beyond the tarmac-and-boondocks version of an airport, Montana stretched in a wide expanse of snow-dusted, midday tranquility. Cows stood in a field off to one.

Queasiness rolled through her stomach at the sight of the lumbering animals. She smoothed the cuff of her jacket. She wasn't the ragtag kid anymore, wondering if she'd scrape together dinner for her siblings—wondering if the neighbor's steers would trample her as she collected fallen, unwanted apples from the orchard where they grazed.

Suppressed images of falsely smiling lips whispering insults dotted her memory again: neighbors who were the opposite of neighborly. All those years ago, buzzing, waspish tongues in Ebony Cove hadn't affected her until she'd lost her childlike naïvety on that horrible afternoon in the speed boat.

And here she was, enroute to another small town. If her sister-of-the-soul, Miranda, hadn't frantically called, she'd never have flown in to offer moral support and informal legal coaching.

The clatter of luggage and bodies charging the aisle announced the airplane cabin exodus.

She rose from her seat.

Twenty rows up, the paunchy guy in first class who'd bolted late onto the Seattle to Three Falls flight turned and eyeballed her again. He caught her looking and headed out the forward exit.

Bristling alarm sent cold chills down her spine. Colder than jumping into Puget Sound to escape the boat attack. She'd blocked the blasted memory for years, but today it flooded her brain.

She hoisted her bag from the floor and balanced it on the armrest. Knowing Miranda had barely dodged a hitman would cloud anyone's subconscious. Especially anyone dumb enough to catch a flight to the scene of the crime. It might have helped if the FBI had caught the remaining dirty cop, but they hadn't. She slung her stuffed bag to her back and tromped the aisle in the opposite direction of first class, ignoring the urge to run to the back of the plane.

Surges of frigid air shot through the rear exit.

Miranda's amazement two days ago when she'd trudged through snow in this godforsaken state hadn't sunk in until now.

Chalk that oversight up to distraction because your BFF has a bullseye on her back, Corrin concluded, and snapped shut her thin suede jacket.

She turned right in the airplane's galley and lifted a plum-colored Prada mule over the sill of the cutaway door.

Shimmering patterns of frost glistened on the boarding stairs pushed against the regional jet. Her stiletto-heeled shoe skated across the slick surface.

"No. No. No." Icy spikes from the steel handrail stabbed her flailing hand as she tightened her grip. Her chest teetered over the edge until she threw her shoulders back.

Safe. Prickles radiated from her exposed toes perched on the metal precipice. She scanned the area and let out her breath.

Thank goodness they'd all dashed out and not witnessed her awkward backbend. Her thumping pulse dropped a notch.

The other passengers continued tramping single file to the airport, intent on managing assorted packages like worker ants scurrying to their hill.

The line passed by Paunch Guy, holding open the terminal door and smirking straight at her for the third time. Receding hairline, dark suit—maybe another guy from the bureau sent in to guard Miranda from the mobsters until she reached a Seattle courtroom. He turned his head away and went inside.

How did Miranda stay sane, knowing there was a price on her head? A troupe of agents might help.

Corrin narrowed her eyes. Not many beer-bellied FBI agents, and even fewer first-class passengers who'd play doorman for people in steerage.

Nope, he'd clearly waited for her to exit the plane. Unease rippled through her. Ever since leaving the office at ten last night, she'd endured the weird suspicion of being watched. The bumps on her skin from the bone-biting cold doubled.

Get a grip. Paunch Guy acted too dumb to be any version of a stalker.

One motivation remained. Well, she wouldn't allow his lecherous ogling to intimidate her. At least not right now, in the middle of a public place, with at least twenty people watching. Squaring her shoulders, she pried her hand from the rail and braved the empty stairs.

Her seatmate stood by the lower platform, rummaging in his backpack. He popped out his ear buds, turned his head her way, and shot her a smile. "Welcome to the first cold spell in Three Falls."

"Cold spell." She descended, hovering her hand above the metal rail. "Right."

The flap-eared Elmer Fudd hat he plopped on didn't appear out of place. "Enjoy your visit, ma'am." He strode toward the terminal.

Ma'am? Either he considered the ripe old age of twenty-eight past prime, or she'd truly landed in cow country.

"Thanks." Another sharp gust whipped through her. Heat. She needed heat. The sleeveless angora shell she'd worn underneath the light jacket suited her law office, not a flight to the set of *Frozen*. Hearing Miranda's panic during their last phone call had thrown her into overdrive.

Just thinking how Miranda had witnessed a mob hit in Seattle and fled for her life made Corrin walk faster, challenging as that became. Rock salt crunched beneath each calculated step to the glass doors and shelter. Finally, she stepped inside the open concourse area. Blissful warmth enveloped her, along with the smell of stale coffee and teenage bodies.

Behind a group of shrieking kids from the plane, a glass case held a nine-foot-tall stuffed grizzly, jaws open wide, claws outstretched.

"Geeze," she muttered, "nice mascot." She tilted her head. *You know you're in Montana when . . . taxidermy suffices for artwork.* She grinned. Making a game of the funniest Montana offerings could entertain little Corey and Willy the next time she visited her sister's home. She scanned the room. No men in suits.

Assorted wall posters indicated the spring rodeo galloped to town in April, and the Globetrotters performed in May.

No sign directed travelers to taxis or shuttles. Judging by the assortment of Stetsons and cowboy boots on the locals, a covered wagon might be the transportation du jour.

One of the kids from her plane stood apart from the other loud teens who were all wearing matching hoodies, sweatpants, and Nikes. He stepped near their circle, but two ponytailed girls closed ranks and elbowed him out.

He dropped his head and shuffled to the side. The loner's frayed jacket, scuffed boots, and stained jeans suggested the poverty she'd endured as a kid. "Excuse me," she said, as she approached him.

He raised his head. "Yes, ma'am?"

"I need a taxi or shuttle. Any idea where to find one?"

He squared his shoulders and pointed to a young man in a gray uniform wearing a silver badge. "He'll help you. We're waiting for the team bus, or I'd ask if someone could give you a lift."

To hell with her strained budget. She pulled a twenty from her purse, handed it to him, and smiled. "Thank you."

"It's hard to be in a strange place," he said. His young eyes showed wisdom beyond his years. "You needn't pay me." He held out the bill.

She would've done the same. Proud to a fault. "I insist. Study hard, you'll be surprised where an education can take you."

A shy grin crossed his face. "Yes, ma'am."

She marched toward the vestibule where the freckle-faced security guard and a janitor chatted.

The guard paused mid-sentence, mouth agape. He puffed out his chest and adjusted the big flashlight clipped to his belt. His perusal began at the top of her blond head and stopped at her chest.

Ugh. She pulled her satchel around to cover her front. "Excuse me, can you please tell me where I might find a taxi?"

"You bet." He straightened his scrawny shoulders.

"Where you headed?"

"Emma Springs."

"I'm willing to drive home that way. I'm off duty in an hour." The guard raised an eyebrow. "No charge, if you can wait."

No freakin' way. "Thank you, but I'm already late. Lyft?"

"Don't know him, but I spotted old Ben, our Thursday shuttle driver, a few minutes ago in the Runway Grill."

"Is Ben a reliable driver?"

"Yes, ma'am." The guard nodded. "Pillar of the community. I'll show you where to find him. Such a tiny girl can't be too careful."

Oh brother. She'd trounced men twice his size in defense class. "Lead on, please." Her heels tapped double-time on the linoleum floor as she followed him into an empty corridor leading to the exit. At SeaTac, she'd be battling throngs of travelers.

The Runway Grill's lone occupant, a gray-haired man whose belly comfortably hung over his belt, stood as they approached. "Got a fare for me, son?" He set his coffee mug on the counter.

"Yup." The guard smiled. "She needs to go out your way. This here's Ben, Miss . . ."

"Thank you again." Corrin nodded politely at the security guard and turned to shake Ben's weathered hand.

"Happy to be your chauffeur, miss. Where to?" he asked.

The mobsters who'd chased after Miranda might have the residents on edge. She lowered her voice to a courtroom whisper. "Do you know Grant Morley? I need to get to his home, a few miles from Emma Springs."

"Sure thing." Without hesitation or a raised eyebrow, Ben casually tucked a couple of dollar bills in the restaurant tip jar sitting beside the cash register.

Corrin tried to read Ben's demeanor. Nonchalance radiated from the old guy. Either Grant's FBI operation transpired off the radar, or smoke signals hadn't been sent discussing the recent criminal activities.

She rolled her shoulders to ease the muscle kinks acquired by working on the cramped plane. "I'll pull the address on my phone."

"No need. Seems our local boy did alright after moving to the big city." Ben winked and pulled on a knitted cap.

"I've never met Agent Morley. Glad you have." She flashed her version of a cheerleader smile, trying for girly casual. "My best friend's visiting him. I'm excited to surprise her."

"Well, we better get you to your gal pal. Your luggage should be at the carousel."

"I packed light." She adjusted her satchel, and the strap dug into her shoulder. "Everything's in my carry on."

"It's below freezing today. You okay in your thin coat?" That sorry verdict had been declared. "I'll be fine. Thanks."

"Okay. Follow me. On the route to Emma Springs we'll see—"

Her attention veered to Paunch Guy, who stood at the car rental kiosk.

Judging by his suit, he'd not checked the forecast either before catching the flight. He took a step backward toward their pathway.

She stared at his vaguely familiar profile. A client from her Seattle office?

The guy raised a sheaf of papers, blocking his face and disguising his eavesdropping.

What a lot of nerve! She beat Ben to the door and held it open.

He led them to a muddy Ford Explorer and pulled a gold pocket watch from his vest. "Here's my rig."

Alongside his SUV, a row of silver vehicles occupied the rental car area.

He popped open the watch. "Ideal timing to make my grandson's second birthday party."

Offering friendly eyes and a rumbling voice, he'd be just the type of grandpa to tuck a kid into the crook of his arm and read a bedtime tale.

Not that she would know what that was like. She'd never known cozy story time. She yanked open the vehicle's rear door.

"Stow your satchel, and join me up front," Ben offered, and wrote his mileage on a notepad. "We're friendly here, and the view's better." The motor rumbled to a purr, and a country voice on the radio crooned about a farmer tan.

You know you're in Montana when . . . the AM station's blaring "She Thinks My Tractor's Sexy," and your driver knows every word.

They wound through the outskirts of town. Businesses fronting uncrowded parking lots were scattered like buckshot. A red brick building advertised rooms for a third of Seattle prices.

You know you're in Montana when . . . the first hotel you spot has a chopping tomahawk in red neon lights to welcome guests. Willy, her nephew, would appreciate the flashing design. To her, it radiated all the charm of the Bates Motel.

As buildings became sparse on the flat landscape, she realized Ben had continued talking.

". . . the foothills to the south have remnants of stone medicine wheels. It's amazing they carried water so far to their camps." Ben merged onto an empty highway and headed into the sun.

She'd tuned out some of his running banter featuring the Blackfeet tribe and wagon trains, but she couldn't ignore him checking the mirror for the umpteenth time in forty minutes.

"Something going on behind us?" she asked.

"Not really," he scoffed. "Had a silver car following us all the way from Three Falls. Not one I recognize."

Following them? Corrin's creep-sensor buzzed to alert mode. She glanced out the back window. A barn and silos blocked her view of the curving road. "Where?"

"He hung back after we turned off the highway and got stuck behind a hay truck. Probably visiting a local."

She released her grip on the leather seat. "I bet out-of-town company for dinner in Emma Springs makes the gossip grapevine. It did in the little town I grew up in."

"Yup." Ben agreed. "This here's Grant's spread. He's got a beautiful view of Mount Hanlen." He wheeled onto a long gravel drive leading to a log house and a barn sitting fifty yards behind it on the edge of a meadow.

"I assumed the trip took longer," she said, and unbuckled.

"Nope. And we arrived in time for me to enjoy birthday cake in front of a cozy fireplace."

"Glad it worked out." She scanned the area. Fresh tire tracks dented the snow and continued to the barn. A pond sat on one side of it and on the other side, distant foothills led to the mountain.

They parked beside a short, straight walkway, which ended at a front door inlaid in light and dark woods.

"Amazing." Corrin shook her head. "My friend has a picture of a similar house on her fridge."

Ben tapped on a handheld calculator. "Probably reminds her of Grant's."

As far as Corrin knew, Miranda first visited this area a few days ago. "Uh-huh." She pulled a tube of lipstick out of her bag and swiped it across her lips, mentally calculating the dent the trip made in her tight budget. She'd eat ramen for a month before she'd scrimp on winter coats and boots for Willy and Cory.

"Nineteen even, miss."

"That's all? In Seattle the fare would've drained my bank account."

"Montana's friendly and economical," he stated, wearing a satisfied grin.

"I'll get my purse." She shoved open the car door to find two inches of snow. Her consignment store shoes could be replaced—she needed to be certain Miranda was okay.

"Hold on." Ben pulled her bag from the back seat, groaning at the weight. "You're strong for your size, same as my grandson."

"I guess." She opened her wallet to retrieve his nineteen bucks and added an extra five to the fare. The grandpa and toddler should be wearing blue party hats soon. "Here you are."

"Thanks." He stuck the cash in a dashboard clip. "Whadda you know." He pointed to a Jeep parked under an awning beside the barn. "Doc Kyle's visiting."

Doctor? Miranda's wound was supposed to be healing.

She stretched her right foot onto the edge of the cement, pushed off the car door, and step-hopped twenty feet on a freshly shoveled path to the covered porch. "Thanks for the ride."

Ben waved at her as he turned around and drove away.

Bloody hell. She'd failed to notice the totally dark house. Had they taken Miranda to the hospital? Chills permeated much further than her fingertip as she pushed the cold doorbell. The chime echoed.

No one knew she'd left Seattle. She swallowed hard, rubbed her palms over the sleeves of her jacket, and rang again. Shouldn't someone have answered the door by now?

She gripped a cold post and leaned out from the end of the porch. The closed doors on the barn appeared locked. No nearby homes, only a hawk circling overhead and a mountain behind it. A ten thousand-foot, covered-in-snow mountain.

Her fingers skimmed her skirt front, the thin wool ending above her shaking knees.

She'd landed as unprotected as it got. At work, a security guard hovered in the background, and at her apartment, the manager lived on site. She'd flown here impromptu and ill-prepared for the mind-numbing, dangerous cold.

The hawk made a final screech and flew away.

Montana wasn't the end of the world, but you'd certainly see the Canadian border from atop craggy Mt. Hanlen, looming in the distance.

Corrin shuddered again. Miranda had been left for dead on that mountain. She huffed on her fingers, thawing them before searching for her phone.

No service bars.

No taxi.

No parka.

No Miranda. Where was she in this Arctic cold?

You know you're in Montana in September when . . .the events of the day are frozen into your mind like a tongue stuck to a flagpole.

Approaching vehicle tires scrunched on the driveway. *Hallelujah.* She turned.

A green Suburban approached and stopped at the edge of the sidewalk.

Her exhale formed a puffy cloud of relief at a friend fix. She picked her way to the end of the cement walkway and raised her hand to wave at Miranda.

The passenger window opened. No passenger.

Her hand dropped.

The driver appeared near thirty, but minus the linebacker physique Miranda assigned to Grant. She glanced around uneasily and then back to the man at the wheel.

He leaned closer to the open window. An ID badge showing *DOCTOR* printed at the bottom swung from his collar.

Vibrant blue eyes shone through strands of disarrayed blond hair. "Hi there." His enthusiastic, wide grin belonged on an ad for surfing on Venice Beach. "Can I help you?" he asked politely.

Quite the switch from the lawyers and lewd clients she dealt with as a paralegal. Unfamiliar tingles of attraction distracted her. She tilted forward.

But then, the creeps in the boat had looked okay at first. "No, thank you." She backed away and checked her phone again for service bars.

None showed. Not one, single, rotten bar.

Piercing gusts of cold penetrated her unprotected neck and legs, and stabbed into the ten years' worth of armor she'd perfected to discourage amorous men.

"Are you certain I can't help you?" he repeated. "It hasn't hit twenty degrees today."

She planted her feet and stretched to her tallest height on the three-inch heels. "I assume you're not Grant Morley. Is this his house?" She clenched her jaw to keep her teeth from chattering.

"Yes. I'm a friend." Wind scattered his words.

"I'm here for Miranda. Where are they?" She wiggled her tingling bare toes, then stomped each foot.

"I took them to catch the Seattle flight." He pointed to the Jeep beside the nearby barn. "I'll get my rig and be right back. This metal behemoth is Grant's." The window rolled up.

Her mouth dropped. Miranda had left. Shivers shook her body. She watched the Suburban disappear behind the barn.

Clutching her leather satchel to her chest didn't block the blustery weather or her growing panic at the sheer stupidity of jetting unannounced to hypothermia territory, dressed for balmy fall weather. She blinked back a tear.

This stranger must be okay. He'd chauffeured Miranda, which upped his cred. She stomped her feet again to force blood to flow, hopefully also to her brain.

A door shut in the distance. The driver ran to the Jeep, then backed it to where she stood.

The front seat, passenger door flew open. "Kyle Werner, Grant's friend. Happy to be at your service, Ms.—"

Miranda had mentioned Grant's helpful doctor friend. With the wind kicking up, his name sounded familiar enough for her to hoist her freezing butt into the bucket seat. She dropped her bag next to a black case on the floor.

He averted his eyes from her legs while she climbed in.

The doc got bonus points for courtesy. She yanked her door shut, not allowing one excess molecule of warmth to escape the smaller, sporty Jeep Renegade. "Corrin Patten, Miranda's friend."

"Ah, she mentioned your name several times." His breath smelled minty fresh. "I didn't peg you for the Goldilocks burglar," he jested.

"Nope, and nothing in my plans are just right. Can I impose on you to transport me to Three Falls? I hope you're available."

A wide grin made him cuter. "Available?"

Heat flared in her cheeks. "I need to catch the next flight. Miranda shouldn't be alone in Seattle. I came to help her prepare for the trial. She's like my little sister."

His face took on a faraway look, transforming his uncomplicated and almost boyish charm to a handsome, serious man. "She won't be alone anymore."

Like hell. Didn't he understand her concern? She rubbed her temple. "Miranda needs a trusted friend right now. I know it's an inconvenience, but my taxi driver left to attend his grandson's birthday party. I'll pay you."

"Sorry, there's one flight a day to Seattle, and it's twenty thousand feet above Idaho by now."

Corrin rolled her eyes skyward. "This day keeps getting better."

His mouth twitched, fighting another grin. "You're welcome to use the guest room attached to my office."

Over her dead body she'd ask another favor of a drop-dead gorgeous guy who must be adept at beating off women by the dozen. Her luck the nearest booming metropolis rated ghost town compared to Seattle. "Oh, I couldn't bother you. Please take me to the closest hotel, and I'll call Ben, my taxi driver, for tomorrow."

"Sorry again. Ben only works on Thursdays."

He didn't sound sorry, so why'd his deep, solid, male voice warm her better than an angora parka? She tried to ignore the fuzzy feelings and keep her tone businesslike.

"Maybe you know the Friday driver for hire? I'm sorry to be such a pain."

His blue eyes flickered over her appraisingly. "An unexpected diversion, but not a pain. Let's sort it out during lunch. You work in the legal field, don't you?"

"Yes." She tried to hide her surprise. "Guilty as charged. I'm a paralegal."

"Right." Kyle rested his elbow on the console.

Up close, his shoulders seemed plenty broad and plenty attractive.

Those kinds of thoughts she didn't need. She shifted away until her upper arm met the cold window. "You treated Miranda's gunshot wound, didn't you?"

"Gave her a checkup after Grant's stitches. Soon as she realizes she missed you, she'll be disappointed."

Miranda needed her big time. Her chest tightened. "I don't want to trouble you any longer, Dr. Werner. Maybe there's a local bed-and-breakfast?"

His full lips spread into a kindly smile. "Please, call me Kyle. And trust me, it's no trouble. During hunting season, nearby rooms booked out weeks ago."

Her face must have betrayed her distress, because he lifted a large hand as if to reassure her. "No worries, though. We'll find you suitable accommodations. My dad has two guest rooms. We both live a few miles from here. He's an attorney, and he'd be thrilled to engage in legal discourse. He cooks dinner for the two of us on Thursdays. Care to join us?"

"Let me check my schedule."

"You do that while we sit tight and let the engine warm up."

She let out a nervous laugh and pulled out her cell. "Sorry. I'll turn off auto-lawyer."

"Fine by me." A mischievous smile showing perfect white teeth boosted his appeal to off the swoonometer.

She blinked to clear her head and glanced at her phone. "Service bars. Hallelujah." Her finger scrolled through her phone log. "Oh brother, what an idiot."

"What?"

"Sorry, I'm an idiot." She reread the last message and sent a reply.

"Something wrong?" he asked.

She tossed the phone into her open satchel on the floor and slouched into the seat. "Miranda texted. She's doing okay in the bureau's care. Her updates on flying home got minimized beneath another message. I asked her to call me as soon as she lands. My own operator-error on a stupid new company smartphone."

"They should offer classes on new phones."

"I haven't even memorized my login on the dumb thing yet." She'd probably lose the sticky note holding her password, stuck to the back.

"Passwords are the plague of the modern world."

His steady voice relaxed her and brought a sense of protection she'd missed for so very long. Written into a medieval story, he'd be seated on a white charger, ready to joust against the evil knight. Evil, same as the man pursuing Miranda. "Did Grant get word the FBI apprehended Karpenito, the crooked cop?"

"Not yet. The bureau's on alert regarding Miranda's dangerous situation. You can relax. She's being guarded by the best."

Her body tensed. "Not my impression. I put her on the bus, called the dude ranch, and assumed she'd be safe in Montana. Wrong call. Poor Miranda got chased, shot, and left for dead on that bloody mountain. I left unexpectedly today, to prep her for testifying and to check out Mr. Agent's capabilities for myself."

He lifted his right hand. "I understand your anxiety."

"I hoped you might."

"Miranda told me how close you two are." He raised his dark blond eyebrows, and his gaze flicked to her bare legs. "She also told me you're a top legal researcher. Not my impression of the impetuous type."

A smooth change of subject, or a dig at her unsuitable clothing? She straightened. "Miranda's being hunted. I'd do anything to relieve the pressure she's under. I should've come sooner."

"I understood she kept her getaway plan a secret."

"She'd scribbled a phone number on her wrist. My job is research and reading people. This time literally. She vanished to survive, and I wanted to keep track of her."

Kyle's face tightened. "We've all been doing our best to keep Miranda safe."

"Safety hasn't happened to date," she snapped.

"We can agree to disagree. Seems everything's warm on the vehicle front." He grasped the shifter knob, and the Jeep crept away from the house. He stopped at the end of the driveway, his glance to the right scanning oh-so-briefly across her exposed knees.

She dragged down the hem of her skirt and stared out her side window. A silver car sped toward them from the right, traveling well over sixty.

Ben had noted a car in the same color. Corrin lowered the visor as a precaution and watched the lone driver as he sped past. Her pulse spiked. *Bloody hell.* Paunch Guy from the airport again. She clutched her shaking hands in her lap.

"Where's the fire?" Kyle shook his head, then met her eyes.

Those baby blues could sway any jury, on any count, any day. Only a stupid coincidence, but Kyle readily spotted her unease. She tore her eyes away from him. The car faded into the distance.

"Miranda told me you became her rock, the friend who kept cool and collected. Are you certain you're okay?"

"You're witnessing my frustration. I can't believe I travelled here and missed Miranda. She must be terrified. I won't relax until she's safe."

He glanced at her hands. "She's being protected by a top FBI agent, who also happens to be my best friend. We grew up together like brothers. I'd trust Grant with my life." He accelerated onto a two-lane paved road.

Relax your fingers and breathe, she instructed herself and concentrated on empty pastures out the window.

She'd known country naïvety too. Her nose wrinkled at the memory of smelling cow manure on the trek home from school. "You're not scheduled to testify against a mob boss. The agent better protect her, or he answers to me."

Kyle cleared his throat. "Yes, ma'am. Grant told me you'd directly voiced your concerns to him. He's a big presence, even on the phone. Made me want to invite you here myself." He circled his finger over her satchel. "Anything closer to shoes in there?"

"I didn't pack my spare mukluks. I worked a couple of hours at my office and spotted open seats on today's flight. What you see is what you get."

"I'll plan accordingly." He kept his eyes focused ahead, but his fingers tapped lightly on the top of the steering wheel. "Hungry?"

"Yes. I need brain food after this debacle. My treat. I appreciate your assistance."

"Your debacle's my rare opportunity to be debonair. There's a nearby spot for lunch. Not quiet, but good food."

"Great, noise doesn't bother me. Oh jeez, I left my phone volume shut off. I won't hear Miranda's call from my bag." She unclipped her seatbelt and reached forward.

A huge elk and a fawn dashed onto the road.

Kyle veered to the right, braked, and flung his body across the console with his arm thrust out to restrain her.

Her body pitched into him. The Jeep jolted to a halt, lodging her chest against his back.

The mama elk stopped on the centerline and bounced from right to left on her front feet, then mother and baby loped to an empty field and trotted away.

A stress-induced giggle escaped her lips. How ironic— she'd never thrown herself at a man in her life.

"You hurt?" Kyle twisted his head around, which put his lips inches away.

She'd grabbed his sleeve, and her body remained plastered against his warm, solid male back.

Bloody hell. Hurt didn't come to mind.

CHAPTER 2

Kyle's shoulder harness cut into him. Thank God, he'd blocked Corrin from hitting the windshield. Heartbeats hammered in his chest. Her gasps from behind sent wisps onto his neck. "Are you hurt?" he repeated.

"No. Thanks to you, I'm okay." She let go of his coat sleeve. "The seatbelt must be choking you."

Egad! Her generous breasts remained pressed into his back. He dropped the hand he'd flung out to pin her into her seat and slid back into his. Heat rose from under his collar. "Good, no injuries."

She secured her own belt. "Thanks again for the . . . support," she said, and pulled her satchel to her lap.

His pulse continued to race. "You could've gone through the windshield."

"I, I ah, I never unbuckle driving at home." She shoved a blond strand into her bun and adjusted her skirt. "So much for the placid countryside."

"Elk and cars, bad combo. The mother probably weighs a good six hundred pounds. Wildlife makes seat belts mandatory in Montana."

"Duly noted." She angled her legs awkwardly to the side, avoiding his black satchel.

"Oh, sorry, I forgot my medical bag is by your feet." He reached for the handle of his leather case. She did the same.

Their fingers touched, sending a jolt to his core, stronger than any defib paddle delivered.

She yanked her hand away as if she'd received the same spark.

Kyle grinned. "My bag's heavy. I'll lift it out."

"Sure," she stammered, and pushed her butt into the door.

The move indicated shy, angry, or fighting interest. He lifted the case and stowed it behind her seat, avoiding contact. "I'm ready for lunch."

"I'm truly sorry to interrupt your day off." She extracted a small leather purse from her satchel and shoved her phone into it. "The first time I revisit rural, chaos erupts."

Kyle studied her pale, taut face. "Were you raised in the country?"

"Yes. Ebony Cove, Washington. It's near Seattle. I grew up on the outskirts of the area's last shuttered coal mine. I broke free at eighteen." She raised her chin and smoothed her suede lapel.

If poverty drove her success, that answered a few questions. "Independence requires courage. On this trip, I bet you didn't imagine you'd be stranded on a doorstep miles from a city, needing to depend on a stranger."

"No." Her body relaxed. "I wanted to comfort Miranda." She rotated her bracelet, fingering a variety of shiny, polished stones. "Handling mishaps is good practice for travelling abroad, though."

The world better start preparing, because it didn't appear she would. His gaze skimmed her flimsy jacket and high heels. She needed a handler. His pulse jumped at the thought before his brain kicked in. "Travel has never appealed to me."

"It's my aspiration to explore, once I make partner."

"I'm a homebody, except while entertaining a guest." He pulled back onto the road. "The Red Horse Tavern serves food buffet-style alongside a live band playing honky-tonk music. Generally, a good introduction to Emma Springs entertainment."

"A bar," she mumbled, then faked a perky grin. "Well, music's always a good diversion. I mean, a pleasant diversion."

Like a diversion to kill time when you're bored. The snow angel he'd envisioned at first sight of her on Grant's sidewalk melted faster than the slush from his boots. He'd been wrong about mutual attraction—her comments didn't indicate interest, more likely disdain. "Food and entertainment, next stop."

"Great."

Her voice sounded too chipper. He turned onto the highway and accelerated. Go figure. On first sight he'd considered her an unexpected gift from Grant, an attractive female dropped in front of him.

He considered her tightly clasped hands. Not dropped on him, but displaced because she tried to do a friend in danger a favor. He took his foot off the gas pedal. "After lunch, we can drive around the lake. If you can stand an evening listening to a couple of old bachelors, I'll call my dad and alert him to expect two for dinner."

"Sure." She tapped her manicured fingers on her purse. "I usually work late and eat alone in my apartment." The drumming sped up. "It occurred to me that Miranda's room may be available for the night."

At this rate, she'd need a sedative. Knowing overnight options might relax her. "Concerning lodging,

I can't offer you the Ritz, but no one's booked my guest room where Miranda napped before Grant's rescue. Big Red, the mule with miraculous ears who led Grant to Miranda, hung his halter in my garage, if that helps." No smile appeared.

"I've never been comfortable around farm animals." Her hands clutched her purse as if she'd taken a seat on the New York subway and he'd donned a dark hoodie. Her eyes darted to check every car in oncoming traffic.

A city girl shouldn't be this skittish, even following the recent criminal activity in Emma Springs. "The barn where Big Red resides is miles away and Miranda's hitman is behind bars. Things are back to blandly normal in our little town."

"That Karpenito cop guy is still gunning for Miranda. Could you stop at the Lazy K Ranch if it's on the way?" she asked quietly.

Kyle fought a frown. This high-maintenance urbanite didn't match Miranda's description of her tenacious best friend. Maybe something he'd done? "They're shut down until spring. Miranda booked at the end of the Lazy K's season."

Corrin unclenched her fingers. "Lucky for me you arrived," she conceded in an honest tone.

Damn straight. Grant owed him. Airplanes to start the day, and now this. "No problem. I'm not on call tomorrow, I'll drive you to the airport." His stomach tightened. Planes were not his forte. Why in hell had he offered?

"It's generous for you to transport me on your day off," she said.

He cleared his throat. "It's gentlemanly, under the circumstances."

"Thank you for your assistance." She stiffened. "I'm concerned entertaining me may inconvenience you and your father."

Wow, she took formal to a completely new level. Possibly low blood sugar? She'd checked out his ring finger twice—maybe a married guy jilted her recently. "Dad enjoys entertaining."

"Sounds nice."

His gaze dropped to the stitched cuff of her expensive and unsuitable thin suede jacket. "Dad probably hasn't dusted lately. My home isn't fancy, but it's cleaned weekly and the spare bedroom's comfortable, even though it lacks monogrammed sheets." Would she catch the dig?

Her hands flew to her cheeks. "Oh! I apologize if I acted unappreciative. My sisters and I slept noses to toes in a variety of shacks posing as houses."

And she'd retained a junkyard dog attitude, which worked well at keeping men at a distance. A looker like her probably got hit on constantly. Most likely her issue. "Must be nice being from a big family. I don't have any siblings. My mom died last year, and my dad gets lonely."

"I'm sorry," Corrin said. "Losing your mom must've been terribly difficult for both of you." Concern softened her face.

She'd known loss, too. He met kindness in her eyes. "Losing Mom sunk us."

"I can't begin to imagine. I've been worried sick over Miranda's safety, and now I'm irritated I missed her again." She spun her bracelet on her wrist. "Your plans for the evening sound nice."

She sounded sincere. Nerves affected people differently. He'd make it his job to soothe hers, to make her welcome. "Actually, your accompanying me in public does me a favor. Our appearance shall be reported to the editor of the local newsletter." He met her eyes again and raised his brows.

"Tell me what to do to make the next edition." A smile tilted the corners of her perfectly shaped lips. "Years ago, my uncle and I did a mean two-step at weddings."

Years ago? If schmucks hit on her, it justified the prickly exterior. "Seattle's known for premier nightclubs. Not your style?" He downshifted and turned onto a road leading to a one-story building outlined in white lights.

She shook her head. "I haven't possessed the luxury of free time for a decade. I relocated to Seattle after high school and promptly began university night classes to attain a Juris Doctorate degree. I've worked full time since I hit town." Her eyes flicked to her stuffed satchel. "I officially graduated last quarter and next is the bar exam."

"An accomplishment to be proud of. Good luck on passing it the first time."

She rubbed the front of her graceful neck. "I aspire to. I plotted my financial independence after hearing a lawyer during 'Bring Your Parent to School Day.' Her children's father had skipped out years prior. Considering her family's lifestyle, the single mom attorney managed well minus the deadbeat."

Another discouraging view of men. Well, he had twenty hours to send her back with a positive view of Montana's gentlemen. "Interesting. We've seen the opposite. Emma Springs has recently attracted single women from California who are supported by wealthy ex-husbands. They escape here for weekends."

"I guess miles of woods and weeds classify as an escape for divorcees."

He chuckled. "No outdoorsy bones in your body." He threw her an exaggerated side eye. "Regardless, my porch should be free of casseroles in Corning Ware next week."

"I've been known to ward off negative publicity before, but none involving food stuffs." She flashed him a crooked grin.

"Game on." He laughed and stopped the Jeep.

Several inches of snow covered the tavern's sidewalk.

If she'd bothered to check a forecast, she'd have been wearing snowmobile boots instead of the minuscule amount of leather posing as footwear. He parked close to the walkway, hopped out, and opened her door.

Brows furrowed, she surveyed the snowy path and the flawless nap on shoes that probably cost a car payment.

However, she'd presented his first opportunity to be gallant. "I'm happy to carry you to the door." He rocked back on his rubber-soled boots and kept his hands stowed in the pockets of his jacket.

She peered around him, no doubt gauging the distance and damage factor. "I couldn't." Her color paled.

In an instant, she'd morphed from diva back to distressed.

"There are other restaurants," he offered.

"It's a short walk."

"Your feet will get soaked, and here, that's dangerous. Please allow me to play Prince Charming." He opened her door and stopped.

Her pale lashes framed eyes colored a dark indigo blue.

What in hell was causing her involuntary response of fear? Kyle's jaw tightened.

She exhaled and unclenched her fist. "Prince Charming, one of my favorite childhood heroes. Is my laptop safe in your car?"

Good, he'd gained a dram of trust. "Yes. I've got a prowler alarm, due to my medical bag. When you're ready, put your hand on my shoulder." He'd mustered his best physician-in-charge tone to calm her and stepped closer.

"I'm ready." She clenched his jacket collar and slid toward him.

He wedged his fingers between the car seat and her legs. A slab of granite would've been softer in his arms. He kicked the door shut with his foot and steadied his hands under her skirted thighs and back.

At the end of twenty feet of walkway, he set her down, opened the door, and ushered her inside. "I took my weekly bath last night," he drawled, trying to relax her. "Sorry if my coat needs a scrubbin'."

She shook her head no, giving him a glimpse of her deathly pale face.

A trauma victim's reaction. He swallowed hard, braced for an appalling possibility. "Did a doctor hurt you?"

She wrapped her arms around her chest. "No, nothing like that. Music sounds nice."

The connection hit him worse than a swift gut punch. He clenched his fist. She'd been brutalized on a date or by a boyfriend.

A foreign sensation raged through his body, hammering out an intense need to find the bastard and inflict pain during a non-medical operation with a scalpel.

~ ~ ~

Emma Springs. The backwoods name sounded vaguely familiar. "You lost sight of her, Mikey?" H.P. squeezed his cell and turned to look out his condo's window. Another passenger car ascended to the top of the Space Needle, the upper level remaining obscured by drizzle and distance. Patten had thrown his life onto a similar path.

"There's hardly any traffic, so I couldn't tail two cars behind."

H.P. pressed his fingers into the cold concrete of his kitchen counter. "Where are you now?"

"On a highway surrounded by farmland," Mikey said. "I cruised past the house where the old guy driving her from the airport stopped. No sign of Blondie."

"Backtrack and find her. No more excuses." His jaw tightened. "She couldn't fly out of town."

"I couldn't fly over the damn hay truck blocking the road. When will I be able to access the phone-tracking app your guy planted?"

"Shortly, if his promise isn't worthless, too."

"Don't sweat it," Mikey crooned. "Soon enough, she'll learn the squawking bird gets its neck wrung first."

"If we're sharp. Hold on." He stuck his cell on speaker and laid it on the table. "My old man's mentioned Emma Springs a time or two." He thumbed through a sheaf of real estate contracts. "No way." He let out a low whistle.

"Did we get a lucky break?" Mikey said.

"Not luck. Fate. She's landed in one of our potential resort sites for the California crowd. My old man positioned one of his advance teams there last week. I hadn't had time to cancel their explorations. I'll text you an address. First, you need to find her."

He hit the 'end call' button and smiled. The retribution that money-grubbing Corrin Patten's deserved would be finalized prior to the board of directors officially voting him in as CEO at the next quarterly meeting—an appointment which should've happened sooner.

His fist clenched, recalling exactly why it hadn't. Fourteen years ago, a mandate had been delivered by his enraged father. "I'll pay her the money," he'd yelled. "You damn well better destroy any proof you touched her and vanish. My company image is at stake!"

H.P.'s gaze travelled out to Puget Sound and stopped at the stretch of water where he'd hammered a hole in his brand-new MasterCraft, his last birthday present from the family.

He'd watched the red metallic beauty sink into ugly gray water.

Cutting off communication with his friends and girlfriend had collapsed his life. He'd bottomed out, transferring to Podunk U in the boring-as-hell Midwest.

Time for Corrin Patten to pay for all he'd lost.

CHAPTER 3

The entry to the Red Horse Tavern reverberated with beats from a kick drum.

Breathe. Corrin forced the in and out count she'd learned.

"Are you certain you're okay?" Kyle asked.

Genuine concern prompted his actions. He'd be the guy who'd face the dragon unarmed to protect the damsel. Moments ago, he'd protected her stupid shoes, and she'd acted mortified.

She let her arms drop to her sides. His face radiated worry or maybe misplaced guilt. "Being carried took me off guard is all."

Kyle stepped to the door. "If you want to stay, I'll park the car."

She wanted to hear Miranda's voice and assess her fear level. She smoothed her hair and shoved in a pin. "Yes. Let's stay. The band sounds fun. I'm sorry I acted prudish."

The beat slowed to a smooth tempo.

Warm air surrounded them.

"I don't believe you're a prude." Their eyes met, and she recognized concern in their blue depths. He clenched his keys in his hand and returned to the Jeep.

The noisy tavern elicited a friendly vibe.

On the left side of the crowded room, an expanse of carved wood framed a mirror. Below it, a shelf held assorted booze bottles. A wooden bar long enough for a dozen stools faced it. On one of the short ends of the bar sat an array of covered metal chafing dishes for food.

The bartender stood in front of the booze and ran his hand through slicked-back hair. He handed off two beers, the first to a man in a cowboy hat, the second to a woman wearing a short skirt and tooled western boots.

Across the room, a singer dressed in black fronted a four-piece band. His husky baritone rasped out the tale of lonely nights. Several dancing couples circled an area ringed by tightly packed tables and chairs.

Smells of stale beer and spent cigarettes mingled amongst tantalizing aromas of barbecue.

Corrin's toes tapped to the music. She closed her eyes and recalled chattering cousins, sawdust floors, and old men's coal-stained hands playing fiddles at family weddings. Memories eased her tension.

The door whooshed open behind her, and before she turned her head, her nose detected the scent of freshly chewed mint. She smiled at her protector. "I'd bet if you wore a ten-gallon hat, it'd be white," she teased.

His rosy cheeks magnified the azure blue of his eyes. "I hope so." He took off his gloves and stuffed them in his pocket. "Let's find a place to sit." He pointed to an empty table in the center of the room and held out his hand. "The floor's probably slippery."

Kyle's attentive nature held no hint of ulterior motives. The final edges of her unease melted. No one had safeguarded her since she'd been a little girl. She placed her hand into his.

"Your hands are chilly." He briskly rubbed his warm hands over hers, then clasped her right hand in a firm grip.

She trailed behind, allowing him to guide her through narrow spaces between chairs, allowing the notion of slipping back to when trust held a place in her world.

He nodded to patrons, leading her with the dignified posture of a man receiving a prestigious award.

The spectators smiled back. Without exception, the men's eyes dropped to the level of the third snap on her fitted jacket.

New town, same old story. City or country, she'd endured boob checks since her body had developed from its pre-adolescent shape to an hourglass figure, all in the space of her eighth-grade year. Irritation from leering eyes annoyed her more than usual. She squared her shoulders and marched behind him. Conversations in the room paused for a few beats.

"That spot should work," Kyle pointed to her left, did a double take, and proceeded to bump into the next table.

His wide eyes unhinged her, his reaction the result of how much her anger had backfired. He'd interpreted her chest out, get-out-of-my-way attitude wrongly as strutting her stuff. Heat crept into her cheeks. Between embarrassment and the warmth from the surrounding packed bodies, she might've stepped into a sauna. She slipped off her jacket and hung it on her chair.

Kyle cleared his throat. He took off his parka and opened the top button on his white dress shirt. "Your entrance skills earned you a beverage of choice. Hushing drinkers in a honky-tonk isn't easy," he joked. "What do you prefer?"

Time for damage control. He'd wanted to send a signal to casserole-bearing women, but he looked shocked. She pulled her purse against her chest. "The least I can do to compensate you for escorting me today is to purchase drinks and lunch." She plastered on a pert smile. "What may I acquire first to quench your thirst?"

He let out a deep honest laugh. "A root beer suits me fine. I'm on call until midnight. I'll go scope out the buffet." He stepped around her, on a direct route to the narrow end of the bar.

"Divide and conquer. Good battle plan." Bad rebuttal, she mused and wove through occupied tables toward the bartender.

Fifteen feet from him, Kyle and a couple of women took turns lifting lids off silver servers heated by Sterno. Corrin's nose twitched. "Hot wings, yum," she whispered, and approached the cash register, sitting beside a row of beer taps mounted to the bar.

"Hi honey, can I help ya?" the bartender asked, in a voice as slick as his hair.

"Two root beers please, and add two lunch buffets to the total," she said. He leaned over and held out his hand. "Twenty even, honey."

She handed off the payment, and he grasped Corrin's wrist.

"Anything else I can do for you today?" His thumb stroked her palm. "Or tonight? The doc's a nice guy, but I'm known for fun in these parts."

She pivoted, facing Kyle, and stepped back, her bare arm stretched across the bar.

Kyle dropped a metal lid and strode toward her, glaring a warning to the bartender that he'd sever the sleaze ball's limb if necessary.

Corrin shook free. "Thanks, I'm spoken for." She grasped the long-necked bottles of root beer and frosty glasses. A good scrubbing might remove the ick from her hand. "Be right back, Kyle." She waved the empty glasses at him.

"Awkward times ten," she mumbled to herself, feeling the room becoming stuffy to the point of suffocating. Too many male eyes. Too far to the table. And Miranda should've landed by now and called. She set the drinks down and grabbed her phone. No calls.

Her stomach rumbled. She took a deep breath and followed his route to the buffet.

Kyle stood awkwardly, his back pressed against the end of the bar holding the food, blocked in by the two women.

The femme fatales faced him with the tilt-shouldered stance of conquest. He caught her eye and did a mock backbend over the high counter.

Help signal received. The competitiveness she'd experienced preparing legal arguments burned in her gut. She beelined through the last two tables.

The taller huntress swished glossy brown hair and leaned toward Kyle. An expensive pair of saline-filled sacs pushed against her low-cut top. Her friend, a puffy-lipped blonde, tee-heed at a remark.

Kyle offered up a choice morsel to the middle-aged feline predators. She'd helped represent their type in divorce settlements. They ought to be ashamed of cradle robbing.

He'd grabbed dinner plates and held them at chest level as shields.

Game on, all right. "Excuse me." She elbowed aside Big Lips and sidled in next to Kyle. "We have restaurants in Seattle specializing in wings. I can't wait to try these, Kyle."

Two sets of cold eyes stared at her. The brunette flipped her hair to expose huge diamond studs. "And you are?"

"Ladies, please meet Corrin." Kyle grinned and handed her a plate. "If you like wings, they have a steaming supply of drumettes." He lifted the nearest silver dish cover, and the aroma of sauce spiced the air. He put two on her plate.

"I prefer this size to a big piece of old stew hen," Corrin announced. She dropped her eyes to the taller one's high-heeled boots, scanned up the leather skinny jeans, and then ignored the faint scowl on her taut face.

"My preference, too," Kyle chimed in. "In fact, I'll choose a simple cupcake any day to a slice of layered, decorated cake." He smiled at Corrin, a smile radiant enough to melt a glacier.

Heat levels in the room rose another notch.

The women crossed their arms in unison. "Nice to meet you," Big Lips mumbled.

"Meeting you both has been a pleasure." Corrin smirked.

"Later, doc," said the brunette, and tilted her perfectly bobbed, stuck-up nose higher. She strutted off, her heavy perfume lingering in the air.

Corrin stifled a giggle and held her plate for Kyle. They'd managed to best LA transplants flaunting implants.

"A sample of beef?" Kyle'd moved to the pan of saucy brisket. "I don't want to spoil your appetite for later."

Her cheeks heated. "Thank you for reminding me of our plans." She turned her attention to a tray of fudge bites and popped a piece in her mouth.

"Nicely done, Ms. Patten." Kyle smiled at her. "Although I don't remember the last time I split my attention simultaneously between three women."

Victory tasted sweeter than chocolate. Corrin raised an eyebrow. "Might've been more than your attention. You're lucky they didn't each grab a pant leg and pull."

"Ouch." From a stack at the end of the bar, he pulled off two plastic bibs emblazoned with a rearing red horse. He held one to his chest. "I may have to report in today, and we don't want any stains on your sweater." His playful grin took her back in time.

Back to when she'd enjoyed cutting loose. She plucked one of the bibs from his hand. "I appreciate your concern for my apparel."

Men's heads swiveled to track her return to their table. For once, it didn't irritate her. Only Kyle's opinion mattered.

Since when? She stumbled, he grabbed her arm, and then he pulled out her chair. "Thanks," she said.

"Concern for your well-being highlights my month." He bowed before sitting.

She did a mock eye roll and fought the lingering buzz from his touch, a distraction she didn't need during this phase of her career. *What the heck.* Twenty-four hours wouldn't constitute a commitment, and their back-and-forth wisecracks beat the heck out of legal arguments. "You're the most devastatingly unoccupied man I've ever dined beside at the Red Horse Tavern."

"I'll free future dates on my calendar then," he murmured in a low undertone.

"Your prerogative." She gulped a swallow of root beer. "So good. The taste sparks a memory of me and my little sisters slurping ice cream floats in front of the TV." She positioned her bib and held the ties to the back of her neck. One dropped.

"Allow me to assist, Ms. Patten." He leaned over and deftly tied a bow at her neck. "Took me years to master scrubs." His light touch remained on her shoulder for a deliciously long moment.

Tingles made her squirm in her chair.

This day became more complicated by the minute. It was a trial of wills, and no bail would set her free.

~ ~ ~

A confident Corrin sat opposite him, tapping her fingers to the beat of the music. Kyle chewed his last bite of brisket and scanned her face. No trace remained of the frightened creature he'd carried earlier, while championing the cause of her dry shoes. In turn, she'd cleverly discouraged a determined divorcee. They made a fine team.

The song ended, and Corrin stacked their empty plates and took them to a nearby dish tub.

His eyes studied the shifting movements of her balanced gait while the drummer pounded out a sexy beat. Possibility danced in his chest.

Corrin returned to their table, her perfectly aligned hips keeping time. If he knew women at all, she wanted to join the dancers.

The crack of glass hitting wood snapped him back to reality.

The rancher at the next table gave a sheepish shrug and righted four empty beer bottles in front of him and his foreman.

Kyle recalled giving the rancher a tetanus shot last year and treating the other guy for an STD. Both had eyed Corrin from the moment she'd entered the building. Both nervously tapped their table, ready to make a move.

She slid back into her seat. "Great food. There's prince-worthy fudge for dessert."

He'd watched Disney movies with Mom. Prince Charming never hesitated, not with glass slippers or dancing at the ball. He wiped his clammy hands on his trousers. "Time for candy later. Care to spin around the floor and determine if you remember any steps?"

"Oh, don't you worry. I'll keep pace."

Her alluring smile implied she'd accepted the challenge. He pushed out of his chair. "Time will tell."

"We'll see how your rubber-soled shoes shuffle," she jested, and sauntered to the edge of the dance floor. Her bouncy sway satisfied him better than a warm bed on a cold night. He inhaled, let it out slowly, and strode to her.

His hand fit perfectly at her waist. Fluffy softness met his fingertips. He raised her palm. "Ready?"

Her creased brow hinted at efforts to convince their audience this typified her behavior. "Ready and willing." She placed her other hand on his shoulder. "To dance. You're the perfect height," she confided quietly.

Didn't all women dream of taller hunks? His fingers settled into the small of her back. "You mean you don't prefer a six-foot-three, Grant-sized leading man?"

"Definitely not. I've found their clamoring egos match the stature." She met his eyes. "Haven't met the bureau boy, but I favor a man who's comfortable knowing who he is."

Whoa! She'd easily make him well above comfortable, the way his nerve endings energized. "I'm a simple country doctor who's been blessed to practice medicine among lifelong friends." He nudged her into a back step, joining the counterclockwise parade of dancers.

Corrin nodded, keeping her gaze centered above his left ear. Slight movements of her lips coincided with the music's tempo.

Beat counting. He knew the trick. Kyle kept his first few moves simple before he cued her to promenade. He smiled. She may have needed a refresher, but her blissfully fluid responses suggested they'd partnered for years. "Nice footwork, counsel."

Her grip on his shoulder relaxed. "Surprised?"

"Au contraire. I'm certain you're full of them."

Several couples strolled in unison, staying attached at the hip. Others needed a wide berth for showy footwork.

He and Corrin advanced around the floor precisely like gears of a clock, one turning and propelling the other.

A crackling awareness pulsed sparks deep into his core. He'd never been this attuned to another human being. Never.

His realm needed this woman. He'd be her prince, her page, whatever she asked. The verbal sparring energized him. Their synchronized steps, acting and reacting on sheer instinct, proved physical compatibility. His base impulses demanded more of the unexplored.

He swung her out to his side, carefully avoiding her open-toed shoes. Impractical, expensive, urban Seattleite shoes dashing out of his life tomorrow morning. The image jabbed him worse than a dull needle piercing tender skin.

In all of life's uncertainties, one fact secured his existence. He'd never leave Emma Springs, not for Three Falls, or Seattle, or London. Town residents had become extended family, and they relied on his medical skills, especially his own dad, if he'd interpreted the warning signs correctly.

The song's tempo sped up, blurring the faces in the crowd while they whirled as a single entity.

What if her life reached a crossroads between a loving family and her precious career? What if she needed someone to champion her, or heaven forbid, protect her?

Fading guitar notes ended the piece.

"Last song of the set, and we'll make it slow for you lovers." The singer smiled at Kyle and rubbed a spot above his left brow.

He'd sutured the bandleader after his recent fall on ice. Kyle scanned the packed room. He'd doctored more than half the occupants.

Corrin could practice law in Emma Springs. He tightened his hold onto the curve above her hips. An unfamiliar need sped through his veins, intense and demanding. "One more dance?"

"Yes, please." Several shoulder-length blond tendrils grazed her cheeks.

His fingers itched to slide out wire hairpins and free all her silky hair from the bun. He caught himself and stepped into the waltz position.

She'd depart in the morning, back to her preferred city life of plaintiffs and precarious heels. From the cutting remarks, she didn't yearn for country living.

The music slowed to a sensual pulse, and she leaned on him without hesitation, pushing hope into his chest.

No more proper dance positions. He'd cast his rope and pull her in slowly. He drew her body in close enough to feel her warmth, and damn his luck, she relaxed further.

His chin rested against her temple. Scents of coconut and spices lingered in the soft strands brushing against his cheek.

Thumping heartbeats and her seductive appeal told him he'd found the perfect woman, and important minutes to convince her ticked away.

He wanted much more than a wife who knew what he took in his coffee. He needed a friend to talk to, or to tease into smiling, and deep in the night, a soft form he'd spoon against with sleepy, loving eyes that he'd kiss awake each morning.

He dropped his head, keeping his cheek nestled against her skin. Their bodies swayed—every drop in his veins willed her to let go and free-fall beside him into the unknown future.

Somehow, some way, he'd convince her they'd land safely.

~ ~ ~

Music enveloped Corrin in a protective shell against time and space. She closed her eyes. Kyle's firm guidance unwound her tightly strung cords to divinely slack.

Moving in unison, a simple concept. She'd let the drunks in the boat define her aversion to men. Until now. Until trusting Kyle and letting her spirit soar.

Her palm rested on his strong, solid shoulder. She thumbed a wrinkle in the fabric of his cotton dress shirt, not starched and pressed to lawyerly impersonal. An image of him in an old sweatshirt, throwing a ball to a blond toddler, flashed in her mind.

She adjusted her hand and the linked stones on her bracelet jangled a reminder of her goal since she'd ridden the bus out of Ebony Cove. Her body stiffened.

The music ended on a low, somber note. Kyle kept holding her after the last chord faded.

Heated waves swirled between them. She dropped her hands to her sides.

Other couples left the dance floor and flowed by, as river currents avoided a boulder. She'd be the rock, determined not to let a fleeting desire sweep her away.

Kyle's hands slid down her bare arms, slowly reaching her wrist. "Those stones are unique."

The ambition to visit foreign countries propelled her through the worst days at work. She swallowed to wet her dry throat. "Each one signifies a different continent I plan to visit." She fingered the African topaz.

His mouth tightened. "Long flights on airplanes."

"Yes, to exotic destinations. I read colorful stories as a kid."

He'd dropped his eyes, as if discouraged.

Not everyone took vacations. "Have you traveled much?" she asked.

"Very little after I attended the University of Washington for medical school." He entwined his fingers into hers and led her back to their table, their hips bumping to squeeze through a narrow path.

"Another root beer?" he asked over his shoulder.

Nothing would quench the strong desires dancing with him had awakened. "A soda sounds refreshing."

He released her hand and pulled out her chair. "Two more cold ones, coming up."

A considerate yet steamy-hot man shook her world. She fought the impulse to kick off her shoes and run, preferably straight out into snowy darkness. "Thanks. I need to check my phone." She grabbed it from her purse. "Blast. Still no message from Miranda. I'm going to find the ladies' room, back in a minute."

"Bathrooms are to the left of the bar." He touched her arm. "Did I twirl you too much?"

Escaped strands of her hair concealed her eyes. "Nope, you dance well." Her feet couldn't move fast enough to distance her from his spell.

Laughter carried across the room. A hand-holding pair stood in the entry, brushing fresh snow from each other's shoulders, both ruddy-cheeked from the cold.

She rubbed her bare arms. Nothing could freeze away the memory of her time near Kyle. Dammit, she'd try.

Couples mostly occupied the tables, their foreheads angled together like poles in a tepee, probably whispering plans for the chilly evening. She turned into a hallway.

At the end, she pushed open a door with *MARES* printed in bold letters. The scent of Chanel No. 5 filled the bathroom.

The dark-haired cougar from the food buffet stood at the sink. "I don't believe I recognize you as a local," she purred.

"Not likely." Corrin turned to leave. Confrontation took energy and tamping the wonderful sensations Kyle aroused drained her.

"Visiting from nearby?" she persisted, while powdering her nose. In brighter light, age spots suggested she'd hit at least forty-five.

Corrin grabbed the door handle and hauled it open. "I'm not a Montanan."

"That's right. You mentioned Seattle. Hold on a minute. I left California and I'm dying here in Dudsville. I need another urbanite to survive. I'm willing to share Kyle. He's got plenty of energy for the both of us. When your pop's the nosey town lawyer who has contacts on every corner, the concept of friends with benefits is more clandestine." She winked.

Corrin recoiled, and the scent of the woman's heady perfume gagged her. "I wouldn't know the local swinger rules." She left and jerked the door shut, then stood in the empty hallway.

Anger rose in her chest. *Bloody hell.* Did she look like a sleaze?

She needed to talk to Miranda. She must've landed and gotten the text she'd sent asking her to phone immediately. Why hadn't she called?

The spicy barbecue churned in her stomach. *STALLIONS* denoted the men's room on the opposite door—precisely the macho type Miss Fresno of 1999 deserved, presently fumigating the bathroom.

Corrin balled her fist. If she were a local cowgirl, she'd go back in and defend Kyle's honor.

Not her battle. Her shoes thudded against planked wood. She rounded the corner and spotted Kyle. Was he too perfect? The cougar knew about his dad being a lawyer. Could Kyle be expertly hiding the deception? Her fingers dug into the sides of her purse.

His gaze followed her movements shoving empty chairs aside to reach the table.

She came to a stiff-postured stop at their table. "I'd prefer to leave soon."

He met her request with a composed face. "If you forgot to pack anything, McPherson's General Store is open."

"Ugh." She rolled her eyes. "I need a hotel and an aspirin. I ran into one of the women from the buffet preening her whiskers in the bathroom, and she implied you're involved."

His eyes widened. "What? I haven't dated anyone since college, and I'm certainly not seeing anyone, in any way, now."

"Not according to her, the one flaunting the expensive pair of huge . . . earrings."

"Betsy." Nothing in his manner changed. He casually poured frothy root beer into two glasses. "She's not my type, never has been, regardless of her repeated hookup hints. In the produce aisle last week, she shared her affinity for cucumbers. I ignored her tasteless joke." He slid out her chair. "Please sit for a minute."

"Betsy's dead serious and not craving salad." The cold chair seat hit her thighs. "She offered to share your energy. I didn't ask for details."

"Sorry that happened." He leaned forward. His eyes shone, clear and gentle. "Other men might be flattered. I'm not a player."

The honesty took her off guard. He wanted her trust. She took a swig of cold soda and let the spicy brew linger on her tongue. "Why's a catch like you single?"

"I concentrated on other priorities. First medical school and later earning patient confidence by providing optimum care. The closest doctor retired. He'd practiced for more than forty years."

Priorities she understood. "Donning his stethoscope must've been a challenge. I struggle against preexisting attitudes."

"I bet you do. The folks living here knew me growing up. Adjusting their perceptions after I'd become their physician kept my social life on hold. Didn't matter. The few single women in this county are either too young or too jaded."

"In Montana there is a lot of pasture between the fence posts. I'd imagine distance complicates dating."

"If you let it." He perched on the edge of his seat to get closer.

She'd curtail his thoughts of them dating before her own fantasies gained traction. Like the one, right now, where she ran her fingers down his jawline to touch his lips. She pulled her coat off the back of her chair and onto her shoulders. "I hate long drives. My preference is public transportation."

"Opinions can change," his deep, smooth voice suggested. "Betsy's one of dad's clients. Rumor has it she put a pin on a map, it landed near Sunrise Lake, and she built a McMansion to irritate her wealthy and soon-to-be third ex-husband."

"I figured she didn't moonlight on a John Deere. At least not the tractor version."

Kyle laughed. "She's toughing it out at her three-thousand square-foot cabin until her divorce settlement's finalized. Dad's not accustomed to her type."

"Lucky him," Corrin stated. "I've handled a few Betsys and more repugnant male versions."

"She probably has sterling attributes, but I'm not interested in what she's offering. Family life appeals to me. I'll be thirty-one shortly. You look young for all you've accomplished."

"I'm twenty-eight." She set her purse on the table and twirled a loose strand of hair. "You're lucky to recognize what you want."

"Each of us has to figure out what brings true joy."

Joy hadn't factored into her existence for years. "Agreed. My focus is narrow until I make partner."

"My practice has settled into a routine." He rotated his glass. "Dad's jokingly requested tots to bounce on his knee."

She smiled and waved her forefinger. "Better keep him away from Ben, the taxi driver."

"Too late. Wednesdays they go fishing. Dad already owns a paddle boat for his future grandkids."

Boating, another negative. "Nothing beats preparation. He must be a lawyer."

Kyle grinned and thumbed a path on his frosty glass. "I wish I embraced such optimism about raising kids in today's world."

"At least your family had their life in order. My parents aren't the plan-ahead types. They got married and I appeared before Mom got through high school. My sisters and brother followed in rapid succession. Mom and I never talked much between diaper changes. I chose education."

"Careers are motivating, but isn't it hard living in a city away from family?" His eyes stayed on her. "Dad and I hike or paddle kayaks on the lake most weekends."

How many years since she'd seen her parents? "I go home regularly to visit Corey and Willy, my niece and nephew. They'll get a great college education if I have to scrub floors to fund it. My sister's a widow."

"I'm sorry. Do your folks help her out?"

She shrugged. "Not a lot. Dad's committed to whiskey, and Mom always struck me as the unhappy kid on the tricycle at the bottom of the hill. Peddling back to the top took too much effort."

"That's a strong statement." He met her eyes, seemingly intent on searching for answers buried deep inside of her. "I've learned you can't always understand how others react if you haven't walked in their shoes."

He dared to rebuke her, after having a perfect childhood. She cleared her throat. "I've walked in plenty of second-hand shoes." She held out her foot. "Like these."

He tapped her bare toe. "And you wear them well. Next time you visit I'll loan you a pair of wool socks."

Next time? She ignored the remark. "Did you always plan to be a doctor?"

"Nope." He pointed to his black, waterproof half-boots. "My feet fell in behind others—namely Grant going into law enforcement. Early on I did a couple police ride-alongs and realized I wasn't cut out to arrest criminals. My folks suggested medical school. Science and the human body consistently fascinated me."

"You found your life calling."

He gave her a two-fingered salute. "From babies to seniors, I enjoy treating patients. Now I believe, parents are the luckiest people on earth." Anticipation radiated from his smiling face.

No need for a court interpreter's translation of his stance. She took another long swig of soda. "I'd surmise your future dreams include children."

He leaned back in his chair, his hands behind his head. "They do now."

Could he possibly consider her mommy material? Longing for a family struck a deep, deep chord. He'd be the kind of dad who'd enjoy bouncing a chubby tot on one of his practical shoes.

Shoes worn by a loving, responsible husband.

She imagined a myriad of other possibilities in his crystal blue eyes. Swallowing became difficult.

~ ~ ~

"Damn!" Mikey slowed to a crawl, passing under the blinking yellow light and into Emma Springs. No sign of the Explorer from the airport. And no sign of Blondie. He squeezed the steering wheel. H.P. would be furious.

Google Maps led him past a handful of closed shops on Main Street and a few well-kept old houses.

Only money justified camping out in the boonies, and he'd better earn a pile from the overflowing Piersall family coffers.

He re centered the address from H.P. and steered uphill, past a lake. The directions ended at a farmhouse. An identical rental car sat in the drive.

Must belong to one of old man Piersall's advance teams, he determined, while he parked and studied flat water on a breeze-free afternoon. How to word the text message admitting failure? No matter, there'd still be steam coming out of H.P.'s ears.

Lost her, he wrote. He sent the text and kept to the edges of the bowed wooden stairs. A shiny keypad contrasted against the weathered doorframe. After punching in the code number, he removed the key.

Another day, another alimony check, he brooded, and entered a kitchen still harboring a 1950s white enamel stove displaying side-by-side ovens. An overflowing garbage can sat alongside it.

A cough blasted from the next room, the same hack he'd heard from Piersall's geotechnical engineer.

Crossing the kitchen's creaky wood floor stirred aromas of peanut butter and play dough into the still air.

An arched opening provided a view of a computer station on a table. Overstuffed chairs had been pushed to the corner of the living room.

The stench of smoke hit his nose.

A few weeks ago, he'd met the smoker who currently leaned over graphs and charts. He hadn't bothered to remember his name.

"Decent flight?" He raised his head and asked. He pulled a drag from his cigarette, then snuffed it out in a jar lid.

"Uneventful. The way I prefer it." Mikey dropped his carry-on bag to the floor.

The guy tapped a topographic map. "Good thing the senior Mr. Piersall started buying half the West's available mountain sides decades ago. Can't picture an exclusive resort in this county, though. Hell, there's nothing to offer high rollers and rich techies within a hundred-mile radius. Why's Junior suddenly interested in these parcels?"

"Not your concern. If you want your job, don't let H.P. catch the 'Junior' tag. Did you investigate the county council members yet?"

"I added it to the list. They're not exactly LinkedIn types. I understand H.P. hired a fancy Seattle law firm in case there's any environmental squawking on his daddy's legacy project." His smirk showed dark teeth. "My hunch is this little area won't pan out."

Not the way H.P.'s old man envisioned for the last forty years. "Doesn't matter. I'm stuck here indefinitely. Meet any interesting locals?"

"I pushed the realtor to encourage the owners to sell this dump and the one next door. A broad going through a divorce owns another lakefront property. Found out at the nearest watering hole she's a bored California transplant we can use to our advantage." He cupped his hands under his pecs. "You know, the plumped out and pedigreed type needing to sink her teeth into fresh meat."

"Just your style."

"You bet." He lit another cigarette. "I'll grind beans for a fresh pot of coffee." He rose and stepped into the kitchen.

Whirring erupted, then stopped.

"I've got a couple things to go over. Afterward, I'll show you the sights," he called. "Former owners left a Carhartt jacket in the closet, unless you prefer to freeze your ass off."

"Got sent here on short notice." Mikey's phone beeped an incoming text. *Your login for her tracker… burythebitch … is active. Follow every move she makes.*

Blondie would learn the penalty for leaving her new phone charging overnight in her office with a mop-jockey on their payroll.

He opened the site and studied the moving arrow on the screen. "Skip the coffee. We need to head to a spot outside of town." He folded the maps where dollar signs from commercial development should be floating on the pages.

A skull and crossbones seemed more appropriate. The angst in his gut wasn't from the reek of stale cigarettes and greed.

The tracer app blinked on a destination. He should've severed ties to H.P. a decade ago. Should've known Blondie equaled trouble. If he didn't need the money, he'd bail on the lunatic who was hell-bent on exacting her punishment.

CHAPTER 4

Bobby Bell watched the two men in the silver car drive downhill to the highway. Mommy always warned him about strangers, and he'd not gotten anywhere close to them. He wrinkled his nose. One of them had pitched a cigarette into the snow and it stunk.

"Let's go." He released his hold on Daisy's dog collar and skipped out from behind the shed where they'd hidden. Together they scampered past the empty farmhouse. "Mom won't let me go near the lake alone, but she never said not to climb Mt. Hanlen."

Daisy wagged her tail, circling his legs.

"We're following the trail where I watched the guy drive toward the old mineshaft on the ATV yesterday." Bobby held his hand to his forehead, shading his eyes to scan the foothill leading to Mt. Hanlen. "Maybe they're searching for arrowheads, like we found with Daddy last summer."

Daisy darted ahead under a clump of snow-covered bushes.

His feet slipped and slid trying to catch her. Fading afternoon sun reached patches of the shaded hillside. They'd made it to where climbing got steeper and rockier. He zipped the snowsuit to his chin.

"The guy I saw yesterday must've come from the farmhouse." He pointed at another cigarette butt. "Litterbug. We won't leave a trace if we walk on the frozen part of his tire tracks." He pulled on a pair of mittens and gazed downhill.

The farmhouse seemed way, way below.

The beagle's nose dropped to the ground. She darted uphill and stopped abruptly, sniffing and yipping at a tall pile of boards in front of a rock wall.

"Hey Daisy, what you got?" Bobby's bulky snowsuit rubbed against his knees while he ran.

Daisy barked.

"Someone's building a fort!" He dashed to within a foot of the stacked boards, looking for a door.

His cowboy boots skidded into an open hole the size of a manhole cover. "They uncovered the mineshaft!"

The ground under his butt gave way, and he dropped to his waist. "Help!" His boots busted through wood underneath him. He threw his arms out and pawed, but his thick mittens slid across the frozen edge of the hole.

Daisy grabbed his cuff. The ribbed material slipped through her teeth.

"No!" He crashed through crisscrossed pieces of wood, the rough edges poking and scraping during the plummet into darkness.

He thumped onto hard earth. A hot pain jabbed his leg. "Ouch!"

Yipping sounded from far above. Daisy's toenails scratching on wood echoed in the narrow chamber.

Splinters and cold dirt smacked his head.

"Stop digging, Daisy!" He shook off the debris and stuck out his tongue at a board a few feet above his head.

"I'll climb out." He tried to stand, winced, and grabbed his leg. "I need Mommy, Daisy." The dog barked twice.

"Doggy bone. Go home and get a doggy bone."

She let out a loud whine, then silence. A faint bark sounded from far away.

"Good girl," he whispered. He raised his hand to wipe away a tear. Pain shot from his wrist. "Ow!"

The cold wall pressed into his back for what seemed like hours.

Light dimmed at the top of the hole. Did clouds block the sun, or had Daisy forgotten him? His lips trembled.

"Mommy!" No response. What if she never found him?

"Mommy!" he yelled louder.

Chunks of rotted wood fell onto his shoulder.

Another hot tear washed down his cheek. What if the shaft caved in?

~ ~ ~

Loud voices competed with canned music in the Red Horse Tavern.

Corrin feigned ignorance at hearing Kyle's remark concerning children. He could dream until the proverbial cows came home, featuring another woman playing the wifely role.

She'd done her time mothering her younger siblings. Anyway, Corey and Willy deserved her commitment to pay for school clothes now, and four years of college later. "Why hasn't Miranda called?" She checked her watch and took a swig of root beer. "She should've landed an hour ago."

"The airport's probably slammed. So, any wish for a husband and family?" Kyle asked.

She rotated the glass between her fingers and watched the band reassemble. "I learned a lesson from my impoverished sister, who flips burgers to support two kids."

His face showed the pity she'd dealt with in childhood. "Her life must be tough." He leaned forward, prepared to say more.

The first chords of *Somewhere Over the Rainbow*, chimed out from her purse. She dove for the phone.

"Miranda's ring tone! Excuse me, Kyle."

He nodded. "Of course."

Corrin stuck her cell to her ear. "Too loud. Hold on a minute." She trotted to the entrance. "Are you safe?"

"I guess," Miranda mumbled. "A team of agents stand guard in the hotel hallway."

Guards should instill more confidence. "A team. Wow. Your FBI guy gets a gold star." No response. Corrin clenched her fist. "Has something else happened?"

"Not yet. Hey, am I hearing twang music in the background?" Miranda's voice sounded closer to normal.

"Yes indeed," she said. "You'll never believe this, I'm being entertained by Doc Kyle."

"I read your text. Kyle's a great guy. He's kind, loyal, and oh-so-cute."

"He wants kids. He'd be perfect for you." Lunch dropped to the pit of her stomach. He *would* be perfect for her best friend.

"Nope. You're interested. I can tell," Miranda teased. "Give him a chance."

"I gave him several dances."

"Good start, and I'm proud of you. Consider dating him," she insisted.

"Geographically undesirable by six or seven hundred miles," Corrin released a long sigh. Through the glass door, endless fields stretched out from the parking lot. "You sound weird. What haven't you told me?"

"I overheard Grant's boss saying they believed Karpenito returned to Seattle. The crooked cop is here to off me."

Corrin flinched. *Bloody hell.* The mobster who'd ordered the first hit would likely kill Karpenito if he allowed Miranda's testimony. "Kyle swears Grant's the best. I'll be on the flight tomorrow."

"I miss you."

"You're going to be safe," Corrin said, forcing confidence. "We'll be hugging in no time."

"If anyone can protect me, it's Grant," Miranda murmured.

Corrin swallowed hard. "Not a positive response. Spill."

"Just tired. Gotta go, Grant wants to prep us for tomorrow."

"Okay, you rest. Night." Corrin thumbed the back of her phone. Why did a small piece of electronics-stuffed plastic have to provide the only link to her best friend? She leaned against the wall. Damn phone, the lifeline that choked when you couldn't do a thing to help.

"Please keep Miranda safe," she whispered out to the clear sky. Movement caught her eye in the parking lot.

A silver car parked, and two men got out. Her body tensed. Paunch Guy from the plane slammed the passenger door. He'd thrown on an old jacket. Maybe a local returning home from a business trip?

Still. The nagging suspicion he'd followed her made her hurry back to their table. She sat beside Kyle and glanced over her shoulder.

At the entrance, Paunchy pulled a ball cap out of his pocket, caught her watching, and tugged it low over his face. He hustled from the doorway to the bar.

Buzz off, sucker! She gripped the edge of the table.

Kyle put his hand on hers. "We can continue sightseeing, unless you'd prefer dancing more."

"May we leave?" She slipped on her jacket and caught hurt displayed on his face. "I enjoyed dancing. I'm simply maxed out on loud music for one night." She turned away.

Both men from the car stood opposite the bartender. The unfamiliar one pointed toward Betsy. Paunch Guy shot a look in Corrin's direction, then bent to tie his shoe.

Too many coincidences for one day. She clenched her purse. Why did he make her so nervous?

Kyle stood and removed several dollar bills from his wallet. He anchored them under his mug. "Glad you noticed my footwork from mandatory junior high sessions," he said. "Something else bothering you?"

Did all doctors possess a tension radar? "I keep seeing a guy from the airplane. The beer-bellied one at the end of the bar."

Kyle eyed the two men. "Not locals, probably hunters."

That made sense. "Hunters, sure. And about your fleet feet, I knew you'd graduated dance class the minute you put your hand firmly on my shoulder and assumed the 'ready' stance."

"All the effort paid off." Kyle took her hand before guiding her to door. "You stay inside, and I'll grab my car."

"Thank you."

He settled his parka around her shoulders. "The sidewalk got shoveled, but there are icy patches. I'll pull to the end of the walkway and escort you out."

"Okay." His blond head disappeared into the dusky parking lot, and she directed a tiny pang of resentment at the shovel leaning against the outside wall.

The tavern offered her a needed reprieve, until the last few minutes. She scanned the room.

Paunch Guy tipped his coat collar, pulled out his cell again, and began typing.

What the hell, was he writing a book on other tourists in town? She thrust her arms into the sleeves of Kyle's puffy coat and zipped it to her chin.

Kyle maneuvered his Jeep to the curb, and true to his word, he gripped her forearm walking out.

"Whoa." Her foot skidded on a patch of ice.

Kyle held her upright. "I've got you."

She faced his caring eyes and smiled gratefully. Caring eyes were a novelty after avoiding men the past fourteen years. No man affected her like Kyle, who stimulated her brain and her body, yet put her at ease.

After a few careful steps, she'd scooted onto the car seat. "Thanks for the assistance."

"Anytime. Next, a tour through town en route to Dad's."

She buckled her belt. "Before I meet your dad, I'd appreciate a little family background."

"Okay, chart notes on my folks." He grinned and made his way around the front of the Jeep and into the driver's seat. "Dad thrives on serving the legal needs of community residents. My mom was amazing—funny, nurturing, and a tomboy." He started the engine.

"You can't be squeamish raising boys."

"Not Mom. I had the perfect childhood and got through med school before the cancer axe fell. Despite painful treatments, Mom never lost her sense of humor or her compassion for other people." His voice cracked.

An ache formed in Corrin's throat. "As a doctor, that must've been unbelievably difficult. I'm very sorry, Kyle."

The windshield wipers swished away snowflakes while they sat in silence.

He let out a long sigh and twisted the heater button to high. "I'd begun my residency at the hospital in Billings." A pained expression crossed his face. "Everyone in Emma Springs helped Dad. He's incredibly lonely now. Do you have family in Seattle?"

"A special aunt of mine lives nearby." She flicked a minuscule piece of lint from her skirt. "Do you think your dad will remarry?"

"I hope so. He's still active and healthy, but there's a distinct void in his life I can't fill." He drove across the parking lot and turned onto the highway.

No senior centers sat amongst the empty pastures, serene in fading light. "Most men don't do well alone," Corrine offered.

"Particularly after they've been happily married. He'll enjoy discussing your Seattle practice. If he and Mom hadn't left Cambridge and settled here, he could've been a high-profile attorney."

The road curved, and they passed a barn and house sitting back from the road. Smoke rose from the chimney.

"Sounds like your dad attended Harvard. How'd they land so far west?"

"They both graduated from Harvard and were on their honeymoon when their car overheated outside of Emma Springs. Mom decided this beautiful setting and the friendly folks created a perfect place for raising a family."

The kiddie thing again. "Unlike a big city."

"Precisely." He slowed and pulled off the road and onto a driveway flanked by a wrought iron gate. "Here's the Lazy K Ranch."

"They could've called it the Drunken K Ranch, with how the letter's tipped. Lazy to me is a book and a couch, but I guess that would be hard to weld into a brand."

Kyle laughed. "I like your image better."

A 'Closed for the Season' sign hung on the rail. Behind it, a meadow ended at a group of closely packed evergreens.

He grinned at her. "I didn't call to alert them. Or send a text or a telegraph. Honest."

She rolled her eyes, then giggled. Where'd that come from? After meeting Kyle, dignified comportment flew out the window, and instead, easy banter tumbled between them. "I bet you sent a smoke signal telling the owners an urbanite needing a room was on the way and they'd better high tail it to Florida."

"It wouldn't require much prodding, after they'd coddled guests all summer teaching them to ride." He pointed to one of the horses grazing in a pasture behind the fence. "I can coax over a pony to pet."

"No thank you, and that's not a pony." One of the large animals raised its head. She grasped the edge of the seat. "I don't have my pills."

"Oh, allergic to horses? Usually it's their dander."

Two curious, brown giants ambled to the rail and stretched their necks out, aimed at her.

She dove away from the window and leaned over the console. "Not allergic, deathly afraid. Miranda promised to help me acclimate."

Kyle turned sideways, his back to his door, as if knowing she needed space. "I never noticed a horse in Seattle," he said.

Stop acting stupid. She returned to the center of her seat. "We figured I might encounter the beasts during travel. I'd planned to visit the pony ride area at our zoo. My doctor prescribed mild anti-anxiety meds for the first trip there."

A horse whinnied. She flinched.

"Hey, you're safe." Kyle touched her forearm and then steered onto the road. "We'll try equine desensitizing during another trip."

The beasts returned to grazing. She blocked out the childhood memory of her mother screaming at the giant horse. "Good luck, I get hives imagining I'm touching one."

"I enjoy a challenge."

His resolute tone both calmed and excited her. A hasty decision to help a friend and now she found herself indebted to a man who attracted her like a malpractice lawsuit to a cash-strapped attorney.

The Jeep topped a hill. At the bottom sat a placid lake. A small inlet held brown cattails, and a dead tree poked out of the water. A tiny house sat close to the shoreline with a large one further down.

Kyle pointed. "My folks gained their first essence of Emma Springs while living in that little cottage." He slowed to almost a stop.

She craned her neck. Not a single barn in sight. Corrin smiled. "The lake's charming. Straight out of a storybook featuring a tiny, enchanted cottage on its shore."

"Nice description. Sorry, no fairies in residence, or humans either."

Enchanted cottage? She blinked. "No renters? What do people do for a living besides farm and guide hunters?"

"Sunrise Lake's a summer draw to tourists, being one of the cleanest and warmest swimming lakes in Montana. Hot springs flow into the north side. My folks bought the cabin first, and once Dad's legal practice took off, they also purchased the bigger home across the street. He has an office for his practice on the main level."

Inviting lights glowed from the front windows of his dad's two-story house. Stone pillars framed the wide front porch.

She'd grown up dreaming of being loved by sober, functioning parents in a stately home. "Aunt Iris lived next door to a similar Craftsman in Seattle. I used to imagine having a bedroom there all decorated in peach tones."

Kyle's eyes searched her face. "My folks welcomed newcomers to Emma Springs into their home."

"And you carry on the tradition."

"I try to. After I obtained my medical license, my parents celebrated by providing the down payment for my place."

Contrasted to her family. "I got a graduation card from my parents." She turned to the window, a hollowness forming in her chest. "You're lucky to own a home."

'Kyle Werner, MD' was printed on a sign out front of a white clapboard rambler sitting in the middle of a big lawn.

"Until I get loans paid off, the bank and I are co-owners. The townspeople were excited to have a young doctor and helped remodel it to hold my office."

"Couldn't you have converted the tiny house next door?"

"Not really. Your enchanted cottage accommodated guests, barbecues, and birthday parties while Mom was alive. It holds too many memories for Dad to make any changes."

"The cottage deserves an occupant who appreciates the charm."

He gave her an appraising look. "It does." He pushed the button on a remote and drove into his dad's three-car cement-walled garage. Interior lights flicked on, and the door slid shut.

She opened her car door. "Your dad's not a mob lawyer, is he?" Corrin blurted, surprised at the volume of her own voice inside the garage. "The steel door leading to the house should hold off marauding vikings." She scooched off the seat and stood beside Kyle, watching him press his thumb into a sensor pad.

"Dad and I were both Boy Scouts. Be prepared." He held up two fingers in the bunny ear pose.

"You probably surmised I wasn't a Girl Scout." She pointed to her shoes.

A green light blinked on the pad.

"Hadn't crossed my mind." Kyle twisted the door handle. "My dad collects valuable clocks and secured the house according to his comfort level."

Clunks reverberated as bolts retreated from their holes. "Solid gold, diamond-encrusted clocks?" Corrin asked.

"I wish." He rolled his eyes. "Rare antiques. Dad came from a tough town and also wanted Mom to feel protected if he traveled overnight." He opened the door into the next section.

Vines decorated the windows of the enclosed walkway from the garage to the house. The winding tendrils climbed heavy, wrought iron scrollwork, resembling the covered entrance to a Spanish fortress.

Kyle spoke into his cell. "Hey Dad, the mystery guest has arrived."

Corrin peered through the greenery to the road. Her eyes widened. The silver car slowed at their driveway, then sped off. "Kyle—"

A thick wooden door to the house swung open.

"Enough mystery. I want an introduction." An older man stepped out. Smile lines creased the edges of his honest, welcoming eyes, the same shade of blue as Kyle's.

"Dad, please meet Miss Corrin Patten."

"So nice of you to invite me to dinner." She offered her hand.

"My pleasure. I'm Roy Werner." His warm hand gripped Corrin's firmly but gently. "Your hands are freezing, young lady. Step in from the cold passage."

Same as Kyle, he put her strangely at ease. Precisely what she needed after seeing the damn car again. Had they been followed from the Red Horse? "Thanks," she mumbled. She raised her foot, caught the step, and the heel broke off her shoe. "Blast. I just bought these." She pulled off the shoe.

Kyle picked up the heel. "Nothing two-part epoxy can't fix. You'd begun to tell me something?"

Paunch Guy probably struck out with Betsy and headed to his bunk to lick his wounds. "It can wait."

"I'll get the glue," Roy said, and ushered them into a room bearing the tantalizing aroma of mashed potatoes and roast beef.

Assorted caps and jackets hung from a mirrored hall tree standing watch in the entry.

Kyle rotated her shoe in his hand. An image of Cinderella's prince flashed in her brain. No animation captured Kyle's brand of charm. "You're also a cobbler. My, my, Dr. Werner, you're full of surprises, too."

"While Dad organizes dinner, I'll get your shoe healed. If you stick around, I'll be happy to keep you on your toes." He took the tubes of glue from his dad and winked at her.

She swallowed hard. "I bet you would." Her eyes followed him while he disappeared into a hallway. Corrin directed her attention to Roy. Like Kyle, he shared the classic profile of a Brooks Brothers shirt model, completed by a determined set to his well-defined jaw.

"Kyle's a fixer. Make yourself comfortable, while I throw another log on to get you toasty," Roy said.

Childhood fantasies she'd concocted while staring at the home beside Aunt Iris's rang true—disturbingly accurate in fact. She would've given anything to spend her childhood here, protected by men who spoke and acted respectfully to one another, father to son and man to man. "Your home radiates comfort," she whispered.

Dark cherry columns separated the living and dining rooms. Flames from a glass-fronted stone fireplace basked overstuffed chairs in a warm glow. An inlaid coffee table held a stack of dog-eared magazines.

Kyle returned, holding her taped together shoe. "We'll give it time to dry. By tomorrow you'll never know the difference."

Oh, she'd know the difference on a growing number of distressing, life-changing concerns. The broken heel came in last. Leaving charming, funny Kyle and returning to a bland life topped the list. "Thank you."

"My pleasure." Kyle turned to Roy. "Dad, Corrin's on the brink of joining your profession. Could you share some highlights of your career while I check in on a patient?"

"Glad to. Take your time," Roy said, and grinned at Corrin.

Roy's attitude lacked any trace of the pretense displayed by MFB partners. She didn't miss that, either. "I enjoy a good story."

"Perfect. Please excuse me for a moment," Kyle said, and left.

"We'll chat in the dining room, so I can keep an eye on dinner." Roy stepped into a room glowing under soft light from a brass chandelier with dangling crystal prisms. Beneath it sat an oval dining room table, set for three with real china. From one of the longer sides, he pulled out a padded chair, its cushion decorated in needlepoint roses.

Corrin slid onto it and Roy sat at the narrow end of the table, his back to the doorway leading into a pale-yellow kitchen.

"Which school are you attending, Corrin?" he asked.

"I graduated from the University of Washington School of Law and passed the Multistate Professional Responsibility Examination. I'm scheduled for the February bar."

"You can't be old enough. Are you one of those child prodigies?" Roy's exaggerated wide eyes made her smile.

"Afraid not," Corrin replied. "College has taken me ten years to complete. I've worked in a land use law office to support myself." A linen napkin at her place held a silver fork. She straightened the handle, which was embossed by a spray of roses.

"Hard work pays off, my dear. Good for you," Roy said. "Property contracts are part of my practice, too. Our town's going to need a younger lawyer soon who knows their way around a deed of trust."

She smiled and considered his comment. The Werners resembled the fictional happy and perfect families she'd read about as a girl. And he'd hinted at offering her a job. Why'd she discover the real-life equivalents now, with Seattle career plans on track? "Kyle's made my missteps into Montana enjoyable."

"Glad to hear. Relax and join me in a glass of wine. Kyle's on call." Roy indicated a half-empty bottle on his end of the table.

Alcohol. Nothing was totally perfect. "No thanks, I prefer water."

"I'll get you a glass and check on the roast." He rose from his chair, raised his chin, and sniffed. "Uh-oh, I smell something burning." Roy bounded to the kitchen.

Across the room, framed photos sat atop a long buffet. One of the closest showed handsome and confident Kyle wearing a graduation gown. He held a diploma in a firm grip.

A grip she knew too well. Her arms craved to be held by the man who'd supported her during the waltz and would hold her tight through any challenge, unlike her father, who'd chosen to support a bottle of cheap whiskey instead of his family.

She straightened her bracelet. Bringing a man, no matter how perfect, into her life jeopardized her focus. She'd witnessed actions of other women in the office after they'd become engaged.

Their goal wasn't partnership. She'd be logging in sixty-hour weeks for another five years to prove herself to the partners before the next door opened.

Escaping the small-town confines of Ebony Cove initiated her first step to freedom. Corrin stretched her toes under the table. No way would she trade in her Pradas for cowboy boots. Broken, secondhand, or otherwise.

Roy returned, carrying a tray of fresh-baked biscuits and her glass of water. "I saved one pan from burning. Darn oven."

He set the rolls on the far end of the table and pointed through the columns to the living room's wide picture windows. Yard lights from the two houses abutting the lake cast a ghostly glow onto a dark, dangerous expanse. "The lake's beautiful at night. We're lucky the cottage and Kyle's home are far enough apart to allow our view between them," Roy said.

She'd avoided bodies of water since the attack. She swung her head and took a deep breath. "Yes, very serene," she fibbed. "The dead tree at the water's edge is spooky, though."

"Not to our resident wood ducks. They nest in an open cavity midway up the trunk. You'll spot it in daylight." Roy left again and reappeared holding a platter of pot roast and a bowl of steaming carrots.

To heck with duck gazing. He'd brought comfort food. She licked her lips. "Smells delicious! In my world, infrequent dinners at my Aunt Iris's provide my only homemade meals." The linen napkin she placed on her lap had softened from many launderings.

"No boxed shortcuts here." Kyle brought in a boat of rich brown gravy and a bowl of creamy white potatoes. "Dad, your oven's fine. Set a timer."

"A timer, right. Hand me your plate, young lady, and I'll fill it up," Roy said.

She passed her plate and noticed lights out a side window, shining on dormant flowerbeds outlined in stones. "Appears someone enjoys gardening."

"Kyle's mom, my sweet, sweet Flor, did. This yard remained her pride and joy until she got too weak." Roy's face suddenly lost its animation. He refilled his wine glass and took a swig.

"My Aunt Iris enjoyed what she called, 'puttering in her posies.' She gifted bouquets of her prized Tropicana roses to neighbors."

"Mom's garden provided fresh flowers to our neighbors from June through September." Kyle buttered his roll. "You probably have a longer growing season in Seattle."

Corrin blinked. Thoughts of the Emerald City and Miranda's plight had receded. Might've been relief knowing a team of agents protected her. Even so, she'd never zoned out like this before. "Milder weather, yes. I remember her fresh flowers in November."

Kyle shifted in his chair and unclipped his phone. "Excuse me a minute, dining companions. I have a call."

"Dr. Werner here . . . I see. Your exact location?" Alarm sharpened his tone as he stepped into the kitchen.

Roy topped off his wine glass and took a couple of gulps.

Kyle returned to the dining room, tapping on his phone screen. "Can you send an ATV to get me? . . . Okay, I'll wait for you at the bottom."

"What's going on?" Roy asked.

"Bobby Bell fell into a twenty-foot shaft on the ridge above his house," Kyle said. "It'll take multiple ATV trips to get the firefighters and extraction equipment delivered to the site. I'll be transported after they are in place. Bobby's conscious but may be hurt."

"I hope he's okay." Roy looked at Corrin. "Cute kid. A nice beagle's always tagging behind him, Norman Rockwell-style."

Kyle stuck his phone on his belt. "It's funny, I've hiked the mountainside across the lake, and the old mine shaft appeared well covered. You recall other holes the rescuers should be aware of, Dad?"

"No. Odd events at the two houses across the lake that sit below the hill, though. Heard the first family sold their place and moved out in the middle of the night. A day later, the folks next door to them complained a car followed their kids home from school. Next thing the townspeople knew, the second family vacated without telling anyone goodbye. Offended a few folks."

"I did school checkups on those kids." Kyle stood at the foot of the table, his eyebrows furrowed. "Neither family lived here long."

"Correct. Got the update during my haircut yesterday."

"Guess I need to visit the barber more often." Kyle ran his fingers through his own shaggy hair.

Corrin rubbed her thumb and forefinger together under the table, imagining the texture of his unruly locks. "An uncovered mine and families vanishing in the middle of the night sounds rather menacing for your quiet little town."

"A concern to discuss later," Kyle said. "I'd better head out to get in line for a ride."

Roy lumbered to the hall tree. "Bundle up, son." He grabbed Kyle's coat.

The urge to observe Dr. Werner on duty in real time struck her chest like a gavel on a judge's bench. She rose from her chair. "Kyle, can I go along to help? Maybe borrow a pair of boots and a jacket?"

"Good idea," Roy said. "Flor had tiny feet for her size. There's a pair of her work boots in the garage." He struggled to focus glassy eyes at Corrin. "Gardening bibs and a jacket should be in a storage tub."

Kyle hadn't answered.

~ ~ ~

Kyle opened his mouth to object. Corrin wouldn't know a carabiner from a clove hitch knot. Her attentive face stopped him. Curiosity, excitement, or an honest desire to help animated her to stunningly beautiful. "Sure. I'll grab gear for you," he said.

Four tubs sat on a shelf in the garage. Mom's printing marked the top one 'Outdoor Clothes'. He lifted her jacket and brought it to his face, remembering her excitement pointing out the first emerging daffodil of spring. The smell of Shalimar still perfumed its collar even after the three years she'd been gone. He'd given her a bottle for her birthday every year since he turned nine.

He stacked the clothes on top of the boots and headed inside. Dad and Corrin stood in mom's former art studio, transformed into a clock repair space. Both their heads were tipped over a disassembled automaton mantle clock.

She gently fingered a tiny carving of a deer. "It's a local craftsman who creates replacements?"

"He's more loco than local, if truth be told." Roy chuckled. "He lives on the mountain—way above where you're headed."

"I hate to drag you away from the painted toothpicks," Kyle said. "Here's the clothing. Bathroom at the end of the hallway. Clock's ticking."

Corrin took the bibs and left.

"I recognize the optimistic expression, Dad." Kyle twirled his keys in his fingers. "But she's a city girl, and her heart's set on making partner in a big, fancy law firm in Seattle."

"You've told me you're ready to settle down. A perfect young lady appeared. I'll never forget how your mom described single women in this town—the odds are good, but the goods are odd. Women carrying too much baggage."

"Yeah, well, Corrin carries a three-piece designer set crammed full." Kyle checked his watch.

"We all do, son. I admire her tenacity, so would your mom," his dad said. "You can monitor your own life, and you can direct the treatment of your patients. Because a young woman has aspirations that are out of your control, it doesn't mean you can't compromise."

His dad never rambled or preached. Kyle stared at the lake. "Don't book the church yet. She's not the country type."

"Neither was I. In my prayers tonight, your mother's going to know we might have another lawyer in the family."

"Okay, give her my love, Dad."

Steps came from the hallway. Kyle put his finger to his lips to warn his dad.

"Sorry, I rolled my pant legs to avoid face planting." Corrin hustled into the entry. Five inches of cuffed fabric stuck out at her ankles. A shoe-less, hesitant Corrin peered at Kyle. "Now I understand what my younger sisters endured wearing my castoffs."

He'd always been self-conscious around Grant, his mondo-sized best friend. Corrin made him feel taller than an NBA star. "Oversized beats out freezing. Time to meet our ride to Bobby."

"Thanks for the warm clothes." Corrin smiled at Roy.

"She'd be thrilled, Connie. If Flor were here, she'd be joining you on the adventure."

"Her name's, Corrin, Dad." Kyle patted his shoulder. "Please keep dinner warm until we return." He handed her the pair of ladies' winter boots. "We'll be cold and hungry."

He watched her slip them on and he evaluated three disturbing and challenging facts—Dad was losing his memory, this wasn't a normal emergency call, and Corrin had offered to help outside in the cold. He held the coat out for Corrin.

His fingers touched her soft neck as he adjusted the flipped under collar.

"Ready for action," she announced.

An image of her and his mom, standing arm in arm, wrenched his heart. "You look the part," he said softly. "Let's go."

Roy opened the door, and Corrin stepped into the breezeway.

Her golden hair hung in a single braid outside the jacket collar. He resisted the urge to give it a tug and instead dashed ahead and opened her door of the Jeep. "It'll be windy on the hill."

"Is it far? The poor kid must be terrified if he's alone in a dark pit."

"We'll be there in a few minutes. Chances are he's hurt." Kyle's stomach clenched. "He's a tough little guy. Cute freckle-faced sister, too. His dad's a plumber, and his mom teaches school. They foster rescued miniature horses." His descriptions of a favorite family spilled out.

Corrin nodded. "They must be frantic."

Wearing those clothes and the worried expression, she could pass for one of the locals. He wheeled onto the highway.

Her finger drummed her cheek. "You mentioned a shaft. Any recent mining exploration nearby?"

"Nope. Mostly they tried further west in the state. There's a gold exploration borehole from the 1800s on the hill. Abandoned and boarded up."

"If gold didn't bring people here, what did?"

"Trappers traded with the Blackfeet tribe, who camped near Sunrise Lake. The beauty of these mountains made them permanent residents. No lawyer before Dad."

"Not uncommon in rural areas."

"I suggested he limit his practice and maybe retire. What did you think of Dad, his alertness?"

"Reasonably alert. Enjoys vino. Why?"

"Alzheimer's runs in his family. He's forgotten things lately. I'm hoping it's the stress of losing Mom three years ago."

"Stress can cause self-medication."

She'd judged Dad's drinking to be excessive. Kyle's spine stiffened. "I've scheduled him to see a geriatric specialist next month. Dad's always enjoyed a glass of wine during dinner."

"I noticed he consumed more." Her lips pursed. "Where does he find clients to maintain a practice?"

Geez. They weren't in Antarctica, the most remote continent represented by a stone on her wrist. "People from a hundred-mile radius are willing to wait for his legal expertise. He's determined to find the best lawyer to bring on as a partner."

"I noticed. Hopefully his issues are minimal."

"Or treatable." He checked the crossroad for traffic and sped under the blinking light. "His clients help fill the loneliness gap."

She rotated her bracelet around her wrist again. "He won't have trouble finding an attorney to buy a successful practice."

Someone who appreciated Emma Springs. "Those are unusual stones. Is your bracelet a family heirloom?"

She squelched a snort. "Not from my parents. Aunt Iris's husband, Uncle Charlie, admired my goals and created the custom piece for me." Her hand dropped to her side. "You attended school alongside Grant?"

Another subject change from anything involving family.

"A year ahead. He's one of the few who moved away."

"Not many kids leave here for careers?"

"Nope. In-migration keeps the population stable. It's strange the two families Dad mentioned vanished. One of the mothers who left suddenly had recently told me she'd become the fourth generation to live on the family homestead and felt welcomed back by townsfolk."

Corrin dropped her chin. "Ebony Cove never welcomed anyone."

Her childhood must've sucked. What he wouldn't give to erase those ugly memories. "Montana's unique in a few ways." He softened his voice. "We're remote in winter. Everyone's protectively friendly here for safety's sake, not nosy. I grew up knowing in an emergency our neighbors would help me. Like now."

"Safety." Corrin murmured. "Miranda and I live next door to one another, and we call ourselves sisters-of-the-soul. I hope she gets a good night's sleep. If anything happens to her, I'll—"

"Grant's the best," he asserted. "He's my brother-of-the soul. We hiked the whole county as kids, did Scouts together, and roomed together at the U-Dub."

"So you said." She thrummed her armrest. "If I can do anything to assist getting this kid out, don't be afraid to ask. Not much bothers me. I pretty much raised my younger brother and sisters."

Judging by the set of her jaw, it hadn't been by choice.

~ ~ ~

Corrin waited in silence for Kyle to respond, probably defending Grant again. Undeservedly. Miranda repeatedly sounded nervous on the phone, bureau boys stationed beside her or not.

Kyle never spoke. His lips formed a tight line while he turned the Jeep into a cul-de-sac of split-level homes. Six vehicles sat parked at hurried angles, flanking the first driveway. He parked at the end closest to the road.

Half the town must've assembled to help rescue Bobby from the freezing pit. She zipped her jacket to the collar.

A man ran to Kyle's door. "Hey Doc, glad you're here. The emergency crew from the fire station won't proceed without you. They're working on a contraption to pull out Bobby."

"Thanks for the update, Mase. I'll grab my bag." Kyle turned to Corrin. "You can wait here until I learn more."

Headlights flashed into her window. A truck rumbled by.

Frissons of danger jolted her to full alert. No way she'd be stuck alone this close to the road. "I'm not a wait and see type." She hopped out.

The man pointed to a pair of fume-spewing ATVs. "Drive the red one, Doc. The seat's better for riding double," he said, and gave Corrin the once-over.

"Thanks." Kyle secured his medical bag to the back, jumped on, and motioned for Corrin to climb behind.

She eased her leg around his rear and squeezed her butt onto the seat. The cold frame pushed into her back.

The other rig roared ahead of them, tilting and swaying. They disappeared into near darkness.

Corrin clung to Kyle's waist. Blond hair on his chest? Maybe curly? She'd never itched to explore more of a male body, only batted away unwanted advances from wealthy clients.

The front wheel hit a rock and pitched her butt sideways.

"Whoa!" Her foot flew off the peg, and her hip slid. She dug her fingers into solid abs.

Kyle slowed the rig, grabbed her hand, and held her in place. "Could be more hidden rocks. Hold me tighter, I won't tip."

What irony. Her life began tipping the moment she'd slid off the airplane, each interaction resembling the blindfolded woman holding the Scales of Justice. She laced her fingers together and molded her body against his back while they climbed a steep incline.

Thrilling and terrifying at the same time, the exhilaration woke a suppressed quest for adventure. She pushed her face into Kyle's jacket, picturing his kind eyes, genuine smile, and temptingly toned muscles.

Kyle slowed to a stop and shut off the engine. She lifted her head. Fifteen feet away, a steel tripod held ropes dangling above a hole. Firefighters in turnout gear adjusted a winch. Nearby, a group of people huddled together.

"Those are Bobby's parents." Kyle pointed to a tall couple.

The father rushed over. "Hi, Doc. We have faith you'll tell us what to do." Panic strained his boyishly round face.

"Is Bobby alert? In pain?" Kyle's erect posture and sharp eyes radiated authority.

"If we crawl to the edge, we can talk to him," the father said. Bobby's too scared to move. We're all too big to fit into the shaft without pushing against the wobbly supports."

"Okay, I'll speak to him first." Kyle stepped to within a few feet of the hole. "Hey Bobby, it's Doc Kyle. How you holding up, buddy?"

Corrin bit her lip. He'd employed the tone of a doctor calming a child before a Band-Aid got ripped off.

"I'm cold and my leg has jabbing pains," a squeaky voice pleaded. "I want Mommy."

Kyle dropped to the ground and inched slowly to the edge on his belly. He tipped a flashlight into the hole.

Whimpers from the boy squeezed Corrin's heart.

"If we lower a rope swing, can you hold on for us to pull you up?"

"Don't think so. My arm hurts. I want Mommy to help me."

"You'll be out soon, bud." Kyle scooted back slowly and spoke to the closest firefighter. "He can't safely hook himself into a sling."

Bobby's mother pressed her pasty-white face onto her husband's shoulder. Like the others, both were tall and broad, sturdy country stock.

Kyle scanned the gathering of local men and women. "I'm concerned about one of our shoulders hitting a support." His face paled.

The tautness on Kyle's face mirrored Corrin's growing apprehension. Her Grandpa Patten nearly died in a collapsed mine in Ebony Cove. She shuddered, recalling the worst part of his story, the pitch-blackness and his description of being helplessly trapped, a fear she understood too well.

"Mommeee." Bobby's moan pierced the air.

Surges of adrenaline rushed through her body. She walked over to Kyle and lifted her chin. "Lower me."

All eyes turned to her.

She let her arms hang at her sides. "My shoulders are narrow."

Kyle moved behind her. He gently laid his splayed hands across her back. "I believe you'll fit." He stepped to face her and clasped her forearm. "This is dangerous."

His eyes searched hers, worry lines creasing the corners. "You don't have to go. We'll figure out a harness for Bobby somehow."

Corrin placed her hand atop his, squeezed, and removed it. "We can't risk him falling again. I trust you, Dr. Werner."

"That means a lot to me. Miranda told me how tenacious you were. I thought she meant in court. Action speaks so much louder than words," Kyle slid his hand to her wrist. He stopped at her bracelet. "You're going to conquer the world."

"Hey, does the hole go to China? If it does, it'll save me a lot of money." She threw Kyle her best cheeky grin, then motioned to the tall, female responder who held the harness.

"Gear me up."

"Mommy?" A faint, heart wrenching plea came from the hole.

"He's got to be in pain," Bobby's mom declared in a shrill voice. "He's never sobbed." She used her coat sleeve to swipe tears from her eyes. "I'm Rachel Bell. Thank you, thank you."

Corrin held out her hand and squeezed the mom's gloved one. "Corrin Patten, and I'm honored to help."

A firefighter rigged a rope sling. "This will support you and Bobby." He showed her how to work the clasp. "Tug the rope for us to stop lowering you and again to be lifted. Keep your voice and movements quiet. I don't trust the walls." An EMT opened a red medical supply case for Kyle.

"Corrin, here's a neck collar and temporary splints for Bobby's arm and leg," Kyle said. "Secure them snugly using the Velcro straps, please." He turned to the parents. "Mr. and Mrs. Bell, I can't guarantee he won't be jostled coming out of the hole and sustain complications."

"We understand the danger. Our prayers will be for our son and your girlfriend's safety."

Corrin waited for Kyle to correct them. He said nothing. Her heartbeat drummed in her chest.

"You're our rescue angel, Corrin," Kyle said in that deep, assured tone. He fitted a helmet bearing a headlamp onto her. He fastened the chin strap and cradled her jaw. "I'll be right there with you, every moment." His intense blue eyes backed up his words.

Sparks of confidence rose in her chest. No way she'd disappoint him, not if she needed to throw the kid on her shoulders and climb out bare handed. "I know you will. I'm ready."

"We'll lower you slowly to enable you to minimize contact with the broken beams. We don't want dirt on your halo." Kyle leaned in and brushed his lips against her cheek.

The gentle kiss melted away the remnants of cold dread in the pit of her stomach. He believed she'd succeed.

A firefighter cranked on a winch. Her feet left the ground. She squeezed the ropes and sought out Kyle, their eyes now level.

His strong hands steadied the harness. "Be safe."

They maneuvered her to the center of the shaft. Into the earth she went, plunging into cold, damp darkness until Kyle's flashlight became a dim glow in the eerie forest of broken boards.

A jagged piece of wood poked her calf and scraped to her thigh. She straightened her knees and pointed her headlamp below. Her light shone on the outline of a little kid. Freckles stood out on his pale face.

Dirt couldn't hide a gap-toothed smile. "Are you a ninja come to save me?" His voice reverberated against the walls.

Another believer. "I lift weights like a ninja commander," she whispered. "I need you to follow orders, warrior."

"Yes, Commander." His wobbly salute went straight to her heart.

"Dr. Kyle gave me a protective collar in case your neck got bumped and splints for your leg and arm. Working together, we'll get out of here in no time."

"Yes, Commander," he squeaked.

"You made a miraculous landing, warrior." She pushed off from the edges to center herself. A shower of dirt and sticks hit her shoulder.

Bloody hell. It'd be a miracle if they got out alive. "Dirt attack, sorry."

"We won't get buried, will we?" His eyes glistened from tears.

"Not on my watch." Her feet hit the ground, landing on either side of his snow-suited body. Her butt hit the back wall. She tugged the rope to stop.

She splinted him and buckled his harness to hers. "Wrap your good arm around me. We need to be two arrows in a quiver, toes pointing straight down. Okay, tug the rope and up we go."

Bobby's grubby hand pulled the line.

The rope lifted them a foot off the ground, jerking his sling. "Ouch, my leg." He scrunched his eyes shut, his body rigid.

Poor kid. Corrin adjusted her legs to allow more dangling room for his. "Even warriors have pain. It's okay for you to whisper it hurts."

"Okay."

His fine hair tickled her nose. She gripped the rope beside his head and smoothed a dusty strand using her pinky finger.

A child's hair—she'd smoothed her kid brother's many times to soothe skinned knees and hurt feelings.

Her back bumped into a sharp point. Boards creaked and a shower of dirt hit the floor. A broken stick brushed his back. "Am I caught?" he cried.

Her heart thumped in her throat. "No. Hold me tight. We're close to the top."

Bobby tipped his chin. "I see light. We made it, Commander."

"Yes—"

Wood cracked and the rotted framework wobbled.

"Hold on tight!" Kyle yelled.

Boards and dirt hit her shoulders. She hunched over him.

"Close your eyes, Bobby."

Wood slammed into her while the shaft collapsed.

CHAPTER 5

A yipping dog's happy barks echoed into the last foot of mineshaft and bounced around Corrin's head. Her arms relaxed.

"Daisy!" Bobby squealed.

Cheers erupted.

Up they went, up the last few inches to freedom. Tears welled behind her eyelids. "We made it, Bobby." She kissed his forehead and raised her head.

Two men in yellow-striped turnout gear swung Corrin and Bobby away from the hole and unhitched the harness.

A foot of the bank gave way, and the hole belched a cloud of dust. The sound of cracking boards pierced the air.

She gulped in fresh air and scanned the smiling faces.

Men and women hugged and high-fived.

Kyle blew her a kiss.

"Thank God, you're alive!" Mrs. Bell cried and ran to Bobby. Her shaking fingers stroked his pale cheeks.

Bobby leaned against Corrin until they unhooked the strap holding them together. She held his shoulders, her knees wobbling.

Kyle pressed his firm hand into her back. "Thank you. You're amazing." His sincere smile utterly disarmed her. "My turn now." He lifted Bobby from her grasp. "He gets a quick family moment before I stabilize him."

Bobby's parents kissed him gently and paused, heads bowed, hands clasped together. "Praise be to you all. Amen," they said.

"My little warrior needs a blanket." Corrin hugged her arms to her chest.

Kyle took an emergency blanket from a firefighter and tucked it around Bobby. "Please get one for our heroine." He met her gaze, his eyes radiant.

She managed a shaky return smile. Comforting Bobby, she'd re-experienced how she'd shielded her innocent siblings from ugliness during her father's drunken tirades and her mother's depression.

A fireman draped a silver sheet across her back. "Doc's orders. Great job rescuing the child."

"Thanks. Team effort." Her lungs expanded, with deep, satisfied breaths. She'd been told that before, long ago, and the same sense of pride filled her. Upon her return to Seattle, she'd plan frequent outings including Willy and Corey. No more working every weekend.

The thin blanket warmed her back. She brushed dirt off her pant legs and stretched out each arch, relieving claustrophobic cramps.

While she rolled her shoulders, her gaze shifted to the quiet valley. A light flickered in the window of a darkened farmhouse partway downhill. She grimaced at the glow, reminiscent of her dad's cigarette lighter.

Kyle had maintained the house was vacant.

The trunk of a silver car stuck out from the far side.

Goosebumps rose on her arms. The people who'd moved out quickly might've forgotten stashed belongings and returned in a rental car.

Something tapped against her leg. She looked down and spotted the wagging, white-tipped tail of the beagle.

"Daisy, don't jump on Ninja Commander!" Bobby yelled.

Corrin bent and stroked Daisy's velvety, brown ears. The dog barked and darted back to the murmuring group surrounding Bobby.

Kyle squatted, allowing Bobby's faithful pup to lick his smudged cheek. Safe kid, happy dog, relieved parents. This part of the scene brought her peace, and she'd done her part. Later, she'd mention the light in the house to Kyle and Roy.

The firefighters dismantled the tripod and secured equipment to a small trailer hitched behind an ATV. One of them waved his hand. "Dr. Werner! The aid car's five minutes out from the Bell's house."

"Great news!" The grinning father tousled his son's hair. He turned to Kyle. "I can drive steady while you sit behind me carrying Bobby."

"Good plan." Kyle held the boy tight to his chest on the way to a bigger ATV. "Corrin needs a ride," he called out.

"I've got room." The tallest fireman smiled and pointed to the quad. "I'm Mason Connolly. My friends call me Mase." He stuck out a gloved hand.

"Guess you're my driver." Corrin palmed a quick handshake and climbed behind him.

He pulled her hand to his waist and revved the engine.

"Take good care of our heroine!" Kyle shouted.

Corrin opened her mouth in a fake scream, then shouted over the noisy engine. "Wait a minute, Mase." She released her grip from the fold of his coat. "Daisy, come here." The beagle jumped onto her lap. "Okay, ready. The real heroine deserves a ride." She caged the dog between her arms.

Mase pulled alongside the other quad and let the engine idle at a quieter pitch.

"Never chose a favorite beagle until Daisy," Kyle joked. He settled Bobby in his arms. "Real easy to avoid jostling Bobby, Mr. Bell."

"Sure thing, Doc." Bobby's dad throttled forward at a slow speed.

Mase twisted his handle grips to full throttle. Corrin's head snapped back.

"Careful!" Kyle shouted.

"There's a short cut," Mase yelled over his shoulder. Their vehicle cut a sharp right off the path.

Pointy nailed paws gripped her legs. Wind whipped her face. Not the kind of excitement she craved. She juggled the dog and held onto Mase's jacket. "Slow—"

The quad's front wheels skidded across something under the snow. A loud crack sounded, and they tipped, their butts sliding off the seat until Mase jolted them to a stop. They'd landed in a low spot of the rippling hillside.

"What the hell?" Mase shouted and cut the engine. "Sorry! You okay?" He reached out for Corrin's arm.

She brushed his hand away and stroked Daisy. "We survived, Speed Racer."

"Wanted to be certain." Mase threw her a cocky grin. "I better check what broke," he said, and lifted a corner of the big wooden board.

Two four-by-four posts stuck out from a half sheet of white plywood lying on the ground.

Corrin leaned out. "It's bigger than a typical 'For Sale' sign."

"Yup. We cracked the bottom." He set it down and swept a wide stroke using his gloved hand, revealing a phone number and printed information. "I think it's a county sign."

Unease rolled through her stomach. "I need to get photos. Documenting anything unusual proves essential in the legal game." She climbed off the ATV and patted the seat until Daisy lay down. "Good dog."

She turned to Mase. "Don't remove any more snow yet."

"Ah, sure thing," Mase said sheepishly. "No permanent damage."

Corrin pulled her phone out of her pocket and snapped close-in shots of the writing on the board. "Please gently remove the snow from the bottom of a post."

Mase took off a glove and used the fingers to dust the nearest leg.

Her eyes widened. "It shows no evidence of having been pounded into dirt."

"Nope," Mase said. "Someone dropped it here, in the swale."

She took two more photos and leaned back to get a perspective shot of the town, far in the distance.

"I'll come back tomorrow and hammer it in properly on a high spot. That's the right thing to do, isn't it?"

She hovered the flashlight on her phone above the board. "Correct. This is a 'Significant Interest to the Public' notification. In my state, they're posted in plain view prior to getting an area rezoned before development. The public comment period expires in a few days. From here, even upright, this sign isn't visible from below."

"Townsfolk should be alerted to changes on the mountain," he said.

She scanned the downhill slope. "Possibly their intention, to hide the notice and prevent anyone from submitting objections."

"Sounds illegal."

Cheaters topped the group of miscreants she hated above all others. "If proven."

"You a lawyer?"

"I plan to be one soon." She hopped on the seat and pulled Daisy to her chest.

"Sorry I jostled you and Daisy. I couldn't see the boards." Mase threw his leg over the engine cover and put his hands on the throttle.

"Slower, please." She caught hold of his jacket in one hand and cradled the dog with the other.

He nodded and gradually released the clutch. As they putted downhill, she considered an unsettling hypothesis.

What, or who, would've convinced someone working for the county to deliberately suppress proper notice of zoning to Emma Springs residents? The disturbing question sank in as Mase parked their quad next to an ambulance. An EMT stood watch by an empty gurney.

She patted Daisy. Her little explorer's fated trip had exposed more than the mineshaft.

Daisy jumped off and barked. Three more ATVs rolled in, their headlights illuminating the front yard, outlining a sled and child's plastic shovel stuck in a snowbank.

The open hillside should've been a safe place for children to play. Roy's mentioning families leaving town after possible threats signaled cause for alarm. Honest country folk hadn't hidden the sign out of view.

Charming Emma Springs was being threatened by someone despicable, and she'd bet that tonight they'd been watching from the house below.

~ ~ ~

Kyle spotted flashing lights. They parked the ATV close to the ambulance.

Bobby had not issued one whine or cry on the bumpy descent. Kyle rose from the seat, holding the child snugly to his chest. "You've earned a gold star for courage."

"Really?" Bobby's trusting eyes melted some of the icy angst lingering in the pit of his stomach.

"Don't be afraid to tell the doctor what hurts," Kyle said, then handed him over to an EMT, who secured Bobby onto the stretcher.

Kyle loosened the makeshift brace, ran his fingers across Bobby's shin, and wrapped it again. No more trembling, but the boy's face remained a pained shade of pale.

"Is it broken?" Bobby asked.

"Probably your tibia, the bone above the ankle. You did a good job keeping it straight, and I'm proud of you." He secured the blanket around him. "Tell the doctor at the hospital that Doc Kyle recommended a waterproof cast."

"Okay." Bobby chirped, then waved his good hand. "Ninja Commander, I get an ambulance ride!"

The group of firefighters and medics parted for Corrin.

"You earned one, my brave little warrior." Without her spiked heels, she stood at a perfect height when she leaned in and kissed Bobby's dirt-smudged cheek. "Next time you and Daisy decide to go out, be certain to ask your mom if it's okay first."

"Yes, Commander." Bobby saluted. "Maybe you and me can go exploring together?"

"Maybe." She smiled and stuffed her hands in her pockets.

Mase and the other firefighters stood off to one side, wearing satisfied grins on their faces.

The medic slid the gurney into the ambulance.

When Corrin blew Bobby a kiss, Kyle rubbed his palms together. *Yes, indeed.* His patient and his guest shared a bond, and judging by her glistening eyes, a strong one.

Bobby's mother approached Corrin. "Thank you again."

"Daisy is the real heroine." Corrin suggested.

Mrs. Bell bent and lifted Daisy, kissing a long ear. "You both deserve halos. I'll pray you never suffer being cloaked in fright while searching for your missing child."

"Sounds horrible." Corrin patted her arm. "Bobby will be fine."

"Doc Kyle brought us an angel." She smiled at Corrin and then grabbed her husband's hand. "We need to stash Daisy in the laundry room with the mini before we follow the ambulance." The two parents ran to the front door, the dog following.

Kyle tipped his face skyward and gave a silent prayer of thanks for Corrin's courage and Bobby's seemingly minor injuries.

"You're new around here," Mase said, and sidled in next to Corrin. "Join me in a drink after I change out of my gear?"

A sinewy knot twisted in Kyle's gut. He snapped his medical bag shut.

"I have a date for the evening," she said. "Thanks for the plummet, I mean ride, Speed Racer. I bet you're a familiar patient of Dr. Kyle's." An impish grin lit Corrin's face.

Mase shrugged. "Yeah. By the way, you were brave to enter that hole. Sorry we tumbled on the ride down."

"No worries," she said.

Kyle put Corrin's hand in the crook of his arm. "Tumbled?"

"We slid across a board buried under snow," Mase shuffled his feet. "I'll straighten out what I broke. See ya." He headed to his ATV.

Kyle scanned her frame. "Corrin, are you hurt in any way?"

"No. Mase is harmless unless he's controlling a throttle."

"He's an overloaded single dad controlling two young daughters. He needs a wife."

A low grumble came from Corrin.

Had she groaned in disgust? Kyle opened the passenger door of his Jeep. "It's been a night of challenges."

"Yes. I hope Bobby's injury isn't more serious." She slid onto the seat. "My kid brother cracked a few bones."

"A broken leg will put him out of the exploring business for a bit. Amazing, considering the fall." He shut her door and climbed in. Maternal instincts resided inside her, whether she'd admit it or not. She'd heard Bobby cry out and jumped into action. "You have a younger brother?"

"Yes, and Bobby reminds me of Mitch. He pushed himself to catch his sisters. I wasn't always successful monitoring his attempts." Corrin's voice trailed off.

Protectiveness verified. "You deserve the Ninja Commander title. By tomorrow, Emma Springs will salute your courage."

She twisted toward him and fastened her seatbelt, then searched his eyes, as if doubting her own bravery.

He leaned on the console, her lips so close he felt her warm breath on his neck. All he wanted was to kiss her and show her how much she mattered. He tilted his chin, his mouth so, so ready.

Her breath hitched. "Glad I got to meet Bobby." She shifted toward her door. "He'll be back exploring beside Daisy in a few days, hindered slightly by a grubby cast."

She'd clearly sent the back-off message. He strapped on his seat belt and guided the Jeep onto the road. "There's an orthopedic doctor covering ER tonight. Bobby's in good hands."

"Glad to know." She pulled out her phone. "Wait until you read what was posted on the sign Speed Racer and I found." Her voice sparked with eagerness. "Between the exposed shaft and the zoning announcement, I'd wager there's development coming."

"I skimmed a recent article in the Billings paper. Years ago, an LLC bought property rights on a bunch of mountain slopes throughout the state. By next year, they plan to break ground on a ritzy private ski resort. I wasn't aware Emma Springs was in the running."

"Interesting," she said.

Kyle considered the right wording to perk her interest. Her law firm specialized in land use, which could benefit Emma Springs. Determination filled his chest. "Lift towers—an ugly blight on a hillside. This community needs affordable housing to grow the community, not a bunch of billionaires building gaudy eyesores they live in for two weeks out of the year. We need your expertise."

"I'm not an expert in recreational land use. However, investigating the terrain stability would be a logical reason to reopen a shaft."

The no-nonsense tone of her voice indicated that her principled nature itched to investigate. "Expensive homes push taxes up." He checked for traffic and turned onto Main Street. "If you wanted to stay a few extra days, I'd help do research."

Corrin's brows knitted together in deliberation, and her face tightened. "I wish I could. I'm outlining closing statements on an important case for a senior partner," she said. "Studying for the bar and taking this futile trip to support Miranda put me way behind schedule."

Kyle flinched. There was a lot more to life than schedules. "Bobby's family thinks differently. You'll be featured in the *Emma Springs Newsletter* next week. I'll send you a copy."

"I'm glad I helped Bobby." She rubbed her temple. "My niece and nephew would get a kick out of seeing the story in print. I brought business cards in my purse." Her stomach rumbled. "I'll be grateful if your dad saved dinner." She put her head back against the seat and closed her eyes.

The glow from streetlamps gently illuminated homes along Main Street. It also revealed the mud remaining on her delicate hands.

"I'll guarantee dinner's waiting. Dad's used to my calls taking a few hours. I'm certain he'll be interested in the board you and Mase uncovered."

"He'll determine what to do," she sighed.

Might Corrin's programmed brain ever consider alternate career prospects? His little town couldn't compete against Seattle. A bleak pall settled in the pit of his stomach.

Still, images of her and Bobby clinging together and her tears after she blew the goodbye kiss wouldn't leave his mind, no matter how hard he tried to erase them. He rounded the last corner.

Floodlights brightened Dad's yard. The garage door rolled up before they turned in the driveway. The Jeep entered the garage, and immediately the heavy metal door from the breezeway swung open.

Roy lumbered out and yanked on Corrin's door. "How's Bobby?"

"I believe he has a broken tibia and sprained wrist," Kyle said. Leaning over, he took in the earthy scent of mud in Corrin's hair, and another smell. Wine. "Nothing life threatening, Dad."

"Thank God," Roy exclaimed. "Young lady, it appears you crawled through a sawmill."

Pride welled in Kyle's chest. "Corrin made the daring rescue. Bobby's calling her 'Ninja Commander.'"

"Can't wait for details." Roy offered his hand to assist her out and brushed sticks off her back.

She struggled to unzip her jacket one-handed while extracting her phone from her pocket. "Bobby fell through rotted wood. I fit into the tight opening. Occasionally, my petite size becomes an asset." She worked her jacket off, gingerly flexing her wrist and elbow.

"Good things come in a variety of packages." Kyle moved to her side. "Sore arm?"

"I held tightly onto Bobby with my free hand. It'll loosen up."

"Come under the light. There will be no injuries to a town hero on my watch." He carefully maneuvered her arm and shoulder, briefly kneading her trapezius muscle.

His fingers longed to continue. "If the ache persists or you experience sharp pain, you need to let me know."

"Your ministrations helped."

"Probably a strained muscle. Might be wise if you cancelled your flight to recover fully." *And got a back massage at the least. Bad doctor.*

"I'll be fine, guys."

"I'm glad Bobby will be okay, and Flor's duds kept you dry," Roy said. "Did he fall into the old mineshaft?" He ushered her into the breezeway.

"Yes, some idiot uncovered it," Kyle said. He stopped at the back door and delicately removed a slender wood strip from her silky hair, then held it out for her to examine. "You procured a few souvenirs."

"Thanks for removing the evidence of my unexpected descent." She took the twig and closed her fist around it, then handed her phone to Roy. "On the trip downhill, my quad driver and I discovered a sign holding a notification to the community of a request to change zoning. I took a bunch of photos. Where they'd thrown the sign, it might've alerted a mountain goat."

Kyle steadied her elbow while she slipped off her loose rubber boots. He'd use any excuse for contact. *Bad, bad doctor.*

"Leave the boots on the mat and help her in, son." Roy grinned knowingly at Kyle. "We'll hang onto Flor's favorite wellies for next time."

A flicker of longing crossed Corrin's face before she took his arm. "Mmm, I still smell dinner."

The aroma of roasted beef brought Kyle's taste buds to full alert. Nervous energy burned calories. He ran his free hand through his hair. "More than a few strands of my hair turned white watching Corrin being lowered into the pit."

"Appears all shiny and golden to me." Corrin's mouth dropped open. "Ah, I need to freshen up in your bathroom." She grabbed her purse and tucked the sliver of wood inside, then trotted into the hall.

"Towels under the sink," Roy said. "Please help yourself to whatever you need." He pulled half specs from his chest pocket and scanned her phone screen.

"Shiny and golden." Kyle patted his hair. "I'd bet the town might require a land use attorney to assist you."

Roy nodded. "Now you're talking. A property scouter snooped around a dozen years ago. They paid a few of us lakeside owners five thousand dollars apiece for the first right of refusal on our lots."

"Mom was a card-carrying environmentalist," Kyle reminded him. "She'd never have let them develop the mountain."

"We retained the right to pass it to our children. Considering the price of college tuition, we accepted their check."

Corrin stood in the doorway, her cheeks scrubbed clean. Damp strands of hair surrounded her lovely face. "The town's lucky you're their lawyer. Those contracts are complicated."

"Money talks," Roy said. "A few neighbors copied us. They dreamed their kids would plant roots here."

"Land's never been valuable around here," Kyle said.

"Sometime in the 1970s, a rich city slicker who'd vacationed at the Lazy K tried to buy the original Calderon homestead." He raised his eyes to Corrin. "Rane, Chayton, and Katherine Calderon-Langley live on adjoining properties which their ancestors homesteaded in the late 1800s. They wouldn't sell an inch."

"A classic Old West story," Corrin said.

Kyle peered over his dad's shoulder "Kat Calderon meeting Tray Langley is a fun tale." He scanned Corrin's cell screen. "I believe the shaft sits on Stan's property, Dad's mountain-dwelling hermit friend. What's C-A1 zoning?"

Corrin leaned in to view the tiny photo. "I'm not familiar with that. Interesting. They're not changing the zoning but assigning one."

"Large swaths in Montana are unzoned," Roy said. He grabbed a notepad from the bureau and copied the information. "I think C-A1 is an agricultural and recreation classification. Stan will blow a gasket if he realizes they're plotting to construct anything below him."

"He might scare them off with his old rifle and his cantankerous attitude." Kyle rubbed his chin. "Maybe whoever purchased those two farmhouses didn't realize the exact boundaries," Kyle said.

"Or didn't bother to check," Corrin scoffed.

"This week, a realtor I'd swear was retired left me several phone messages," Roy said. "Bragged about a client who wants to buy our lake cabin and waterfront strip. He suggested the parcel's in high demand, possibly worth double or triple the assessment." He tipped the wine bottle unsteadily and poured what remained into his glass.

The rabbit ear bottle opener and a cork sat on the buffet.

Dad must've polished off an entire bottle tonight. Kyle rubbed the back of his neck. "Possibly enough money to fund the expansion to my office."

"I have no intention of selling any lake frontage. We'll figure out financin'." His dad slurred the last word.

Kyle winced. Not the time to address the drinking issue. "Might be good to find out who the client is. Did you see the article about someone wanting to build another ski resort in Montana, Dad?" He headed to the stove.

"Sounds familiar. I'll contact the county and old Don Underson, the realtor, first thing tomorrow." Roy pulled out a dining room chair for Corrin. "Time for you to set. I mean sit."

"Thank you," Corrin replied and looked up as he returned.

Her eyes flicked to him, displaying earnest and sincere worry from someone who cared. He gave her a subtle nod. "Hey Dad, write down what Underson says." He placed one foil-wrapped plate in front of Corrin and unfurled the covering. The second plate he put at his customary seat.

"Pilates never gave me an appetite like the one I have after hauling an injured kid out of a deep hole. Bon appétit," she quipped, before forking in bites of meat and potatoes.

"You deserve fillet mignon, not a measly chuck roast, despite this being the Wagyu beef Rane raises on his ranch," his dad decreed loudly. "Kyle should invite you to a fancy restaurant dinner."

"Never underestimate the value of home cooking." She waggled her fork in midair at Roy. "I understand you've practiced law here for over thirty years, Mr. Werner."

"Correct, and please, call me Roy. If you run into questions studying for the bar, don't hesitate to contact me. I'm going to retire one of these days, and this is a mighty nice place to live." He pulled a card from the buffet and pushed it toward her plate.

The moment froze in time. Kyle waited for her response. "You are kind," she said.

Kyle intercepted the card. "I'll put my cell number on the back." He jotted his number and pushed it to her. "Now you have two contacts." He reached into his pocket and pulled out his key ring. "I carry a thumb drive for phones. Mind if I copy the photos?"

"Not at all." She tapped her phone screen and slid it across the table.

I'll send these photos to Dad's email. "We'll print them for future reference."

Her eyes flicked from one man to the other, then out toward the lake. "Great idea. I'm glad I could help. It's a pleasure to dine among men who genuinely respect the welfare of others." She pocketed the card and her phone.

Roy eyed her clean plate. "Seconds are standard in our household."

"My stomach's sufficiently suffuncified." A lopsided grin removed any inkling of her legal demeanor. "I've never recited my father's silly line before. Tonight, it's appropriate."

"I enjoy cooking for friends." Roy refilled her water glass. "Any possibility you'd be interested in becoming a partner in a successful law firm in a beautiful part of Montana? I'd hire you tomorrow."

Kyle choked on his last bite of meat. Oh. My. Goodness. A job offer.

Corrin's lashes fluttered. She carefully placed her knife and fork on the plate and slipped her napkin under its edge. "My compliments on a delightful and delicious dinner, Mr. Werner, I mean, Roy."

Whether she'd admit it or not, her bright eyes verified Dad's job offer flattered her. He sat back and contemplated her possible responses.

"My question's serious, Corrin." Roy leaned forward, his forearm resting on the edge of the table. "I need a trustworthy partner to continue helping our community. I plan to work part-time, though."

All traces of the relaxed Corrin vanished. She folded her hands primly in her lap. "I never considered living anywhere besides Seattle. Myer, Fitch, and Brine are prepping me for partnership." She blinked several times.

"Well, our community already appreciates you. Keep Emma Springs in mind. In the meantime, if I need help doing research, maybe I can hire you as a consultant."

She shifted in her chair. "If time permits, I'd be happy to assist."

The doorbell chimed.

"Not expecting guests this late." Roy rose and zigzagged to the front door.

Corrin smoothed the linen napkin between her thumb and forefinger. Her eyes shifted from the photos on the buffet to the fireplace in the living room. She leaned back in her chair.

The ambiance affected her. Kyle did a fist pump under the table. All he needed were a few key ways to sway her.

"I hear friendly voices. Our heroine has visitors." Roy threw over several locks and swung open the door. "Step in, folks." Bobby Bell's family trooped inside.

"Bobby wanted Miss Patten to be the first to sign his cast." His father tucked the sleepy-eyed boy in the crook of his arm, using his hands to hold a flat board supporting the child's outstretched legs. "Miss Patten, please meet my folks, Ed and Julia Bell. They want to thank you."

Kyle swallowed hard. Julia's help preceding his mom's funeral had been a blessing. He ushered Corrin to the living room. "The Bells reside at the top of my favorite patient list. Julia manages church events with compassionate expertise. Ed's our veterinarian." He turned to them. "Evening folks. Dad and I are giving our heroine reasons to visit more often."

"Try really hard." Julia smiled. "Your blessed girlfriend brought light to our Bobby, trapped in darkness." She unwrapped an etched, white brooch bearing the likeness of Sunrise Lake. "Corrin, please keep this token of our gratitude. My father did scrimshaw on elk horn he found in the woods, and I want you to have my mother's favorite."

"Oh, it's beautiful! But it's a family heirloom," Corrin voiced her objection quietly.

"Given with heartfelt thanks," Julia said.

Corrin stood solemnly while Julia pinned the delicate badge to her sweater. A piece of inlaid turquoise represented the lake. She lifted her finger to trace the grooves in the pin. "Bobby's a special treasure, like your gift. Thank you."

Twice now, she hadn't denied a reference to being called his girlfriend. Kyle put his hand at her back.

"Thank you again, for saving my grandson," Julia's voice trembled. She leaned in and kissed Corrin's cheek.

"Our grandson found a worthy heroine," Ed broke in. "You've earned free lifetime animal care from me." He choked on the last words, and then patted Bobby's shoulder.

Corrin nodded, not a word leaving her lips. Her glistening eyes, though, held wistful longing.

Powerful silence filled the room.

Bobby stuck out a felt pen. "Ninja Commander, please sign my cast."

Corrin swiped her finger at the corner of each eye and grinned. "I'd be honored. You realize those firefighters and Doc Kyle get equal credit, though." She wrote her name and sketched stick figures of the two of them hanging in the rope harness. "Don't forget to give Daisy an extra treat. She's the real hero."

Bobby nodded and yawned. "She sleeps beside me. Tonight, she gets two doggy bones." He snuggled into his dad's shoulder.

"Speaking of treats, can you folks join us for dessert?" Roy said.

"Time to get our explorer home. It appears the pain medications have kicked in. Thank you for the offer, though." Bobby's mom reached out for Corrin's hand. "When you have children of your own, you'll understand why we believe you're the angel sent to us on purpose."

"I'm thankful I could assist," Corrin said. Tenderness softened her voice.

Kyle sketched a rendition of Daisy on Bobby's cast. "I'll review the hospital report and call you folks later tonight to check on his pain tolerance."

"Thank the Lord it's just a broken leg and sprained wrist," Julia said.

As the guests filed out the front door, Corrin put her hand over the pin, her mouth curved into a satisfied smile.

Happy chatter resounded from the family heading to their car.

"I can't believe they gave me a family heirloom." She tipped her head toward him.

"You saved Bobby. Nothing else matters." Kyle brushed a wisp of hair from her cheek.

Corrin closed her eyes. "You're absolutely right." She pulled away and returned to her seat.

"We need a bakery in town." Roy moved a pie from the buffet to the center of the table. He pointed to the unevenly rippled crust. "My dessert skills are sadly lacking." He cut a slice and placed it in front of Corrin.

"We'd touched on job possibilities before our visitors arrived."

"I'll keep your employment proposal in mind. Offering to be my personal mentor is generous. Thank you." Corrin smoothed the edge of the tablecloth. "I'm currently assisting the senior partner in a big case. At night I study." She ate a bite of pie and returned her fork to the plate.

"I understand. Call me anytime." Roy smiled. "Coffee, or do you want to call it a night?"

"The latter," Corrin said.

"I noticed you've got your spare beds piled with stuff, Dad. Sorting time?"

"Umm, yeah," Roy mumbled.

A yawn escaped Corrin's mouth. "Well, I guess it'll be Kyle's bedroom, then." Her ears turned a dark pink. "Guest bedroom. I've got to hit work after the flight lands tomorrow." She dropped her head and stabbed another bite of pie.

Kyle grinned. "Wouldn't want to keep our new town idol out too late. She might never want to return."

Corrin smiled shyly.

Not returning might be her intention, except her eyes held hints of yearning. Kyle found himself formulating a plan to make the next visit happen. First, he'd talk to Grant.

"You've earned a good rest," Roy said. "Make her comfortable, son."

How he'd love to.

Corrin's shoulders sagged. "Fresh air does have an effect." She stood and pushed in the chair.

"As does saving a life. My humble abode awaits." Kyle moved from the table and stopped in the entry hall. "Your shoe should be stable if we leave the tape on."

"Thank you again for your hospitality, Roy." She slid her feet into her high heels and brushed past Kyle to step into the cold breezeway.

Kyle admired her swaying hips.

"Next time you come to town, Corrin, I'll be more prepared to negotiate partnership." His dad gently poked Kyle in the ribs. "Don't stand there, son, unlock the door to the garage and get her tucked in for the night."

Kyle poked him back. "On it." He unlocked the deadbolts and held the door to the garage for her. "After you, milady."

"You know, we could easily transform Flor's studio into Corrin's office," Roy said. "Fighting the zoning may become a battle."

"Emma Springs doesn't realize how lucky they are to have a caring lawyer." She held out her hand to Roy. "And a great cook."

Roy took both of her hands in his. "Thank you doesn't convey our gratitude. Good luck with your case. Come again, real soon."

Dad would help convince her.

"Lovely meeting you," Corrin said in a heartfelt tone. She climbed in the Jeep and slouched into the seat.

A streetlamp illuminated his driveway across the street. If only he could peer into her mind. "Penny for your thoughts?"

"Oh, my reflections command a much higher rate."

Any amount of cash it took, he'd pay to know. He'd seen her entire demeanor change holding Bobby. He backed out, drove ten feet, and swung into his own drive.

Corrin checked each stone in her bracelet. "I reserved a seat on the eleven o'clock flight tomorrow morning. What time do we need to leave?"

He could try to win her over by action, to infuse her with a positive impression she'd remember in Seattle. Instead, he said, "No hurry. Nine should get us to the airport plenty early." His key rattled in the door to his clinic.

Corrin remained in the shadows.

No time for a long-range strategy to treat the malady she incited in him. How to make her want to return to Emma Springs?

He pushed the door open and flipped on the light. A deep-seated, unfamiliar ache settled firmly into his bones. He needed a chance to show her his off-duty life. "Corrin, in spite of living far apart, we could date."

She stumbled, grabbed the reception desk, and stopped. "It's been quite the exciting day." Her lower lip trembled. "You've gone above and beyond. Show me the bedroom, I mean guest room, and I'll be out of your hair." Her cheeks bloomed to a warm pink.

Visceral reactions didn't lie. His dating offer brought on the lovely blush. He swung her satchel on the desk.

She extracted her purse from her bag, her eyes lowered.

Kiss her hesitation away? She'd taken the first step by not giving him a negative response to dating. He wouldn't push. He'd used the ask and back-off strategy successfully to get his shyest patients to discuss their ailments. Presuming she'd been assaulted, he'd try the technique and tread lightly. "The spare bedroom's on the right. Do you need to call anyone to inform them where you're staying?"

"Miranda and Aunt Iris know." She turned and walked in the direction he'd indicated, head held high, her spiky heels clicking on the wood floor.

His eyes followed her. Studying body motion never made his hands sweat before today.

"Is this the correct room?" She paused at the first one.

"Yes ma'am." He answered. His bedroom was next. "I keep it guest-ready."

She hesitated at the door, cracked open a few inches.

He approached slowly. "It has a private bath. New toothbrushes are in the medicine cabinet, and clean T-shirts and sweats are in the top drawer."

"How convenient." Her voice sounded high-pitched. She leaned against the doorframe.

"I invite patients to stay here if I ascertain they don't need to travel to the Three Falls Hospital." He pushed the door wide open and faced her. "Call out if I can provide anything else. I'll be awake until I get the notes on Bobby from the orthopedic surgeon."

"Such a sweet little boy," she murmured.

"In a dangerous pit. Thank you again." He lifted her hand and gently brushed his lips across her fingers, inhaling hints of earth and coconut.

She didn't pull away. Instead, she tilted forward a fraction and froze. Her pulse fluttered in her neck. "Thank you, Kyle. You've been a consummate gentleman."

"To a brave lady." He dropped her hand.

She looked away, into the dark room.

He reached behind her to find the light switch, brushing her shoulder. A shock jolted through his body much brighter than the light.

"Sleep well," she said.

"You too." He pulled his hand back before she nudged the door closed and caught a glimpse of her widened blue eyes. *Yes!* His chaste kiss had produced global warming of the snow princess, and he hadn't gotten near her lips yet.

He two-stepped into his bedroom and stopped. The memory flashed of how she'd clung to him on the quad ride. He removed his shirt in front of the mirror and smiled. Faint bruises covered his lower torso.

Eleven years of medical study had included treating patients' mental and emotional needs. He'd research how to calm Corrin's anxieties involving men and convince her that intertwining their lives strengthened both of them.

He tapped his finger on his cheek. How to bring her back to Emma Springs? His eyes landed on a photo from college of Grant, John, and him, in their dorm at the University of Washington.

Miranda would connect them. Lucky Grant, to have found a woman who truly loved him, if he'd read the signs correctly.

He tilted his head back. The crescent moon shone brighter than usual. Corrin must feel something. Should he tap on her door for one last check?

CHAPTER 6

Corrin's body craved more of the unfamiliar pleasure. She leaned on the dresser in Kyle's guestroom. Waves of delight still radiated through her from his mere kiss on her fingers.

Wow. One set of warm lips dissolved her fourteen years of resolve to squelch any reaction to the male species. If she'd been cast in a scene in a 1940s movie, she'd swipe her hand across her forehead and swoon. Instead, she stared outside.

Hundreds of miles away sat her apartment. In a decade, she'd never welcomed a man through the door. Not even for coffee. The experience in the boat eliminated all her teenaged desires for romance. Her adult self justified the absence by saying she was focused on her career plans.

Kyle and his easy grin had unsettled her life with the impact of a summons served on an unsuspecting defendant. Only she wasn't unsuspecting.

Not anymore. Every move he made showed his concern for people: maybe too much, too soon, in her case.

Dancing with him rated nothing short of mesmerizing when harmonious precision between their bodies effortlessly responded. She stroked her arms, remembering his touch on her skin. Her fingers moved to her purse, where she'd stowed the sliver from the mineshaft. The top ended in an arrow point. Was travelling to Emma Springs the best or worst mistake of her life?

His bright eyes revealed attraction and all indications were that he was not a player.

She sat on the edge of the bed, staring at the moon above the dark, shimmery lake. If only they'd met earlier. If only he'd stayed in Seattle to practice. No *ifs*. Only a fool rejected the attention of a man like Kyle in a place as beautiful as Emma Springs.

She tugged off the angora shell and pulled on one of the T-shirts from the drawer. Had his skin ever touched the soft, white cotton?

Her limbs relaxed on the flannel sheets, her well-trained brain did not. Too many new options to be weighed and measured, balanced and noted.

The physical sparks from merely touching him shouted chemistry. A normal response, or elevated by the stress surrounding Miranda, Paunch Guy, and Bobby's rescue?

By now, Kyle should've received an update on her little warrior. Her feet touched the cool floor, while her heart pounded in her chest: one part of her not ready to let the night end.

~ ~ ~

Mikey released his breath and held the phone away from his ear while H.P.'s snobby tone blathered a request to leave a voicemail message. A recorded update might save his ass. "Wanted to give you a heads up," he began. "Blondie and a crew of locals brought a kid off the mountain tonight and put him in an aid car on a stretcher. Your engineer thinks whatever happened took place in the area uphill where he hauled out ground samples. He's unsure if they found the posting for the rezone. He supposedly paid off the right people to ensure nobody objected. Thought you'd want to know. Cell service sucks here. I'll call tomorrow."

He hit the 'end call' button, checked the new spy app, and threw the phone onto the worn comforter on his designated bunk.

His back bedroom's window faced the mountain. He pulled aside the curtain and sighted in on the patch of ground uphill. Half the town knew they'd dug soil samples. So much for being inconspicuous.

He took a deep breath and coughed. Even this room stunk, but the chain-smoking engineer seemed to have half a brain. Hopefully he'd greased the right palms. He put the phone on the charger. Blondie's green blip hadn't moved for forty minutes.

If H.P.'s intel on her being an early riser proved correct, she'd hit the sack for tonight. Tomorrow the game continued. Keeping out of the fray presented the problem.

~ ~ ~

Soft light edged through a crack in the drape. Corrin rubbed her tired eyes. For too long she'd lain awake last night, deliberating on whether to disturb Kyle for Bobby's prognosis.

Chickening out had been smart. She'd probably never see Bobby, or Roy, or Kyle again.

Her fingertip brushed the spot on her cheek where she'd felt Kyle's warm lips kiss her before the descent to reach Bobby.

She rolled to her side and spotted a clock. It was five a.m. local Montana time, the same time she'd rise at home. A few more hours and she'd leave Emma Springs.

Maybe Kyle rose early, too. She tugged off his T-shirt and got dressed.

The bedroom door creaked open. The aroma of coffee perfumed the hallway.

Kyle sat with his back to her at a kitchen table in a windowed breakfast nook. A mug and empty plate lay next to a newspaper folded in front of him.

How many other women had taken the same steps? Women who'd *not* slept in the guest room. She set the shoes he'd repaired on the floor. "Good morning."

He jumped in surprise and tipped his chair. "I'm not used to healthy guests."

She smiled. Only patients slept here. "Is Bobby okay?"

"His injuries are what I expected. I recommended quiet for a few days, before he resumes exploring."

"That's a relief. I grew fond of his little boy charm."

"Hard not to," he agreed, smiling. "Do you prefer coffee or tea?"

"I drink tea."

"Perfect. A client gave me this for my birthday." He lifted a flat wooden chest from the counter and held it out to her.

"I barely recall my doctor's first name, let alone her birthday." She scanned a rainbow of colored packages in individual sections, then picked an orange wrapper. "My favorite, tropical orange spice."

"That flavor description suits you." He ran water in a mug and placed it in the microwave. "I'll fix us an omelet and hash browns if you'll join me."

"An offer I won't refuse." *Bad wording.* She pretended to study the programmable choices on his multi-cooker, sitting on the counter in a kitchen twice the size of her own. "It appears the men in your family excel at cooking."

"Mom taught us simple things." His eyes dropped to a knitted potholder. "On winter evenings when I was a kid, we'd fix dinner together and then I'd listen to her needles click while we watched TV." He removed a couple of items from the frig.

His hollow voice told her the loss still devastated him. She put her hand on his arm. "Your mom sounds amazing. I wish I'd known her."

"You'd have been friends." Kyle let out a slow breath. "I can't imagine how Dad manages. He puts on a good front, if you don't know him well."

"Aunt Iris and sweet Uncle Charlie took me in before I found my apartment. Charlie died of a heart attack, and Aunt Iris attempts perky while her eyes remain sorrowful."

He gave her the steaming mug, and she dunked the tea bag.

"Most couples never experience such a depth of love," he said, and turned to face the smooth lake.

Her parents had been too busy having kids. "I'd imagine it takes work in the beginning."

"Great things are worth the effort." He flipped a section of hash browns and poured eggs into another pan.

She waved her hand in front of her nose. "Smells divine."

"I thrive on recognition." His grin proved it. "If you'd like, I can show you around the community before we head to Three Falls." He handed her lined leather gloves. "Dad wanted you to have these for the trip back. They were Mom's favorite pair."

A farewell gift and goodbye tour. Her appetite disappeared. "Another thoughtful gentleman. Please tell him thanks from me." She blew over the cup before taking a sip of hot tea. She'd be happy to wait until it cooled, taking in all things Kyle.

Leaving this town would be the polar opposite of leaving Ebony Cove. Painfully, chillingly opposite.

~ ~ ~

Kyle's pulse thrummed. Corrin managed to chat casually over breakfast, but it seemed that her eyes darted excessively from the lake to him if she truly was an uninterested visitor.

"Need help cleaning up?" she asked.

"Sure." Their movements in the kitchen flowed together in an undercurrent of awareness. "All done." Too soon she'd thrown her satchel onto her shoulder. He locked the house and opened the door to his Jeep.

What could he do or say to solidify her return? He downshifted to cruise Main Street. At the turn to Bobby's cul-de-sac, a coal black mini horse bolted onto the highway.

He slammed on the brakes and threw out his arm again. The seatbelt held her in place. "Sorry, habit." He pulled his hand back.

Corrin twisted to look around him. "A baby horse?"

"Bobby's family fosters abused and abandoned miniature horses. This little girl's their youngest rescue yet. She's about eight months old and a mini Shetland." He pulled the Jeep to the shoulder. "Give me a minute and I'll trot her home."

Corrin pushed open her door. "She's so small, I bet I can shoo her your way. A good first step to conquering my fear."

"That's the spirit." He pulled a length of rope from behind the seat. "Might really help if you stopped oncoming traffic. Minis don't always follow orders from strangers. I'll coax her using the power of suggestion." He shook mints into his palm.

"You know you're in Montana . . . when the minis cross the road for mints," she joked.

"I appreciate your optimism." Kyle squatted a few feet from the black filly. "Hey little filly, want a treat?"

The horse stretched her neck, her tiny nostrils flared. She took two steps, stopped, and pawed.

Kyle crept closer, his hand outstretched. The little horse pivoted and headed straight to Corrin. Her hooves slid and her shoulder rammed her shin.

"Hey." Corrin pushed the horse's neck, and her bracelet caught in the long mane with reddish-brown tips. She blinked rapidly, then turned to Kyle. "Guess I'm caught. And, what's a filly?"

The mini stood still, resting against Corrin's knee.

"Good job, horse wrangler." He looped the rope around the mini Shetland's neck and freed the bracelet. "You caught your first female horse. She's called a filly, I think, until she's three, then she'll be a mare."

"Learn something every day." She touched the mane. "She's kind of cute." She gently stroked her tiny cheek, a thoughtful look softening her face. "I think she senses my anxiety."

The horse nuzzled Corrin's leg and let out a low whicker.

The pony got a gold star. "They're popular for therapy animals."

"Her fur's really soft," she moved her fingers across her back. "The tiny version isn't terrifying." She scratched her rump.

"See how her muzzle's moving? She's showing contentment, and they don't act that way toward everyone. You made a friend."

She bent her head close to her dark ears and whispered, "You be good, so you find a forever family."

The horse shook her head, the mane fluttering against her bare knee.

Corrin giggled. "That tickles."

Nothing matched the sight of her relaxed and grinning. Warmth filled his chest. "Bobby's parents will be looking for her. I better trot her back to her temporary home."

Kyle returned the mini horse and continued their tour. "One blinking light keeps order in our town."

"No city hall." Her eyes skimmed the church and row of shops. "Is Emma Springs part of a county government?"

"Correct. Our county council makes decisions on zoning issues, if you're wondering."

She'd cocked her head, her signal that she'd engaged in strategic analysis.

"It'd be awful if Sunrise Lake lost its small town charm," she said. "Escalades don't belong in those parking spaces."

A pinprick of optimism spurred him on. "Agreed. I bet Dad will grill the county on not properly posting the notice board."

"I hope he gets answers from the realtor, too." She pointed out the window. "Is the huge bird an eagle?"

"Yup, they grab fish out of the lake."

"How wonderful to be free, soaring into endless sky."

He never wanted to leave town, and she aspired to travel the globe. Physically in sync, with an endless difference in aspirations. "Sometimes home is a great place to be," he offered quietly.

"I wouldn't really know." Her shoulders dropped.

Given the chance, he'd show her. To Corrin, life included condominium cocktail parties, not two-stepping and root beer.

She'd shrunk into the seat, her arms wrapped around herself.

What did a simple country doctor have to offer her besides down-home values and devoted love? "Want to borrow my spare coat?" he asked and held his breath.

"Thanks. I'd better not."

The clock had run out. A lump rose in his throat.

~ ~ ~

Kyle hadn't responded to her turning down the offer of a coat. His square shoulders emanated confidence, but the typically agreeable look on his face had gone to bad-news serious. Precisely how she felt.

Corrin honored his silence while they drove past the horse-free meadow adjoining the distinctive metal gate at the entrance to the Lazy K Ranch. This morning, she felt like the tipped K in the brand. "I should've accompanied Miranda to the dude ranch and ignored her insistence I'd be in danger," she confessed. "I let her persuade me. Stupid, stupid. I'm the closest she's got to family. I could've worked on my horse aversion and kept watch for the hitman." Her voice trailed off.

"Past history. I firmly believe Grant's keeping her safe. He's trained in defensive tactics." If his grip tightened more on the wheel it would shatter.

Her comment about the hitman must've hit a nerve. Miranda's name still topped the hit list because Grant hadn't done his job. She opened her mouth, then closed it.

"Why the horse fear?" he broke the awkward silence.

Another ugly memory. She shifted in her seat. "It's a strange story, in part because it's also one of the last pleasant days with my family."

"Okay, you've captured my attention."

"We visited a country fair when I was around five years old."

"I can picture your blond curls."

"Probably. No money for school photos, cameras, or photo albums in my family. Anyway, Mom insisted on petting a huge draft horse before we left the fair. Dad held me in his arms, while the twins sat in a stroller. The big horse snatched Mom's straw purse. I can still see the horse's huge, yellow teeth chomping while Mom shouted for help. He ate everything except her wallet and the handle."

"That's horrible. It seems strange for a horse."

"The owner said his horse went nuts over apples. Mom had an opened bag of those blasted apple-infused soft candies and an envelope of cash for our rent stashed in her purse. My parents had a big fight in the car. Dad dumped us off at the house and then he took off while Mom stood crying on the front porch."

"Wow, a lot for a child to witness."

"He came home drunk and smashed the TV. I don't remember him sober the rest of my childhood."

"What a shame he didn't get help."

"No substance abuse services in Ebony Cove. Dad could stay sober long enough to paint houses in exchange for a few months rent. We moved nine times before I hit eighteen, graduated, and escaped to Seattle."

"I understand the negative association to horses. Minis can be pushy. I'm sorry she rammed you."

"More of a nudge. I think she wanted my attention."

"Don't we all," Kyle grinned and gently bumped her elbow.

The simple action sent a vibe deep, deep down—awakening sensations buried for too long. In another life, she'd appease her traitorous heart and reach over to tug on a strand of his hair or snap her finger against his solid bicep. In another life, she'd thumb her nose at unfriendly, bustling, and litigious Seattle.

Rotten, crappy, timing.

Concentrating on small talk for the forty-minute return trip to Three Falls demanded more effort than unearthing facts from a legal brief. She glanced ahead.

To the right stretched the airport. Reluctance overwhelmed her.

He parked the car opposite the entrance to the terminal but dropped his keys on the sidewalk after shutting the door. "I'll get your bag." He shouldered it, retrieved the keys, and followed a few paces behind her through the glass doors.

She slowed for him to catch up. "You've been so generous with your time, Kyle." They'd reached the cordoned off area for bag check. She stopped by a pillar. "Thank you."

"Can we continue getting to know each other? Our invitation for you to come to Emma Springs remains open ended."

A charming, pointless invitation. "There must be other women in your life," Corrin said.

"Nope. You could testify that the available ones make it known they prefer Tinder-types. Not my style." He placed his hand on her forearm. "May I visit you in Seattle?"

Every cell in her body urged to pull him closer, tell him how much she wanted to stay. It'd be totally unfair to encourage him. "I've enjoyed this reprieve more than you'll ever know."

"That's a yes?" His hand gently squeezed.

Another current of longing charged through her body. Certainly, she'd be less affected by him on home turf. "Sure." She pulled out a business card. "If you're in town, give me a call."

He pocketed the card. "I'm willing to work out travel wrinkles."

Parts of her were buzzing to don an apron and wield an iron at a moment's notice to smooth the path between them. She tried to meet his eyes, which flicked between the scanner tables to the tarmac visible out the wide windows. "Your career goal is to be Emma Springs' doctor. I have a career goal too."

Perspiration dampened his brow. He ignored the comment.

"Are you okay?" Corrin asked.

"Airports and flights put me on edge."

"Maybe you need to fly a remote-controlled plane," she suggested. "Similar to me and the little horse." He finally looked her way.

She gave him a bright, fake smile. "We'll cross paths if Miranda and Grant get serious."

A plane revved and took off, the air shifting with the vibration. He took deep breaths. "What? Oh, right. I assumed they were serious. Either way, it doesn't mean we can't correspond."

It'd be tough to glamorize her life, even in writing. "Sure, I'm glad to have met a new friend."

From his grimace, he did not like being called a 'friend.' He gazed into her eyes, searching for a clue. "Friend it is. Small towns aren't for everyone," he said.

He'd gotten the point. She forced away barbs of regret piercing her composure. "You're trained to understand."

"Home's where the heart is." He threw a fake smile and patted his broad chest. "I wish you the best of luck in passing the bar and getting your sheepskin." He set the bag on the floor between them and then kissed her cheek. "Goodbye."

"Goodbye." She stood on tiptoe, and sighted in on his mouth, willing her nerves to kick in. He tipped his head and his lips found hers, caressing tentatively, waiting for her. A luxurious glow spread through her. She relaxed and parted her lips. He tenderly kissed back until she broke free. Free from what could be her downfall.

She shoved on her dark sunglasses, slung the bag on her shoulder, and bolted toward the TSA station. "Thanks again."

"Don't forget, you're the town hero, Commander," he called after her in a cheerful voice. "Peaceful Emma Springs awaits your next visit."

Traffic and crowds used to sing her siren song. They didn't anymore. Not after experiencing his sensual, awakening kiss. She twisted around and caught Kyle brushing his fingers across his lips, astonishment shining in his eyes. For her. For them. For what could be.

He waved and stood watching.

Agonizing hesitation made the bag she hefted onto the conveyor belt feel loaded with bricks. She waved back. To Kyle, Seattle consisted of lifeless steel and glass buildings, indignant toward intruders. A correct diagnosis in comparison to Emma Springs.

The dullest shade of overcast colored the sky. She approached the airstairs, head bowed, her light suede jacket no match for Montana weather. She should've taken the coat he'd offered.

The lined gloves gifted to her from Roy protected her fingers from the cold handrail. Another cherished heirloom from a devoted family. She swiped at a stray tear.

She needed an impenetrable glove to protect her heart.

That appeal had been filed too late. Kyle Werner had thrown her flat life into an overnight roller coaster of infatuation, self-worth, and fun.

She slid into her assigned seat and faced the window while they took off and sliced through clouds.

Meeting Kyle infused her tasteless life with tempting treats. And his funny cake analogy to taunt Betsy back at the bar rang true. She'd always preferred cupcakes. If her life were a vanilla one, on this trip she'd sampled a rich double chocolate confection topped by decadent ganache frosting. She brushed her finger against her lower lip, remembering how he'd gently begun, tempting her to kiss him.

Parts of the past twenty-one hours had been a blissful reprieve of letting someone else make decisions.

Her mind wandered to a fulfilling life, working for Roy, dating Kyle, growing into a member of a community.

The beverage cart rattled by to dispense drinks to the front of the plane first. Daydreaming didn't pay bills.

She pulled out her legal pad and the top file and concentrated on Mr. Meyer's upcoming case.

"Sorry, ladies and gentlemen," boomed a voice from the PA. "The flight will be delayed. The tower cleared us to land in Lewiston to check out a light on the dash. Shouldn't take long. Flight attendants, prepare for landing."

No root beer today. Corrin shoved her notepad into her satchel. Maybe travel wasn't so awesome.

Three hours later, the delayed flight departed for Seattle. She stretched her fingers, cramped from jotting notes on ridiculous arbitration over a swampy lot.

Someone in front of her shuffled a deck of cards. A child's tiny voice called out for his mommy. A woman murmured a response.

She put her head back, shut her eyes, and listened to snippets of life. Visions slipped in of Bobby propped up in bed with brown and white Daisy curled beside him. He'd feel safe and warm. And loved.

~ ~ ~

The bump of tires on the runway indicated arrival at SeaTac Airport.

She gathered her things, headed to the exit, and stepped out of the plane. Chilly air whirled around her. The sunny days and late summer temperatures had surrendered to fall. The outside cement stairs leading to the concourse seemed endless.

She moved to the side of the wide corridor and blinked at a sign directing travelers to public transportation. The faster light rail cost more, but it was late. The strap on her bag dug into her shoulder. She shifted its weight and took a step forward.

"Ouch." A blow from behind spun her into a quarter turn.

Five steps ahead, the jogging oaf toting the offending backpack never turned around to acknowledge he'd clipped her arm. "Jerk," she muttered. Another man had turned her way, then ducked his head. A ball cap and glasses hid his face.

Same tan Carhartt jacket Paunch Guy wore! Her pulse raced as she dodged roller carts to get a better look.

He passed a group of hustling flight attendants, and despite her fast steps, she lost him.

People wearing assorted coats and jackets traversed the hallway. Carhartts were popular with the yuppies in her office. She rubbed the back of her neck.

Loud cell phone conversations, overhead announcements, and clacking luggage wheels assailed her ears. The volume increased while the crowds in the hallway sucked her in.

Each step took her further away from the quiet pace of Emma Springs. Her instincts told her not to get on the light rail to the office, but to head home. Too bad instincts didn't pay bills.

People on the train hunched over electronic devices or sat vacant-eyed, with their earbuds in place.

Cold from the molded seat penetrated her skirt fabric. She pulled out a manila file folder and balanced it on her lap. Hours, not weeks, had elapsed since she'd placed the documents in her satchel. A pen in her hand wavered above the pages where she'd written notes that were important—at the time.

Yesterday, her hand had calmly smoothed the hair of an injured child. She clenched the pen and held it to her heart, pressing the brooch into her chest.

Bobby's family and the volunteer firefighters all epitomized the meaning of the term 'fine folks.' The townspeople of Emma Springs deserved Kyle's devotion.

And her? Determined to make a life of stripping down legal pages and turning them into unemotional arguments for faceless clients in an indifferent city. *Bloody, rotten hell.*

All in the name of money—her motivation until this trip. If she hadn't sent the six hundred dollar check for the February bar exam in Washington, she'd consider taking the test in Montana and working a second job to bank enough for Corey and Willy's future.

She exited the rail car and caught a bus to a stop near her office building's parking garage. Her Firebird sat in its usual spot.

The freight elevator rumbled to her floor. A quiet Friday night equaled efficiency. She walked the deserted hallway past a row of empty offices and flipped on her desk light.

Here she was, pushing thirty without anything except a standard issue desk in a steel tower to show for her life.

A typical gray sky outlined dark buildings through her window. Tonight, it shouted drab, same as her work. She plugged her cell in the charger on her desk. The file from her bag needed research. Roy's offer faded while she concentrated on pages upon pages of facts. Three hours later, she rubbed her burning eyes.

Enough work for tonight, she decided. She shut off her light.

As she stepped into the hall, she heard a cough. The cleaning crew never worked this late. Hair rose on the back of her neck.

CHAPTER 7

The newest janitor rounded the corner, saw her in her office doorway, and abruptly stopped. He pushed something into his uniform pocket. "Evening," he kept his head bowed.

He'd come from the IT room. No cart, no other crew members. They typically were packed up and gone hours ago. She'd worked enough late nights to know the drill. "Why are you here so late on a Friday?" She locked her office door.

"I'm making up for a missed shift." He waved her off and darted into the men's bathroom.

Doing what? The urge to get home intensified. She buttoned her coat and hustled to the elevator. The doors opened to the garage, where a huge black SUV had pulled in beside her car.

"Learn to park," she muttered, squeezing in between the poorly angled Lincoln Navigator and her door.

A shadow moved behind its dark, tinted windows.

What nerve. A hundred parking slots, and some jerk had parked in one reserved for MFB employees, a hairsbreadth from her car.

She slid onto her seat and drove to the exit. Overhead lights threw off an eerie blue glow on oilsplotched cement in the empty garage. She tapped her fingers on the steering wheel, waiting for the night gate to rise.

Hitting every red light on the commute home and parking a block from her building didn't enhance her mood.

She unlocked her apartment, set her laptop on the Formica kitchen table, and booted the computer. While email loaded onto the screen, she microwaved leftovers. Aromas of basil and tomato made her mouth water.

A red exclamation point on a new email caught her eye. A companywide memo—sent after she'd left the office. She swallowed and pursed her lips.

Subject: MANDATORY COCKTAIL PARTY. Attendance required.

Tuesday 5 p.m. Business formal attire.

No doubt a man conceived the ridiculous dress codes. He'd be able to wear the same suit to any function. She swallowed a spoonful of rich soup.

Her head throbbed—from either fatigue or the impending dog and pony show for a new client, as well as the partners. She pulled her phone from her purse and dialed the person in her life who'd never let her down. "Hi, Aunt Iris. Can you join me at Couture Consignment tomorrow? I need your expertise."

"Sure, honey. Shopping for anything specific?"

"Attire radiating business formal."

"Silly description. How'd the trip go? Is Miranda okay?" Iris's kindly voice soothed better than warm soup.

"Miranda's fine, I guess. I missed her in transit."

"Oh dear. You were alone in a strange city overnight?"

"Not exactly. The local bachelors entertained me. One's the town doctor, and Miranda vouched for him."

"Your tone implies cute."

Either Iris and Miranda knew her too well, or in twenty some hours she'd become giddy over a new boyfriend.

Kyle as her boyfriend. A smile came to her lips. "His widowed father invited me to join them for dinner. Father and son are both charming. Hey, it's late. I'll give you all the details tomorrow."

Iris chuckled. "I've waited a long time to hear you use 'charm' to describe a man, instead of a 'snake charmer'. Get a good night's rest and be prepared to spill."

"I will." Corrin pressed her palm into the scrimshaw brooch. "Let's meet at ten. Night."

Iris signed off, and Corrin set the cell on the table.

She studied the party notice issued by the most senior partner, Phil Meyer. He never worked past six o'clock. She grabbed a package of soda crackers from the basket of takeout extras she kept on the table and fingered the cracker label.

The creepy custodian's working late story seemed off. Had the giant, new SUV held someone waiting until he finished?

Not her business who chauffeured the janitor. But a new client who warranted a coming out party meant kid gloves, more unpaid overtime, and imitating the groveling from the partners. Time for her to mimic that time-honored practice. Her jaw tightened. What if Mr. Meyer had decided on the next partner and this constituted a meet and greet?

The soda cracker wrapper burst in her hand, crumbs scattering across the table.

It couldn't be, not after he'd promised she'd be the fourth and final partner. She swiped the table clean, grabbed her phone, and pulled up next week's calendar.

At nine o'clock on Monday, she'd slotted in meeting Miranda at the Federal Building before the hitman's arraignment. She kneaded the tight muscle in her sore shoulder. Her brain needed Kyle's wisdom. Her tight muscles needed his fingers. She typed in the cocktail party for Tuesday and swiveled to face the window.

Outside her apartment, streetlights fought through cold, ominous fog rolling onto Capitol Hill.

She hugged herself, missing Kyle's deep, steady voice. A wave of longing for simpler pleasures seeped into her soul. She pulled Roy's card from her purse and flipped it over to where Kyle had written his number. Time to inquire about Bobby's progress.

Kyle's voicemail clicked on immediately. "Corrin here, I wanted to thank you again for making my overnight in Emma Springs memorable. I hope Bobby's okay. Give me a call when you get a chance, dance pro. Bye."

A normal, single, male would be out on Friday night at nine o'clock. She bit her lip. It was an hour later in Montana.

~ ~ ~

For a Tuesday, the building housing MFB bustled. Corrin hung her dress over her arm and squeezed into the elevator car behind a man pressing the open-door button. "Hit fifty-five, please?" She unmuted her phone. Still no return call from Kyle.

Smells of perfume and nerves took her back to the crowd she'd left yesterday, waiting outside the courtroom doors for a prime seat at Venom's trial and a glimpse of the hitman's snake tattoo.

The vision of a pale, skinnier version of Miranda soured her stomach. She'd given hugs and a few words of comfort. Had yesterday's visit been enough to enable Miranda to survive the grilling from mob lawyers, or calm her angst of being the only one who could identify the crooked cop who still hadn't been arrested?

When Kyle called back, she'd ask him to recommend supplements for gaining weight and calming tension. Grant should've noticed Miranda's decline, whether they were dodging killers or not. How drastic were the charges for kicking an FBI agent?

She left the elevator and passed the unattended reception desk. A clear garment bag hung from her bookshelf. Her sigh ruffled the thin plastic. The jacket completing this evening's armor had been delivered and now looked perfect.

She lifted the bag and ran her fingers across the expensive raw silk fabric of a couture navy garment woven with gold and cobalt blue, sold cheap due to scorch marks at the original hemline.

The attached bill for tailoring seemed low. She'd throw in an extra ten for her seamstress, who'd rushed to hem the cuffs and shorten the length.

Two sharp knocks sounded. "Come in." She hooked the dress onto the jacket hanger.

"Your new jacket's beautiful," Kelly said. "The silk sheath you brought matches the blue threads perfectly."

"Thanks. I'm not schooled on business formal attire."

"You'd impress Wall Street," the receptionist teased. "Have fun, and scope out if our newest client's young and eligible."

Her body relaxed. Tonight was not a partner introduction. "For you, I'll pay attention." She twiddled her fingers in an affable wave and sat at her desk. Entering her password and bouncing the mouse woke her laptop. She hunkered down for a marathon session.

Late in the afternoon, an unfamiliar email address flashed in a side bar, with Werner in the username. She double clicked.

Dear Corrin,

Hope all is well.

The old realtor, who should be retired, called yesterday and made a purchase offer I 'shouldn't refuse' on my cottage. He sounded desperate.

An unfamiliar SUV almost ran me off the road tonight on my way home from a Lions Club meeting. If you have time, I'll hire you to research Harlan Piersall and give me your opinion. His LLC is the registered owner of the development company that bought two homes above Sunrise Lake. Keep track of your hours, and I'll compensate you generously.

Best regards,

Roy Werner

Hair lifted on Corrin's forearms. Why threaten Roy? She dialed Kyle and left another voicemail, then copied the correspondence onto a flash drive and slipped the tiny stick into her pocket. Hitting shift and delete, the email disappeared, but not from the backup server.

Mr. Meyer frowned on personal emails at work.

She'd frequently bought slushies for the computer brainiac stuck in a closet-sized room. Nothing wrong with asking his assistance now.

"Good morning," Corrin stood at the door marked 'IT.' "I need a favor. I received a personal email. Drinks and donuts for the next week if you can permanently delete it," she offered.

He flashed a shy smile before dropping his eyes. "You don't owe me anything. You're the only team member who acknowledges me as human." His fingers tap-tapped on his keyboard. "Found it, from someone named Werner."

She leaned against the doorframe. "Yes."

"Consider the message scrubbed." He keystroked furiously. "What the heck? Someone's hacked your email."

She leaned forward. "Bloody hell."

More typing. "I've eliminated the problem." He sat back in his chair.

"Someone illegally accessed my account?"

"You'd never believe what I see in electronic espionage. All it takes is keyboard talent and money," he said. "The bug's been squashed."

She bit her lip. "Thanks for fumigating my, ah, pests."

"No worries. I discovered a cell phone glitch on our system this morning. I'm working on clearing that up."

"You deserve a corner window," she said, and stepped into the hallway. The low whir of a vacuum set her teeth on edge.

The creepy new custodian kept his head lowered while he vacuumed a spotless carpet. Were they entertaining the president?

Kelly waved from her desk. "T-minus ten minutes," she announced.

"Okay." Corrin scooted into her office. She slipped the thumb drive containing Roy's message into her bra, then unwrapped the pair of pristine designer stilettos. Both those and the blue dress were consignment store gems she'd planned to wear after making partner.

Roy wore cords and flannel shirts. The female equivalent for Emma Springs might be her jean skirt with a pair of Frye boots. She grabbed her toothbrush, draped the dress over her arm, and headed to the bathroom. After brushing, she slipped into a stall.

Soft-soled shoes padded in, and the whoosh of liquid spraying onto mirrors infiltrated the quiet room.

She fought the back zipper and stepped out.

Ramona turned, dressed in her gray uniform. "I'll help you, Ms. Patten." She ran the zipper pull to the neckline. "I noticed your beautiful dress when I tidied your office a few minutes ago," she said, without her typical smile.

"Thank you, Ramona. You're here early. Did it disrupt your schedule?"

"No. Mr. Meyer needing an extra clean before the reception is no trouble."

Corrin dodged Ramona's supply cart. "We appreciate your efforts."

"Ms. Patten?" Ramona's gaze dropped to the floor. "You are so very kind. A pretty woman alone, like you, needs to be careful." She bent to rummage in her tool caddy.

"Thank you for the reminder. I'll remember." She'd mull over the weird comment later. Right now, duty called. Corrin shouldered open the door.

Tinkling glass echoed from near the freight elevator, where a man balanced three racks of stemware in his arms. He headed into the conference room.

Maybe Ramona had seen the amount of booze they typically supplied for these parties. She slipped inside her office, shut the door, and kicked off her black pumps. Her foot fit perfectly inside stiff fabric atop three inches of spiked status. The days of dressing up in Mom's scuffed pumps from the bin in the church basement were over.

She unwrapped a peanut butter cup and nibbled on the chocolate, her go-to snack before a presentation. It did nothing to quell the jitters in her stomach after visiting her IT friend. It would've been smart to have asked him if he knew who'd hacked her. Being in a hurry always threw her off. She downed the candy and chucked the wrapper.

Male voices came from the hallway. Meyer, Fitch, and Brine bantered en route to the reception. Fitch's whiny voice stood out. He and Brine typified card-carrying elitists.

For multiple reasons, the trip to Emma Springs had stripped off their veneer. She opened her purse and pulled out a tissue-wrapped bundle. Julia Bell's brooch anchored her to good men. She pinned it on, admiring the delicate grooves and tiny piece of turquoise.

More voices trailed into the empty hallway. She locked her door and headed to the makeshift bar in the conference room. Her throat felt like sandpaper. "A glass of seltzer with a lime twist, please," she requested from the bartender.

"Corrin, join us," ordered Mrs. Meyer from the circle of spouses preening themselves like proud blue jays admiring their feathers. The more ambitious the attorney husband, the less fabric covered the well-toned body of his trophy wife.

Corrin squeezed a napkin around her highball glass and slid into an opening next to her boss's wife.

Mrs. Meyer drew her rail-thin frame to full height. Even wearing flats, she pulled off the stance of a teacher glowering at a third grader. "Philip tells me you rooted out a few statistics for our newest winning lawyer," she stated.

Corrin placidly smiled at the backhanded compliment. She'd formulated the entire defense and written the closing statement for the newbie. "Team effort."

Mrs. Meyer continued, "Considering his expertise, the opposition didn't have a chance. Phil told me he can practice in several states." A vulturine smile appeared on her lips while she ogled the broad shoulders of the recently hired California transplant, who stood beside her slim, elderly husband.

What did you call a woman who took care of bropriating? Any attorney with cash and half a brain could be licensed in more than one state. Corrin squeezed her chilly glass. "Mr. Meyer assembled a good crew to win that case."

"Quite an accomplishment for a lawyer new to our state." Her eyes narrowed to slits, now scrutinizing Corrin's jacket. "My incompetent maid ruined a garment exactly like yours using a hot iron before I ever wore it."

Chap Brine's wife swirled scotch in her glass. "None of my help can read tags." She cleared her throat. "Instructions should be printed in Spanglish."

Corrin stepped back. These women set the bar for microaggressions against immigrants. Her own seamstress had educated her on respecting fine silk while she'd pinned the six inches to be cut and hemmed. "A Latina friend warned me never to iron this fabric."

"And I believed my jacket to be haute couture from the designer," Mrs. Meyer snapped.

The one-of-a-kind garment must've originally cost a fortune. Too close a call though, Corrin realized. From now on she'd shop at a consignment store in a different wealthy neighborhood. "Hmm." She sipped her drink.

"Obviously a lie I need to address." Mrs. Meyer aimed her buzzard eyes toward Corrin's shoulder. "Interesting pin." She pointed to the brooch. "A souvenir?"

Corrin covered it protectively. "It's an antique scrimshaw likeness of a peaceful town."

"How quaint." Mrs. Meyer puckered her lips and turned away to verbally bulldoze Brine's wife, the spouse of MFB's most junior partner.

In a perfect world, the trio of wives would rise above such behavior. The pin warmed under her fingertip. It'd be a relief to leave the vulturettes and head to the circle of men. "Excuse me."

Phil Meyer tapped his glass and the room quieted. "H.P. texted. He regrets he must cancel meeting everyone tonight."

Corrin scowled into her seltzer. She'd blown her budget and wasted an hour of work time on entitled ingrates.

Mr. Meyer waved his hand toward Brine. "Chap's landing of this prominent client warrants a celebration. He'll be the lead attorney and Corrin will assist. Please enjoy the refreshments." He raised his hand in a salute to Chap.

H.P.? A demanding client named after a printer. She twisted her lips, mulling the fact they'd already stuck her on the project beside leave-by-three Brine.

"Chap's delighted to be in charge," Mrs. Brine crowed.

Corrin put on her happy face. "Nice chatting with you all. I have briefs to finish."

"So late?" Mrs. Meyer's steely eyes challenged. "Well, we women do have to prove ourselves." She looked down her nose. "Good luck helping with the new account."

She'd need longer days, not luck. "Thank you."

Conversation rose in volume before she exited. Drinking and bragging would continue for at least another hour.

On the plus side, it'd be fun telling Aunt Iris whose garment they'd scored, luckily untraceable. If cold-blooded Mrs. Meyer spit fire à la her scaly ancestors, Corrin would've been singed worse than the jacket they'd resurrected.

Something always irritated the woman. Might be Mrs. Meyer's jealousy of Corrin's respectful working relationship with her husband. She'd seen resentment displayed by other lawyers' wives.

The cleaning cart stood opposite Meyer's office, the closest to the lobby. Corrin walked the silent corridor, stopping at her cracked-open door. She clearly remembered locking it.

She shoved it open.

The new janitor stood over her wastebasket, holding a fistful of papers.

"What are you doing?" she asked.

The man jumped. "Thought you'd be at the party for a while." He shoved a sheet into his pocket. "I, ah, dropped my list." He grabbed her shred bin and dumped it into a gray plastic garbage bag.

The janitor wrote lists on legal paper? "Those need to be shredded."

"Yeah, new system," he mumbled before he ducked out. "All clean. Night."

Corrin took out the key to her desk. She leaned closer to the locked drawer.

Scratches marred the area around the keyhole. Had the creep tried to jimmy her drawer open? She'd report it tomorrow. Purse in hand, she switched shoes, jammed her arms into her winter coat, and stomped to the elevator.

Ramona transferred a basket of fluttering sheets to the bin in the center of the cleaner's cart, labeled *SHREDDER*. No gray bag in sight.

"Are you using a gray plastic bag for shredding?" Corrin asked her.

"The new man, he has a different system," Ramona tsk-tsked under her breath, then met her eyes, "Challenging day, Ms. Patten?"

Magnified by the email hack, the desk lock, and now her stolen trash. "Yes, I'm ready to head home," Corrin said.

"Remember our conversation." Ramona scowled at the new guy ambling into the copy room, then locked Meyer's office with her pass key. She spritzed a spot on the spotless mirrored glass and swiped it clean.

"I'll remember. Thanks." Corrin got in the elevator, punched the garage button, and leaned back. So freakin' weird.

Wait. Hadn't Ramona said she'd tidied Corrin's office earlier? Whose microscope was she under? A knot formed in her empty stomach.

Tomorrow she'd ask Mr. Meyer. One thing she knew for certain—the founding partner wanted everyone on the same system. His business, his rules.

Expensive booze had kept the parking garage unusually full. Corrin rounded the trunk of her Firebird and stopped.

A scoop of pink ice cream sat on the pavement beside her driver's door. Strawberry, her favorite flavor. She bent over and studied the perfectly shaped mound, straightened, and scanned the quiet rows of cars.

No kids nearby, and Meyer's Mercedes sat next to hers. An icy chill went up her spine. She shoved her key in the ignition, backed out, and squealed around the garage's corkscrew exit.

Damn the weird coincidences. She squeezed the wheel on the drive home, then dashed into her building. Her feet beat hollow thumps on the empty apartment hallway.

While she pulled on sweats, her brain struggled to tie pieces of the strange events together. Pranks or a jealous coworker? Crap happened in every industry.

She opened her laptop and plugged in the thumb drive holding Roy's email. A vision of him and Aunt Iris picking flowers together popped into her brain. The image disappeared after she reread the threats to him.

She typed 'Harlan Piersall,' and watched as the screen filled with links to him and his son, who'd been given the 'Junior' moniker. Pictures of 'Senior' espoused the flabby excess of an elitist. No photos showed the son's face. Not one. Camera shy or clandestine? She tapped her finger on her cheek and scrolled further.

Piersall Enterprises had begun in mining. They currently specialized in building exclusive resort communities, covering half the western states. They were described as ruthless, untrustworthy business moguls in reviews.

Her empty belly rumbled. While she spread almond butter on an apple and let her favorite spicy tea steep, she opened links. She popped the last bite in her mouth and waited for another screen to load.

"No!" She shoved her hands against the table, propelling her chair into the center of the kitchen.

H.P. was one of Harlan Piersall Jr.'s nicknames. Her cursor blinked at the unthinkable.

Another coincidence? The odds were stacked against a Seattle developer picking on the complaisant townspeople of Emma Springs. Her pulse jumped while she clicked on the next website.

A faint knock sounded on the apartment door.

"Who is it?" Corrin growled, then walked over and stood on tiptoes to see through the peephole.

She jerked the door open and pulled in the teary-eyed figure. "Miranda, what happened to your celebratory dinner with bureau boy?"

Her friend sniffled and wiped away tears.

Corrin shut the door and hugged her. "What did Grant do? Did he hurt you?"

"Only my pride," she stammered. "He took a dangerous job in Reno."

After Miranda's shudders subsided, Corrin maneuvered her into a chair and slid her the steeped cup of tea. "Sip this."

Grant, Mr. FBI, the big, handsome, alpha male. She'd seen this coming. Damn his hide! Corrin listened to how the night had played out, how he'd proposed after bragging he'd taken a wonderful promotion, and how Miranda had thankfully bolted.

Bolted. Exactly how she'd left Kyle. Tenderness softened her approach. "I understand. Kyle's great, but imagine me in a cow pasture." Miranda never moved.

Corrin minimized the screen on her laptop. "If you wanted to return to college, we could be roomies to save money. Peruse the upcoming U of W courses while I tell you the story of the kid I rescued from the mineshaft. Call me Lassie's lassie."

Miranda's color improved while she sipped tea and listened to the tale. "I knew you'd enjoy Doc Kyle. He's grounded, charming, and cute," she needlessly asserted.

A triple threat. "Roy offered to mentor me and give me a job. They both belong in uncomplicated Emma Springs."

"What I saw of it looked appealing."

"And peaceful." Corrin stared into her mug. "But I promised my sister Grace that I'd fund Corey and Willy's education. Partnership in a big firm's the only way to earn enough money for their college tuition. And I hoped to bring them along on parts of my world tour." She fingered a piece of black shale from Antarctica on her bracelet.

"Kyle's the type who would understand if you spelled that out."

"Probably, but he lives to treat Emma Springs residents. A doctor needs a supportive homebody for a spouse." She heated another mug of water, needing her own dose of comfort.

"Did you ask Kyle what he needed?" Miranda pointed her finger.

"Did you ask Grant?" She pointed back.

Miranda dropped her hand and shook her head.

"We've both avoided romantic involvement for good reasons." Dark under eye circles emphasized the stress in Miranda's green eyes. "You went through hell last week."

"Forged stronger from the heat," Miranda wrapped her fingers around the mug. "I remember those words from counseling a few years ago."

At least she'd gotten something out of it. Corrin ruffled the pages of the course catalogue. "Lease out your plant care business. A degree opens doors."

"I'm tired of watching from the outside of life. You're heading to the legal summit, and my life's at the bottom of the mulch pile."

Corrin squeezed her hand. "Seriously? You battled mobsters while impressing FBI agents."

"There's still a thug out there after me." She met her eyes. "The bureau's watching for Karpenito, but keep alert."

Mr. FBI's former Seattle partners better shield Miranda. Corrin shuttered the blinds on the window. "I will, and I'll reconsider Kyle's offer of being more than pen pals after I pass the bar exam."

"I wonder how MFB will react. You do their work for a fraction of what they charge. I bet they haven't offered to mentor you."

"Correct. Mr. Meyer compliments my work, but never offers anything more." Roy and Kyle certainly had. Corrin brushed her lips, recalling the kiss goodbye. "I'm going to accept Roy's help, if I'm not put in too close contact—"

"With the rock-solid doc," Miranda teased. "You fell for a guy with a brain to challenge yours and a great bedside manner."

She threw the thumbs up sign. "Unfortunately, I need to avoid furthering the frustration for a couple of months, and he's probably ready to sign up with farmersonly.com. Their dating site motto is 'City folks just don't get it.' Saw the ad in the Three Falls airport." Her wise crack didn't even rate a smirk.

"I enjoyed the quiet of Emma Springs, and Grant's family is wonderful." Miranda rubbed the crook in her nose. "I wish he understood what he's blowing off."

Too bad the agent didn't warrant the effort. "You're the gardener. If the main branch of a plant withers, another shoot appears," she said. "We've both sprouted new growth, thanks to Montana. Let's unfurl one leaf at a time."

"I accept your offer of being roomies," Miranda sighed and tucked the U-Dub booklet under her arm. "Finishing college could be my first leaf."

One of them had a plan. Not a single plant survived in Corrin's care, due to her notoriously black thumb.

CHAPTER 8

Corrin shivered, despite the wool coat buttoned to her chin. In a few weeks Seattle's climate had changed from pleasantly chilly to downright frigid. She adjusted her satchel, ready for the elevator car to stop at the MFB floor.

The bell dinged, and she straightened her shoulders, prepared to greet Kelly with a smile.

The doors slid apart. A man who had been poised to enter stepped to the side. He stuck his hand against the edge of the steel panel, forcing it to stay open.

Eyes in his tanned face skimmed her with the intensity of a predator sizing up the next kill.

A distinctive scent hit her nostrils. Corrin's smile faded. Smug satisfaction crossed his thinned lips.

No! It couldn't be him. Other men wore the musky cologne of the man who'd lured her onto the boat.

"Getting out?" he said, in the snobby voice scorched into her memory like hot steel branding tender skin.

Her eyes darted to his hand, a few inches from her face. *No. No. No!*

He wore the horrible ring.

Corrin bolted past him. She locked her office door and dropped her computer bag.

Her body shuddered. Fourteen years had passed since he'd tried to get her drunk on his boat and attacked her. When her girlfriend intervened, he'd pushed them overboard and left them in frigid waters to die.

She yanked the phone receiver and hit the reception button. Controlled anger replaced the insecurity of a traumatized teenager.

"What's up?" Kelly asked.

"I need the name of the man who just left. Six-foot, dark hair." Corrin pressed her nails into her palm. "He's not a regular client."

"Oh, the one in the Ferragamo coat. I'm not certain whose office he came out of. All the partners' doors were closed when I arrived."

Corrin grabbed her pen. "Can you look up appointments for today?"

"I'll check the calendar," Kelly said. "He's handsome."

"No, he's pure evil." Could she face the bastard alone and press charges? She gripped the edge of the desk. The other girl who'd accompanied her that awful day had insisted they never tell a soul about their deadly boat trip with strangers. Shortly after the ordeal, her friend moved out of state.

"He did give off a cold vibe. Are you okay?" Kelly asked.

"I don't know yet. Please keep this confidential for now."

"Of course." Keyboard taps disrupted the silence. "No partners had an appointment scheduled. What's going on?"

"I'm not certain. Thanks. Call me if you find out. Gotta make a call." The statute of limitations had long passed. She'd check for a police report. Her pen doodled a broken dagger and smashed stone onto her yellow pad. She tossed the pen aside and dialed Mr. Meyer.

An out-of-office recording took her message to voicemail.

Her shoulders tensed.

Recognition had glinted in the eyes of her attacker.

~ ~ ~

H.P. sauntered through the underground garage and threw open the door to his Navigator.

Corrin Patten would be served to him like a seven-course French meal, with strawberry gelato for dessert.

Muscles relaxed while he rolled his neck from shoulder to shoulder. He'd waited a decade to sink his teeth into the satisfying taste of revenge. Waited until it became personal. A little longer, and he'd devastate every level of her pathetic life.

He rubbed the dagger on his ring. He'd been pushed away from his family because she'd demanded hush money. He'd be avenged for the destroyed boat, the friendships he'd lost after the college transfer, and the years of missed business opportunities involving his old man's money.

Tapping calls and tracing her whereabouts via her new company cell had paid off. He made a note to give his snitch on the cleaning crew a bonus for spotting her password and loading the app.

The janitor sifted through trash like a real spy. Hell, he even tracked how many peanut butter cups she ate before she assisted on a deposition.

Paybacks would be to the bitch.

~ ~ ~

The molester in the elevator had been gone for hours. Murmurs of colleagues in the hallway hummed through Corrin's closed door. "Concentrate," she grumbled to herself and adjusted the height of her man-sized office chair to relieve both aching shoulders.

Kyle could work out the kinks. She imagined his hands kneading her neck. Why hadn't he called back?

A siren blared from the street below.

Daydreams and what-ifs didn't pay bills. The litigation on her desk took precedence. At least for now. She stared at her monitor, willing herself to focus on six pages of detailed strategies.

At the bottom of the fifth page, the print on the computer screen ran together like white caps on water.

Another ugly memory. After the degenerates had left them to drown in Puget Sound, the old couple who'd rescued them had motored through choppy swells to a dock. They'd been wet, cold, scared, and unable to give an accurate description to the police. No report filed, if she recalled correctly.

Corrin rubbed her temples. Her attacker might be a client. She dialed and reached Phil Meyer's voicemail again. She shifted her weary eyes to a view of Puget Sound, a sliver of gray-blue between towering buildings. The 6:30 p.m. Bainbridge Island ferry pulled out of Colman Dock, probably chock full of island residents sailing off to houses scattered throughout a rural community.

The ship left her field of vision. She pulled open her desk drawer for a tissue and spotted her nameplate. Aunt Iris's present for her twenty-fifth birthday had been purchased in anticipation of her receiving a mahogany partner's desk. The shiny brass no longer inspired her.

Dusk shaded her office, normally her best time to work after everyone else had left. *Bloody hell, she should've headed home earlier.* She hastily packed her satchel, walked the empty corridor, and hit the down button.

The elevator opened onto the deserted parking area.

A shadowy figure slid behind a pillar. No other cars remained in the MFB spaces.

She hit the button to unlock her Firebird, and hustled the ten feet to the driver's side. Her eyes dropped to the sticky pink residue beneath her car door. Stepping over it, she opened her car, slid onto the seat, locked and shut the door, and checked her mirror.

A man in a suit ducked out the well-lit pedestrian exit. The attacker?

Her tires squealed when she jetted onto Sixth Avenue.

Two quick turns, and her car reached the arterial leading uphill to her building. "Please, oh please, be home Miranda," she whispered.

She parked close and ran into the apartment they now shared. Her blessed roomie stood at the sink. The door squeaked as she shut it and then let her body rest against the solid wood.

Miranda turned. "You're paler than my cauliflower. Are you sick?"

If only. She put a courtroom-worthy, composed expression on her face. "Weird stuff going on at work, and a new client's a monster I met a long time ago."

Miranda dried her hands and grabbed her phone. "Do you need Grant's help?"

Like hell they'd contact the heartbreaker. "Nope. I'll straighten it out through work."

"What weird stuff, and who's the monster from your past?"

She'd blurted too much. "I truly appreciate your concern and your help. Thank you," Corrin said.

"Remember when I assisted you in escaping to Montana and didn't ask questions?"

"Yes, and now you're making me more nervous. I had a killer after me."

"No hitmen, I promise." She unpacked her satchel on the kitchen table. "I haul too much stuff back and forth."

"Quit diverting. You know you can trust me with anything."

The dirty cop who was after Miranda remained at large. She didn't need any more angst in her life. Corrin forced herself to chill. "Let me talk to Mr. Meyer, to see if I can discuss it. You know, the client privilege thing." She laid her notepad beside her laptop.

Miranda touched her shoulder. "Are you sure talking about it won't help?"

"Yes." Corrin's pen tapped a swift beat on the table.

"It's my night to forage, so I picked up tuna and vegetable subs. I thought you'd be late, so I downed mine." Miranda pulled a wrapped package out of the refrigerator and set it in front of her. "Panic's familiar to me. Want company while you eat?"

She needed time to think. "I'm fine, just super hungry." The wrapper trembled in her hand. She gritted her teeth and slit the tape on the bundle with her fingernail. "Why don't you soak in a relaxing hot bath?"

"Good idea."

"I'd flip you for the tub, except my brain's in high gear. I need to work on a project for Roy. Happy bubbling."

"Glad you're working with at least one appreciative lawyer." Miranda headed into the bathroom with a robe and a book.

At least one of them would relax.

The first web site loaded. Piersall Enterprises' reputation darkened the more she dug. No personnel photos or different shots of the son in any search. She took several gulps of water and bites of the sandwich.

Harlan Piersall Sr. managed a large portfolio of *Right of First Refusals* in Montana, the first drawn up in the late '70s.

She pulled maps which revealed that all the parcels he owned fronted a lake at the foot of a mountain. Emma Springs could've been used as the advertising poster.

Had Paunch Guy been sent to Piersall's Emma Springs job site, or was he just an out-of-town hunter like Kyle had assumed?

He wouldn't be a random stalker who'd followed her back and forth from Seattle to Three Falls. Chills hit, unaffected by warm air blasting from the heater vent beside her chair. She sent an email to Roy, closed the website, and stashed her sandwich back in the fridge.

The right side of the refrigerator door held treasured photos of Willy and Corey. Below them were tiny pictures of Sydney's Opera House, the Great Wall, and the Taj Mahal. A getaway sounded good, and even Kyle must vacation sometime.

Next to Miranda's dream house photo on the left, a gavel-shaped magnet held Roy's business card. She checked her watch. Too late in Montana to call. Tomorrow she'd phone Kyle to check on Bobby. Maybe he'd missed her earlier message, same as she'd missed Miranda's.

Two more workdays until the weekend. What a dump week, topped by her hacked email and horrid elevator encounter. Once she spoke to Phil Meyer, she'd mentally light a fire to the rotten mess and quit worrying.

A niggling sensation warned her. A blaze couldn't destroy the wreckage.

~ ~ ~

Corrin scowled as she passed Mr. Meyer's office and pushed the down elevator button. Learning her boss had met with her attacker, and then jetted to a remote island without cell service, stunk.

She walked to the bus stop, caught the Number 10 to Capitol Hill, and slunk into a window seat. Life sucked when Friday rolled around, and a dental visit rated as the week's highlight.

Residue of cherry-flavored fluoride lingered in her mouth. Cavity-free teeth were a plus, considering the money she'd be spending to pay off the new car tires they'd installed today.

Air brakes groaned while the bus lurched to a halt at the curb. She grabbed the railing on the seat ahead and steadied herself.

A police car jetted past them, heading downhill. She relaxed her grip and the interior lights hit the opal in her bracelet, revealing a rainbow of colors in the pale stone.

Australia should be an easy first continent to explore. Corey and Willy both adored kangaroos, and Kyle would rock a Speedo if he joined them at the Great Barrier Reef. She pictured his blond hair slicked back by salt spray, droplets running down his abs . . .

The bus lurched again. She took a breath and pinched her nose. Faint smells of diesel and unkempt bodies hung in the air.

Buildings and alleys blurred together out the window, muted by another blustery day. She zipped her coat, hopped off at her stop, and let the wind push her to the corner.

A mule bugled, loud and clear. Not a live animal, she assured herself and moved forward.

It brayed again as she rounded the corner of their building. Tied to a tree in the yard stood a huge, reddish-colored mule. No horse trailer or cowboys in sight.

Corrin shielded her belly using her satchel and approached the walkway. Twenty feet and she'd be inside her building.

The behemoth eyed her and tilted his head forward. She put her key between her knuckles and dashed across the remaining sidewalk toward the entry. His long, furry ear came within inches of her elbow.

She scrambled up the steps and pulled the outside door shut behind her. Miranda's laughter and a deep baritone voice drifted into the hallway. *Grant's voice?* A big mule had led him to Miranda on the Montana mountain.

It had to be him. Damn if she'd let him break her heart again. She pushed open their apartment door. Grant and Miranda stood with their arms wrapped around each other's waists.

"Corrin, I have wonderful news." Rosy shades warmed Miranda's cheeks while she explained that Grant had decided to leave the bureau. The police car she'd seen had held the crooked cop, whom they'd apprehended in their apartment less than an hour ago.

Corrin shook her head. "The thug underestimated my roomie."

Grant grinned, his eyes on Miranda. "I'm grateful for the arrest, but I travelled here on a different mission." His hand went to a lump in the chest pocket of his coat.

A marriage proposal. "I'll leave you lovebirds alone. I'm truly happy for both of you." She stepped into her bedroom and shut the door.

Her brain struggled to process the turn of events. She wrapped her arms around herself. In Kyle's embrace she'd felt safe and cherished. Her butt sank into her dresser while she stared through the window at the mule.

"We're engaged!" Miranda trilled from the kitchen. "Corrin, will you be my maid of honor?"

She yanked open her door and hugged her friend. "I'll be your maid of anything, silly."

Grant stood in front of the refrigerator, wearing a sloppy grin on his face. He looked closer to a lovesick schoolboy than a former bureau boy.

"Congratulations! Grant, did you know she'd tagged you Agent of Interest before our long-eared yard ornament brought you two together?" Corrin asked him.

"I'll file that away for when I need it." He held out a big paw to Corrin.

She squeezed his hand and stood on tiptoe to peck him on the cheek. "Glad I didn't need to follow through on my warnings."

Grant pulled Miranda to his side. "I understood your concern and slept better knowing Miranda had a sister-of-the-soul for a wingwoman."

"Thank you. Go have an engagement dinner. You two have earned it," Corrin said.

"Grant's thought, too. Big Red will be housed for the night soon, so don't worry about him. And don't wait up," Miranda's teasing voice trailed out through the doorway.

"Not on your life," Corrin whispered.

The door closed, leaving morose emptiness in the apartment.

There must be a reason Kyle chose to ignore her messages. Like, if he'd found a nice country girl. She conjured a fate worse than torture—dancing the bridal party song together and afterward surrendering him to another woman's willing arms. A prickly ball of jealousy formed in the pit of her stomach.

She scrunched the hem of her sweater in her fist, blocking thoughts of the doctor who'd haunted her dreams and kindled a spark of desire, for him and a real life. She'd run out of excuses to call him and not appear needy, or Lord forbid, desperate. Then why did her chest ache?

"Think," she muttered. Roy deserved a verbal update and maybe he'd spill details on Kyle. Her finger trembled while she scrolled through contacts.

The phone answered on the first ring. "Roy Werner," stated his friendly and efficient voice.

"Corrin here. More than a few negative issues have emerged regarding Piersall Enterprises."

"Great. Say hello to Kyle while I get a notepad."

"Absolutely." Corrin sensed the moment Kyle's hands held the phone. Strong hands, gentle hands.

"Hey counselor-to-be, how goes it?" His deep, smooth voice revved her from the inside out. "I tried to leave a message on your work cell, but I got dropped out of the system twice."

Corrin's pulse jumped. "You did? I get calls from clients and lawyers all day. I never saw yours."

"I worried you had me blocked," Kyle laughed. "Glad it's not true, right?"

Weird to both have corrupted phone lines. She rubbed a blemish off the new cell's screen. "I left you a couple messages. I'll talk to my IT man on Monday. So, ah, how's Bobby doing?"

"I didn't receive your messages, either," he stated. "Bobby's fine. Hey, I'm on duty, and they flashed me an emergency code. Can I catch you when I have time to talk, maybe Sunday?"

That'd be two more days of wondering. "Sure."

"Gotta grab this call. Bye."

For once in her life, she wanted male attention. Kyle's attention. Could he have weekend plans?

Her body went numb. Kyle wouldn't string her along if he'd started dating.

~ ~ ~

Another crap week completed. Kyle hadn't called back over the weekend or all week. Again. Corrin stepped into the entry of her apartment building.

A red, vinyl bike tassel hung from the small brass door of her mail slot. Her old Schwinn had sported a similar pair of streamers hanging from each handle grip. She fingered one of the thin strands then let it drop.

No kids lived in their building. Someone must've found it outside and randomly taped it at eye level. Doubt crept up her spine. The last time she'd ridden that bike, they'd gone to the marina and boarded the molester's boat.

So long ago, she and her teenaged girlfriend spent hours pedaling all over town. The attack had ended biking, too. Damn the pervert.

She pushed aside the tassel and removed her mail. Miranda had sent another postcard from Montana on their leisurely return trip, dated three days ago.

While she read about her BFF's happiness in returning to Emma Springs, she hustled to her door and into her apartment. Her keys clunked onto the table. Next to them lay a pink folder labeled 'Miranda's Big Day.'

Seven o'clock Seattle time should be late enough in Montana to reach Miranda and be sure she and Grant had finished any horsey chores.

Imagining big horses furthered the unease in her empty stomach. That and knowing IT hadn't been able to pinpoint the cell phone issue of missing calls. And the phone company challenging her statement that every time she called Kyle, his recording engaged on the first ring. Every damn time.

Soon enough she'd get face time with Kyle at the wedding in Montana. She bit her lip, contemplating the possibility of him having a girlfriend. Could she manage a placid demeanor during the reception?

She took a deep breath. Miranda would've said something if he'd started dating someone. Unless she'd become too wrapped up being a temporary guest in Grant's house, counting the days until her wedding. She hit speed dial.

Miranda answered on the first ring. "Seattle sis! How do?"

"Hey B2B, or bride-to-be, I have the hall reserved at the church and a woman who'll bake your cake," Corrin said. "Planning your wedding so fast has been a refreshing challenge."

"So glad. Gotta run right now. I appreciate your rushed labor of love," Miranda said.

This time, she needed to chat. "Of course. Call me later."

Miranda would soon embark on a real life Happily Ever After, and scads of photos would document the radiant bride posed next to her Maid of Honor, Corrin Patten, a.k.a. Miss Coulda-Woulda-Shoulda.

~ ~ ~

"You may use your cellphones," the airline pilot announced. "Sixty-one and clear in Three Falls. Enjoy your day."

Corrin reached between her feet and Aunt Iris's and removed her leather satchel. Securely inside sat detailed notes proving that from two states away and just in the last couple of weeks, she'd envisioned, planned, and executed the perfect wedding reception for Miranda—at least on paper. If all else failed, Aunt Iris would conquer last-minute emergencies. The woman resonated with assurance. She'd proven herself when Corrin had arrived in Seattle, when Miranda needed work contacts and sympathy, and following Uncle Charlie's death.

She zipped her bag shut and unclipped her seatbelt.

Iris peered out the window as the plane parked near the terminal. "I'm excited to visit Montana!" she exclaimed. "Not excited to join the airplane exit dance."

Dance. Corrin's throat went dry. Maybe she'd change the bridal party dance to one with a faster tempo.

No, Miranda had insisted she honor Grant's request of John Legend's slow, sexy ballad of romantic bliss.

"Don't forget our stowed carry-ons," Iris chirped. "I hope Miranda and Grant get plenty of use out of the crystal vase we bought for their wedding present."

"Miranda mentioned that he brings her flowers regularly." Corrin rose and wedged her butt in the aisle between a man wearing a cowboy hat and a business-type, both tall enough to easily retrieve her garment bag from the overhead compartment.

The suit pulled out his cell phone. The cowboy flashed her a grin and raised an eyebrow. She balanced her weight evenly on tiptoes to unlatch the bin and lifted their heavy bags out.

Aunt Iris shook her head. "It's okay to accept help, honey."

"I guess." Corrin slipped on her wool coat. "Button up, it's parka and long john season in Montana from now until May, I'd expect."

Iris peered at her phone. "The three-day forecast still shows we hit a fall warm spell. Sunny and above sixty degrees tomorrow."

Corrin faked a smile. "Good news. Otherwise, Miranda's ride to church on Big Red wouldn't work for her wedding day."

"I'm honored she invited me. Miranda holds a special place in my heart." They shuffled toward the front exit.

"The three of us have a mutual admiration society."

"You're both family, dear. You and your siblings are the children we never had, and Miranda's special to me. I'm glad she and Grant worked things out."

Part of Corrin rejoiced, while the other part already mourned losing her roomie. "Even over the phone, she radiates happiness."

"And love," Iris said, and nodded goodbye to the flight attendants.

They stepped onto a dry platform of the mobile stairs, pushed tight to the front of the plane. Sun warmed Corrin's shoulders. Halfway down, she spotted activity in the terminal window. "I see our B2B girl enthusiastically flailing her hand."

"Your bride-to-be day will come, honey. Trust me," Iris said.

Corrin shrugged, bounded through the doors, and passed the crowd milling in the waiting area. No lapse in communication from Kyle would spoil Miranda's celebration.

"Whoopee! My buddies have arrived," chortled Miranda, from outside the tiny TSA area. "I never figured I'd be nervous marrying Grant. Here I am, wavering like an arrow knocked in a bow, right before flight."

Corrin glanced at the stuffed Grizzly in the case behind her. "Anyone who uses an arrow analogy must live in Montana. Give me a hug." Corrin squeezed her tight. "We're here to hold you steady. Seriously, you're glowing."

"Of course. I have Corrin and Iris, the perfect cure for tautly-strung nerves." Miranda shook a car key on a horse-shaped key ring. "And we get to cruise in Grant's Mustang. It's a manual transmission, so cross your fingers it's not a teeth-jarring ride." She looped her arm across Corrin's shoulder and aimed them toward the exit.

"You know you're in Montana when . . . the possibility of being bucked by a Mustang doesn't bother you, 'cause it has wheels instead of hooves." Corrin laughed and sidestepped to avoid a man carrying a toddler on his hip.

Iris grinned. "I'm impressed you learned to drive a stick."

"Grant's an excellent teacher." Miranda blushed.

"New worlds await you, dear." Iris smoothed a lock of her curly, silver hair. "Enough pillow talk. I adore this state. Two men have tipped their Stetsons at us."

"No surprise." Corrin grabbed her aunt's hand, linking the three together. "Runway-ready Miranda and irresistible Iris can't help enticing the locals."

"You should talk. Country doctors don't stand a chance," Iris declared, while they grabbed luggage and exited to the Mustang.

How she hoped that was true. Corrin slid a leather binder out of her satchel and dropped the bag on the back seat. "Please swing by the church first. I sketched out dimensions and placements for food tables and the band." She tugged her ear. "I need to confirm the logistics."

"We'll be there tonight rehearsing," Miranda said. "Kyle and his dad anxiously await your arrival. When I left they were beaming broader than toddlers on Christmas morning."

Those biceps of Kyle's were long past childhood. Corrin repositioned the clip restraining her hair. "I need to see the space in daylight. Afterward, we can move on to the sleepover. Roy's a gem for offering."

"You girls get the front." Iris hopped into the back seat with the agility of a woman twenty years younger. "I'm eager to meet this Roy fellow, the way you've extolled his virtues."

Virtuous, or did Roy still harbor ulterior motives to get her and Kyle together? Corrin deliberated while she settled into her seat. "You'll have Roy's full attention wearing your chiffon overlay dress to the wedding."

"Tomorrow we'll see Grant and Kyle in tuxedos, oh my." Miranda fanned her face and started the engine.

Not knowing who'd be adjusting Kyle's bow tie killed her. "Speaking of Kyle, is he dating anyone?"

"You can ask him yourself," Miranda proposed.

"You avoided my question." Corrin swallowed.

"Yup, I did," Miranda laughed it off. "Prepare to gallop to Emma Springs, girls."

What the heck? "Okay, BFF with questionable motives," Corrin chided. "I'd appreciate a detour to the church."

"Okay, nervous wedding planner of the century," Miranda teased, and pulled away from the curb. She drove pro style on the highway.

Familiar roads returned them to Emma Springs. They braked at the blinking light, then cruised to the church.

Corrin descended the steps to the reception hall. "Punch and drinks left, band in the corner." She paced off the distance for tables. The closer she got to the dancing area, the faster her heart raced.

"Everything okay, Corrin?" Miranda asked.

"It'll be fine." She scratched a note. "I need to adjust where to put the cake table."

"I meant you. I've never seen you jittery."

"Doing great." She snapped the folder shut.

"Then off we go." Miranda propelled her to the car.

Several folks on Main Street saluted their classic car while they cruised toward the reunion with Kyle.

Corrin clenched her hands in her lap. "Miranda, you're an expert driver, it's only been a couple of—" her mouth dropped.

Both Werner men stood in the middle of Roy's driveway.

Kyle's smile left no doubt of his interest.

Iris leaned between the seats. "You should've warned me. Those two should be in the movies. I imagined Roy to be the balding, portly type."

Goosebumps rose on Corrin's forearms. "Not in this family." Her grin broadened, watching Kyle rush to her side of the car. She jumped out, protected in the tight space of the open door. She folded her seat for Iris and turned.

Roy stepped forward and held out his hand to Iris.

"Iris, please meet Roy, and his son, Kyle," Miranda said, and unloaded the luggage.

"Lovely to meet you both." Iris's eyes flicked to Kyle and then rested on Roy. She flashed a shy smile and took his hand.

Roy raised Iris's hand. His lips barely brushed her aunt's fingers. "I'm delighted to meet you, Miss Iris," Roy said. "It's my pleasure to host you ladies." He tucked her palm in the crook of his arm and escorted her to the front door.

Iris's skin tone deepened. Within seconds, she'd succumbed to the Werner charm.

Kyle raised an eyebrow. "Whoa. I haven't seen my dad act cavalier for a helluva long time. Do you two have pixie dust you throw on us?"

Watching Iris stroll away beside Roy, Corrin leaned against the car frame, saying, "I could ask the same. Aunt Iris instantly regained her glow."

Miranda laughed. "Appears all is well, Kyle."

"Very, very well," he replied.

Had she missed something? Corrin stepped aside and shut the car door.

"Miss Wedding Planner made me stop by the church first and deemed the space sufficient for the reception. I'll meet you back at the sanctuary."

"We'll be there," Kyle said.

"Bye." Miranda left with another chuckle and a wave. "Love thrives in Emma Springs," she called from the end of the drive.

Corrin pressed her palm to her heart. Nothing would quell the galloping.

"Shall we?" Kyle picked up a suitcase and held out his arm.

The question of the day, the night, and maybe the future.

CHAPTER 9

Kyle needed a moment alone with Corrin. He slowed his steps to match the organ music, escorting her reservedly to the front of the old church as his pulse thumped double-time. Every atom in his body jumped to vibrant awareness at the mere touch of her fingers on his forearm.

If a scientist could reproduce a pill to match the euphoric exhilaration, they'd make billions.

Their minister smiled. "After you reach the altar, Kyle, you two will separate and move to three feet on either side of the pulpit."

Kyle slid his hand to overlap hers on his coat sleeve. Soft skin beckoned to him. He couldn't help it, he stroked above the meaningful bracelet on her diminutive wrist.

Her eyes sparked.

Every nerve ending longed to pull her close and kiss her, long and passionately, as if they were lovers torn apart and suddenly reunited. Probably not the best idea in front of the minister and the wedding party. Although no one in this room would object, he thought, and fought a smile.

"So." Corrin cleared her throat and stepped to her position. "I take Miranda's bouquet when she reaches the chancel."

"Correct, and you're set until the service concludes and the bridal couple leaves. Please follow a few feet behind them." The minister raised his head and signaled for Miranda and Grant to come forward.

Kyle listened to the timing of the wedding band handoff and acknowledged the minister's nod excusing him.

Patricia, Tom, Ike, and Shirley grinned from the front row. Both couples personified the description of proud parents, ready to watch their offspring tie the knot.

On the opposite pew, Corrin fake smiled with her hands clenched in her lap.

He headed to her. "I told Dad we'd swing by for Iris and him before we headed to the rehearsal dinner. I'd enjoy your company in the meantime, unless you prefer to wait here."

Corrin motioned to where the pastor stood in discussion with Grant and Miranda. "Appears I'm not needed anymore."

Just as he'd thought. "I don't agree."

She retreated to the entry and shoved open the double doors leading outside. She stared at the parking lot. "Dusk settles differently here than in hazy Seattle."

"Having your best friend move away sucks. I can listen if you care to discuss a non-weather topic."

"Thanks." She headed for his Jeep parked in front of the church. A blast sounded from nearby. Her head whipped around. "Gunshot?"

Kyle grabbed her hand and ran them to the passenger door. "Yes, from the direction of Dad's house. No one shoots in town." He jumped in, threw it in reverse, then cranked the wheel before peeling out. "Dad might be in trouble." His pulse thumped in his chest.

Corrin braced her hand against the dashboard. "More problems?"

"Dagger Realty made Dad a bigger offer on the lake frontage property, and after he refused, more incidents occurred."

"Roy mentioned a black SUV tried to run him off the road."

He checked the intersection and hit the gas. "Add in slashed tires and his mailbox leveled. The sheriff couldn't find any fingerprints. Our county council president, Sharlene Underson, doesn't want negative publicity to mar the town's reputation. She maintains its kids."

"Kids don't force you into a ditch."

"Sharlene suggested Dad hit an icy patch." Kyle wheeled past the lake. "The sheriff's been doing extra drives through town."

Corrin held on while he swung into the drive.

His dad stood on the front lawn, jaw clenched, a shotgun teetering in the crook of his arm. His free hand supported Iris's elbow.

Kyle sprang out of the car. "Anyone hurt?"

Binoculars dangled from Iris's neck. She put her thumb in the air. "We're fine." She leaned into Roy.

Kyle scanned the two of them and blew out through his mouth. No blood. "What were you shooting?" He eased the rifle from his dad's grip and laid it aside.

"I'd pointed out to Iris where the wood ducks nest. I thought we'd spotted a coyote."

"Roy fired a skedaddle warning into the air," Iris said.

"Turned out to be a two-legged varmint, some guy with a big package skulking in the reeds." Roy ran his fingers through his hair.

"I watched through the binoculars," Iris said. "He slogged off, wearing hip waders."

"Iris tripped and twisted her ankle." Roy sputtered. "Wouldn't have happened if the blasted intruder hadn't shown up."

Kyle stepped next to Iris. "Any pain, tingles, or numbness?" He took her warm hand. "Please sit on the porch step while I check your ankle."

"Certainly." She smiled at Roy. "I'm fine, boys."

Roy brushed off the carpet runner and took her other hand. Together, they lowered Iris onto the step. His dad sat by her side, concern darkening his eyes. He projected defender again, a role sadly missing since Mom's death.

Optimism welled in Kyle's chest. His dad deserved happiness. Kyle squatted and raised Iris's pant leg. He gently touched her anklebone. "This hurt?"

"Nope," Iris said, and scooched over for Corrin to sit on her other side. "I know that look. What else do you need to know, honey?"

"Did you see the man's face?"

"He wore a ski mask. I saw writing on his bag."

Corrin got out her phone. "Exactly what, please?"

Iris closed her eyes. "It had the letters HgC and the word 'poison.'"

"You don't waste any time, counselor," Kyle said, and rotated Iris's foot. "Any pain?"

"Not a smidgeon," Iris chirped.

"HgC." Corrin thumbed her phone's screen. "Water-soluble mercuric chloride is toxic to lakes."

"Have you called the sheriff?" Kyle released Iris's foot.

"No, my concern centered on Iris," Roy said. "Probably should, though."

"Agreed," Kyle sat back on his heels. "Time to ignore Sharlene Underson and her bad publicity worries."

"Let's see if your trespassers left any evidence," Corrin said.

"Good idea." Roy took Iris's hand. "I'd planned to show Iris the cottage next." He gallantly pulled Iris to her feet. "If we stay on the pavement, will you be okay? There's a walkway all the way to the lake."

"I'm structurally sound," Iris declared.

He liked this lady more by the minute. Kyle clasped Corrin's hand and held her back to let Dad get ahead, then crossed the street.

Corrin stopped in the driveway. "It really could be a seven dwarf-style cottage, complete with a whitewashed exterior." Her eyes narrowed. "Too bad all isn't bluebirds and bunnies in your fairytale land," she stated.

Kyle nodded. "Precisely, counselor. I'm getting worried. I need someone to research Dagger Realty."

"I've already begun researching Dagger, per Roy's instruction," Corrin said. "It's newly registered. A man named Donald Underson is the principal broker. Related to the councilwoman?"

"Her husband," Kyle muttered.

"What a beautiful lake," Iris exclaimed from the other side of the garage.

Kyle squeezed Corrin's hand and led her onto flat, wide paver stones alongside the garage, which continued to the shore.

Roy and Iris stood side by side on the last stone.

"Up close, the serene lake sparkles," Corrin's voice held wonder. She cleared her throat. "Does your father know the realtor?"

Warmth filled his chest. "Hey Dad? I thought old Don quit thumping for business ten years ago."

Roy turned. "Guess not."

"What's in the reeds?" Iris pointed to a slim, lime-green piece of plastic. "See, the bright-colored thing, about three feet out."

Roy tiptoed into soggy ground and bent to pick it up from between two cattails.

"Wait. Please don't touch it." Corrin snapped photos with her phone. "We may need fingerprints off that tear strip." She pulled a tissue from her purse and handed it to Roy. "Lift it out by the corner with this, and we'll bag it at your house."

Seriously? Kyle grimaced. "Crime show junkie?"

"I don't own a TV. My office relies on evidence from our in-house private investigator, and I comb through her findings." She took another photo. "There's part of a logo."

Roy shook his head. "I've never dealt with crooks before."

"Thankfully." Kyle's chest tightened.

"These are slap-in-the-face warning signs. Staying alert is paramount," said Corrin.

He had to face facts. Corrin reacted from big city experience. "Scope out front more often, Dad."

"Right, right." Roy smiled at Iris. "While we're here, allow me to show you our first home in Emma Springs." He ushered the group to the picture window on the lake side of the cottage. "Flor brought her paintings here to finish."

Iris placed her hand on Roy's arm. "I noticed the lovely watercolor in your dining room."

Roy smiled at her. "I'll show you more of her work." His gaze dropped to the ground. "The yard needs TLC."

Iris pointed to brown stalks in the shrubbery. "You've planted bulbs." She broke off dead stems. "Someone needs to tidy this bed."

"Oh, are you interested in gardening? If you delay leaving, we could tackle fall maintenance together." Roy took the dead foliage and dropped it into a bin. "I'll handle the scuttle work."

Corrin gently elbowed Kyle and backed away from Iris and Roy. A quacking bird circled overhead. "Those two are birds of a feather. Where do the ducks nest?" She stepped onto a flat stone leading to the lake.

"It's one of the wood ducks. They live in the snag you thought was spooky," Kyle replied. "Nice going, matchmaker. I haven't seen Dad this enthusiastic since Mom's diagnosis."

"Wasn't all me," Corrin whispered as Roy and Iris approached from the back of the cottage. "Miranda insisted Aunt Iris come to her wedding, and we needed a budget-friendly hotel."

"I'll give Dad extra points for offering the Werner Inn," he whispered back.

"Corrin, honey, I assume you're capable of flying home on your own." Iris stood with a hand clasped on Roy's forearm. "I've accumulated vacation days, and I miss my flower garden. Even cleanup."

"Please stay." Corrin's voice became feather soft. "Roy doesn't know what a gardener he's getting."

"I know a good thing when I see it, young lady," Roy said. "My eyes may be older, but my instincts are solid." Roy winked at Corrin and checked his watch. "We're due at the rehearsal dinner in fifteen minutes. Let's head back to the house and I'll get it locked."

Dad and Iris weren't afraid of mutual attraction. Kyle knew from the tenderness in Corrin's eyes her defenses were weakening. Emma Springs versus Seattle.

He needed to present his case to counsel, and he had three days to win the dispute.

~ ~ ~

Best man. Precisely who sat next to her at the rehearsal dinner. Not only the best dancer, but also kind, smart, and achingly handsome. Her fingers itched to touch his hair, trace the curve of his jaw, and pull those lips into kissing range. Corrin folded her hands into her lap before she looked away.

A wall of windows in the dining room of the Springs Cafe afforded a panoramic view of Sunrise Lake.

The lights in Kyle's home shone, and next to it sat the dark Werner family cottage. Across the lake were the recently vacated houses, also dark. Mt. Hanlen towered imposingly in the background.

She adjusted her napkin and slipped off her tight half boots. Next time she'd thoroughly break in new footwear.

Seating the bridal party side by side had seemed logical from the safety of her Seattle apartment. She'd placed herself to Kyle's left, forgetting a critical trait. He was left-handed, and while eating, their elbows routinely bumped.

She anticipated the next Kyle connection. He raised his fork, and she followed suit. Yup, there it came, his arm caress.

"Excuse me, again." His mischievous eyes held no regret. "I'm glad we're finally able to catch up."

She'd second that emotion. The cell phone fiasco hadn't been her fault. Or did he mean alone time in person? "I'm stumped as to why you missed my voicemails. I left at least two for you on a standard recorded message."

"If we were playing poker, I'd raise you two voicemails and call your hand with a letter and the Emma Springs Newsletter I sent."

Her chin jutted forward. "Really? I never received anything. Where did you send the letter?"

"To your office." He thumbed his wine glass. "You never gave me personal information."

For stupid reasons she regretted. "Old habits die hard." She flattened her tired feet onto the floor. "I should've received your letter."

Concern radiated from Kyle's face. "Something else is bothering you."

The degenerate from her past wasn't his problem. She twisted the napkin in her lap, realizing the anxiety caused by seeing the pervert had become obvious to Kyle. "There have been a couple of phone glitches. I'll investigate the mail issue."

"You'll alert me if there's a problem?"

She forced herself to relax. "I will. Thank you."

"Fair enough, and dad says he enjoys your case law conversations. I'll contact my cell carrier, too. Until we get it straightened out, I'll call you from Dad's phone."

"Great idea. Roy's been extremely helpful," Corrin said.

"That's an understatement." Kyle's glance flicked to where Roy and Iris sat, with their arms touching.

"Dad hasn't worn that suit in years, and I've never smelled cologne on him." Kyle leaned close enough for his breath to warm Corrin's ear. "Your free-flowing hair is beautiful." He slid his finger down a lock, then let out a long sigh.

Belly flutters launched. His dating status required clarification, before this flirting went any further. "Thank you. You make a dashing best man. Any younger, casserole-carrying, bedazzled Californians move into town?"

"Not that I'm aware of," Kyle smiled. "I've looked forward to spending the weekend together, celebrating Miranda and Grant's happiness."

Relief flooded through her. "So, there's a chance you'll be available to be my escort for the reception? Aunt Iris and your dad appear spellbound, and I don't want to be an old maid."

"I attempted to pose the same question. Several times." He leaned closer, shoulder to shoulder. "You may be a maiden, but never, ever, old." His eyes traced a sinfully slow path down her neck to the aquamarine birthstone necklace at her throat.

Her body thrummed. If his perusal amped her up this much, what would . . .? "Glad one of the questions is settled," she managed.

"Technology isn't foolproof," he said. "Odd, though. Anything else strange happening?"

He'd worry if he knew the facts. A cold wave swept over her, colder than the mysterious dropped ice cream. "There's always craziness in a city the size of Seattle."

Kyle's lips parted, as if to press further.

A fork clanked on a wine glass.

Tom Morley rose. "Pat and I appreciate your role in making Grant and Miranda's wedding day tomorrow special," Tom began. "We've come to love her as a daughter."

Ike stood. "And we're thankful she's found a Montana family. Shirley and I are blessed to have sweet Miranda in our lives. She's the dear child we never had. Grant is a fine young man, and we're happy to have the chance to become acquainted. We couldn't imagine two people better suited for one another."

Everyone clapped.

Shirley motioned to the bridal couple, and both sets of parents at their table. "Present married couples excluded." Cheers and laughter erupted in the room.

Aunt Iris and Roy had their heads tipped together, smile wrinkles enhancing their relaxed ease.

Corrin managed a grin. Outside, joy radiated for her best friend. Inside, she faced the prospect of no Miranda sharing her apartment, Iris falling for Roy and moving here, and days ahead without Kyle. An empty cavern grew darker with so many impending losses.

~ ~ ~

The rehearsal dinner wound down. Kyle sat back, mentally flipping through conversations.

Corrin's blond lashes shuttered her eyes. She'd mentioned a sister and kids she helped support. He rubbed his chin. No mention of girlfriends besides Miranda.

Time alone with her would prove how he could be a good listener and help fill the void. "If you're ready to call it a night, I can return you to Dad's."

"Yes, thank you," her voice wavered.

"It's fun observing Grant and Miranda, and now Iris and my dad. One couple blissful, the other bashful."

"With your dad's charms, Iris is a goner." Corrin's focus sounded miles away. She fumbled under the table to put her boots on. She stood up and scrunched her face.

Aching feet? He rubbed his hands together. Given the opportunity, he could remedy the affliction. "They're mutual goners. Dad's spark has returned." He offered his arm, and she tentatively placed her fingers on it. "Grant's never looked happier."

"Miranda, either," she murmured.

Kyle guided her to the four happy couples at the head table. He nodded to Tom and Pat. "Thank you for dinner."

"You're very welcome. Won't you two join our group for a nightcap at our house?" Pat offered. "Your Dad and Iris are coming."

"I'm beat," Corrin said. "Excellent dinner, thank you." She nodded to Pat and clasped Miranda's hand. "You, B2B, I expect at ten," her voice lacked any authority.

"It's a date." Miranda tugged at a strand of Corrin's hair. "Everything's perfect. Get a good night's sleep."

"I will. See you all tomorrow for the big day." Corrin waved goodbye.

Kyle took her hand and caught sight of her lip quivering during the walk to his Jeep. He bit back what he'd practiced saying to her. Now wasn't the time for declarations, but for respectful silence.

She kept her head down.

Her withdrawal became worse than charting an unfamiliar infection not responding to treatment.

~ ~ ~

Kyle remained oddly silent on the short drive from the rehearsal dinner. Corrin smoothed her calf-length skirt, feeling the tightly woven wool strands. He had to be ecstatic Grant would be living close by again. And he got Miranda, too.

She waited patiently for him to unlock Roy's home, then followed him through the breezeway and stopped at the hall tree. Methodical tick-tocks broke the silence. She rubbed her arms, fighting unaccustomed desolation.

"I'll turn on the fireplace." Kyle pressed a button on a remote and flames danced in the hearth. "You'll get warmed up if you sit on the couch. A cup of tea might help, and feel free to ditch your boots."

"You never miss a thing." She sank into velvet cushions.

"Please go to the Morley's and celebrate." She pulled off her spike-heeled boots, removed her short socks, and rubbed her cramped toes.

"There's nowhere I'd rather be than here, with you."

He rated the best-ever-man title. "Thanks, I'm experiencing withdrawal pains from losing Miranda. I'd appreciate hot tea."

He ran water into two mugs and stuck them in the microwave. "I felt the friendship void after moving away from Grant and John. Why don't you describe working in a prestigious law office and your apartment? It will give me a better picture of your life."

"MFB's a typical law firm run by a multi-partner dictatorship. Our attorneys don't engage much with lower-level employees. Your dad's an anomaly in the trade."

"I know, he's a friend to me and a father figure." Kyle set the mugs on the coffee table, along with a pump bottle of hand lotion. "If your aching arches could use a massage, I'd give it a try." He sat near the middle of the couch, anticipation in his serious eyes.

Very, very, Best Man. Splurging on a mani-pedi last week had been worth every cent. "I'm a willing subject." She swung her legs to the middle cushion.

He pulled her right foot onto his knee, bent forward, and filled his palm with lotion. "I'm glad Iris agreed to join the gathering at the Morley home tonight. Dad doesn't socialize enough."

She sunk into the couch corner, his thumbs kneading the ball of her foot into relaxed bliss. "I hope you aren't annoyed that I encouraged Aunt Iris and your dad to spend time together."

"Quite the opposite." His warm, deft strokes caressed her ankle, then stopped. "May I loosen your calf muscle?"

Those fingers would loosen while she lost her grip. "Please do."

He folded the hem of her skirt and worked more magic. His little finger brushed the underside of her knee. Tingles shot into her.

Just a little higher, her body whispered.

"Sorry if I hit a tender spot," his deep, low voice murmured.

Mind reader. And that voice didn't contain one note of apology. "Sorry my . . . I mean, you're a master masseuse."

His lips twitched while he worked to the ends of her toes.

She tipped her head back, absorbing each movement from his strong, capable hands. Where had the conversation ended? She forced her brain to reengage before she dropped into la-la land. "Glad you approve of Iris."

"Dad needs companionship, and Iris is a sweetheart. How's she related?" He moved his hand to her right foot and began the methodical and oh-so-satisfying motions again.

How slowly could she speak? "She's my mom's older sister. She and Uncle Charlie were childless and became a second set of parents, until in a drunken tirade, my dad told them never to set foot in our house again."

His fingers left her foot, the air suddenly feeling chillier. "I'm sorry." He unfolded her skirt and handed her the mug of tea. "That must've been tough." His left hand rested on her ankle, still propped on his knee.

The intimacy didn't feel awkward or forced, simply warm and comfortable. She inhaled the earthy scent of chamomile before sipping the soothing liquid. "Aunt Iris sent me books to read every month. I chose to live in Seattle, knowing she'd be there to guide me."

"And if she and Dad deepen their relationship, you might lose her again."

His gentle voice smoothed out the last rough edges of the day.

"It's not about me. Aunt Iris and your dad deserve happiness." Her fingers tightened on the mug handle.

Kyle's keenly intelligent blue eyes met hers. "Agreed," he said. "We all deserve happiness and someone special to love. Don't you think?"

This close to him, sure. "You've got a calming bedside manner." Heat rose to her cheeks. "I mean, your patients must be comfortable talking to you."

"I hope so," Kyle said. "You deserve to be loved, Corrin. No debate."

Flutters of possibility drummed against the thinning barriers she'd built deep, deep inside. "Thank you again, Kyle. I'm ready to turn in. It's a big day tomorrow."

"I understand." Kyle stood up and offered her his hand. "I'm always here, whenever you need to talk."

His warm clasp pulled her steadily to her feet. Even barefoot, she wobbled, her chest grazing his jacket. "I appreciate you." Her lips brushed his cheek. She smoothed his lapel.

Kyle froze in place, while his eyes burned for more. "I want you to be happy. Dad's serious about partnership with you. And I'm serious, too."

If she kissed him again, she'd be sunk. Her palm lingered, resting over his heart. "I know. Let me get through the bar in February. Then we'll talk." Each step away took effort. "Goodnight." She flicked on the bedroom light.

"Goodnight. I'll lock you in, to the house and our talk." Kyle's steps faded down the hallway. The outside door clicked shut.

Kyle wanting her here tempted in too many ways. Tempted her enough to consider a move to Emma Springs if she passed the exam.

She rested her elbows on the bedroom windowsill. A porch light glowed from his house, fifty feet away. Tonight, the distance seemed infinite.

No sound from the garage door. He must've left his Jeep here. She caught movement near the end of Roy's drive.

Kyle crossed the street—his broad shoulders and determined steps declaring he knew his precise path.

If she gave the signal, he'd offer a strong grip and help to guide her. Was she ready to make that declaration? She raised her hand, preparing to rap on the window.

CHAPTER 10

Calling Kyle back last night would've verified his genuine offer to be loved, she chided herself again. Her gaze flicked around his old room, the morning sunshine brightening the blue walls. She let out a long sigh.

Emma Springs welcomed morning solely with light, not clanking garbage trucks or revving engines.

Corrin watched while Aunt Iris puffed out regular breaths of peaceful slumber.

Her feet pushed against twisted sheets, evidence of her indecision. She sat up.

Next to her twin bed hung a series of school photos featuring Kyle missing a tooth, Kyle wearing a turtleneck, and Kyle the handsome graduate. All big-smiled and confident, the same man she'd watched cross to his dark house eight hours ago.

Cool wood met her feet. She rubbed her bare arms.

A purple hoodie hung on a row of hooks next to the closet. She tugged on the sweatshirt and smoothed the material hanging to her knees. Kyle, oh Kyle, give me some of your courage. Her hands paused, picturing the honest, fun, and drop-dead gorgeous owner.

Would his father be awake? She turned the glass knob to open the bedroom door. Aromas of sweet rolls and coffee wafted in the hallway. The apple didn't fall far from the pie in their family.

Roy stood in the kitchen, staring out a window. Three place settings lay on a table. A slim crystal vase held tall orange flowers. Were they chrysanthemums? Iris would know.

Corrin cleared her throat, and Roy turned. His engaging smile greeted her. "Hope you both slept comfortably."

"I did, and Aunt Iris never made a peep. She's generally up by six."

Roy lifted a china cup from the table. "Country air's relaxing. Tea, right? Kyle brought these over for you." He waved reddish-orange packets.

Kyle had remembered her morning tea preference. "Yes, please." She smiled and looked outside. "I'd guess those raised beds are for vegetables."

"Correct. Flor made me promise one thing before she died. Well, actually two. She wanted me to marry again, hopefully to a woman who'd help me tend her plants."

"I figured she enjoyed gardening by the gear you lent me for Bobby's rescue."

"This may sound corny." He pulled out her chair. "Truth be told, the moment I touched your aunt's hand, it struck me I'd met a kindred spirit. That was Flor's second request, to find a loving partner."

How lucky to embrace that awareness. "Aunt Iris must enjoy your company to accept your invite." She lifted her cup to meet the floral teapot Roy offered.

"I'm flattered." His cheeks grew pink while he poured. "Your aunt's a special lady."

She inhaled orange and spice scents. Kyle was a special man. "When I came to Seattle, Aunt Iris and

Uncle Charlie opened the front door and their welcoming arms."

"Flor did the same with countless people in the community."

"Must be a gardener trait. Aunt Iris took pride in her beautiful flowers. Charlie never knew she had to sell the house to pay his medical bills."

"Dedication under pressure is a true sign of devotion." Roy turned his spoon in his hand.

"She volunteers to fill her extra hours, not that anything can satisfy loneliness."

"Boy, is that the sad truth. I miss Flor's company at the oddest times. I turned to commiserating through wine. Drinking stopped the day after the Bobby incident. Kyle and I discussed my wine consumption, and I agreed with his concern."

Another plus. "Alcohol never proved beneficial in my world. Before I forget, thank you for hosting us, and for providing a place for Miranda and me to get ready today."

A door closed in the hallway.

"Your timing's perfect," Roy beamed. "I needed a good dose of female."

"We're happy to oblige, aren't we, honey?" Aunt Iris kissed the top of her head. "I peeked in the other guest room. Well-stocked with hair spray and whatnots for preparing a bride." She slid into the empty chair.

"I told Corrin, no overloaded suitcases if preventable. McPherson's store has more if I missed anything."

"Can't imagine you did." Iris fingered a flower petal. "How splendid to have fresh chrysanthemums."

"Yes, they were Flor's favorite fall centerpiece." Roy poured coffee into Iris's teacup, decorated with roses.

"If I remember correctly, you prefer a drop of cream." He bobbed a tiny pitcher over the dark brew.

"Thank you." Her smile radiated more than mere appreciation. "My Charlie always fixed our coffee." Iris said tenderly. "Little things make you feel cherished."

Cherished and cared for. Exactly her reaction to Kyle.

Damn the distance, damn the timing. Damn, damn, damn.

~ ~ ~

They finished using hairpins and styling gel. Corrin stood back and watched while Miranda slipped her arms into her wedding gown.

She turned, her hands on her hips, her eyes bright. "Move to Emma Springs, Corrin. Please?"

"MFB's grooming me for partnership."

"I overheard Kyle and Grant endorsing your potential partnership with Roy," Miranda said. "Not that he needs any encouragement to hire you. Roy appreciates and respects you."

Did she receive respect from anyone at MFB besides Mr. Meyer? Corrin looked at her hands, which had prepared umpteen briefs credited to thankless lawyers. "Roy was kind to offer lodging for Iris and me. He used the term "girly" when he insisted on a supply list."

"Your tactic of dodging questions doesn't work on me. It took me awhile to realize small towns protect their inhabitants."

Memories of taunts describing her drunken father resurfaced. "Ebony Cove ignored my family, and we needed help," Corrin said.

"From what I've witnessed in Emma Springs, everyone's treated as extended family," Miranda stated. "The good, the bad, and the quirky."

"I saw that in action."

"Speaking of action, Kyle worried you were avoiding his phone calls. I didn't want to bug you, so I stayed out of it. All cleared up?"

Cleared up, massaged to putty, and ready for a repeat. "We both wanted to talk. Annoyingly, calls weren't connecting through our cell phones."

"Sounds strange. Kyle's a great guy." Miranda threw her a megawatt smile. "By your blush you're more than aware. I officially request you show him you're interested today. Please? It'd make my wedding extra special." She twirled in her gown, delicate beads rippling with the movement. "Can you believe it's happening?

A request from Miranda couldn't be ignored. Her stomach flip-flopped. "Uh-huh. Let's get the back closed." Corrin zipped the dress but fumbled hooking the loop onto a covered button at the neck.

"I'm lucky height runs in Shirley's family." Miranda studied the hem grazing the toe of her shoe.

"It fits like a designer created it for you." Soft material brushed against Corrin's fingers. She turned Miranda to face their reflections in the full-length mirror. "By arranging your hair in the Greek upswept style, you do the goddess look proud, Miss Miranda."

"I feel regal standing alongside my striking maid of honor."

Corrin smoothed her blue silk dress and glanced down at her shoes, chosen especially for dancing. That wish would come true. "A sweet compliment. Thank you. However, no one will question who owns today."

Miranda swished the folds of the skirt from side to side. "Shirley's mother took her wedding vows wearing it in 1922, Shirley in 1961, and now me. I'm grateful to wear it."

"You own this style."

White chiffon aged to a delicate cream had been overlaid onto the silk, column-style gown. Pearl beads flowed in a scroll pattern from the waist to the fitted, elbow-length sleeves.

"Someday, you'll have a daughter who'll appear equally gorgeous in it." A fierce longing burned in Corrin's heart for Miranda's happiness and for unlimited possibilities involving Kyle. If she hadn't made a financial promise to Grace and the kids, she'd act immediately.

How lucrative was Roy's practice? Enough so that Willy and Corey wouldn't endure the same childhood shame? Emotion ripped through her, pulsing two courses of action, running in opposite directions. Her vision grew misty.

Miranda rotated in front of the mirror. "The coronet headband you bought me is perfect." She pivoted and clutched Corrin's arms. "Hey. No tears. I need you always in my life. You've been my savior since I lost my family and found you in Seattle."

"Grant pays attention to little details, and he clearly treasures you. I trust him." Corrin slid a bobby pin into Miranda's glossy auburn hair.

"Our sisterhood bond is different. We've risen like the phoenix, remember? We'll call all the time, and I promise I'll come to visit you in Seattle."

So much change. "You'd better." Corrin straightened a bead on the shoulder of the wedding gown. "I'm elated you'll have a wonderful life, soul sis." She handed her the bridal bouquet.

"I'll be your matron of honor on your day."

"Deal." Corrin forced a grin. Her best-ever friend would be walking the church aisle and out of her life. She lifted her bouquet from the Petal Pusher Florist's box.

An ear-splitting bray trumpeted from Roy's front yard.

Corrin's knee bumped the dresser. "Sounds like your four-hoofed limo arrived."

"Stan Johnson gifted us a handwoven Native American saddle blanket for my ride. The long white fringe will be a beautiful contrast to Big Red." Miranda pulled aside the lacy window curtain. "Come see. The pale blue and green designs match our velvet capes from Shirley."

"Uh-huh." Corrin peeked out and shuddered.

Red pawed the ground, his big head dwarfing Stan, the reclusive mountain man.

Miranda squeezed Corrin's shoulder. "He's a puppy dog in a big mulish body."

"You mean Stan?"

"Big Red, silly. I imagine Stan is, too."

A knock on the front door jolted Corrin.

"Hey girls, it's parade time by my watch," Kyle called. "You ready?"

"Be right out." She kissed Miranda on the cheek and watched her beautiful and confident best friend glide into the hallway.

"Riding to the church on Red's my idea of a fairy tale entrance. Thank you for managing the mounted part," Miranda said to Kyle.

"I got lucky. Stan descended Mt. Hanlen and insisted on leading Red after hearing his part in your harrowing story. Animals worship him."

"I'm still worried I'll slip off and ruin my dress. I've never ridden sideways."

Big Red spotted her in the doorway and nickered He stood still, as if he'd heard.

"You're going to do fine. Red's a careful boy," Kyle spoke in his calming tone.

Corrin lifted the longer of the two heavy capes Shirley had provided. She draped the garment across Miranda's shoulders and secured the clasp. "You're ready, my gorgeous bride."

"Because of your unfailing help." Miranda hugged Corrin and then hitched up the short train of her skirt to exit off the front porch.

"Dad will walk next to you, Miranda." Kyle turned to Corrin. "Back in a minute."

Her fingernails dug into the stems of the flowers. She stepped outside and raised her face skyward. "Keep Miranda safe atop her giant beast and bless her new life," she whispered.

She pictured the procession to the church's open side doors, allowing Grant and the congregation a view of the approaching bride, seated atop Red.

A black SUV cruised in front of the cottage and slowly passed behind Big Red. She leaned forward too late. The mule's rump blocked her view of the license plate.

There were plenty of people in town for the wedding. Still, a warning jarred her.

The mule brayed, and Kyle laughed.

"Your ride's honking, almost-married lady," Kyle teased. "I'll set you atop Red, and you're off to your new life."

"Red didn't care for that car by the tone of his call," Miranda looked back at Corrin and forced a tight smile.

They'd keep in touch, they had to. Corrin stared at the unfolding scene. Kyle and Miranda stood beside the mule.

"Dad will help you off, while Stan holds Red. No worries, okay?" He boosted her to sitting sideways.

Miranda waved. "I'm balanced. I forgot what a broad back Red has."

Corrin gripped a post and shuddered while Miranda exuded confidence. If she'd only toss a backbone her way. "You're a princess bride," she yelled.

"You made me into one!" She waved her spray of flowers.

A prince of a groomsman patted the mule. Kyle wore his tuxedo well, stunningly well. He simply needed a crown and a scepter. And a damsel to kiss. Her hand went to her lips.

"Off to the church, Stan." While Kyle raised his arms in a salute, the fabric stretched across his rounded rump.

She flexed her fingers at the novel urge to explore a guy's glutes. Her bouquet dropped onto the sidewalk. Warmth spread to her cheeks. She'd blushed more in the last month than in her entire life.

Kyle ran up the driveway and picked up her bouquet. "You're flushed, Corrin. Inhale a couple of deep breaths. I'll be right next to you, and Red's already half a block away."

He handed her the flowers, grabbed her cape from the hall tree, and helped her into it. "Take my hand?"

If he knew where five of her tingling digits wanted to explore, he'd be either insulted or excited. His steady grip enfolded her fingers, her thumb imagining a firmer cushion. Had she rubbed a circle on his palm? *Oh crap.* "Thanks."

He met her eyes and did a double take. "Wow, your pupils are huge." His sexy grin held a challenge.

Busted. The doctor knew her thoughts weren't innocent. "You don't look half bad in a tux." She raised her chin.

"I'll settle for half bad from the honorable maiden. Come on, the church is close." He squeezed her hand.

"You haven't walked a mile in my heels," she quipped and took the longest strides she could manage.

He shortened his steps, his warm hand providing a reassuring grip. His eyes held a distinctive spark of playfulness. "I'm happy to carry you again."

Held tight in those muscular arms? She licked her lips. "Sidesaddle?" she teased.

He raised his eyebrows and gave her a most disarming appraisal, sending quivers deep, deep down. "Your choice."

"Hey besties!" Miranda had dismounted. She removed her seafoam green cape and leaned against Red, her hand on his cheek, the delicate cream of her dress a stark comparison against his glossy, russet hide.

The photographer snapped shots.

Corrin leaned into Kyle. "That pose would rate top billing at a photo shoot capturing the elegantly dressed bride and the smart, long-eared mule who found her future husband."

"Focus on Big Red's heroic attributes," Kyle said.

She nodded and averted her eyes from the polished hooves, the mouth capable of chomping a Smart car, and twelve hundred pounds of untethered equine.

"Good job. We'll do this together." Kyle's lips tickled her ear.

She inhaled his sexy, citrusy cologne and released her death grip. "Oh, sorry."

"I admire a woman possessing strong hands," he whispered.

The notes of *Pachelbel's Canon* wafted onto the lawn. Miranda's dreams would soon come true. Tears wet Corrin's eyes.

Ike poked his head out the church door to check their progress. He smoothed out his gray hair, straightened his cummerbund, and waved them forward.

Miranda touched Stan's arm. "Thank you." She crossed the sidewalk and kissed Corrin's cheek. "We did it, my forever sister-of-the-soul."

"Forever," she whispered back.

"You're a beautiful bride." Kyle and Corrin spoke in unison.

Corrin shucked her sapphire blue cape and handed it to Stan. "Great job handling Red." She brushed away a tear and faced Miranda. "A perfect day for your wedding, and the start of your happily ever after."

"Don't forget my request," Miranda prompted.

"Signed, refined, entwined," Corrin said, and smiled at Kyle.

His eyebrow shot up. "Oh-kay. Shall we?" He offered his arm and led Corrin to the short flight of steps. She turned and mouthed, "I love you."

"Me, too." Miranda patted her heart.

Kyle's footsteps metered the slow anthem while they passed Ike. Corrin's shoe sunk into the pristine white bridal runner splitting the two rows of pews. Folks twisted sideways to see Miranda and Red.

"Mom! There's Ninja Commander. Oh my gosh! She's wearing a dress." Bobby's squeal created a ripple of chuckles. His round eyes remained riveted on her.

She felt as if her head brushed the ceiling. When she reached his row, she winked.

A grin spread from ear to ear on his freckled face.

Grant beamed at Bobby and Corrin before directing a look of loving anticipation to the door.

In a few more steps, they'd reached the chancel. Kyle lifted her fingers and leaned in. "Someday," he whispered.

She nodded. He hadn't issued a proposal, had he? Her foot bumped onto the upper carpeted area holding the pulpit. She swiveled his way.

Kyle took his place next to Grant, a satisfied smile flicking across his face. He looked sideways and winked at her, solidifying she'd been correct about his flirtatious proposal.

Two could play the game. She tipped her nose and fluttered her eyelashes in an attempt at coyness. Joking or not, her imagination jumped to a life with caring people, many of whom she'd come to admire, and who genuinely liked her. Nothing stopped her from passing the bar and requesting a leave of absence.

The opening chords of the bridal march drummed her to attention.

The crowd stood to watch Miranda and Ike enter. Walking the white runner in measured steps, they resembled one another: bound by their proud carriage and their broad smiles.

Corrin studied the joy they radiated, deeper than for the happy celebration. Both seemed to project to the faces turned toward them an underlying gratitude for their survival. A shudder shook her flowers. Both had come so close to death.

At the altar, Ike pulled Shirley to her feet. Together they placed Miranda's hand into Grant's outstretched palm.

Corrin drew a tiny handkerchief from under her bouquet and dabbed her eye.

Miranda deserved tender acts of devotion and a fresh start. Grant would supply both.

Kyle would too, if given the chance. What really stopped her? She never heard the ceremony.

~ ~ ~

Their pastor repeated the signal word. Kyle jolted out of a daydream featuring Corrin wearing white, smiling up at him. He slipped the two wedding rings out of his coat pocket, the cool gold heating in his palm.

Miranda had told him her grandparents had given her folks the simple bands. They all had passed on, so she and Grant had decided it would be fitting to wear the treasured wedding rings to link them to her family.

A tiny shock from the rings touched Kyle's skin. Another man might think it nerves, but he knew how close Miranda had been to her family. Serenity filled him. They were present, and angels consecrated this wedding.

He handed the rings to the minister and nodded at the cross hanging behind the pulpit.

At the conclusion of the ceremony, Grant and Miranda faced the exuberant audience of well-wishers. Her body tilted into his and connected subtly from shoulder to knee. He tenderly tucked back a loose tendril of her hair and pulled her into a kiss.

Kyle longed to do the same with Corrin. Instead, he stood at his post behind Grant, smiling heartfelt joy for his best friend, and fighting envy, knowing Grant would soon begin sharing a love-filled life with Miranda.

His future involved Corrin. The smart, loyal, and sensitive woman needed his love, and he'd move mountains to deserve hers. For now, he'd patiently show how two people could complement one another.

Familiar faces occupied the crowded room, except one. A man in the back of the chapel caught him looking and then rushed out through the open side door. He resembled the paunchy guy from the bar.

Why would a stranger attend Grant's wedding?

~ ~ ~

Corrin pulled her cheeks into a practiced smile and moved to her position in the post-wedding party pose.

The best man radiated elation, except for the frequent blinks.

She knew his secret. He fought an emotional knot. The same one she fought, for the same reasons. Timing, their godforsaken enemy.

The photographer nodded and backed up.

The newlyweds exchanged hugs amidst Grant's folks, Ike, and Shirley. Miranda's radiant smile beamed onto her loving new family.

"Our pastor did the service proud." Kyle fell in step and offered his arm to Corrin.

"Simple ceremonies are meaningful," she replied, through lips frozen into an album-worthy smile.

"Agreed. Allow me to escort you to the reception." They descended the stairs.

Bright lights shone on lacy white tablecloths adorned by vases of gladioli. "The decorating guild will get a nice donation," Corrin whispered.

A man in a pale blue tuxedo lifted a saxophone from a case in the band area. Three other men in matching garb attended to a keyboard, a guitar, and a drum set. One held the yellow diagram sheet she'd provided. He motioned the others into positions.

"The band came highly recommended," she said.

"Carl and the Crooners can play almost anything," Kyle said.

"Shirley and Ike requested slow songs, and I passed them the word,"

"Remind me to thank them," Kyle whispered, and squeezed her hand. They took their seats at the bridal table.

A four-course dinner progressed in a blur. She managed to nod her head when guests stopped by and acknowledged the beautiful decorations and excellent food she'd planned.

A shock of unplanned energy surged through her exhausted body each time Kyle's knee brushed against her leg.

Happy chatter filled the room.

The seductive piano notes of *All of Me* rang out, and the crowd quieted to hear Grant's requested song for the first dance.

He led Miranda to the parquet floor, took her in his arms, and began singing her the words in a deep baritone.

Tears wet Corrin's cheek. Curves and edges—the lyrics rang true. She pulled out a tissue and dabbed, while watching her best friend serenaded by a man clearly and utterly in love with her.

Kyle rested his arm across the back of her chair.

After a few verses, Grant waved to invite the remaining members of the head table. His parents, Ike, and Shirley rose to join them.

Kyle leaned over. "May I have this dance?"

The dance, and so much more. "I'd be honored." There were enough butterflies in her stomach to lift her off her feet.

Kyle guided her skillfully, their bodies effortlessly swaying together to the slow rhythm. When the night ended, she'd need a reality check. This wasn't

Cinderella's ball, and she'd return to a life devoid of the handsome prince.

Forget the future. She tipped her head back while her hair swung. Music and freedom swirled into her.

Kyle pulled her closer. "Give us a real chance," he whispered.

The song ended.

She clung to his shoulder, knowing both their hearts pounded double time. Could she? Should she? "You're constantly on my mind."

Surrounding guests clapped and the band thumped out a livelier tune.

"Let yourself feel, too."

His statement sunk deep. "I do. Trust me, I do." She released her hold. "Miranda asked me to watch out for wallflowers. Want to help?"

"February can't arrive fast enough. Right now, I'm scheduled to organize the champagne glasses for the toast, as noted on your list."

"I admire dependability in a man. I'll return after playing party enhancer."

"I'll be waiting." His hand lingered on her waist.

She needed to distance herself before she caved and committed to a life here, from this moment forth. "Counting on it," she whispered, and headed toward her first loner.

Straight ahead, a lanky man wearing a gray, Western-style shirt leaned against the stairway door. He held a black cowboy hat in one hand.

Corrin began her assessment while she approached. He'd be pushing forty, judging by the sun-earned wrinkles on his chiseled face.

"Hi, I'm Miranda's friend, Corrin." She tilted her head and stuck out her hand.

He compressed her palm until she pulled back. "Sorry. I'm Rane Calderon, Grant's cousin." The words disengaged haltingly. "Ah, nice to make your acquaintance, ma'am." He looked at his boots.

Might be country shy. "Beautiful weather for a wedding. Do you live locally?" she asked.

"Yes, ma'am." His focus moved to her shoes. "And you?"

"I live in Seattle. Emma Springs is a pretty town to visit." Mentally she checked him off her list of dutiful conversations.

"Seattle, you say. A port city known for boatbuilding." He rubbed his chin. "I'll be needing a live-in welder for my cattle ranch soon. If they cook, I'd pay extra." He pulled out a wallet and extracted a card. "I'd be mighty obliged if you passed on my mailing address to any hard workers interested in a clean place to bunk and generous wages." His russet brown eyes sparked with intent.

Corrin scanned the card. "Can I get your phone or email?"

"No consistent service at my spread." He checked his wristwatch. "Tell them to write."

"I don't exactly have shipbuilders on speed dial." She waited for a response to her joke. There was none. "Well, if I meet an unemployed welder, I'll point them in your direction."

"Past time to feed the cattle. They'll be mooing for supper. Gotta run."

"Bye," she snapped, after being dismissed. Apparently, she rated low on his farm-to-female scale, she deduced while watching him leave. They grew 'em big in this part of the country, particularly the rear part holding up their pants.

He ducked his head to negotiate through the narrow passage leading upstairs.

"Cake time!" high-pitched, girly voices announced.

Grant and Miranda swapped bites of cake in the traditional mode.

Mase, her ATV driver, grabbed the shoulders of two little girls. Both their fingers wavered near the pale green buttercream frosting of a cake designed in the shape of Mt. Hanlen.

Their excited pixie faces stretched close to the gingerbread cabin and tiny figurines.

Corrin caught the eye of the photographer.

The man kneeled to get perspective and smiled when he'd finished the photo putting Hansel and Gretel to shame.

"Hey girls, would you help me hand out cake slices? I'll make certain we save you each a piece containing lots of frosting." Corrin used her body to move them back a few steps.

"What do we do?" the taller munchkin asked.

"Wash and dry your hands in the ladies' room and reappear." She pointed to the hallway.

Mase blew out his breath in one whoosh. "You're good. Say, I'm searching for a live-in housekeeper and nanny for my daughters. Any chance you need a job?" He thumbed the lapels of his suit.

"Nope." She rolled her eyes. "You're the second man at this event scouting for a worker to fill multiple roles."

"Can't vouch for the other guy. I'm a fair employer on my wheat farm. I can't juggle both girls and grain."

She pulled out a pen and flipped Rane's card. "Print out your phone number and email."

Dark waves of thick hair outlined a classic profile while he wrote. Mase would be considered attractive, in a desperate-daddy sort of way.

"I've got a couple of ads running. Boy, there are lots of wackos."

That fact she knew too well. "You need to investigate their backgrounds thoroughly." She checked the legibility of the writing and slid the card in her pocket.

"I call references," he said, and as if on cue, the two grinning waifs skipped to his side.

"We're ready."

Corrin instructed Mase and watched the girls handle their first delivery.

Miranda slipped her arm around Corrin. "Brilliant idea. Poor Mase, he's raising them alone."

"He's scouting for a housecleaning nanny, and Grant's cousin needs a welder who can cook."

"Rane, the tall cowboy who exited at a frightened pace after speaking to you?"

"Record the day a human female scares Rane Calderon. His hungry heifers at the ranch required immediate attention. Between him and Mase, I should be interviewing for a new reality show, *Rural Prospects,* a cross between *Hee Haw* and *Here Come the Brides*. If you meet anyone seeking agrarian employment, contact me."

Miranda's giggles shook the beads on the antique dress. "Maybe you should vacate Seattle to start a company. Iris and Roy are your newest pair of dove-gray love birds."

"I'm pleased for them. I'm usually dealing on the other end of the spectrum."

"Not today." Miranda squeezed her arm. "Gotta run, Grant's holding a pair of flutes for our champagne toast. Don't forget my request regarding Kyle." She pointed two fingers at her eyes, then at Corrin.

"Quit watching me and show those pearly whites for the next photo. I'll disassemble your cake and wrap a piece for your freezer." Corrin's gaze followed Miranda as she took her place with Grant.

In a year, they'd be reminiscing. Where would she be? In a cozy home or a lonely apartment? Her trembling fingers struggled to remove Stan's intricately carved figurines of a man in a tuxedo, a woman in a white dress, and a mule. If Big Red hadn't found Grant, Miranda might've died.

She looked closer at the tiny bride and groom. The old carver had managed facial features bearing an uncanny resemblance to the actual couple. Even the mule wore a wise look. She placed the figurines alongside the top layer in a bakery box.

Saxophone notes signaled the quartet had begun another set. She tapped her toes and closed her eyes. A familiar scent of mint drifted to her.

"Be my dance partner?" Kyle whispered.

That 'P' word again. She sighed. "Yes, please. You've surpassed stellar wedding date."

Other men lived for the chase. Kyle, heaven help her, wanted permanence. Connected to her.

~ ~ ~

Kyle watched Corrin's sexy version of the twist, wishing he held the key to permanently unlocking the carefree woman dancing for him.

She caught his eye and winked.

He winked back and matched her quick turning movements to get his butt nearly on the ground.

"We're going to slow things down for the final song of the night," the singer announced. "Grant and Miranda want to thank all of you for joining them in their celebration."

Silky notes echoed through the hall. The dance floor filled.

Kyle rested his hand at her waist, with his palm above her softly rounded hip.

She leaned in and tipped her chin, her nose tickling his neck. "Entrancing cologne," she whispered, and smiled up at him.

He'd buy a gallon. "I thought of you when I picked up the hint of orange."

Her murmur of appreciation drove desires deep to his core.

Velvety tones drifted around them. He wrapped his arms tighter, closed his eyes, and swayed to the old tune, feeling each strand of her hair brushing against his cheek. Her breaths drew in and out, her chest rising and falling against him.

The sax player's long, pleading notes captured his yearning. He'd give anything for this moment to continue for hours. The song ended, leaving him wanting more.

Corrin slid her arms off his shoulders, her fingers falling across the front of his tux. Regret shone in her eyes. "Let's visit the Gilsons for a second."

The night wasn't over. He squeezed her hand. "Thanking them is in order. Slow dancing with you has been one of my greatest joys so far tonight."

"Mine too." Color stained her cheeks. Her eyes sparked.

He let her lead, keeping his hand firmly clasped around hers.

Shirley put her fingers to her lips and blew a pretend kiss. "Corrin, marvelous job of planning details for Miranda's special day. We're eternally grateful."

"My privilege," she said.

Kyle stepped forward. "Wonderful old songs. Thank you for the suggestions."

"We think Miranda fell for Grant during a slow dance." Ike's face became serious. "Grant guarded Miranda from my assailants and encouraged her to fight for a real life. We're forever indebted to him."

Moisture beaded at the edges of Shirley's eyes. "After Ike was shot, Miranda's quick thinking allowed him to be standing here next to me."

Kyle nodded. "Few realize how Miranda saved Grant twice, once from the hitman and again when he took the new job. He couldn't fully function in Reno without her."

He understood too well the power of loss, and damn if he'd lose Corrin.

CHAPTER 11

All the wedding guests had departed from the church hall. Kyle took Corrin's arm and led her up the stairs and stopped outside the door. The sun still shone above Mt. Hanlen, but not for long. How would it feel to be happily married, like Grant, and literally riding off into a gorgeous Montana sunset with the woman you loved?

His car alarm buzzed again from his jacket pocket. Weird. Everyone had vacated twenty minutes ago. He plucked out the remote.

"Did I hear something?" Corrin balanced a basket of wedding cards over one arm.

He held up the key fob. "It appears someone must still be in the parking lot. I stowed my medical bag at home and forgot to turn off my prowler alarm. It's motion-activated, forming a perimeter around the Jeep. Maybe an engine needed a jump, and someone brushed against my car." A brisk wind circled them.

"I see." She pulled her sapphire-colored cape shut, resembling Little Blue Riding Hood en route to Granny's.

With her hair tumbling around her pink cheeks, and the tired drop of her shoulders, he wanted nothing more than to take her home, throw in a movie, and curl up together on the couch. Tonight, the cold didn't faze his wolf-worthy thoughts of nestling her beside him and nibbling those lips again. He slid the basket off her wrist, the need growing to extend the evening.

Corrin extracted a piece of yellow paper from her purse.

Her brows furrowed. "We've turned off the lights and closed the front door of the church. I believe we're done."

"Yup. The rental fee covers clean up. The Red Horse has a band tonight if you care to dance more, or maybe watch a movie at my house. I excel at making popcorn."

"Rain check? I'm too tired to concentrate. I appreciate your bringing the car to the church."

No couch time or slow dancing her into his world tonight. He eyed her lower heels. "I hope I managed to avoid your toes."

"All ten are untrod. Your graceful moves were worth the long wait of dance-free years. I picked appropriate shoes for a change."

Walking to the Jeep, her fingers pushed into his sleeve as if she were falling, and his arm held her aloft. "I'd never have guessed you've avoided dancing."

She didn't respond.

Time for a different tactic to convince her to keep hold of him and consider the leap of a lifetime together. "We're a great team, Commander, while dancing, mini horse-wrangling, and rescuing kids."

"Uh-huh." Corrin stopped and pointed. "Something's hanging from the windshield wiper."

"I find feathers all the time." He leaned over the hood. "That's strange. Who'd put a fishing lure on my car?" He reached toward a red spoon holding a treble hook.

She jerked his sleeve. "Don't touch it, Kyle!" Her voice held a frightened edge.

He pivoted and caught fear in her eyes before she lowered them and pulled out a tissue. "What in hell's going on?"

She pressed her fingers to her temple. "I think there's a connection. Between the creep from my past, the ice cream by my car, and my electronic problems."

Needlelike pricks skittered up his spine. "Creep? Ice cream? Please explain."

She plucked off the lure using the tissue and dropped it into the basket holding the cards. "I need to consider client confidentiality and talk to one of our lawyers before I do, or say, anything."

"Not if you're in danger." His fist clenched. "When I carried you into the Red Horse, I sensed your reaction stemmed from an assault. Does this concern him?"

"I can't discuss him until I'm certain." Her eyes turned the deep, deep blue again.

"It's the assailant." His pulse spiked. "Stay in Emma Springs. Dad's house and my determination can keep you safe."

She bit her lower lip. "Seattle holds the answers I need," her voice had wavered.

"No one watches over you there. I'll go back with you." He touched her cheek.

"These aren't threats," she responded, failing to convince him.

"Not my impression, based on your response." He opened the Jeep, then scanned the empty parking lot and the shrubs beside the church. "No one here."

On a deserted Main Street, they traveled in silence, which challenged him. He needed to talk things through.

Not Corrin though, her internal processing took time to gauge all the options.

The realization didn't make his arms ache any less to pull her to his chest and protect her from whatever or whomever frightened her.

The inside of his dad's secure garage never appealed more. He thrust his finger onto the touch pad. "I'll get Fort Knox opened for you," he said, while he found the next key and escorted her into the house.

"I had a wonderful evening." Corrin stood in the entry, a strained smile on her face. She stood on tiptoes and aimed her lips at his cheek. "I promise I'll enlighten you when I can."

Enlightening wasn't nearly enough. Kyle shifted and kissed the edges of her lips. She tasted sweet and right now he needed her close. "Let me help protect you."

"I feel safe when you hold me." Her arms circled his waist, her palms warm on his back.

He skimmed through tendrils of her soft hair. She tenderly kissed him, and he struggled to keep things slow, to let her go at her own pace. Holding her in his arms felt right. Her tentative lips tasted so good.

"Oh, Kyle," her hands pushed against his chest, "you've opened my world." Tears welled in her eyes.

"We have something special. Accept it, Corrin."

"I do, believe me." She slid her fingers over his lapel. "After the exam, I'll put in for a leave of absence and do a test run assisting your dad."

She had to be one of the law firm's best employees. Would they let her go? "I'll count the days. What about us in the meantime?"

"I didn't ignore your calls. From the day we met, you've turned my world to moments of torment and bliss. I can't handle more tilting right now." She dropped her hands and plodded down the hallway, head lowered.

Kyle reached for her, an instant too late. "I'll be here to catch you," he called. "Day or night. Here or Seattle."

"I know." Corrin's shadow passed a hall night-light, and a door clicked shut.

Should he push for more details? He couldn't protect her from two states away. He shoved a fist against the door frame.

Those kisses had seared her initials onto his heart. How would he convince her to share joy, fears, and whatever lay in between?

Hesitation couldn't be treated by a round of antibiotics. The fact she'd consider Emma Springs was huge. He'd keep in touch by phone and drive there nonstop the minute she sounded worried. If need be, he'd have Grant pull in favors from his FBI friends.

Night air cooled his cheeks crossing the street, his body weary and drained of reserves. Corrin presented a bigger challenge than med school. He fished out his key and slid it into the lock on the side door of the clinic.

His house quietly awaited the methodical closing ceremony he performed each night. Locks clicked into place and lights flickered out. He walked into his kitchen and filled a water glass.

A dark sedan cruised by his dad's house, slowing when it got directly in front. Kyle leaned over the sink, watching. The unfamiliar vehicle drove to the end of the block and off into darkness.

He drummed his fingers on the counter and pulled out his cell. What would he tell the sheriff? Driving through town wasn't illegal.

Another car approached from the opposite direction. The lights swung onto his dad's driveway. He took a deep breath. *Dad and Iris were home.*

But his intuition screamed Corrin was in danger. Bad, bad danger.

~ ~ ~

Couldn't be jealousy causing the unsettling feeling so early in the morning, Corrin determined. She dunked a Danish pastry into her tea, half-heartedly listening to Roy and Iris plan out their upcoming gardening and sightseeing.

Kyle entered the kitchen, his face taut. "Morning. Did any of you notice the stranger in the dark suit at the back of the church yesterday?"

"No son, we were facing forward during the vows. What's your point?" Roy said.

"I called Tom and described him. No one they'd invited. He ducked out early and a car cruised past your house late last night. Please keep your security system fully armed."

Corrin gripped her napkin. "What'd he look like?"

"Maybe six feet, beer belly, receding hairline, wearing a dark suit."

Bloody hell. She bit her lip. "Was it the guy I pointed out at the Red Horse Tavern, right before we left? The paunchy guy from my plane flight?"

"Damn it! I think so." Kyle blurted. "I should've paid more attention."

Kyle swore? He'd cancel her flight if he knew she'd encountered the attacker in Seattle. She put on the bravest face she could muster. "Well then, Paunch Guy isn't a local resident or a hunter."

"Maybe the impending development brought him to Emma Springs," Roy said, and patted Iris's hand. "I chatted with Julia Bell yesterday. Bobby saw a man leave that empty farmhouse and head uphill on an ATV the day before he fell into the mine. Likely a Piersall Enterprises worker."

"Not an invited wedding guest, either." Kyle frowned. "Don't take any chances, Corrin or Dad, and immediately call me if you see him," he insisted.

Warmth radiated throughout her body. She had a protector, but she'd never yank him from his life for her past blunder, especially if Roy was fighting Piersall in Emma Springs. "Will do," she managed. "The night we rescued Bobby, I saw a light inside the farmhouse, too."

"I'll ask around town to see if anyone else is having trouble or has seen any new faces," Roy said, while he collected plates. "Let's enjoy the rest of the day and take the scenic route to the airport."

On the car ride, Roy and Kyle expounded on all the community functions, à la football recruiters.

"You haven't said much," Kyle leaned in close after they entered the terminal.

She clenched her boarding pass in her fist. "If I were an undecided star athlete, I'd sign on for Werner U."

A plane took off, the noise pausing conversations.

"Kyle, you're pale." Aunt Iris stopped the group in the lobby.

"He can't tolerate the thought of flying." Roy shook his head. "Kyle refused a scholarship to Harvard Medical School because of the distance he'd be from Flor. She'd recently been diagnosed."

"Oh dear, I've never cared for airports and flying either." Iris squeezed his arm.

"Technically, I fear heights." Kyle stated flatly. "Watching airplanes climb into the air causes me mild anxiety."

Cruising by ship to all seven continents might be fun. An image of Kyle reclining on a deck chair flashed into Corrin's mind.

"Let's see what new books are out." Iris took Roy's arm and led him to a gift shop.

"I think we need to talk." Kyle stepped closer, his voice husky. "There's more than mutual attraction between us, and kissing you reached a pinnacle for me. I want to give our relationship a try over the next few months." His finger traced the curve of her cheek. "There's always a halfway point, you know. Maybe we can meet on common ground, instead of running away from it."

His touch sent shock waves against her carefully built shields. Nothing staved off his soul-searching blue eyes.

"Halfway between you and me is in the Idaho Panhandle. Keep in touch, and I promise, we'll talk seriously in February, Kyle." She unzipped her purse and pulled out her sunglasses. Her fingers shook while she shoved them on her nose.

"I'll send a telegram if I have to." Kyle's voice held the determined confidence she'd grown to admire.

Add it to the list. "A singing one would ruin my reputation." Corrin turned away, struggling against unfamiliar dreams, struggling to stay out of his arms, and struggling not to shred her return ticket to Seattle.

"Hey, kids, want to grab a quick beverage before the flight leaves?" Iris and Roy approached.

Dedication to her aspirations fought against desires to explore a brighter world. She leaned in to give her aunt a kiss on the cheek, ready to snap. "Thanks. Time for me to surrender my shoes to TSA."

"Sure, honey." Iris stroked her cheek. "Allow your heart to guide you to happiness," she whispered.

Infatuation hadn't worked for her mom, but Kyle wasn't her dad. "You, too. Roy's perfect for you." Corrin squeezed Iris's hand. "Have fun, and I'll call you when I get home."

Roy pulled Corrin into a relaxed hug. "Don't forget the offer to join my firm."

"Thank you. I'm keeping it under consideration." She inched away.

Kyle reached into his pocket. "Miranda wanted you to have this." He placed a bundle in her palm and held her hand. "Please be careful." He leaned in and brushed her lips with a feather-light kiss. "Dad's spoken of how cutthroat big law firms are, that money overrides integrity. If anyone bothers you at MFB, I don't care who they are, I'll take them on."

Tears wet her eyes. His pledge unraveled more heartstrings. "I'll never forget, Kyle." The hem of her pencil-slim skirt cut her thigh with each stride, taking her away from people who wanted her. Kind people. Concerned people. Ethical people.

Four feet from the conveyor belt, she flipped off one pump, took a step, and pulled off the other. Her belongings disappeared into the X-ray tunnel where privacy was no longer sacred.

She rushed through the screening area, pulled on her shoes, and darted to the end of the boarding line. Don't look back, she told herself and dabbed a tissue under each side of her sunglasses. Nothing would wipe away the pain pounding in her chest.

Why did her carry-on, no longer holding the wedding gift of a lead crystal vase, weigh twice what it had when she'd arrived? Because every inch of her knew she shouldn't be leaving.

Corrin stumbled outside, up the steps, and found her seat. Through the airplane window, flat land became mountains. Gray clouds surrounded the ascending plane.

She removed the package from Miranda and fingered the square of wedding paper. A rubber band secured a note to a stiff object.

Dearest Corrin,

Remember, it will take many tough strokes to carve out your happiness.

Love, Miranda.

Stan's carved cake topper copy of Big Red, Miranda's miracle mule, fell onto her lap. Red had guided Grant to Miranda, saving her life. She held the treasured keepsake to her heart, wondering if Seattle had any spare service equines.

The black mini horse flashed in her mind. Had she found a home? The little horse had not crossed the road for Kyle's mint treat, but to calm her, precisely what she'd needed. Animals she'd met in Emma Springs showed devoted support—as did the humans. If she had any brains, she'd book the next return flight.

~ ~ ~

The trip from Three Falls to Seattle was a blur. Corrin paid the cab driver, unlocked her apartment door, and dragged her suitcase into her kitchen. No one could've predicted the effect of a Montana weekend, noted by doodled wedding bells on the calendar stuck to her refrigerator. Another square, outlined in pink, caught her eye.

Her niece, Corey, turned six on Wednesday. The little girl shadowed Corrin every waking hour during her visits to Ebony Cove.

Two books, ready to be mailed, sat on the back corner of her desk, *Junior Scientists* and *The Gossamer Guide to Fairies.* Each package she sent to her niece and nephew on their birthdays contained a special letter outlining the deal— read the book, write a description, and mail it to her.

Aunt Iris had encouraged reading. Her own bookcase now held a collection of Nancy Drew mysteries, one of her best investments.

A binder clip attached to the bulletin board above her desk restrained an assortment of drawings and a few letters boldly printed by wobbly fingers. Corey and Willy received five dollars for each sketched or written book report. Her sterile apartment was decorated only with their art, nothing like the warm ambiance of Roy's home. She rubbed her arms and upped the thermostat five degrees.

~ ~ ~

Corrin woke the next morning to rain beating against the window, perfect weather for her mood.

After dropping off her package at the post office, she sat in bumper-to-bumper traffic for the rest of her commute to downtown Seattle. She parked in the last MFB slot.

"Good morning," Kelly said, after Corrin exited the elevator. "Must've been a great wedding, I seldom arrive first." She grinned and pushed a memo across the raised countertop above her reception desk. "Sent after you left on Thursday. Glad I caught you first thing."

All legal staff: Monday 9 a.m. mandatory meeting in the conference room.

Corrin frowned at the memo before pulling a jar of Montana huckleberry jam out of her satchel. "I appreciate you." She slid the glass jar across the glossy wood.

"Yum, huckleberry's my favorite. Thanks. Glad you view me as more than an answering machine."

"I value friends." Corrin patted her heart and entered the hallway.

Bits and pieces of hushed conversation escaped through a crack in Brine's door.

The overhead light in her office illuminated her Montblanc pen and yellow legal pad on her desk. She grabbed the pen, heavy from empty prestige. Her legal pad wasn't centered the way she'd left it. Had the new guy snooped again? Ramona never touched her desk due to company policy.

The intercom buzzed a meeting warning.

During the session Brine and the new kiss-up California attorney droned on about pleasing this client. They mentioned potential environmental issues on the proposed Virtue Valley development.

The frog she'd doodled in the lower corner of the empty yellow page sprouted teeth. She flipped the sheet over.

"Enough of initial findings." Brine shuffled papers into a stack. "Corrin, you'll meet the LLC representative first."

Her head bobbed to alert. She mentally kicked herself for inattention. "Whenever." Crap, she'd fallen into a jam, and not Kelly's jar of huckleberry.

She exited and approached the lobby. Kelly nodded toward a woman seated on the visitors' couch, facing the windows. "She asked to see you, said she knows your aunt."

"Oh-kay." Corrin shifted to get a better view of the unfamiliar woman. "While we're meeting, would you please pull anything on Virtue Valley for me?"

Kelly threw her a friendly salute.

The woman rose, "You must be Corrin Patten. I'm Elon Hardy. Iris insisted I speak to you. My parents owned the gardening center next to Iris and Charlie's jewelry store." She straightened her scarf. "Is this a good time?"

Corrin smiled. Iris had spoken fondly of Elon for years, and recently expressed worry regarding her divorce. "Absolutely." She ushered her into her office and closed the door. "Please sit."

Elon perched on the edge of the guest chair. "Thanks for seeing me."

Corrin tapped her pen on the pad. "What's this concerning, Ms. Hardy?"

"Please call me Elon. I wish to hire you to represent me in divorce mediation." She forced a lock of her hair behind her ear. "There are extenuating circumstances in my case regarding division of commercial property that my parents owned, and I don't have much cash."

"I'm not a licensed attorney until I pass the bar exam in February. Then, I'll work closely beside a lead attorney on your case."

"Oh." Elon's shoulders dropped. "I read mediation didn't require hiring an attorney in Washington."

"Correct. However, as an employee of MFB, I must follow their rules."

Elon fidgeted in her chair. "I'll try to hold them off until you're available." She rose to leave.

Corrin handed her the yellow pad. "Write your contact information, and I'll send you the initial forms."

"And a cost estimate, please."

"Of course. Here's my business card. Call my cell if you have questions," Corrin slid the card across her desk.

"Thank you again. I'm relieved we connected." Elon returned the legal pad and pocketed her card. "I can find my way out." The door closed behind her, giving a soft click.

Corrin sat back in her chair and pressed her finger to her lip. Elon's need for help had been etched into her likable face.

She bulleted points from the conversation. Maybe taking on this divorce case would be a good start to her career.

Tapping sounded from her door. "Come in." She tore off an entire lake scene from her pad and threw the sheets into the recycle bin.

Brine pushed in the door. "Ms. Patten, please welcome Michael Fernley. He'll be your contact from the development group we reviewed this morning. I'd bet you're anxious to begin."

Bloody hell! Paunch Guy from Emma Springs! Her stomach churned while she rose. "Yes, Mr. Brine."

"I'll let you two get started." Brine ushered him in and left.

Angst built to panic. There had to be a logical explanation. She glanced at him. An expensive suit couldn't hide his flabby gut.

He smoothed back what little hair he had. His eyes shot straight to the third button of her blouse. The one she'd sewn shut to eliminate gaping.

She crossed her arms.

"Well, well." He raised his eyes.

Up close, something struck her as familiar. In a bad way. Her left fist clenched and unclenched behind her back, flexing muscles she'd bulked up. She offered her other hand. "Mr. Fernley."

He gave her fingers a long, clammy squeeze. "It'll be my pleasure to work alongside you."

She discreetly wiped her palm on her skirt. "Let's get to work."

"Suits me, Blondie."

"I prefer Ms. Patten."

Kelly waved a file from the doorway. "I have the documents you requested." She handed them to Corrin and turned toward the door..

Fernley's eyes zeroed in on Kelly's retreating butt.

Hazard pay wouldn't compensate for this lech. "There's more space in the conference room." Corrin unplugged her laptop, and motioned Fernley out.

He stood partially in the doorway.

Swinging her laptop into his crotch as she passed him tempted her. They entered the conference room, and she kicked the door jam in place to wedge it open. "Have a seat at the end of the table, please." She shoved the chair on the side toward the opposite end and sat a safe distance from him. "I'll make notes while we go through your file."

He slid his chair around the corner, inched closer, then pushed a document to her. "Check this out first." His focus remained on her face. "Maybe we can go fishing sometime to celebrate," he sneered.

The bastard had planted a lure on Kyle's car! Why? Corrin fought the urge to bolt. Play dumb and find out more, she challenged herself, managing to will fury into composure. Her eyes dropped to the title of the brief. IN THE MATTER OF APPEAL OF: *The Sunrise Lake Community Association of a Zoning Determination for Piersall Enterprises, Hanlen County, Montana.*

Piersall! The damn attacker was connected to the rezone in Emma Springs! The answer to why he'd been in the MFB office, and why Paunch Guy Fernley had followed her to Montana. Her heart thudded in her chest. Should she let him know she'd figured it all out? She slid the paperwork back, attempting indifference. "What kind of development is your company proposing, Mr. Fernley?"

"Call me Mikey, Blondie." He swung his chair, so his knee brushed her thigh. "An exclusive ski resort." He leaned close, exhaling liquor-tainted fumes.

She picked up her pad and put space between them. "A ski resort?" Her hand shook as she pretended to take notes.

"Between you and me, it's not what the hillbillies think. Although, in the end, they'll see a wipeout or two."

They'd nearly killed Bobby. Her fist clenched the pen, ready to strike.

He leaned over, staring at her chest.

No more! She pushed off the desk and sprang out of her wheeled chair. The force sent it crashing into the next empty seat. *Damn.* "Excuse me, Mr. Fernley. I need to speak to one of our senior attorneys." She grabbed her laptop and notepad before stepping into the hallway and then ran.

Her breaths came in gasps. She made it to her office and leaned against its doorframe. Waves of nausea rolled through her. Why'd the molester choose Emma Springs? She dropped the laptop and pad on her desk.

Mr. Meyer would hear her out and understand her fears. She stumbled to his office and knocked. No answer. She had to tell someone.

Chap Brine's cracked door allowed a view of him seated at his desk, his head bent over a catalog. No way could she work on this project. She stepped forward and knocked.

He raised his eyes and motioned for her to enter. *Yachting*-something was the title of the glossy magazine he slid under his elbow. "Your meeting's done already?"

"Mr. Brine, I have to recuse myself from the Piersall case and MFB should—"

"I didn't know you were going to be judging it." He cut her off and then laughed at his attempted humor.

"Honestly, Corrin, you're the best at research, and they've paid a huge retainer. What's your issue?"

"I've met the townspeople in Emma Springs, and I'm aware of the development. I can't work against my friends. I need to excuse myself."

"Can't or won't? There's a vast difference, and I understand you aspire to be an MFB partner someday." He folded his hands over his gut.

"Mr. Brine, there are extenuating circumstances involving this developer."

"Successful attorneys accommodate clients who don't share their personal views." He attempted a conciliatory pose, or maybe outright mockery.

Nope, he'd smirked. She felt like a kid who had to explain why she'd shoved the bully. A big, ugly, disturbing bully. She raised her chin. "I believe they are not being forthright in the representation they require."

"Phil Meyer and I examined the case, and there's nothing out of the ordinary." Brine's face became a legal mask of indifference.

She fingered the brooch from Bobby's family. "I may have information you should consider."

"I don't want to know. There are circumstances you're not aware of."

Mr. Meyer preached ethics, but apparently not to Brine. Corrin's temper flared. "Then remove me for personal reasons until Mr. Meyer returns. I've worked plenty of weekends and never asked a favor."

"I hadn't noticed, and it wouldn't matter. Mr. Piersall personally requested you on his team."

Of course he had. How could she have been so stupid not to fit the pieces together sooner? Her stomach lurched. No way she'd tell Brine her history with the degenerate. "Piersall has an agenda."

"I'm not certain of his project's details. I missed the 10 p.m. meeting a while back and really don't care about agendas."

Her scalp prickled. She'd sensed someone else in Mr. Meyer's office that night and been edgy since. It had been Piersall, and the man radiated evil through walls. If she stayed employed, she'd keep an eye on his plans for Emma Springs. "I've completed all tasks MFB requested. I won't work on this lawsuit, Mr. Brine. You're the human resources liaison. I'll put my request in writing."

"Don't bother. I'll decline it."

He could take that boat magazine and shove it. A calm wave of conviction spread through her. She leaned forward and splayed her fingers on his dark mahogany desk. "Consider this my verbal two-week notice of resignation. I'll have a written draft by this afternoon."

"As you wish, Ms. Patten." He rocked back in his chair. "Considering your refusal to work for this client and your familiarity with this case, security will escort you out today." He tapped his finger on his thin upper lip. "I'll give you one hour to pack your things and vacate your office."

"An hour?"

"Unless you reconsider."

"Absolutely not."

"Your final paycheck will be mailed." He opened the boating magazine.

She ought to grab the magazine and swat him like a cockroach. He'd dismissed her after she'd spent nearly ten years laboring to provide the funds for a fleet of behemoth boats for the partners of MFB.

The glass in Brine's door rattled as she yanked it shut.

Three file cabinets of researched cases lined the left wall of her office. No other employee had more than one.

She grabbed an empty box and carefully slid the photo of her, Miranda, and Aunt Iris beside her pay stubs.

The brass nameplate topped the pile. Allegiance to men who harbored flexible principles wasn't her style. Still, Mr. Meyer needed to understand her concerns. Her fingers flew over the keyboard, outlining her stance. She printed out the sheet, folded it in thirds, and stuck it under his closed door.

No chatter came from the hallway and no methodical groans from the copy machine in the mailroom. Brine must've sent an all-company alert.

Kelly waved her over. "I've been asked to call security to escort you out in forty minutes." Her voice cracked into a sob. "I can't believe they did this to you."

Corrin patted her shoulder. "For the record, I quit. We can get together for coffee this weekend."

"We can't officially. Brine issued a no contact order of sorts," she whispered. "You're locked out of the computer system. I overheard Brine tell Fitch he would make certain you wouldn't work in Seattle again."

"Watch out for Fernley and his boss, Piersall. They're both thugs." She squeezed Kelly's hand. "Promise me you'll be careful around them. They're the reason I quit."

"Okay."

The reception phone rang.

Kelly swiped her eyes and gave her a quick hug. "I'll miss you."

"Me, too." Corrin returned to her office. She lifted the expensive pen from its place on her yellow legal pad. A gift from Mr. Meyer on her sixth year anniversary with the firm. That day he'd promised partnership. She dropped it onto the pad, sat in her chair, and held her head in her hands.

"Ms. Patten, I'm here to help you move your personal things." Her favorite security guard shuffled his feet in her doorway and tugged at the collar of his blue uniform shirt. "I'll carry them out for you." He pulled the box off her desk.

"I'm sorry to bother you. How's your wife and son?"

"They're fine, thank you." He met her eyes. "It's kind of you to ask."

"I enjoy your photos." She slipped on her jacket and grabbed her spare umbrella. "I don't want to walk past mahogany row." She scanned the office. Nothing personal remained, only the file drawers showing her accomplishments. "To the freight elevator, please."

"A quiet exit delivered by a class act," the guard said.

Coworkers at each desk turned away in awkward poses. No eye contact. No goodbye. From anyone.

Integrity constituted a virtue the last time she checked. Corrin held her head high until they'd reached the elevator. She pressed the down arrow for the last time.

The guard shifted the box and met her eyes. "I'm sorry you're leaving, Miss Patten. I've heard numerous clients speak highly of you on their way out."

Battered elevator doors opened to its dull, gray interior. "MFB and I had an ideological difference of opinion." She punched the garage button. "The newest client, named Piersall, is an unscrupulous thug. Keep alert."

"I will. Things work out for good, honest people."

Not her current perception. "And you're one of them, too." They'd reached MFB's underground level.

Each step onto the concrete floor echoed. She popped the trunk of her car.

He loaded her ten years worth of belongings and pushed the trunk lid shut. "Good luck, Miss Patten."

She'd need more than luck. "You, too." Her best effort to smile fell flat.

Worry lines rimmed his eyes. "When I passed Kelly's desk, Mr. Brine directed her to post your termination on some 'legal eagle' list."

She swallowed hard. "Thanks."

The guard returned to the elevator and saluted her goodbye. The metal door slid shut.

Being named on that list sunk any chance of employment in Seattle's legal field. She swiped at a tear and pulled out her phone. Her carryall slid off her shoulder to the pavement.

Miranda would offer guidance. She dialed her new number and immediately canceled the call. The newlyweds were on a plane en route to a fabulous Hawaiian honeymoon. She pulled the phone to her chest. Aunt Iris and Roy were probably outside planting tulips.

"Going somewhere, Ms. Patten?" Fernley's voice called out.

Her gut tightened. "Yes. I'm late."

"We weren't finished." Mikey Fernley advanced to within a few feet.

"We most certainly are." She threw her bag in, dove in after, and slammed the door shut, missing his shin by inches. It took two tries from her wobbly fingers to get the key in the ignition. She spun the wheel and backed out.

He moved to her empty parking spot, dropped on a pair of Ray-Bans, and pulled his lips into a sinister smile.

The image of jumping off the boat slammed into her. Fernley could be the skinny, long-haired jerk who'd accompanied Piersall that fateful day. He'd used the same unnerving sneer when Piersall gunned their boat, leaving them to drown.

She had no recollection of negotiating traffic to get to her apartment or hauling the remains of her former career inside.

Hours later, she shifted her focus into Miranda's empty bedroom, where she'd dropped the cardboard box from MFB. Now she'd face the consequences from her decision of conscience.

She pulled the sheaf of crayon drawings from Corey and Willy off the bulletin board and held them to her chest before sinking onto a kitchen chair.

Her bracelet jangled. Dreams of money and travel faded while her heart beat stronger at the prospects waiting in Montana. She'd never abandon the innocent, in business or her personal life.

Afternoon light faded, and a thin golden beam floated across the top of the green Formica kitchen table. It ended at the tiny mule in the center. *Tough strokes to carve happiness.* Miranda's words nailed the day. Her first tough stroke had been the decision to walk out of that office, moral principles intact.

Honest people and a legal career awaited her in Emma Springs. Recalling Roy's urging to join his practice lifted her spirits with the strength of the thick rope that had hoisted her and Bobby from the dark shaft and up to Kyle. She laid the kids' drawings on the table and tapped numbers into her phone.

Uncle Charlie had used the saying 'eat crow' when you had to admit being wrong: a distasteful but accurate idiom. Kyle had questioned MFB's integrity, she should've listened.

The phone rang and rang. Was she too late? A crow laid out on a platter topped her page of doodles. She drew a knife and fork next to it.

"Roy Werner," his pleasant voice announced.

"Hello, Mr. Werner, I mean Roy, this is Corrin Patten. How are you this evening?"

"I'm fine young lady—"

"Great, sir," her words tumbled out. "There's been a, um, strange set of circumstances here in Seattle at my firm. I wondered if your offer to hire me to work in your office is still on the table?"

"As a matter of fact, I've sweetened the pot," he chirped.

She pictured the smile creasing his kindly face. A mountain towering over a lake took shape on the bottom of the yellow paper. "Great."

"Iris and I concluded the little cottage needs a caretaker this winter," he began. "If you'll live lakeside, I'll swap rent for help on winter maintenance."

She added rays of sunshine streaming onto a tiny, lakeside home. "Your offer sounds generous."

"You can pay utilities."

"Deal. Now the big question, Roy." She sketched a snake on the grassy shore. "Are you formally involved in the lawsuit against Piersall Enterprises?"

"Yes, and I'd appreciate your immediate assistance while we continue your studies for the bar. It's not too late to register for Montana's February exam. I'll cover the fee. How soon can you be here?"

She pulled the pen to her heart. "Thank you. Let me think. These apartments are in demand at higher rent than I pay, so giving notice shouldn't be a problem." She tapped her forehead. "I can make the drive in two days, depending on the weather, and arrive the first part of next week?"

"Perfect. We'll get organized and create a suitable workspace for you in Flor's studio. Sorry things didn't work out. However, I'm excited to welcome you aboard." His voice hummed with excitement. "Can I give Kyle the fabulous news? He's going to flip."

Picturing Kyle midair in gym shorts wiped away the last sting of dismissal. She grinned. "Sure, and I'll phone him later today."

"You be careful driving. Promise you'll call when you head out and check in when you make stops."

He cared enough to want phone calls. She pressed her cheek. "I will. See you in a week."

She threw the page containing doodles into the trash and folded back the sheets of paper on the legal pad. Elon Hardy's name and address were written on the next page. Iris's friend deserved tips before she left for Montana.

Anything to keep her mind from wandering back to moist lips, blond hair, and a firm . . . handhold. She flipped over Roy's card. As she slid her fingertips over Kyle's handwriting tingles radiated into her palm.

Aunt Iris had told her to allow her heart to guide her to happiness. Miranda had learned to love, couldn't she?

CHAPTER 12

Sultry perfume wafted from the slip of paper Kyle held in his hand, monogrammed by a 'B' at the top of the page. He took a sip of cider and unclipped the sheet from the folder. It revealed the *Children's Research Foundation of Montana* logo. He reread the note while he slid a pan onto a burner and turned on the gas flame.

Hi, Kyle. Congratulations on your Board of Directors appointment. I'm glad I recommended you and anticipate with excitement our monthly trips to Three Falls to help the children. Call me. There are a few things we need to discuss. Maybe over a drink? Fond regards, Betsy

If only the note had been penned by Corrin. Care of his patients had kept her out of his mind during most daylight hours. Nights, not so. He tossed a marinated chicken breast into the pan.

During Bobby's rescue, he'd witnessed the nurturing side of Corrin. The wedding weekend had been promising. She'd dashed out of the terminal wearing sunglasses on a cloudy day for a second time. Regardless, MFB granting her a leave of absence remained problematic if they stipulated a return date.

Kyle took a swig, set the glass down, and pulled his phone from its clip.

He'd keep Betsy at arm's length. He studied her phone number, ending in a zero written in the shape of a heart. The cider soured on his tongue.

The phone vibrated in his hand. He checked the number and sighed.

"Kyle, we have to talk about good news," his dad exclaimed.

"You already got wind of the foundation offering me a seat on their board?"

"Wonderful, son. Hadn't heard."

"Betsy sent me a congratulatory note suggesting we discuss their mission over a drink. I planned to call her and make it coffee in the Springs Cafe."

"Don't encourage her. Betsy's trouble. A drink's not her end game. You're going to dance a jig when I give you an early Christmas present. We need to get the cottage in shape for a beautiful, intelligent inhabitant."

Kyle flipped the chicken and inhaled pungent, seared garlic. "I thought Iris wasn't ready to leave Seattle."

"Your luck this time. Corrin phoned, and she'll be arriving next week to start work. I offered her the cottage to use, and we can get it spruced up enough if we both work hard."

"Really?" He dropped the spatula. "What happened to the legendary firm Corrin pledged her allegiance to?"

"The buggers must've done something awful. She didn't share the particulars. I can tell you one thing, sarcasm won't woo a woman. Corrin's concentrated her efforts on her career for ten years, and I didn't see you offering to relocate to Seattle. It might be smart of you to send a welcome bouquet."

Kyle threw a series of air punches. "Great idea. I bet you can get her home address from Iris. This is the best present you've ever given me." He touched Betsy's note to the flame and dropped it into the sink. The paper sparked for a brief instant before it turned to ashes.

His appetite had returned with gusto.

~ ~ ~

Corrin checked her watch. She placed Rane Calderon's business card onto a file folder labeled 'Hardy, Elon. Mediation Tactics in Divorce Settlements.' She'd taken notes during a phone conversation with Elon and begun research.

Two loud knocks rattled her concentration. She straightened her skirt, forced a confident smile, and checked the peep hole for Elon.

A man wearing a shirt embroidered with daisies on the chest pocket stood in the hallway. A colorful armful of flowers hid his face.

"Miss Patten?"

"Yes. How'd you get inside?"

"The manager, on his way out."

"Hold on a minute." She pulled a five from her wallet and traded it for the unstructured bouquet of tiny pink roses, peonies, and other flowers. The delivery man left smiling.

Familiar scents took her back to Iris and Charlie's backyard. She dipped her nose and inhaled. A white card poked her chin.

I can't wait to lay out a picnic lunch for you in the hillside meadow, Corrin.

Warm regards, Kyle

She grabbed the edge of the table for support.

"So, you were the lucky recipient of the flowers." Elon stood in the opened doorway. "The delivery man let me in."

So much for a secure building. Corrin smiled and set the vase on the table. "You have perfect timing in several ways." She lifted the business card featuring the head of a bull as a logo. "I'm going to shelve the divorce discussion for a moment. You require income and living quarters, pronto."

"An understatement."

"I recently traveled to Emma Springs, Montana, for my friend's wedding, where I met a local rancher, Rane Calderon. His welder's retiring, and he needs a dependable employee. He's willing to provide lodging and a generous wage, and extra money if you'll cook."

"Welding? I've been working in an office."

"Aunt Iris owned metal sculptures you created for your parents' garden shop. I remember being impressed they'd been done by a female welder."

"Under my grandpa's tutelage. I hung up my torch a few decades ago," Elon said.

"Melting iron, a skill set once learned and never forgotten, right?"

"That's a mighty optimistic statement." She smoothed her sweater over her rounded hips.

"Iris explained your situation. Sharing a tiny condo isn't cutting it for you and your collegiate sons."

"No. We're cramped." Elon shook her head.

"Gaining income would allow you to cover their tuition, and your ex couldn't force you to sign off on the commercial property your parents intended to leave you."

"A possible solution." A smile brightened her face. "I'll call your farmer to see what 'generous' means in dollars."

"Not so simple," Corrin said. "He insisted on a written resume."

"I'll put one together and get it mailed."

"Today, I'm a game show hostess," she quipped. "Consider door number two. There's another man, named Mase. He needs a nanny and housekeeper for his two young girls. He's maybe thirty. Rane's older."

Elon rubbed her temple. "Welding and feeding a group of men would be a challenging diversion and probably pay better."

"Your choice. The younger one wrote his phone and email on the back of the card." Corrin placed it in Elon's hand. "There. Not appearing financially desperate will be beneficial in your divorce mediation."

"This is perfect. Tim thinks I'll allow him to play dirty divorce and fold quickly to his threats. I'll hire you in a couple months, if it's okay by your firm."

"I quit MFB and accepted a position assisting the attorney in Emma Springs."

Elon smoothed the tape on a nearby packing box. "I wondered."

"Get the welding job, and we'll be neighbors. My friend Miranda lives nearby. The three of us will have fun together."

"I can't wait to tell my sons. Thank you." She stashed the card in her purse. "It's weird, I believe the opening's already mine."

"Rane solicited my help at the wedding reception, and I'd call his move one step short of desperate. Mail him any kind of resume, and you may win by default."

A mischievous smile brightened Elon's face. "Works for me."

Corrin opened her mouth and closed it. She'd hold off on a description of the cowboy's personality.

"I'll call you when the pony express delivers Mr. Calderon's response. Thank you again." Elon hip-hopped into the hall.

One problem solved. Corrin closed the door and leaned against it, inhaling the sweet fragrance of peonies. Her cell phone blinked to life on the table, issuing an annoying ringtone.

"Corrin, Phil Meyer here. Can you talk?"

Now he'd become available. "Yes."

"I think there's been a misunderstanding." His tone relayed an atypical semblance of an apology. "Chap fired you before consulting me about your workload. Are you available to meet and allow me to straighten out the communication breakdown?"

"No firing, and no breakdown, Mr. Meyer. I offered to explain to Mr. Brine the complications involving deceit on the Piersall Enterprises case. He rejected my offer to put in additional hours on another project to offset declining the work, so I resigned."

"Not his description of the conversation, and I must stand by him."

Must? No sign of the moral compass he proclaimed guided him at MFB. Attaining partnership concealed the brotherhood of the good ol' boys club. She fingered a soft petal. "Now you have both sides of the story. I've been a salaried employee voluntarily working extended hours six to seven days a week without overtime pay."

"We've noted your dedication and anticipate your future consideration as a partner. The client requested your help, so I'm asking a personal favor. The land use division of our office pays a majority of the bills, and this developer's expanding his market."

"Mr. Meyer, I won't work for Piersall. My ethical reasons were met by dismissal before I'd fully disclosed them. I stated them all in the letter I left. Did you read it?"

"We checked this client for conflicts of interest before entering into a contract. Chap Brine is the lead attorney, and after reading the subject line of your memo, I passed it on to him. Mr. Piersall expressly requested Chap to handle his business and I never question such a request. I've drafted a generous salary and bonus proposal. Shall we say lunch at La Grande Bistro at one o'clock?"

He hadn't bothered to read her letter. Piersall's retainer must've been huge. "You should read your mail. I've accepted another position. I wish you the best, sir."

"I'm certain we can mitigate your personal misgivings." He cleared his throat. "We'll beat your other offer."

"Apparently you won't question anything after receiving a large retainer. Virtue Valley doesn't conjure the image of an elite resort." She squared her shoulders. "I pride myself on my integrity. I've made a commitment to another employer."

He snorted with irritation. "Miss Patten, your refusal to remain working at a prestigious Seattle firm is not conducive to your career aspirations. Mail back your company cell." His phone clicked off.

She'd ticked off the most knowledgeable and senior partner. If Piersall's business meant so much, she'd probably spar against Meyer in court.

She dropped the MFB-haunted cell into a padded envelope, stuck on postage, and grabbed her coat. The corner drugstore sold burner phones. Her footsteps were lighter when she walked to the store.

Back at the apartment, she stuck the new cell onto a charger. In half an hour, it showed life.

Her fingers pressed into Roy's card. She studied the numbers on the back, written in confident block handwriting—honest and straightforward letters, same as the writer. "Hi, Kyle."

"Corrin. You got a new number. I've been waiting for your call."

"The flowers are beautiful." Her pulse raced. "I prefer my meal of crow to be poached or fricasseed." She ran her finger along the side of the etched glass vase.

"When I suggested a picnic, I had in mind a few snacks and cupcakes for dessert." His voice dropped to velvety tenderness. "I will never show anything but support for such a beguiling woman."

His words caressed her while she eased onto the kitchen chair. "Oh my."

"We need you here."

She closed her eyes and pictured his outstretched arms. "This has been one of my worst setbacks, and if you knew my life history, that's saying a lot."

"Why don't you tell me what happened." The deep, melodic gentleness of his voice soothed a decade of pent up angst.

"I need to leave Seattle."

"Are you safe?" he demanded.

No questioning his defender instincts. "I'm fine now. MFB threatened to fire me after I refused to assist the developer taking on your town."

"Your firm's representing Piersall?"

"Former firm. I'm no longer affiliated. I wouldn't work the case."

"So, you abandoned the promise of partnership in MFB because of Emma Springs."

She'd have to tell him the truth. She closed her eyes. "Kind of complicated, but yes."

"We'll have the cottage ready. It already has a double bed and a couch."

"I might need a kitchen table and a microwave." She fanned her face using a file folder. "I'll buy some sensible shoes."

"Shoes, yeah," he murmured. "We can hike to peaceful places for a picnic."

A bachelor's button needed adjusting in the vase. "I'm probably not romantic picnic material."

"Why would you think that?"

Kyle would listen without judgement. She rested her elbow on the table. "Do you have time for a Corrin history of sorts?"

"Of course. I just sat on the couch for a break. Please share whatever's comfortable."

His sincere willingness loosened the tight knot in her belly. "You were correct when you carried me into the tavern. I'd been attacked and had a flashback to feeling powerless."

"Damn. I figured you'd been traumatized. Recently?"

"No. A long time ago. I removed myself from our dysfunctional household on long bike rides with a friend. My Dad's an alcoholic and Mom's an enabler." She took a deep breath.

"Must've been tough," he encouraged gently. "Take your time."

The acceptance in his voice erased her embarrassment. She plucked his note from the flowers and held it to her chest. "My girlfriend's parents were super strict. We'd do anything to avoid our homes. The summer before I turned fifteen, we'd often bicycle to Ebony Cove's bait store for an ice cream cone."

"A typical teenage thing to do."

"Neither of us realized we'd reached the age where we attracted male attention. We were nerds in school. A smiling, kinda preppy-dressed guy approached her." Corrin squeezed her eyes shut. "We'd never been into boy crushes. I should've noticed his older age. He must've been at least twenty."

"You were innocent." Kyle's voice tensed.

"And impressed by wealth. He pointed to a red jet boat tied at the dock and asked if we wanted to go for a ride on Puget Sound. I didn't smell booze on them until we'd hopped aboard. The driver sped away immediately, and when we'd motored far offshore, the engine stopped."

"On purpose?"

"Yes. They insisted we'd have fun partying, after we told them we didn't drink." Her body tensed. "In a flash, one creep had my hands held behind my back. The driver reclined my seat, upended a bottle of booze and forced it into my mouth. After I'd nearly choked, he tore open my blouse."

"Holy shit!"

The struggling sensation pounded in her brain. "My friend shoved the driver off me. The guy holding me backhanded her and the force pushed her overboard."

"What happened to you?" he demanded.

"I dove in after her." She rubbed her arms, reliving the first moments in the freezing water. "They gunned the boat and took off, making it hard to see. She'd hit her head on the edge of the windshield and nearly drowned."

"Oh my God. Was she seriously injured?"

"Thankfully only dazed and bleeding from a gash on her temple. An older couple out fishing saw we needed help and rescued us."

"Did the police catch the bastards?"

"None of us got the boat numbers or remembered much more than the color, so the police had nothing to go on." Tears wet her eyes. "They tried to molest me, then left us to die, Kyle."

"Murderous bastards," he growled.

"Almost," she sniffed.

"I'm so sorry. God, I wish I could hold you," he whispered.

She touched the vase. "Me, too. I made a vow that day to avoid men."

"I don't blame you. No one recognized them?"

"No. They bragged about the boat's maiden voyage. An ironic term."

"You remember their faces?"

Her fists clenched. "They both wore sunglasses and ball caps. The driver wore a gold, knife-shaped ring holding a red jewel. I'll never forget his hand ripping my first new blouse. Her throat tightened. "I recognized the attacker last week, exiting our office."

"Did you call the police?" Kyle blurted.

He'd freak if he knew it was Piersall. This was enough for him tonight. "It's too long ago, and I'm leaving town." She set his card back in the flowers. "Now you understand why I flinched when you were being the consummate gentleman by keeping my shoes dry." She gripped the table edge, waiting.

~ ~ ~

Damn bastards! Corrin had been an innocent, helpless girl. Kyle grabbed the couch cushion and punched. Stuffing flew onto the floor.

"Kyle are you there?" her voice pleaded.

"Yes. Sorry." He rubbed his temple. "You need to be careful. Is your apartment secure?"

"There's a locked entry and the manager lives on site."

"Humor me." He clenched his jaw. "Take a kitchen chair and tip it under the handle of your apartment door."

Scraping sounded from her end. "Done."

"Please secure the door that way when you're there and thank you for trusting me." He forced a soothing tone. "You girls did nothing wrong," he continued. "I hope you and your friend got counseling."

"Counseling, hardly. My family's dirt poor and hers ultraconservative. We made a pact never to tell anyone, and I didn't until now."

No wonder she hadn't overcome the traumatic incident. "I want you safely beside me, right now."

"I'll be there soon. Don't worry."

"I've been worried." He scooped batting from the floor. "Have you told your friend that you saw the attacker?"

"I can't. We lost touch after she got married. I'm the weak one."

"You're one of the strongest women I've ever met." Kyle pictured her sheltering Bobby as they'd cleared the collapsing shaft.

"Strong isn't the word at my office. Because of the boat creep, I never dated."

"I'll never pressure you. I only want to make you happy here in Emma Springs."

"Kyle, I'm ready to date you." Her voice remained strained.

"Words I've longed to hear. If a relationship doesn't work out, we'll be friends. Okay?"

And knowing Kyle, he meant it. "Yes. I appreciate your understanding."

"Need help packing?"

"I don't own much worth bringing," she confided. "But there are folks who buy at the Salvation Army who may need my stuff."

He studied the full days of appointments penciled on his calendar. "Seriously, I can drive to Seattle by late tomorrow night."

He waited for her response. She'd held something back.

"Is there more?"

"You're a busy doctor, and you've had to get the cottage ready. I'm capable of vacating the Emerald City in anticipation of what's waiting for me in Emma Springs." Spunk returned to her voice. "And I don't need ruby slippers or Glinda prodding me with her wand to date you."

"I hope so. There's no place like Emma Springs." He leaned back. "Or, there's no one like Kyle. Keep repeating either," he chuckled. "You'll have a move-in ready cottage, a job, and friends who'll protect you."

"I know," she whispered.

Something bothered her. "Do you think your attacker knows where you live?"

"I don't know, but he could've gotten to me in the parking garage, if confrontation was his goal."

He still could come after her. "Please purchase a Taser, or at least pepper spray."

"I bought bear spray for when I walk home from the bus. My normal routine only puts me in the open for a few minutes."

Every minute counted. Now he had some idea of what a transplant candidate endured waiting for a heart. His chest tightened. "Keep your phone charged. I'll be checking your packing progress," he said.

"You'll reach me live for a change."

"Keep the canister of spray close," he stressed. Bile rose in his throat. Only a psychopathic personality left young girls to drown.

~ ~ ~

Corrin watched dawn break over the Seattle skyline for the last time from her apartment window. She deflated the air mattress, tidied up, left the key in the manager's box, and skipped down the stairs.

Boxes and bundles topped the seats in her Firebird. The carved mule faced forward in the middle of the dashboard, his hooves secured in place by poster putty.

She slid into the seat and started the engine, then scanned the radio for a country western station. By the time she'd found one, she'd eased out of the tight space.

Her finger tapped to the beat of a perfect song for Kyle's two-step. She departed Seattle via I-90 and drove four hours east and through Spokane. Various shades of evergreens replaced pavement and steel.

The Firebird carried her over the freeway with an almost human-like enthusiasm, eating up the miles to Emma Springs.

She checked the odometer, recalculated her arrival time, and looked in the rearview mirror. "Bloody hell."

The same slate gray sedan that had followed her out of Seattle remained several cars behind her. Her knuckles whitened on the steering wheel. She'd stretched her legs at a rest area, eaten, and filled her gas tank on separate stops.

Rearview mirrors didn't lie.

A highway sign noted services at the next exit. She accelerated to pass two tractor-trailer loads of baled hay, moved her car into the empty right lane, and floored the accelerator.

Paranoia or stalker, she'd learn soon enough. Her hand trembled on the shifter while she stopped at the top of the off-ramp. A deserted restaurant sat to her left, the town was to her right.

She cranked the wheel and accelerated. A rusty sign proclaiming *Palmeter's Diner* swung in the breeze. She drove behind the building and parked next to a dumpster. The side of the restaurant remained in shadows, perfect for watching.

She slunk alongside the wall until she reached the end. Rolling fields fanned out from the highway.

The gray sedan topped a hill, cruising slowly toward the abandoned restaurant.

CHAPTER 13

Kyle removed the ear tips of his stethoscope and hung the tubing around his neck. He smiled at Tom Morley. "The rib healed, and your lungs sound fine. I am suggesting you hire out your roof cleaning next time."

"Thanks, Kyle. Will do. Pat and Grant will be relieved." He buttoned his shirt.

Kyle's phone chimed. "Excuse me, that's Corrin's ring."

"Hope she hasn't had car trouble."

He nodded and took the call. "Hey, newcomer. Should I get the welcome band warmed up?"

"I'm hiding. I've been followed," she whispered.

He unwound the stethoscope and tossed it onto the counter. "Give me your location, then call 911." He jotted the highway exit and name of the diner. "I'm on my way. Call the police, now."

Tom stood in the hallway. "Caught parts of the conversation. If you'd like a former Stater at the wheel, my rig's gassed and ready."

"You're on." Kyle grabbed his parka. "She's forty miles from here. She's been followed and is scared. Me, too."

~ ~ ~

Corrin ended the 911 call. *Bloody hell.* A jackknifed semi had pulled the Montana State Patrol troopers to a wreck ten miles back. Her gloved finger trembled while she pocketed her phone. She stared at the road and watched as the afternoon light shifted to dusk.

Kyle had to be close now. Cold from the wall of the garage seeped through her coat and into her body while she leaned against it, waiting.

Whoever followed her must not have seen her, or they'd have turned into the parking lot. Never lead trouble to your porch, her grandpa had drilled into them. She wouldn't lead it to Emma Springs.

Gravel crunched.

She clasped the wall and leaned forward.

An unfamiliar SUV crept into the driveway carrying a driver and passenger. The outlines looked male.

She backed up, step-by-step, watching it head straight toward her.

The Firebird sat twenty feet away.

The passenger opened his door.

She readied her key and pivoted.

"Corrin, it's me!" shouted Kyle's deep, reassuring voice.

The best sound ever. "Thank you for coming to my rescue."

"Where's the police?" Kyle jogged to her.

His kind smile and loving hug sent comfort deep into her travel weary bones. "Some big accident west of here." She brushed a kiss across his lips and noticed Grant's dad leaning against the Bronco. "You brought backup."

Kyle smoothed a lock of hair from her temple. "I'm glad you're safe." He pulled her to his side. "Tom was in my office and assessed the situation. Once an officer, always ready to serve. He packs his Smith & Wesson."

"Welcome to Montana, Corrin." Tom smiled. "Sorry you had a tail. We'll get to the bottom of that, don't worry. Montana folks watch out for each other."

Tears of relief dampened the corners of her eyes. "Thank you, Tom."

Kyle rubbed her back. "I'd bet you're tired. You made a heck of a drive today. Want me to pilot your car on the last stretch?"

The best-ever-man had struck again. "Yes, please." She handed off the keys.

Tom followed them on the highway, while dusk became a starry night. Kyle told her stories of commuting home during college, and before Corrin knew it, they neared the familiar homes of Emma Springs.

Roy's garage door rose. As soon as they'd parked, he trotted to her side of the car. "Pat Morley called," he said. "You can stay in my guest room tonight. No more worries." The hand he offered felt warm and welcoming. "We'll set the alarms and sleep soundly."

His eyes darted to Kyle and back to her. "The security company will outfit the cabin tomorrow. I talked to the owner of the business personally."

"Wow. Mighty fast service. I had to schedule a month out for the last update to my clinic alarm system. What prompted the emergency install? Has something else happened, Dad?" Kyle questioned.

"Sam, the gas station owner, called," Roy said. "A customer grilled him regarding a new lawyer in town driving a Firebird. Sam didn't like the guy and played dumb. The name on the credit card he used was Michael Fernley."

"It's Paunch Guy, from the Red Horse. The one who crashed the wedding." Corrin followed the men into Roy's house. "He's one of Piersall's henchmen, working against Emma Springs."

"It's best to know your enemies," Roy said. "Even if he is too dumb to know we'd find out he was snooping."

"I haven't had time to research Fernley's background, but when I see him, my instincts tell me to run." She wrapped her arms around her chest. Another day she'd share her suspicions.

"Trust your instincts and we'll keep watch for him," Roy said. "We have our first appeal in front of the Hearing Examiner in a week. I got the paperwork filed on the last day to submit."

Kyle pulled her to his side. "I've alerted the sheriff. I'll call him again and mention Fernley."

"Thank you." She took a breath and turned to Roy. "One week doesn't give us much prep time. I'll be ready to start working on the case tomorrow."

"You're now my official partner in this law office. Passing the bar's a formality to me." Roy stuck out his hand.

Corrin managed a strained smile. "I can't wait to get started, partner."

His firm grip relayed optimism.

"Let's tour your office," Roy said. "We can change things to your liking."

She followed the men into the square room bordered by windows. They'd totally redecorated Flor's art studio since her last visit.

Facing the lake sat a petite, claw-footed desk. The rich, dark cherry-colored wood glowed.

"I searched until I found furniture I believe will be comfortable for you." Kyle pulled out a matching leather office chair. "In the top drawer, you'll find a spare key to my house. The alarm code is Miranda and Grant's wedding date."

A sentimental date she'd always remember. "Thank you." Corrin settled her back into the curve of the chair and rolled it to the desk. "It's perfect." Her elbows grazed the blotter. "Adult desks are too big, and kids' desks are too small." She ran her finger across the beveled edge. "This one's just right to avoid sore shoulders. I truly appreciate your thoughtfulness."

"Good call, son." Roy winked at Kyle. "He found it in an antique shop."

Besides their thoughtfulness, she'd partnered with men who cared enough to protect her from the likes of Piersall and Fernley. Their ominous vibes shadowed her perfect world.

~ ~ ~

Corrin rubbed her eyes. She'd spent her first night as a real resident of Montana in Kyle's old bedroom. Not exactly restful, after two nightmares. Mulling over the idea she'd brought thugs to Emma Springs, replicating Miranda bringing the hitman, Venom, to town had prevented sleep.

The clock showed seven, sleeping in by her standards. She threw on office clothes and headed to the kitchen.

Roy peered over half specs when Corrin entered the breakfast nook. Between the glasses and his flannel shirt, he projected more grandfather than lawyer.

"You're attired for combat in a Seattle courtroom," he said, bearing a friendly smile.

"My armor's a force of habit. Due to my height, or lack of, I've always dressed on the formal side." She removed the navy suit jacket.

"Your legal brain's what matters." He met her eyes and then thumped his palm on a pile of gardening catalogs fanned out in front of him. "I told Iris I'd find out what plants would survive our winter. With luck, I'll have her here before spring. Kyle's excited at the prospect of her managing his office."

Corrin smiled. "She'll be perfect."

A clippity-clop clattering on wood floor came from the direction of Roy's laundry room.

Corrin tilted her head.

The little black filly they'd found on the roadside rounded the corner, darted to her, and brushed her soft muzzle against her knee.

Corrin inched her fingers to her velvety ear. "You got a pet?"

"Temporarily. The Bell family had to rush to visit a relative hospitalized in Billings. They farmed out their rescue mini. Kyle suggested I could horse-sit this little gal for the afternoon."

"I met this escape artist the first time I visited town." The mini stood still while Corrin touched her fingertip to the white starburst on her forehead. "Does she have a name?"

"Well darn, they were in a hurry this morning, and I forgot to ask. She's house trained to go to the door when she wants out. Still small enough to stay short spells inside."

"A mannerly mini."

Roy grinned. "Ignore her, and she'll leave you alone. I set out your tea and put the kettle on the stove. Fix yourself a cup and a piece of toast. There are eggs in the fridge. From here on out, I'm treating you as family."

And he meant it. Corrin let out a sigh, moved to the kitchen, and stuck the tea bag in a mug. "Aunt Iris would crack up at me sharing quarters with an equine. Come to think of it, you've brought her old laugh back when she tells a story."

"I don't view our relationship lightly." He removed his glasses. "If she'll have me, I'll propose to her next time I see her and marry her when she says the word."

"Wow. Kind of a fast progression. You've spent, what, a week together, Roy?" She popped a slice of bread in the toaster.

"We speak on the phone twice a day and write emails. At my age, I embrace happiness, and your aunt brings joy back into my life. Will a short courtship bother you?"

She knew exactly the joy he meant. "Of course not." She squeezed his shoulder. "Today's Kyle's day off, isn't it?"

"He called and said he'd be available after noon."

Hours away. She spread peanut butter on the toast. "Oh."

"He's been busy lately on Friday mornings," Roy said. "Probably volunteering. I can help you unload your car after you've finished eating. At four, we meet the security people at the cottage."

Kind of disappointing Kyle had plans on her first day in town. "I'd appreciate help. Did I notice a newspaper out front?"

"Yes. I got distracted and forgot to bring it in. The alarm's off if you want that chore."

"On it." She threw on her coat, unlocked the front door, and stepped onto the driveway.

No cars appeared in either direction.

The hair on her neck rose when she bent to pick up the bundled paper. She looked from side to side. Instincts told her someone was out there. Hunting her.

~ ~ ~

In the living room of the farmhouse a tripod held a telescope, pointed out a window at the mountain.

H.P. swung it to take in the breadth of the rolling meadow. "My old man should've known this hillside wouldn't handle enough ski runs."

"So why are we still here?" Mikey asked.

The less he knew the better. "I'm going to show the Piersall Enterprises Board of Directors how to make money on a bad investment. Plan B will prove my point." He swung the telescope to the window facing the houses below. "Well, well." He angled the optical tube to follow the bitch's return to a porch, then shoved it aside. "Patten's staying with the town's doddering old attorney. I googled him."

"I've met my share of lawyers. None built like Blondie." Mikey licked his lips. "She didn't lose any time consorting with the enemy."

"Correct. That's got to be illegal," H.P. snarled. "Get MFB on your phone."

Mikey rolled his thumb across the tiny screen. "H.P. calling for Chap Brine." He switched the phone to speaker.

"H.P.," Brine responded in a honeyed tone. "Always pleased to hear from my Mu Delta Pi big brother."

He wouldn't be pleased in a moment. "I noticed Ms. Patten's arrived in Montana." H.P. fingered his Rolex. "What time's our first meeting?"

"Ahh. Ms. Patten no longer works for our firm. We have our best lawyers and assistants assigned to your case. They'll be in Emma Springs tomorrow noon."

The end of the telescope clanked into the windowsill. "Not acceptable. I made it clear to Meyer I wanted Patten's . . . expertise."

"I couldn't change her mind before she left the firm," Brine grumbled. "She's a paralegal, what's the big deal?"

Another goddamn wrench in his plans. Anger roiled in his stomach. "My contract listed her," he yelled. "I've always found ways to change people's minds." He thumped his fist on a checkbook lying on the table beside geological surveys of Mt. Hanlen. "There better not be any more surprises, considering the retainer."

"That's why I'm your lead attorney," Brine said.

"Right." H.P. shut off the phone and tossed it to Mikey. "No wonder her company cell went quiet. We need to monitor her new routine. Did you discover anything useful at the gas station?"

"Nah. The pump jockey's too busy wondering how tall the corn grew last week to notice anything."

He'd find a way to use Patten jumping ship to his advantage. He always did. "Dumb hicks will make my plans to take her out easier."

~ ~ ~

"Piersall Enterprises can't possibly think they can put ski lifts up the hillside." Corrin studied a parcel map. "The laws are stringent, and they'd need a portion of the land owned by your mountain man, Stan. Still, I've got a bad feeling."

Roy leaned forward in the rocker opposite her desk. The little horse lay at his feet. "Stan won't sell. I wonder if we should try to warn him?"

"Probably a good idea. Send the little filly?"

"This little girl's smarter than that." Roy stroked a black ear. "Tom knows how to reach Stan."

Corrin looked over his shoulder, to her view of the lake and mountain. "Streams, lakes, and wetlands are protected. Moreover, why would they call an exclusive resort Virtue Valley? I'm missing something."

"How hard is it to prove the negative impacts on the lake?" Roy scratched the filly's belly with his foot.

"Miranda's researching the recently overturned proposal for a mine in another state, due to its impact on grizzly bear habitat and bull trout. Piersall's lawyers might attempt to mitigate certain aspects of their project based on low impact. I pulled appropriate cases close to an established town." Roy's back door clicked shut. She looked up.

Kyle stood in the doorway with pink cheeks and windblown hair. "Greetings from the outside world. I brought the fixings for chicken salad sandwiches."

"Have a good morning?" Corrin asked. She raised her eyebrows and smiled, waiting for him to explain his absence.

"Yup." His voice drifted back as he swung a paper grocery sack and headed to the kitchen.

"Not the typical lengthy response from Kyle. I expected him to share his morning exploits."

"He brought lunch to share." Roy shrugged his shoulders. "I can't answer your Virtue Valley question. I think the builders pull names from a hat."

Not this one. "I'll delve further after we eat." Virtue Valley sounded like a tribute. Not Piersall's style.

~ ~ ~

Morning, her favorite time of the day. Corrin had slept well the first night in her cottage, knowing electronic guards were on duty in the form of motion detectors, locks, and a ninety-decibel siren.

No honks or air brakes jarred the peaceful setting. She padded into the kitchen and scanned the lake. No chimney smoke or lights in the houses sitting on the opposite bank. Behind them, the mountain rose in splendid glory, bathed in the pink strokes of sunup.

Her hobbit-sized refrigerator held her personal calendar. Empty squares for the rest of the month, except for Corey's recently passed birthday.

No book report if Corey didn't have this address. She flipped open the 'Welcome' binder Roy had created and lifted out an envelope and paper to jot a quick note.

One of his antique automaton clocks announced its presence on the mantle by chiming to indicate six-thirty. Out pranced a tiny horse and jeweled carriage. Kyle got credit for his multiple approaches of desensitizing her horse fears. The black, carved, wooden horse resembled Roy's little houseguest.

She finished writing and loaded her Pilates DVD into the player. Plenty of time for a workout before her commute, which consisted of precisely fifty-seven steps across the street.

She unfurled her yoga mat. Out dropped another red plastic tassel. She hadn't used the mat since leaving Seattle.

Her feet felt frozen to the ground. Taking deep breaths, she checked the locks and lowered the blinds.

Was Piersall taunting her or did the creep think she hadn't figured out his clues? Regardless, someone had broken into her car or her cottage before the security had been installed. Fernley's sneer came to mind.

~ ~ ~

Kyle rinsed his coffee cup and consulted his cell phone. He contemplated the odd message from the Seattle area code. A Mr. Smith had texted at 7:00 a.m. to get in ASAP for an earache.

Iris couldn't arrive soon enough to be his office manager. He pulled forms out of the drawer and secured them to a clipboard, then looked outside.

Corrin crossed the street, rocking tight jeans under a short winter coat. Jolts of heat zinged through his body.

Promptly at eight, the clinic doorbell rang. His first patient, dressed in a sport coat and tasseled loafers, belonged in a snobby country club, not their countryside.

The man's smug face set Kyle's teeth on edge. "Mr. Smith?"

"Right." He strolled inside. "I have this annoying thing in my ear." From the end of Kyle's desk, he lifted the marble paperweight etched with the Rod of Aesculapius and deposited it near the corner.

Kyle handed him the clipboard. "Fill out the forms, and take a seat, please." He walked to his exam room, pulled on latex gloves, and placed sterilized instruments onto a blue paper.

"It's the right ear." Arrogance accented Smith's irritating voice. He sauntered in and hopped onto the exam table.

"Passing through town?" Kyle stuck an otoscope in the offending ear and tweezed out a hair. He dropped it onto a white towel.

"Here for a while on business. A hot girl crossed the street a few minutes ago. Petite, blond, and stacked. I want to meet her."

"I can't see anything else in this ear." Kyle moved to the other side, his blood pressure surging. His grip tightened on the metal handle.

"You must've noticed her, she's a knockout."

Kyle returned to the first ear, pulled down the lobule flap, and pushed the scope in further.

"Ow, that hurt," the jerk said.

"Removing the stray hair solved your problem."

Smith rubbed his ear. A ring bearing a gold dagger and ruby stone flashed in the daylight.

Corrin's attacker! Kyle clenched his jaw. "The woman you described is in a relationship."

"Never stopped me before." He stood and brushed off his pants. "When I set my sights on something I want, nothing gets in my way," he threatened.

Kyle held his ground. "And I safeguard my community."

The man pulled out a wallet. "Here's two bills. I assume they'll cover this visit."

"We're finished." Kyle crushed the twin hundreds in his palm.

"Not necessarily, Doc." He spun around and strode out.

Kyle dashed after him. His elbow clipped the edge of his instrument cart. Tools clattered to the floor. He retrieved a scalpel and squeezed the handle.

The door to the clinic banged shut.

He turned to the window and noted the license plate before the car backed out and sped away. His fist remained clenched while he ripped the blank forms from the clipboard.

Sheriffs didn't investigate mere concerns. He dialed his father's number. "Don't say anything," Kyle said. "Is Corrin there?"

"Yes."

"Good. We need to talk. Privately."

"Now?" Roy's voice stayed level.

"Yes. Don't raise her suspicion. Lock Corrin in your house and come to my back door."

"Will do."

"Thanks, Dad." Kyle's eyes dropped to his calendar. His next appointment arrived at nine-thirty. He removed his white doctor's coat and the shirt underneath.

Cool air met him on the back porch, where the punching bag hung from a roof brace.

He cuffed the sleeves on his undershirt and pushed his fists into the heavy cylinder. After a few minutes, the rhythmic motion lowered his hammering pulse.

"You've broken a sweat quickly." Roy stood on the back lawn. "What's going on? My gut tells me it's bad."

Kyle pulled a towel from a chair and wiped his forehead. "At fourteen years old, Corrin fought off an attempted rapist who'd trapped her and a friend on a speed boat in the middle of Puget Sound. It sounds crazy, but I'm certain my eight o'clock patient this morning is the same bastard. There were two men on the boat that day. I'd bet she suspects that Michael Fernley's the other creep from the boat."

"Well, hell," Roy said, and planted his legs wide apart in a battle stance.

"She described an unusual ring the attacker wore. I recognized it on a patient named 'Smith' today. Fourteen years have elapsed. She recognized her attacker exiting her former law offices a week before she left Seattle. Same guy, same ring."

"Describe the patient today," Roy said.

"Near forty. Dark hair, aquiline nose, aristocratic looking. He mentioned he wanted to date Corrin, like a big game hunter plotting to bag his next trophy."

"It must've been Harlan Piersall Jr. A contact sent me a college photo of him today. Let me think this through."

"Knowing he wants to be near Corrin is sickening. I'm certain he's not interested in anything above suspicion."

"We've got Corrin's safety and the outcome of a lawsuit potentially hazardous to the community at stake." Roy rubbed the back of his neck. "Corrin did the initial research on the Piersalls."

"Has she seen your photo of Junior?" Kyle asked.

"Not yet. The Piersall family owned the coal operation in her hometown of Ebony Cove until it closed. The color drained from her face at the discovery, and I assumed her grandfather's black lung disease had caused her distress."

"We've got to alert Corrin." Kyle twisted the towel.

"I need to consider the best way to approach this." Roy turned to a view of calm lake water. "If it's sick revenge, we need to plan carefully."

Kyle threw one last punch, swinging the hefty bag to the limit of its chain. "I swore an oath to save people, and all I want is for my fist to bust the smile off Piersall's face."

"I know, son. Me, too."

His dad couldn't match his compulsion to break Piersall in half, bone by bone.

~ ~ ~

"Mikey, listen up." H.P. rubbed his ear. "The town doctor needs to learn a lesson."

"Why him?"

"I verified Patten and the doc are involved." He stuck his ring into a beam of sunlight coming through a clean splotch on the dirty window. Blood red shone from the stone. "Plan and execute something big. I want the whole damn town sent a message. Don't kill him but come close. And it needs to look accidental."

"Double what you're paying me, or no can do."

His fist bunched. Mikey's mercenary streak at its finest. "I'll double what I've been paying you. For one month. You've milked the Piersall cash cow payroll for fifteen years, don't forget."

"Hey, we were buddies before Blondie ruined your life. Don't ever forget how I took care of things."

"A few things." Paying her the hush money hadn't bothered him. Hell, it was Business 101 as taught by his old man. He'd never forget the other ways she'd ruined his life. And neither would she.

~ ~ ~

Roy's front door opened.

Corrin took deep breaths. He hadn't been gone very long, but she'd worked up enough nerve to divulge finding the bicycle tassel earlier and its relationship to the attack and Piersall.

"It's me," Roy muttered.

"I talked to Miranda. She's sourced more relevant DNR studies. I'll see her later today. In Seattle, I resented working weekends. I don't here." She took a deep breath. "Uh, Roy, I've got something I need to discuss."

Roy paused at the entrance to her workspace and avoided her gaze. He adjusted the blinds on her window to shut out light. "Can it wait? I have work to attend to in my office." He left before she'd replied.

That resembled a brush off. She tapped on his cracked door. "Roy, can we talk?" Her fingers pushed the door open.

"In a moment." He looked up from tipping a bottle to fill a crystal tumbler with golden liquid.

The smell of whiskey hit her nose and sent nauseous fumes to her gut. Would drinking early have to do with her? "Is my work unsatisfactory? Tell me straight."

"Your work's exemplary." He twisted the glass. "Why would you ask?"

"It's nine o'clock, and you're drinking hard liquor. You weren't the least interested in Miranda's findings even though they may be critical." She rubbed her shoe on the carpet. "I haven't known you long, but I've noticed your routine."

Roy dumped the vile liquid into a potted plant on the nearby credenza. "You're not to blame, and I certainly don't want you to leave. I value our friendship and our partnership. Please trust me."

"You're one of the few people I do trust."

"I can't discuss my problem right now." He met her eyes. "Did you mention needing to talk?"

"It can wait." She waved her hand and slipped out. Whatever concerned him involved Kyle.

Something bumped her knee. Corrin jumped, then scratched the filly's head. "You know exactly when something's bothering me. They should train you to be an emotional support pony. I wish you could find out from Roy what's wrong."

The horse nickered and dashed into his office.

Geeze, the mini recognized names. If only she'd learned horse-speak instead of Latin.

Roy avoided her the rest of the day. Several hours and too many assumptions later, the front doorbell rang.

"Hey former roomie, or can I say law partner?" Miranda asked, before she pulled Corrin into a nerve-calming, world-brightening hug.

Miranda deserved her full attention. She'd shelve her problem until later. "I won't officially be a partner until I pass the bar. Roy's worth ten of the MFB lawyers. Wait until you see the cottage."

"You deserve a little spoiling. Before your home tour, check out how much I unearthed regarding restrictions on wetlands." She held out two inches of documents. "I highlighted zoning appeals applicable to our county and flagged the pages. We should be able to squash unfavorable lakeside development. The CA-1 zoning that Piersall's asking for clearly states planned development needs to enhance environmental amenities found in rural areas."

Tiny, brightly colored slips of paper stuck out of Miranda's paperwork. The way her stomach roiled, she might as well be strapped to a concrete block flying straight into the center of Sunrise Lake. "You are the official zoning zealot. I need a change of scenery. I'll dig into your rainbow of research after."

"Oh-kay. Everything copacetic?" Miranda asked.

"Somewhat." She ushered them outside.

"Hey, there's Kyle. Let's see what he's up to." Corrin pointed to the Jeep turning into his driveway.

Kyle hopped out. "Well, if it isn't my favorite recent bride and maiden of honorable loyalties."

"I'm making lasagna for dinner tonight. Can you two join us?" Miranda asked.

He put his hands in his pockets. "Darn, one of my favorite meals. I'll be gone tonight to a medical board meeting. Not looking forward to the drive with Betsy, but she had something to do with getting me the position. Maybe you'll grant us a rain check, if Corrin's willing?"

"I can assemble it tonight and stick it in the refrigerator. Tomorrow night?"

He shifted his feet. "Sure. You two work out details." He checked his watch. "Enjoy your afternoon, ladies. I've got an appraiser due here in ten minutes." He waved and headed into his house.

Corrin crossed her arms. "Did he say appraiser? This whole morning's been off."

"I thought he said appointment. Doctors are busy. Want to plan on dinner tomorrow?"

"Sure. I need a cup of tea," she unlocked the cottage, "and your opinion on another incident."

Miranda took the seat facing the lake. "What's bothering you?"

Over steaming cups of tea, Corrin explained her worries concerning Kyle and his dad.

"Grant mentioned Kyle's frustrations of lacking a real medical clinic," Miranda offered. "Roy refinanced his home to pay for Flor's medical bills and Kyle's working with his bank to pull money from the equity he has in his house."

"He's probably meeting a house appraiser right now," Corrin said. "I had no idea. It's not my place to micromanage Kyle's life. Thanks for the heads-up." Corrin turned to the window. "I hope they consider his view."

"They should." Miranda pointed at the tall, gray snag. "Is a duck landing in the dead tree?"

"Wood duck, so I'm told. Roy said they nest in a cavity about halfway up. I heard him quack a time or two. I've seen an eagle flying on the far side."

"Beats the feathers out of the pigeons in downtown Seattle." Miranda rinsed her cup and tugged Corrin's ponytail. "Kyle and Roy both appreciate you. Don't worry."

While she headed to her car across the street, Corrin stood by her Firebird and swiped a path through the brown film on its side. "Ugh, nasty road dirt."

"Get used to it," Roy called from his mailbox.

"In the meantime, can I borrow an old towel?" She walked across the street kicking stones off the road. "Kyle has a meeting tonight in Three Falls."

"I'll give you a stack of old towels. What meeting?" Roy asked.

She grimaced. "With the resident cougar, Betsy. Some medical board."

"Right, I forgot. Hope it's legitimate. She's had her claws out for Kyle since she padded into town." A big grin crossed Roy's face. "I have books on hold at the library in Three Falls. Found some materials specific to zoning that the hearing examiner should appreciate." Roy slapped his stack of letters playfully against her arm. "I think they're open until nine. You can grab them for me."

"Kyle'd pick them—"

A black sports car swung into Kyle's driveway, scattering gravel. Betsy swung long legs out of the driver's seat. Her miniskirt barely covered her butt. A V-neck tank top accented the twin saline missiles bunkered underneath. She leaned against the side with her cell phone pressed to her ear.

"No, I may need you to copy articles and delve into more reference material." Roy grinned at her. "Kyle wouldn't mind if you rode along. I'll pay you overtime."

"No need. You approach him while I change my clothes really quick."

"That's my girl," Roy whispered.

Planning an outfit made her walk all the faster to her closet.

She analyzed the choices lying on her bed—a formfitting black dress, or gray slacks and a pink blouse. She'd worn the blouse once and its droopy bow made her feel twelve.

A devious smile came to her lips.

~ ~ ~

Kyle gripped a sport coat his mom had gotten him. "Thank goodness Corrin's got your spunk, Mom," he whispered.

His back doorbell rang, and almost simultaneously, a knock sounded from his entry. He opened the back door first. "Hey Dad, what's up?" Kyle headed toward the front entrance. "Betsy must be here."

Roy trailed him through the house. "Hang on a second before you open the door, okay? May Corrin catch a ride to do research at the library while you're at the meeting?"

The picture window allowed a view of Betsy in profile, sharply displaying her armaments.

Kyle smiled. "Your request's a relief. Can you let her in?" He stuck his arms into the jacket.

Roy pulled open the door. "Hi, Betsy. We're nearly ready." He waved her in.

"We?" She stood with the open door against her back, tapping her foot.

Kyle pulled his keys from his pocket. "Dad has work laid out for Corrin in Three Falls. We can all drive together." Betsy spun around, and her designer purse nearly whacked Roy. "What? I mean, ah, sure." She pouted. "I guess we can't use my car."

"My Jeep's better in icy weather." Kyle relaxed at the sight of Corrin, walking toward his front door.

"I grabbed my laptop, Roy." Corrin sidestepped around Betsy. "Are the books reserved in your name?"

"This time." He removed a card from his wallet. "You better open an account for yourself. We'll need to do research there on a regular basis. Probably monthly."

Betsy frowned. If she'd had a tail, it would've swished Roy into the couch.

Corrin smirked while she tucked the library card into her purse. "Always happy to assist," she chirped.

Kyle squeezed his dad's shoulder. "Better hit the road." He held the door open for the two women.

"Keep your rig between the poles." Roy grinned.

"I made reservations at my favorite French restaurant. For two." Betsy jumped in the front seat, rested her elbow on the console, and after Kyle got in, leaned toward his ear. "We can drop our little hitchhiker off first." She threw a fur jacket on the seat next to Corrin.

A sneeze threatened Kyle's nose from her overpowering perfume. "I'll bet they can squeeze three at our table. My treat." He adjusted the rearview mirror. "Does the passenger in the back seat enjoy French food?" He raised his brows and smiled, pleading for a 'yes' response.

"I've been known to polish off a croissant or two." She elbowed Betsy's coat into the corner. "I won't touch rabbit."

"You haven't lived in Montana long enough," Kyle chuckled.

Corrin leaned between the front seats. "I watched a TV program recently where a sleek female cougar began hunting. She started stalking this poor little cottontail. You saw her concentrated effort in every muscle. Before she pounced, the rabbit warren sounded a thump, and the bunny leaped into a hole to escape." Corrin sat back. "I couldn't imagine ever dining on a harmless hare."

"You're quite the storyteller." Betsy adjusted her skirt.

Kyle checked the mirror in time to see Corrin flip the two long, rounded bow ends of her blouse. They locked eyes, hers wide open and innocent.

So many hidden treasures. Boy, did he ever ache for a chance at discovery.

~ ~ ~

A sleepwalking poodle could've fired a cannon through the uncrowded Three Falls version of a French restaurant. Corrin smiled to herself, imagining a barrel filled with paint balls aimed at the woman seated across from her at their round table. Josephine Bonaparte would approve of her attack.

"So, how's the wannabe lawyer handling Emma Springs?" Betsy inched her wrought iron bistro chair closer to Kyle's.

He responded by scooting his seat toward Corrin, until his knee touched hers.

Corrin downed half her glass of ice water. "It's a pleasure working beside an honest lawyer. Why'd you build in Emma Springs? Louis Vuitton purses aren't generally strapped behind saddles."

"I'm negotiating a divorce, and my shrink suggested I find a less toxic environment." Betsy flipped her hair.

Obviously, she hadn't lived here long enough. "So, is it?" Corrin asked.

"I'm finding parts of my experience here delightful." Betsy tipped her cocktail glass toward Kyle and thrust her chest out. "Kyle and I committed to help Montana's underprivileged children."

Kyle cleared his throat. "Technically, the board oversees private funding for researching children's lung diseases." He scanned the menu.

"Oh right. Power plants or something." Betsy siphoned the last drops of her second boozy-smelling drink.

A waiter traded out a basket of puff pastry cheese sticks and a pot of pate for Betsy's empty glass. "Our special tonight is bass amandine."

"Find an appetizing entree, Corrin?" Kyle's shoulder gently bumped hers. "I didn't see wild hare on the menu."

"Nope. A bunny-free zone offering a plethora of tantalizing choices." Corrin used her knee to graze his thigh. "But I think Betsy should order first."

Betsy rolled her eyes. "I'll have another martini and the tenderloin. Seared and rare." Color deepened her carefully powdered cheeks.

Stilted conversation bumped along between the three of them until Betsy downed her fourth drink, looked at Kyle, and circled her wobbling pointer finger in the air. "Rumor has it, Corrin, you left a budding career at MFB. Too much competition?"

"Dad spotted the perfect legal partner and jumped," Kyle tersely responded. "I'll signal for the check."

Who'd blabbed to Betsy? Roy? Kyle? Corrin silently mulled the ramifications, her back pressed into a thin cushion. She slid her chair away from the man who'd been playing footsie with her for the last hour.

Finally, the server deposited the black waiter wallet on the table.

"Dinner's on me. I insist." Betsy stuck a platinum card inside, letting the end stick out.

Corrin placed her napkin on the table. Roy wouldn't have discussed her MFB employment. Things had gotten fishy, and not from bass amandine.

If the file notes she'd perused at the office were accurate, Betsy had hooked a potential second husband before she'd divorced the first millionaire. No scandals, simply a quest for bigger sugar daddies. What was her game?

She'd better not still be trolling for a fling with Kyle.

CHAPTER 14

Well-sauced French cuisine churned in Kyle's stomach. They'd become outnumbered, if he'd read the credit card correctly. Corrin needed alerting. He parked the Jeep in front of the Three Falls Library. "I'll get Corrin settled and return in a minute, Betsy."

"Fine." Her lips hadn't relaxed from a tight pout since the last bunny reference.

He jumped out, opened Corrin's door, and took her hand. "Thank goodness you came along. She takes shallow to a new depth."

"You think so?" Corrin pulled away. "You spent enough time with her to discuss my past work history."

"Not so. Tonight's the first time I've spent more than a few minutes in forced conversation. I assumed you had." He opened the library door for her, grabbed her coat sleeve, and towed her into an alcove. "I got a glimpse of her credit card. It said *Piersall Enterprises* on the imprint," he whispered. "My appointment to this board may not be as the community doctor. I think I'm being set up somehow."

Corrin smoothed the creases between his brows with her fingertip. "I'm sorry I assumed incorrectly and I'm sorry you got involved in this mess. Be careful."

If she'd seen who he'd treated for an earache, she'd be a lot more than sorry. He ran his fingers through his hair. "It's not your fault, and we'll fight them together." He scanned the few occupants of the open areas adjoining shelves of books. "Don't move from this building. See you before nine," he said, and left.

What he wouldn't give to throw Betsy in a snowbank, drive Corrin home, and plan a course of action.

During the next two hours, he forced his mind to concentrate on the program. The foundation wasn't a front. Kyle jotted notes on studies concerning updates on sudden infant death syndrome and lung development.

Experts in the field of pediatric medicine oversaw the funding for life-changing research, notably sourced in large part from the coal burning industry.

Judging by the caliber of the other members seated at the conference table, connections secured board positions. How did he fit in?

At the close of the meeting, groups of well-dressed attendees engaged in comfortable banter.

His phone vibrated. Dad had responded that he'd be waiting for a late night consultation. The sooner he got back to Emma Springs, the better. He'd text him a short meeting update and they'd alert Corrin, first thing in the morning, about H.P.'s visit. One of them might sleep tonight. Kyle's fingers tensed while he collected his notes. "Let's go. Corrin will be waiting," Kyle said to Betsy.

The foundation president approached them, smiling. "I'm delighted representatives of our most generous benefactor have joined our board. If you see him, please tell Harlan I hope he agrees to my request."

"Will do." Betsy smiled at the man, turned his way, and flicked a 'let's go' nod toward the door.

Not so fast. He hadn't signed on to be anyone's representative, especially Piersall. Kyle rubbed his chin. "Refresh me on your request?"

"Mr. Piersall's wanting to give back to the community who saved his son forty years ago is a story we'd feature in our brochure. Maybe one of you can gain his approval."

Kyle tilted his head. "What part of the story were you considering?"

"Here's what I've envisioned," the man said. "State the facts in a simple format. A young couple vacations out-of-state in 1978, the pregnant wife falls ill, and a country physician identifies a condition, which left untreated, would have been debilitating to the baby. It's a classic."

"Put the request in writing." Betsy jerked open the door.

Kyle followed her. "Or you can tell Piersall when you give a progress report."

Her grimace thinned to a sneer.

Discovery wasn't always met with fanfare.

~ ~ ~

Streetlights in Emma Springs glowed a bright welcome after the stony silence from Betsy on the way home from Three Falls. Corrin drummed her fingers on her thigh, impatient as hell to hear about Kyle's meeting.

"So long, Betsy." Kyle veered into his driveway and hit the brakes.

"There are things we need to clarify. In private." Betsy jumped out and slammed the passenger door.

"What the heck happened in the meeting?" Corrin asked.

"The Piersalls are the largest donor to the foundation." He rubbed his temple. "I need to call it a night."

For once, he didn't want to discuss an issue. Not the Kyle she knew. Corrin shoved open her door. "Sure."

"No, you don't. Stay put." The Jeep leapt in reverse. "If there's one thing I've figured out, your shoes are important. Besides, the driveway's slippery at night."

Something had unnerved him. "In case you didn't notice, Sherlock, I'm wearing rubber snow boots." She watched for his cavalier grin. Nothing.

He backed into her driveway and stopped a few yards from the door, then shut off his Jeep. "Let's talk first thing tomorrow at your office. Knowing Betsy's on their payroll puts a different spin on things." Kyle's voice held a strained edge.

"So many negatives surrounding boozy Betsy. See you at eight?" She hopped out.

Kyle beat her to her door and waited while she disarmed the security system and flicked on her living room light. "Make it seven tomorrow," he said, glancing at the two closed doors off the hallway. "Mind if I use your restroom?" He flicked on the hall light.

"Not at all." She opened the coat closet and kicked off her boots. Had her bedroom door squeaked? She turned. Both doors were shut.

In a few moments, he returned and pecked her on the cheek. "Lock up tight."

"I will," she said to his backside.

A chilling thought struck. He'd been scanning her home for intruders.

~ ~ ~

At seven sharp, Kyle walked to his father's house, greeted Roy, and faced Corrin. She sat at the dining room table, her fingers tapping her mug. "I need answers. Now," she demanded.

"Believe me when I tell you that Dad and I will do whatever it takes to protect you." He took a deep breath, then let it out slowly. "Your attacker is in Emma Springs."

Her hand jerked, spilling tea onto the table. "No! No! No!"

Kyle placed his fingers on her shoulder. He'd struggled all night with how to break the news. "Yesterday, I treated a patient who'd called in as Smith. He wore the ring you described."

"All the pieces fit together," she muttered.

"Over the years, Flor and I kept up correspondence with our Harvard classmates, several who are now in influential positions. I may not be computer savvy, but I kept the phone lines active yesterday. Harlan Sr. managed the mine in your hometown," Roy offered gently. "H.P. attended the University of Washington for three years. He left Seattle immediately after he attacked you to begin fall classes at a college in the Midwest."

Corrin glared at Kyle. "You told your dad?"

"I had to."

Roy placed his hand on hers. "Kyle wanted to pound his fake patient to smithereens." He squeezed her wrist gently, then squared his shoulders. "It's my fight, too, and I'll carry on as if I'm safeguarding my daughter. Together we'll prosecute the pervert."

"Why's that horrible man following me?" She put both fists to her temples and thumped. "I never reported his attack. As far as I know, my friend didn't either, unless she accused Piersall recently." She slouched into her chair. "I guess that's a possibility. Might be a way to extort money or ruin his chances of taking over the business from his father someday. I'll try to contact her through social media."

"Regardless, we may never identify his issues," Kyle said. "Only your safety matters."

She raised troubled eyes to his. "You're both too good to be true."

"Dad and I want what's best for you," Kyle said. "Stay out of the courtroom if it's too difficult."

"No." She shook her head. "In five days, I need to face him at the hearing to lay out our reasons why Piersall Enterprises should not be granted a C-A1 rezone of the hillside for their ski resort, in order to protect the lake."

"You won't be alone," Roy said.

Corrin straightened in her chair. "No more cowering. We'll expose him for what he is."

"That's the spirit." Kyle sat beside her. "We must agree to disclose everything we learn. I'll start. Yesterday, he asked questions regarding you being here."

"Now me," Corrin said. "He knows that at MFB I met with Fernley, a.k.a. Paunch Guy, a.k.a. the degenerate who restrained me in his speedboat. He must intend to keep me from being able to work on behalf of Emma Springs due to a conflict of interest or something."

"Worse. He bragged he'd date you. That's what brought the vigilante out in me."

Her body shuddered. "He does not want to date me. He hates me. I never connected the boat attack to this legal case, even after I saw him. Then came the fishing lure, and I found another bicycle streamer in the belongings that I moved here. The creep has been watching me and leaving clues."

Kyle felt his heartbeat thrashing in his ears. He stood and pulled her to her feet. He fought to appear calm. "We all miss things under stress. No more worries. The Werner men, Grant, Tom, and our townspeople will shield you."

Eyes darkened from recessed terror met his. Her nails dug into his jacket. "I must face him, Kyle. He's got to pay for the years he took from me, and more importantly, we've got to stop him from whatever he plans for Emma Springs. It isn't only my life's that's being torn to pieces by his irrational vengeance. The man is pure evil."

~ ~ ~

The following day, Corrin pulled into a space in front of McPherson's General Store, next to a new Corvette.

The white sports car had a temporary license plate, and no Montana glaze, what Roy called the dusty film covering every vehicle.

Sharlene Underson exited Emma's Fashion Boutique, carrying three pink- and white-striped bags. She set the parcels at the front of the car, then bowed her head while rummaging in her purse. Her previously mousy hair shone in a rich shade of brown and the fluffy, pouffed out style flattered her bovine face.

"Hello, Sharlene. Hit the lotto?" Corrin tucked her keys into her purse.

The council president's head jerked up. "Oh, ah, no." Her eyes darted from the car to her packages. "I had a relative pass away and, ah, name me in the will."

"I'm sorry for your loss." Corrin took a step forward. "Need help?"

A box holding an Italian espresso machine sat in the front seat.

"Nope. I'm fine." Sharlene snatched the bags and tossed them to the passenger side floorboard. "See you later." She slid her ample butt in, shut her door, and backed up.

There'd been talk of another county council member affording a new F-350 pickup.

Corrin narrowed her eyes. She'd reviewed the records of past meetings. The owners of the new rigs were the two county council members who swung the most influence.

~ ~ ~

Fighting evil, a new use for the reception hall in the church basement where they'd held Miranda and Grant's wedding reception. Corrin scanned the crowded room filled by selected Emma Springs residents. They'd initially met to discuss concerns and submit paperwork to question the zoning request by Piersall Enterprises. This meeting required them to jump ahead.

"Good evening." Miranda tapped a gavel on the podium to quell the chatter. "Thank you for being here tonight to address our stated purpose of, and I quote, 'protecting the water quality of Sunrise Lake for future generations.'" She touched her palm to her tummy.

Belly ache or baby on board. Corrin sketched a baby rattle on her notepad.

"The handout gives the hearing date to present our concerns on the impending zoning of the hillside to a commercial designation. Last night, Corrin discovered a new option. Upon further investigation and after consulting with the helpful Montana planning and zoning folks today, Roy and I agree with the recommendation that the town form a Special Zoning District surrounding Sunrise Lake. The impacted area isn't zoned at all, so it's unprotected as it sits. I know this is a new direction, but there are many advantages in this course of action."

A low murmur rose, then the room quieted.

Miranda's eyes panned the townspeople. "Seventy percent of the property owners who have lake frontage need to sign the petition before it can move forward. The documents we handed out explain the procedure. Are there any questions?"

The woman who owned the Springs Cafe stood up. "I got the impression the zoning hearing should eliminate our problems. Don Underson, from Dagger Realty, told me his client would pay twice what my place is worth. Probably made the same offer to the two families who disappeared."

Miranda nodded. "I'd bet you're correct. Unfortunately, all we know is hearsay that those families felt threatened, sold out, and left. We have proof that trespassers on Roy's property planned to poison the lake and can only assume there's a correlation. Piersall's LLC is looking to build a ski resort in Montana for wealthy clients. His lawyers may have discovered the Special Zoning District and the seventy percent ownership qualifier. Land value here equates to pennies on the dollar compared to where these guys typically build." She smiled warmly at the Springs Cafe owner. "We appreciate all of you who haven't taken the cash and run. Piersall Enterprises has the reputation of being unscrupulous, and we're trying to prepare for the worst, whatever that may be," Miranda said.

Kathleen Langley raised her hand. "It puzzles me why he'd offer double for lake frontage, then try to poison the lake? That isn't good business."

Corrin squirmed in her chair. The townspeople deserved to know her history, to know all H.P.'s possible reasons. She made eye contact with Miranda, and unclenched her hands, preparing to tell her secret.

Miranda gave her head a quick shake no. "We're as mystified as you are. The lake is protected by environmental laws. At the hearing his intentions may be clarified. In the meantime, there's a choice between protecting a lifestyle now and for future generations, versus accepting a quick cash-out and abandoning Emma Springs."

Her hand swept to an easel holding an enlarged photo of Sunrise Lake. "There is an additional option for future tax breaks. It's a conservation easement given by each property owner. The details are in the handout. Basically, you still own the land, pay lowered taxes, and have a document establishing your vision for protecting the lake's natural values by limiting development. You negotiate details with a land trust."

"I can't imagine ruining our hillside with a row of lift towers. My dude ranch customers want pristine scenery," Kathleen stated. "What's the quickest way to squash commercial development?"

"The Special Zoning District. Roy Werner has offered to cover the filing fee. This will give us an added layer of protection, and being landowners, you'll have a guiding document for the zoning authorities to follow, which the county council can't vote away." She set out the petition and a pen.

More discussion rumbled through the low-ceilinged room.

"This isn't the first time," Kathleen piped up. "Around forty years ago, the same realtor tried to force us to sell my family's Calderon spread to an out-of-town client. We didn't do it then, and we won't do it now.

We'll be the first to sign. Guests come to the Lazy K and expect a clean, refreshing swim below a picturesque hillside." Kathleen and her husband, Trey, approached the table holding hands. Others formed a line behind them.

Enough to hit the minimum? Corrin counted the property owners. Relief penetrated her tensed muscles. Where was Kyle? He should be here. He'd said his trip to the Three Falls Hospital would be brief.

Movement in the back corner caught her attention. Feline, cougar movement. Betsy.

The transplant owned a waterfront property. Betsy's thumbs tapped in spasms on her phone. She stopped and pulled the screen closer. Color drained from her tan-in-a-can face. She popped out of her seat and then bolted upstairs.

If Miranda's proposal evoked such a tsunami response from the town spy, they were in for a tempest. Corrin grabbed the edge of her folding chair.

An aroma of mint wafted to her, then Kyle's hand rested on her shoulder. "You and Miranda did well," he whispered. "I knew by Betsy's scowl when she bolted past me at the door. I wish I had a vote."

"You don't?" Corrin asked quietly.

"It's Dad's. The cottage property includes the strip of waterfront adjacent to my lawn."

"Doesn't matter," Corrin said. "We convinced a majority of landowners to sign."

"Good job." A raspy cough drew his focus to the corner of the room. "Excuse me for a moment. Julia Bell picked up a nasty cold," he said.

Corrin grabbed her legal pad and approached Miranda. "I need your opinion on a document." She took her arm and towed her to the side of the room. The second page of the pad displayed the doodled rattle, a diaper, and a huge question mark.

Miranda's cheeks turned pink. "We're not even certain. How'd you guess? Only Grant knows."

"Your secret's safe. It's the happiest request for discovery I've ever made. You'll be a fabulous mom."

Miranda pulled her into a firm hug. "I got everything I longed for, after opening my heart to Grant," she whispered. "He's excited to be a dad," she confided. "You and Kyle are great together. I want you happy, too."

"I am," Corrin replied.

Until Piersall and his ugly vendetta threatened again.

~ ~ ~

Corrin sagged against the outside brick wall of the courthouse. Her brain thrummed with possibilities of what could happen today in court. Never had she been so uncertain regarding a case. Never had she taken on a psychopath intent on revenge.

A copy of their recorded Special Zoning District had been entered into the case file. Doubt inched up her spine while she waited for residents to assemble for the hearing. What had she missed?

Miranda and Grant arrived first. Grant's arm stretched across Miranda's shoulders, their hips touching.

"I hardly ate any breakfast," Miranda said, while twisting an auburn curl around her finger.

"A common problem these last couple days." Grant pulled her closer and kissed her cheek. "I slipped a Ziploc of soda crackers into your coat pocket, love."

"Do they calm courtroom jitters?" Miranda asked.

More likely morning sickness had hit her. "You're going to do great, Miranda. Your evidence is solid." Corrin leaned in close, wanting to bolster her friend's confidence. "This will be simple compared to the hitman's trial."

"So I've been told. Where's Kyle?" Miranda asked.

"Hopefully en route. He needed to check on a patient."

Townspeople filed into the county hearing examiner's chambers, quietly sliding onto padded benches. Familiar faces, now solemn. MFB lawyers sat on a bench closest to the raised desk.

Roy ushered Corrin and Miranda to the other wide seat at the front of the room. He sat on one end, Corrin on the other.

Miranda's fingers trembled while she rearranged the pile of documents on her lap.

Roy raised his chin. "The wrong shall fail, the right prevail," his steady voice quoted.

The hearing examiner emerged from a separate entry and set a file folder on the desk. He explained the proceedings before calling out, "The defendant's wetland expert may present."

A middle-aged man wearing shorts presented his credentials and then placed a photo on the projector.

They'd hired a wetlands expert. Corrin leaned forward to better view the screen at the side of the room. "I dreamt I heard a weed eater the other night," she whispered to Miranda. "His photo shows the shore opposite my cottage, minus the tall vegetation."

"My examination of the property indicates a lack of wetlands," he stated. "Run-off from any development would drain downhill to a retention pond, currently named Sunrise Lake. Rainfall and snowmelt sustain it."

A POND. NO WAY!! Miranda wrote in huge letters on her pad.

"Evidence provided demonstrates no environmental impacts to the pond from commercial development," the presenter continued. He paused to change photos, then nodded to a man wearing a well-cut camel hair coat entering the room.

Blood froze in Corrin's veins. Her attacker now whispered to Fernley. Seeing the two of them together blasted out memories of the groping hands, the strike to her friend's face, and frigid water.

She braced her hand against the armrest, prepared to bolt.

~ ~ ~

Kyle slid in next to Corrin. She flinched at his touch. He followed her gaze to where Piersall sat next to Fernley, the other pervert from the boat.

He unclenched his fist and laid his arm across Corrin's shoulders, feeling her shrink while the two men chatted.

Kyle's nose flared. The molesting bastard had nerve to sit in the front row. He sucked in deep breaths, then snugged Corrin close to his side. Inch by inch she straightened to the rigid-backed, down-to-business version he admired. She gently squeezed his knee.

"Miranda Whitley to the podium, please," the examiner called.

She cited studies and findings. Her testimony raised several questions from the examiner.

The basis of Miranda's rebuttal eluded Kyle, for he'd been too focused on the reactions of the predators seated opposite. Urges to pummel the conceit off

Piersall's face tensed his forearms. One right hook would suffice. Or maybe not.

Corrin unfolded his fist and then stroked his hand. She understood. The realization calmed him more than any tranquilizer.

"The next meeting will convene after December 5, allowing time to adequately assess the information presented today." The hearing examiner removed his glasses. "Parties of interest will receive notification. This concludes today's session. Good day." He gathered his paperwork and exited the room.

"Are you okay?" Kyle tipped Corrin's chin toward him.

Unwavering blue eyes met his. "You're my rock. I want to cut Piersall and his lawyers off at their corporate knees or higher."

"I agree." He kissed her cheek. "You should be proud of yourself, not many people can face their attackers."

Piersall slapped the back of the wetland specialist, smirked over his shoulder at them, and left the room.

"What did I miss?" Kyle asked.

"Their expert contends the lake's a stagnant pond," Corrin said. "If it can be proven, Mr. Shorts will be getting a nice Christmas bonus. Enough to pay for a new reel of line for his weed wacker. I hope someone has photos of the other side of the lake, prior to them cutting every blade of grass on the shore."

"Mom would be furious. One of her greatest joys came from photographing birds perched on the cattails on the far side."

Roy stepped in and shook Miranda's hand. "You did splendidly. Mentioning the new zoning district took their yuppie lawyer down a notch."

"He's the transplant from California," Corrin offered. "A great deal hinges on the wetland determination. They won't be able to put in a ski lodge and parking lot above a protected area. We need to get our own soil tests done, pronto." Corrin leaned heavily onto Kyle's arm.

"I'll handle those," Roy stated.

Grant patted Roy on the back. "Good team you assembled." He pulled Miranda to her feet. "I'm repeatedly amazed at the steel constitution of my beautiful and articulate wife."

"The good news is that the three of you provided enough information to keep the examiner busy until after Thanksgiving," Kyle said. "We can name our turkey Harlan." Faking nonchalance didn't come easy. "Do you think Iris would join us for the long weekend?" He pushed open the exit door.

"I won't be in Emma Springs, Kyle." Corrin dropped her hand from his arm.

The words cut into Kyle like a scalpel.

CHAPTER 15

Kyle tripped on a mat. He'd gone pale.

Corrin grabbed his arm. "I'm not leaving you. I'll be gone a few days is all," Corrin said, while they walked outside.

"Damn straight you're not, partner," Roy's frown had vanished.

"Come on, gentlemen," Corrin teased. "You can't get rid of me so easily. Aunt Iris called this morning to wish me luck and ask if I'd spend one last Thanksgiving with her in the condominium to help her sort through her storage unit. A certain someone's hinting she should move to a more mountainous state."

Kyle lifted Corrin's hand and brushed his lips across the top of her knuckles. "You scared the daylights out of me."

Brilliant rays spread deep into her soul. "I'm sorry. I didn't have time to tell you before the hearing began." She stroked the side of Kyle's face. "I haven't made my flight yet or arranged a ride to the airport."

"And back," Kyle stated.

"Definitely."

"Iris packing means I'm buying lunch," Roy beamed. "We need to convene with Miranda and Grant to discuss a further plan of action against Piersall. I told them to meet us at the Springs Cafe."

Corrin rubbed her temple. "I'm missing something in the regulations."

"If I calculated correctly, they still need another piece of property to move forward." Roy opened the passenger door of the Jeep. "I'm not selling mine. I don't scare as easy as those families who left in the middle of the night."

The image of Fernley striking her friend resurfaced. She curled her fists into tight balls, ready to fight, no longer a scared teenager.

~ ~ ~

"Thanksgiving travel's worse than they said." Kyle wheeled his Jeep into one of the few empty slots at Three Falls Airport.

His movements lacked the hesitation of earlier trips to catch flights. A return date must have merit. She smiled and batted her eyelashes. "I'll pine away until my return."

Kyle tilted the steering wheel and turned to her. "I need a kiss to hold me over, a lasting dose, so to speak."

"High time I provide a binding cause of action." She grabbed the collar of his coat and gently pulled him across the console. "If you'll provide your lips."

He wrapped his arms around her, murmuring agreement. With her body pressed into his, she ran her fingers through his hair.

His kisses pushed sensual warmth into hollow niches. She'd never get enough of him, not in a lifetime. She released her hold. "That may suffice. For the plane ride."

Kyle grabbed her suitcase and gave her another heated kiss inside the terminal. He waved a final goodbye. "I'll miss you. Beyond a reasonable doubt, counselor."

The delicious goodbye moments occupied her attention while she settled into her airplane seat. She'd be returning in a few days to Kyle and a real job. Her eyes drifted shut.

An announcement to prepare for landing jolted her awake. A low bank of gray clouds covered the Emerald City's skyline—the city she no longer missed.

Iris waited at the top of the stairs near the exit to the terminal. "Hi honey. Did you give my guy a hug for me?"

"You bet. I'm sending his hug back to you." She squeezed Iris. "What's the matter, you're tense."

"Grace called. Corey's either developed asthma or something worse."

"Is there anything we can do?"

"Not now. She's scheduled for a battery of tests."

"Poor Corey. Seems awfully drastic for a little kid with a cough."

"I agree. On a positive note, we're invited to join Shirley and Ike for Thanksgiving dinner." Iris looped her hand in Corrin's free arm. "Let's get cracking."

Time dragged while helping Iris sort and pack. Everything reminded her of Kyle.

The tape gun squeaked while Corrin rolled it across another box. "This thing sounds like my spine feels. Are we there yet, are we there yet?"

Iris stood in the hallway with a thick coat draped on her arm. She laughed. "Close, honey. This move hinges on Corey's diagnosis. Regardless, I should get my wool jacket cleaned, if you think blue still works for me."

"Warm's the necessary color in Montana. You'll be fabulous in any shade."

"Thanks honey." The landline rang and Iris picked up the receiver. "Sure, she's here now." She passed it to Corrin. "It's Elon."

Corrin listened to Elon's disheartening story and replaced the handset. "I may have to curtail any further matches of employers and candidates. The last attempt bombed."

"I thought Elon got the job welding and cooking for that tall drink of rugged cowboy we met at Miranda's wedding."

"Yes, Grant's cousin, Rane. Fit only for heifers, if you want my opinion. Elon moved onto his ranch, and all was well for a month or so. Then the cow pie fell. She's crammed in the Seattle condo with her boys again, so we've got to get her divorce paperwork finalized. Can I meet with her here tomorrow?"

"Anything to help Elon. She and her folks were kind when I lost Charlie."

Corrin headed to the guest room. "I need to return to Seattle-style legal mode. I haven't missed it a bit."

The following afternoon, she sat in the alcove lobby of the opposition's law office. The lawyer who represented Elon's estranged husband had readily accommodated a meeting to coincide with Corrin's short trip to Seattle. In lawyer-speak that meant the case favored his client.

Opposing counsel and Elon's ex learned differently in their forty-five minute meeting. Corrin inwardly cheered when the session concluded. She left the building, entered the condominium, and found Iris seated at the dining room table, her face taut.

"Bad news concerning Corey?"

"Thankfully, no. Roy called while you were gone." Her eyes sparked with anger. "He recounted what that horrible Piersall man did to you."

"Roy told you?" Corrin stammered.

"The fact you were unexpectedly meeting a lawyer in downtown Seattle worried him. He wants to be certain you're safe. Why didn't you confide in me?" Hurt rimmed her eyes.

"I'd made a secrecy promise with the other fourteen-year-old girl." Corrin cleared her throat. "And yes, today I managed a successful mediation against the lawyer representing Elon's husband."

"I'm happy for both you and Elon." She shook her head. "I can't believe you've shouldered such a terrible experience by yourself all these years."

Corrin clasped Iris's trembling fingers. "After long discussions, Kyle and I concluded that I retained unfounded guilt. My girlfriend and I were young and naive, and a little stupid. I'm sorry I didn't talk to you. You must realize I consider you my second mom."

"Oh honey. I wish I could've helped."

"Your wisdom always guides me." She kissed Iris on the cheek.

"I'm always willing. Roy said you handled the hearing in Emma Springs with class. Within your petite frame resides the soul strength of a Herculean warrior."

"You planted self-worth in my brain during the second grade when kids started picking on my ragged clothes. I've recalled your affirmations more times than you'll ever know."

Corrin dropped her eyes to the hand holding hers in a firm grip. Regardless of wrinkles, it would always steady her. "For once, picturing Piersall or the boat incident doesn't make me queasy."

Iris smiled. "Kyle?"

"Kyle, Roy, and the community. And of course, you." Corrin patted her hand. "You'll soon experience the welcoming aspects of Emma Springs."

Thanksgiving the next day, without Miranda, began awkwardly. It switched to progressing smoothly as soon as they started talking about the lovely wedding.

Ike carved a slice of white meat from the golden bird. "Miranda tells me you're fighting developers potentially carrying a hidden agenda. I can offer generic advice."

Ike's judicial intelligence and integrity were legendary in Seattle. "Please do."

"Outline your defense and systematically brainstorm any rebuttals for each point in your defense, no matter how insignificant. If something unusual pops into your brain, jump on it. Often, we ignore subconscious hints, and they usually hit you when you least expect it. Stow a notepad by your bed."

"I'll share your tip with Miranda, even if Grant might object." Corrin blushed, and the group chuckled.

Conversation continued about the wedding reception and the beauty of Montana until the group quieted for a moment.

"I'd bet it's time for coffee and something sweet," Shirley announced, then presented three choices for dessert.

Corrin ate her last bite of pecan pie. She folded her napkin. "Thank you for the delicious dinner. Unfortunately, I've got work to do before I fly back to Emma Springs." She gave Shirley a warm hug. "That's from Miranda. Thank you again."

On the drive home with Ike, the same black SUV she'd seen parked across the street during dinner followed them.

Another holiday diner headed in the same direction, or one of H.P.'s thugs?

CHAPTER 16

The flight attendant ushered a last-minute passenger onto the Montana-bound flight.

Corrin tilted her head up, then her shoulders relaxed.

A gray-haired granny excused herself and slid into a seat a couple rows up. The plane took off for an uneventful flight, finally landing in the familiar pastoral terrain.

Corrin shouldered her bag, bounded down the airstairs in sturdy boots, and ran into Kyle's open arms. She tilted her head and his brief-but-intimate kiss soothed her needy soul.

Miranda grinned from beside them. "Welcome home, roomie-turned-neighbor."

"Greeted by two of my all-time favorite people." She released her arms and gave Miranda the news from Seattle while Kyle collected her luggage.

"How's your niece?" Kyle asked when he returned.

"She's on a new medicine. Everyone's hopeful."

"Great." Kyle opened her door and leaned close to her ear. "Dad's worried you're upset with him for discussing the boat trauma with Iris."

"Concern motivated him to warn her." Corrin buckled her seatbelt. "Miranda, there's an incident from my past I need to divulge."

Miranda sat quietly in the back seat while Corrin described the boat attack.

Kyle drove in silence, his free hand holding hers.

"We're truly phoenix birds rising from the ashes." Miranda leaned forward and squeezed her shoulder. "I knew something bothered you. I also know about turning within."

Corrin relaxed into the seat. Another burden lifted. "One of the reasons we're bonded."

"First stop, the Morley home." Kyle turned into the drive. They waved goodbye to Miranda and drove into town. Corrin sat up. "I love Iris, but I missed my cottage."

"Any thoughts of the resident pining away next door?" Kyle jested and parked the car in her drive.

"More than I care to admit."

He set her suitcases inside. "Sorry, I must run. It's not often I rotate into shifts at the hospital to cover a convalescing doctor."

"I understand. I'll get unpacked, and we can have a late dinner, if you're available?"

He drew her into his arms and pressed his lips onto hers, satisfying her need for a physical connection she wouldn't fight ever again. Her mouth and lips moved into a luscious level of exploration. He pulled back, and whispered, "I took a solemn oath to heal people, never imagining I'd find a woman who'd make me question each step I took away from her in moments like this. Please don't ever forget that." He ran his finger down her neck, then gave her one helluva sexy smile.

"Trust me, I won't." Her body tingled to her toes. She closed the door behind him and leaned against it.

The midday sun brightened her kitchen, while peaceful silence enveloped her.

A bird circled the lake and flew into view. It attempted to land near the cavity midway up the silvery tree, jutting out of dead cattails and reeds precisely where Roy had indicated. She grabbed the binoculars he'd provided.

The duck's webbed feet skidded across the branch on his first attempt to land on a limb.

Judge Gilson's comment pinged in her brain. She grabbed her laptop and scrolled through photos of waterfowl.

Birdwatching rated highly with many locals, albeit well below bovine and equine discussions at community events.

Her eyes landed on a wood duck's habitat, and then she looked at cattails on the uphill side of Sunrise Lake. Her blessed ducks had chosen habitat created by a mountain spring flowing into a lake, which discharged into another creek downstream.

Every environmental attorney knew that the Clean Water Act of 1972 protected connecting waters. She threw on her jacket and ran outside, capturing shots of the duck, the trickling mountain stream, and the outflow creek on the other side of Kyle's house. She put the photos on a flash drive and walked the two blocks into town. Roy preferred hard copies, and McPherson's had the newest color copier.

Her pace increased while she headed home with the stack of photos documenting an irrefutable reason to safeguard the lake.

Fresh tire tracks dented snow in Roy's driveway. Right, he wouldn't be home, he'd be attending his Lions Club holiday meeting.

Corrin pulled out her keys and entered the empty house. She grabbed a pen from her pocket.

Across the bottom of the best shot, she wrote, 'Here's our golden goose!' and then slid the photo under the door of his office.

Kyle would be at the hospital, but Miranda should be home. Her fingers danced on her phone. "Hey, Mrs. Grant Morley. I have great news, and I want to celebrate by taking you to lunch." With the details settled, she pocketed her cell, set the alarm, and dead bolted Roy's front door.

A car slid around the corner and braked in Roy's driveway.

An annoyingly familiar and tiny car.

Betsy planted her high-heeled boots on snow-dusted cement, then slid her butt off the seat, aided by tight leather pants. "Well, well, if it isn't Ms. Still-not-a-lawyer.

Corrin curved her lips into a placating smile for their best-paying client. "Roy's gone. May I help you?"

"I've got an appointment in five minutes. I guess I can sit in my car until the senior Mr. Werner shuffles home."

Corrin fought the urge to trip her and instead waved. "Okay." She buttoned her wool coat and strolled to the Springs Café.

Miranda sat at a corner booth with her fingers tented against her tummy. "Grant's students created this inlaid table." She brushed the wood pattern and met Corrin's eyes. "Something's given you a reason to smile today. Kyle?"

"Him, and my feathery neighbors." Corrin slid her the second set of photos, along with the pages she'd copied from the guidelines defining what qualified as 'Waters of the United States.'

Miranda pulled out a pad and pen. "You're a genius! I'll document it and get it submitted to the hearing examiner." She slid the photo into the center of her legal pad. "I'm ordering their five-vegetable lasagna. Triumph inspires an appetite."

"Eat hearty, we're supposed to get flurries, not that Grant wouldn't shovel to the end of the planet for your rescue," Corrin said.

She pictured Kyle doing the same.

~ ~ ~

In a few days, layers of snow had blanketed Emma Springs under a thick crystal coverlet. Corrin gazed out her kitchen window at a squirrel with a reddish tail bounding through the snow, then scampering up the Douglas fir in Kyle's yard.

She'd describe the antics after he returned from his sleigh ride with Roy to attend the annual tree decorating. By now they'd have left the outskirts of town, where a collection of antique sleighs and huge draft horses transported residents from the fairgrounds to the huge ponderosa pine growing in front of the fire station. The flyer in Corrin's hand stated the timeline.

Nothing short of a dire emergency kept a family from participating. Or, in her case, a lingering and annoying aversion to draft horses.

She stared at the photo of the massive animal pulling one of the sleds filled with smiling townsfolk, most of whom she knew by name. Maybe next year she'd be able to face the gigantic beasts and add ornaments to the tree.

All things in good time. The fewer unnerving events she attended, the better. In a few days, they'd make their next appearance in front of the examiner. The stream running in, and out of, the lake would be crucial. She turned to look at the lake.

"Bloody hell!"

Two men wearing hip waders traipsed across Kyle's lawn. One of them brandished a chain saw. They cut through her yard and angled toward the dead tree where her ducks nested.

No! Her jaw clenched while she thrust her arms in her parka and pulled on boots.

Her pepper spray sat on the counter next to her cell. In one swipe, she grabbed both. She left through the front door, rounded the corner of the cabin, and focused her phone.

One of the men stood closer to shore. He adjusted the open mouth of his ski mask, extracted a cigarette from a blue package, and dropped the crumpled wrapper into the weeds. She recorded him while her palms grew sweaty.

The other man raised the chainsaw and waded out to the twenty-foot-tall snag.

A duck flew overhead, quacking.

"Stop!" she yelled. "You're trespassing. Leave! Right now!"

The man nearest her swiveled his shoulders and lifted his foot from mucky water. He grinned, showing a missing tooth through his mask's mouth hole. "You going to hit me with your cell phone?"

Corrin raised the pepper spray and dashed forward.

"Grab her phone, stupid." The man with the chainsaw waved the jagged blade at her.

Toothless pitched his cigarette and charged Corrin.

She stretched out her arm and directed spray into his face.

"My eyes! Shit! They're burning up!" He stumbled to shore while splashing water under his knitted mask.

The other one yanked the saw's cord. "You little—"

The engine roared. He ran at Corrin, jabbing the whirling blade.

She pointed the canister, praying it still had another blast of liquid fire.

He revved the motor and lunged. "Give me your phone!"

The stream nailed him, and the saw dropped. He rubbed his eyes through the slit. "You'll pay, you little—"

Her fingers shook while she punched numbers into her cell and backed up.

"911, What's your emergency?"

"A man with a chainsaw is threatening me."

"Get to a safe location," the operator said. "I'll dispatch an officer."

"Grab the saw." The bigger one splashed water in his eyes, then headed at her. "We're not done with you."

Corrin turned to flee and stumbled. She fell, her hip striking cold ground. "Don't come any closer, I'll fire again!"

The big guy's waders sucked mud with each lumbering step toward her. "Not when I'm done with you!"

A high-pitched whinny pierced the air. The little horse came tearing around her cottage, a leash flapping behind her.

"What the hell's that?" the bigger thug yelled.

The horse beelined to Corrin and bared her teeth at the men. The little filly made a roar-like warning sound loud enough that the men stopped.

Corrin pushed off the ground and grabbed the leash. "Carrots in the cottage." The horse dragged her toward the door.

A siren wailed in the distance, its piercing shriek louder by the second.

"Cops. We gotta get outta here. Run!" the smoker yelled.

The men splashed along the water's edge in the direction they'd come from.

She videoed them, her feet frozen in place.

"Corrin! Corrin! Where are you?" Kyle ran from the side of her cottage. "Are you okay?"

"I think so." Corrin didn't recognize her own shaky voice.

"What happened?" He drew her to his chest.

"I confronted two masked creeps and hit their eyes with pepper spray." She sank against him. "That slowed them down, but the little horse scared them off."

"Come on." He propelled her to the back door of the cottage, shoved a key in the lock, and pushed her in. "We need to get you warm, your hands are icy." The filly followed them in.

Sirens blasted from her driveway, then quit.

"They planned to chop the snag holding the duck's nest," she panted. "Who alerted you?"

"Bobby had the mini horse at the tree lighting. She broke free and dashed this way. I took off to grab her and heard a chainsaw and then sirens."

"Ms. Patten?" An officer stepped in the doorway. "I'm Sheriff Riley. Are you injured?"

"No, just scared."

"My partner went after a motorcycle speeding out of town with two riders and what appeared to be a chainsaw strapped to the back. Can you describe the men who threatened you?"

"They wore masks. One's about six feet tall, and the other's a few inches shorter. He dropped a blue wrapper and tossed a cigarette he'd smoked."

Roy jogged inside. "I'll make certain those items are retrieved for evidence." He took the can of pepper spray from her hand and set it on the counter.

The young deputy pulled out a radio. "They must've been parked behind the café."

"They had on tan camouflage jackets and waders," Corrin said.

More people entered her tiny home. "One's missing—" She stopped, recognizing Council President Underson and her realtor husband.

"Someone trying to cut a Christmas tree without permission?" Mrs. Underson joked, her hands planted on her wide hips.

Kyle's jaw tightened. "How'd you—"

Corrin squeezed his arm. "Might be what happened," she replied.

"Did you recognize them?" Mrs. Underson asked.

The officer clipped his radio onto his belt. "I'll ask further questions, ma'am. Everything's under control." He moved to Corrin's side.

The woman kept watching them.

Geeze, did she need an eviction notice to remove the Undersons? Corrin stepped forward. "Roy, please show the Undersons out."

She'd never let those two hear details. Her snake radar had hissed to high slither.

~ ~ ~

"Thank you for sleeping on the couch last night, Kyle. Experiencing you as my champion is worth taking on a chainsaw." Corrin handed him a freshly brewed cup of coffee.

"Townsfolk believe you're their champion, and I sense so, so much more." His sexy, mellow voice caressed her. He kissed her cheek, pulled her to his side, and faced the lake.

She released a contented sigh. "Mt. Hanlen is striking in the morning, especially standing beside you."

Kyle's tender smile went straight to her heart. "Words I've longed to hear." He nibbled her lips, then pulled back, and yanked his phone from its holder. "It's a text from Dad, and he's waiting for you. I'll lock your cabin."

"Thank you again. For everything. Piersall's behind all this. Time to move him out front to the spotlight." She put on her coat and crossed the street, her lips tingling from his kiss.

Roy met her at the front door, worry lines creasing his brow. "You were brilliant to realize the Clean Water Act of 1972 protects our local connecting waters, which adds to their crime of attempting to poison the lake. Finding out that The Wetlands Conservation act protects the wood duck habitat added another reason for the judge to decide in our favor. Piersall discovered we knew about these laws because of my mistake with Betsy."

Her throat went dry. "How?"

"I turned off the alarm and directed Betsy to my office. She wore a cat-that-downed-the canary face when I picked the photos off the floor. Had her phone in her hand."

"I'd say she's a cougar that downed a duck. Bloody hell." Corrin stepped inside. "I should've handed them to you directly. I wondered how the chainsaw dudes were alerted. I'm sorry, Roy."

"It's my fault." He shook his head. "The good news is that the hearing examiner should allow your waterway findings into the record."

"If Piersall's lawyers understand the ski resort won't happen, why isn't he packed up and gone?"

Ripples from the breeze disturbed the glassy lake.

"Many developers have the 'cut the tree and pay the fine' mentality, which would've happened if they'd been successful eliminating where the wood ducks live," Roy said. "It's not like he can build anything first, so that mentality doesn't apply."

Corrin bit her lip. "This should be a closed case." What Piersall planned next hung over her like the dangling blade of a guillotine.

~ ~ ~

The pad in Corrin's hand bent from her grip. The room quieted while the examiner entered and took his seat.

He opened a file. "Documents provided indicate any development of this parcel will need to be in compliance with the Clean Water Act. The Hanlen County Sheriff's Office alerted me of an attempt to poison the lake and destroy wetland habitat." He looked fixedly over half-specs at the front row, where Fernley, Piersall, and a lawyer sat.

Piersall stretched his arm across the back of his bench seat. His pointer finger tapped the wood. His sardonic return stare didn't faze the examiner. A tic pulled tan skin at the outside corner of the creep's eye.

Unfortunately, Piersall's facial tells weren't admissible, Corrin thought and leaned closer to Kyle.

"I'm imposing a hold on all zoning until the appropriate departments make determinations," the examiner continued.

Angry red colored Piersall's cheeks.

"I have to leave," Kyle whispered in a clipped voice. "Grant has an emergency. Can you get Miranda home?"

Corrin's body went on hyper-alert. "Sure."

Grant stood, turned, and scowled at Piersall.

Kyle bumped his friend's arm, and they jogged out.

The examiner shuffled his papers. "I will personally recommend the prosecution of any individuals tampering with the stream or Sunrise Lake or threatening a resident of Emma Springs. Is that clear to the courtroom?" His gaze traveled to Fernley, their lawyers, and back to Piersall. "This concludes the hearing until further notice." The examiner lifted the thick files and left the room.

Miranda slid over and wrote, *Fire at our shop. No one was hurt.* She turned and glared at Piersall. "He smirked at me," she said. "He knew damn well why Grant and Kyle left."

"He's pure evil." Corrin grabbed Miranda's stuffed satchel, and the two women dashed to her car. She accelerated on an open highway. "Your name is on all the documents we gave to the hearing examiner. They're trying a different tactic."

"Well, if they think they can scare me into not fighting them, they're wrong." Miranda touched her belly. "How far do you think they'll go?"

"I hate to say. You know my horror story. I firmly believe that Piersall is a psychopath."

~ ~ ~

Kyle braced his feet on the floorboards while Grant's truck flew into his drive. "Easy Grant," he said. "Get back to bureau mode, and we'll nail the gutless bastard legally."

"Easy? I'm ready to even the score!" Grant shouted. "Dad was working on a project we needed to ship tomorrow, or my house might've burned."

The Suburban jolted to a stop by a fire engine.

"Your house appears untouched." Kyle jumped out and walked to the shop where Tom stood by the fire inspector. Both faced a scorched wall.

"Go give this to Big Red, son." Tom wiggled a carrot at Grant. "Miranda's mule smelled smoke and must've jumped the fence to warn me, or I'd be burnt toast. I wanted another coat of varnish on the rush order before I joined you. Can't hear anything in the back room with the fan going."

Grant's face paled. "You'd have been trapped by a fire in the main shop," he growled in a low, feral tone.

"If your mother isn't privy to those details, I'd be appreciative," Tom said. "She took Poppy for blood tests in Three Falls."

Charred boards were tipped against a four-foot blackened and wet section of the shop.

Kyle watched the Firebird jet into the driveway. "Corrin's safety worries me."

"How do you think I feel with a pregnant wife?" Grant kicked a rock, shooting it thirty feet.

"Deep breaths, bro. Don't want to alarm her," Kyle said, and walked to their car. "Everyone's okay."

Corrin put her hand into Kyle's. "Was Tom threatened?"

"Could've been trapped inside. Big Red to the rescue," Kyle whispered.

Grant jogged to Miranda and pulled her to his side. "Your miracle mule stood outside and brayed until Dad left the building."

Miranda's hand shook when she took the carrot from Grant. "So much worse than we thought. I'll give him the treat. The fumes are making me queasy."

"What'd they use for accelerant?" Corrin's eyes scanned the charred pile.

"Probably my gas," Grant said, and pointed to a red can. "That belongs in the barn by the tractor."

"There's more evidence." Kyle pointed to a cigarette butt on the ground. "You have zero tolerance for smoking on your property."

"Correct," Grant snapped.

Corrin bent forward. "The blue stripe above the filter on that cigarette matches the one the chainsaw thugs left in the weeds."

"I'll bag it for processing." The fire lieutenant retrieved the butt. "We haven't had an arson here in the twenty-five years I've volunteered."

"The sheriff sent the cigarette from the cottage property to their lab," Kyle said. "They can compare the DNA." An icy lump formed in Kyle's stomach. When his phone vibrated, he flinched.

"Is everything okay?" Corrin asked.

"Yes. Dad's got a pot full of chicken soup and asked you all to dinner."

By the scowl on Grant's face, they'd need more than food to satisfy his urge to find the thugs and end things, once and for all.

He'd put his medical career on the line to assist.

~ ~ ~

Strained described their dinner with the Morleys. Kyle watched Grant's Suburban leave, then returned to the kitchen.

Roy slammed the handset of the phone on its base. "We can't enjoy an evening without Underson from Dagger Reality pleading again. He's badgering me to contact Stan Johnson. Someone told him I knew his whereabouts."

"Point the realtor uphill and hope the grizzlies are out of berries." Kyle noted the deep red coloring on his dad's face. He wasn't the only one running out of patience with the law.

"Piersall doesn't think the fight's over." Corrin wrung the dishcloth in her hands. "Why didn't I connect them before? Dagger Realty's name is a throwback to Piersall's ring."

Kyle swallowed, remembering the ruby hilted sword on the ring. "You're right. Underson hasn't worked in real estate for years. Piersall must've hired him." He dried the last platter.

"Your mountain friend may be in danger." Corrin's voice quavered. "How'd Stan know to arrive in time for Grant and Miranda's wedding?"

Roy removed a container of antacids from the cabinet next to the sink. "Tom Morley knows how to get in touch with Stan in case of an emergency. I'll make the call."

An ache centered at the back of Kyle's neck. "Grant will be furious. Did you speak to the council members who aren't driving new vehicles?"

"Yes. They were approached by phone." Roy shook out a handful of colorful tablets and balanced them in his palm. "Nothing traceable. A man verbally suggested that if they changed the zoning on several pieces of property, they'd be rewarded." He flipped the tablets into his mouth and chewed.

"Title 18 of the U.S. Government Code outlines bribing a government official," Corrin said. "I'll investigate the consequences tomorrow, and then I'll contact the car dealers." The set of her jaw indicated she'd be at work come dawn.

Kyle took three of the antacids from the jug. At least one of them had faith in the law.

~ ~ ~

Corrin leaned back in her perfectly sized office chair and sipped her tea. Nothing quelled the anxiety churning in her belly after yesterday's fire incident—not Kyle couch surfing again last night, not Roy's hovering until he'd left for a lunch meeting.

Piersall fought dirty, and no one knew to what extent.

Roy's frequent four-legged equine guest nudged her ankle. "Thank you again for coming to my aid, little horsey. I hope your permanent home will be nearby, and you get a name soon." She scratched behind the filly's ear.

Her cell trilled out Kyle's tone. She tapped the screen. "What can I do for you, doctor?"

"I need you to fill in where my GPS lags. There's a map in the desk in my bedroom. I'm on a house call—Montana-style. A father and son managed to climb a condemned fire tower by Prairie Ridge and got in trouble."

She rocked forward, tipping the chair. "Trouble in a tower? I thought you didn't do heights. Shouldn't that be the fire department?"

"The father's exhibiting vascular stress symptoms, and he may need to be medevacked. I'll manage. We need to keep the fire team in town."

"Right. I washed my hair twice to remove the burnt shop smell. Be careful. I have a new road map. Will that work?"

"Nope. Left desk drawer. Under a pile of maps will be a dog-eared hiking guide. Please call me when you locate it."

"Glad you gave me a house key. Do you need me to transport medical supplies?"

"I have my bag, and anyway, you'd need four-wheel drive. Snow has melted, so I'm hoping I can stabilize the patient and drive him out."

"I'll find it and call." She clipped the leash on the little horse and dashed across the street. "Stay put." She tied her to the doorknob and tiptoed into Kyle's bedroom. A rustic log bed stood out against terra cotta-colored walls.

A sheaf of blueprints sat on the desk. The heading identified them as plans for a four-bed community wellness clinic.

Someday he'd confide his plans. Maybe, after the frickin' tower rescue. She jerked open the drawer and dug to the bottom of the maps. Faster, urged an inner voice.

She opened *The Hiking Guide of Hanlen County* and punched in his number. Voicemail. Her finger trailed over the ragged map and stopped on Prairie Ridge while she hit redial. No answer. Her throat went bone dry.

Kyle's square, block printing delineated several homes on the map, one of them Grant's. He'd tell her what to do.

"Hey Miranda, is Bureau Boy home?" Corrin asked.

"Nope, he and the folks took Poppy to Three Falls to hit the medical supply store. You quit using that reference to Grant. What's up? Piersall?"

"Nope. Some hiker needed help, and Kyle needs me to confirm directions on a map. I can't reach him by phone." She locked the clinic, unhooked the mini horse, and jogged them to her car. The filly scrambled to get in behind the folded down seat and perched on the back seat. "Sorry, had to get settled in the car. I've sprouted goose bumps." Her voice caught in her throat.

"Okay, don't panic yet, cell reception sucks out here."

"The map shows the location's close to your house. Maybe we can see if he needs help?" Corrin asked.

"Absolutely. I'll tell Grant we might be gone when he gets home."

Corrin's finger wobbled while she put the key in her car's ignition. The closer she drove to Miranda's, the tighter she clutched the steering wheel. She pulled to the shoulder and called Kyle again. No luck. Gravel flew when she sped off.

Miranda stood on her front porch, then peered into the car. "You brought a mini mount?"

"Nope. Roy pet sits her on occasion. And for now, she fits in my car. I think the foster parents worry she'll escape while they aren't home if they leave her in their back yard alone again." She dropped the seat for the filly to jump out. "Kyle told me Prairie Ridge, and it's in that direction." She pointed toward a hill at the edge of their pasture and then spread the map on the hood. "See, there's a road leading to it from your property."

Miranda shook her head. "No road, it's a deer trail. No car can plow through the layer of muck from the thaw." She rubbed her palms on her jeans. "I can go by horseback."

"While pregnant?"

"It's not far, and Kyle said I can do easy rides for another few weeks."

"Nope. I won't let you go alone, not ever again." Corrin tightened her fist. "If you've got two horses, put me on the quietest one."

Miranda pulled her into a hug. "Big Red's given rides to a toddler. I'll use Brasso." She pointed at Corrin's flat-soled boots. "You are acclimating. Give me a minute to collect gear and we'll go."

She'd need to collect a bushel of nerve to ride atop the huge mule. A tremor rolled through her body.

A wet muzzle bumped her fisted hand. "Kyle needs our help," she said to the black pony. "You can trot with the herd if you promise to stick close."

The filly blinked chocolate brown eyes and then nudged Corrin's leg.

"Alright, already."

Miranda pulled their front door shut, a rifle balanced over her shoulder.

"You're packing an antique gun?"

"Not any gun, an Annie Oakley Commemorative Winchester. Grant's been giving me lessons. All part of living in Montana."

"Oh-kay."

"You're on edge, and I'm doing what my husband requested if I ride alone." Miranda led her into the barn. "Technically, more of an Agent Morley-at-arms mandate after the fire."

"There's no better friend than you." Corrin squeezed Miranda's forearm.

"Ditto. So you know, Grant calls me Deadeye." Miranda smiled. "Ten minutes, and we'll be ready. Grant bought me a longer stirrup for easier mounting. I'll put it on your saddle."

"Deal. I'll phone Kyle again. Don't you dare lift a heavy saddle." Her finger shook on the phone screen. "Voicemail."

"You can do the lifting. It's a pleasant ride to Prairie Ridge. Will your mini follow along?"

"The little filly isn't mine, but she gave her pony promise." Corrin followed Miranda into a stall and extended her finger toward the nose of Big Red.

He stretched his neck and nuzzled her cheek.

Her hand trembled while she reached out to pet the mule's velvety nose. She'd do this for Kyle. A really, really bad feeling told her she must.

~ ~ ~

Kyle parked in front of the abandoned fire tower. His eyes traveled up the rickety ladder. Aimed to the sky, the skeleton frame of sixty-five or seventy feet of weathered two-by-fours clung together by rusty screws and luck. Guide wires kept it perched on the edge of the cliff.

Flags printed with *DANGER* and *KEEP OUT* fluttered on a line which zigzagged from near the top to the ground. A huge 'Do Not Enter' sign blocked the ladder—if you weren't an idiot.

"Someone should've demolished it," he muttered, while lifting his foot over a rusted cable stretched to a rotted wooden post. His eyes followed a narrow pair of tire tracks in the slush, leading into a grove of trees. Hadn't the guy said they'd hiked in?

He put his hand to his brow to block the sun. "How's your father?" he called.

"You finally made it." A man's voice shouted from the upper platform. "His color's turned gray."

"Don't move him." Kyle's feet tingled while he panned the deathly drop onto a rocky hillside. "I'll load my backpack and climb to you."

"Glad you showed up in time."

Gray indicated insufficient oxygen. His stomach tightened while he loaded supplies into his backpack. He took a deep breath and hoisted himself over the sign.

The moment of truth after months of fighting his fear of heights. He focused his eyes on each successive ladder wrung and climbed. Minutes counted in heart failure.

His shirt stuck to his back by the time he'd reached the wobbly platform, enclosed by a half wall and sloped roof.

He grabbed onto an inside post and steadied himself.

A man wearing a ski mask stood up.

"What's going on?" Kyle demanded.

"Put your hands slowly in the air, doc." He waved a gun.

Kyle raised his arms.

The thug smiled, showing the missing incisor and cuspid on his upper row of teeth. "Glad you joined us. Hand me your backpack. Real easy, now."

It had to be the same chainsaw-wielding, toothless bastard from Corrin's lawn. Kyle's pulse quickened.

"I need your phone." The dude reached out a grubby hand, yanked Kyle's phone from its clip, and threw it over the wall.

The sound of glass shattering on rock pierced the air.

"Don't want no unexpected visitors, now do we?" Toothless snarled. "You stay tight, until we say." He backed away, shoved the gun in his belt, and pulled out a mallet. He stepped onto the ladder. "You move, I shoot."

"I die, you'll fry!" Kyle shouted.

"Don't move, poet." His head disappeared from sight.

The sound of cracking wood echoed through the quiet valley.

"What the hell!" Kyle yelled over the wall. "Killers are hunted in Montana."

"Don't plan to kill ya." The jerk smashed each wrung above him while he clambered down the ladder.

Another man stood at the bottom, holding a pickaxe. He wobbled a post and raised the axe. "Fire up the bike."

Kyle grabbed a post. Without support wires, the structure would topple into the canyon.

The framework lurched, and pitched Kyle to his knees on the slanted floor. Metal hit wood with a resounding thump.

He hung on, saying a prayer.

~ ~ ~

Riding a mule. Kyle wouldn't believe it. Corrin straightened in the saddle and inhaled crisp, pine-scented air. "If the map's accurate, Prairie Ridge should be visible once we climb this hill," she said.

"Yup." Miranda trotted up the next rise while the little horse followed at her side. "I see the tower."

"Let's go, Red."

The mule lumbered up the last few feet and walked to where Brasso stood, in the shade of a huge boulder and a stand of pine trees.

Corrin squinted. "Someone's climbing down."

"What's that banging noise?" Miranda dismounted. She pulled the long Winchester out of the saddle holster.

"Bloody hell!" Corrin screeched. "He's smashing the ladder, and I can see that Kyle's still above him! The guy walking away has a gun!" She looked closer. "Ohmygod! I think it's the chainsaw creeps!"

"Shh." Miranda put the gun barrel to her cheek.

An engine roared to life, and a guy on a motorcycle appeared. "Knock it down and hop on," he yelled.

Panic flooded Corrin's chest. "Shoot them."

Miranda lowered the gun. "I need to get within a hundred feet for a good shot."

"What can I do?"

"Dismount and hold the horses behind the boulder," Miranda ordered. "If they bolt, let them run."

Corrin jumped off, grabbed a set of reins in each hand, and moved the horses. She peered around the rock and gasped.

Axe man swung at the post.

The little horse raised his head, took off, and whinnied. The motorcycle driver pointed at the horse and both men stopped.

Miranda jogged closer and fitted the butt of the gun into her shoulder.

The crack from the gunshot reverberated across the gap. Red and Brasso jerked their heads and then stilled.

Axe man screamed and clutched his knee. The guy on the bike pulled a gun out and waved it at Kyle, who clung to the outside of the swinging structure.

Miranda fired again.

The gunman's yell pierced the air. His motorcycle crashed into the other short post. The support wire snapped.

"The tower's going!" Corrin shouted. She leapt onto Red and squeezed her legs into his belly. "Run, Red!"

The structure swayed, held by one line.

She aimed Red for the rope tied to the base. "Grab the flag rope, Kyle! I'll use it to pull you in." She'd reached the tower. "By your left ankle!" Corrin slid off, untied the bottom of the line from a wooden beam, and tied it to her saddle horn.

The tower tilted to the right, angled over the cliff. Wood creaked. The rope went slack.

Corrin spun around, "Kyle!" Had he found it?

The thug walked toward Corrin and bent to pick up his gun. "If it isn't the lake bitch."

Miranda trotted in on horseback, swung her rifle, and knocked the gun from the big thug. "Either of you flinch, and I'll shoot!" She waved the barrel between the two injured men.

The post holding the last, groaning guide wire buckled under the strain, and tipped over the canyon, chunks of its cement base erupting from the ground.

"No!" Corrin screamed.

Kyle scrambled over swaying boards toward them, resembling a man atop a moving train. The structure shook, sending debris crashing onto rocks below. He got to within twenty feet of the cliff edge.

Wood creaked. The post shot out of the ground. With an ear-splitting roar, the tower dropped out of sight.

CHAPTER 17

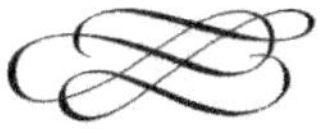

"Kyle, Nooo!" Corrin yelled. Her chest pounded.

Sounds of wood smashing on boulders shattered the air.

Red lurched away from the cliff. The rope stretched tight.

Corrin grabbed the reins, "Good boy," she petted the dancing animal. Was the rope hooked to Kyle or the tower?

"Kyle?"

"Pull me up!" he shouted.

"On it! Are you hurt?" she yelled back.

"No. The rope's fraying."

Corrin tugged the reins. "Move, Red. Please" The mule stepped sideways as a cloud of dust belched up from the edge.

The mini horse ran to Red's shoulder and whinnied. The mule dropped his head and muscled forward. The leather breastplate dug into his chest.

"Walk on, Red," Miranda called.

"A few more steps, big guy, and we've got him," Corrin said, praying for it to be true.

Red lurched. The rope went slack.

"No!" Corrin screamed. She spun around.

Kyle crouched at the edge of the cliff, a big grin on his dirty face. He stood and opened his arms.

Corrin ran to him and buried her face in his chest. "I thought I'd lost you." Tears blinded her as she pulled back to look at him.

"Never." He brushed away a tear and gave her a tender, utterly disarming kiss that went straight to her heart. His fingers glided through her hair and cradled her chin. "You saved me."

"I can't lose you. I love you too much."

He pulled her tight to his chest. "And I love you. Your angel face appeared to me when the tower collapsed."

"You won't think I'm an angel if you ever scare me again." Corrin wiped dirt from his cheek.

"I'll keep that in mind." He kissed her forehead and grabbed her hand. "We've got to help Miranda."

She'd never let Kyle go. Not now, not ever.

He reached under his Jeep and fished out the gun. "Hey! You with the arm wound, move next to your friend."

The guy shuffled sideways.

"Corrin, can you handle a gun?" Kyle asked.

"I can pull a trigger." She took hold of the revolver. "Especially aimed at a gutless murderer."

"Thankfully unsuccessful." Kyle walked to the back of the Jeep. "I'll see what's left in my medical bag. Most of my supplies are at the bottom of the canyon." His voice never wavered.

"I'll find their other gun from behind the cycle." Miranda slid off Brasso.

Kyle tied the axe man's hands behind his back, then opened his black bag and pulled out a long white bandage and applied it to the bloody leg. "Those were pretty impressive shots, Mrs. Morley."

"Thanks to Grant's coaching," boasted Miranda. "Corrin's instincts alerted her that you were in danger."

"Praise be to women who follow their instincts," Kyle said.

Corrin waved the revolver, backing Toothless against the Jeep. "I'll never doubt that little voice again. It was a team effort. The little pony created a diversion, and Big Red pulled you to safety."

Red's ears twitched at the sound of his name, and the mini nickered.

"Team effort." Kyle gave the mule's sweaty neck a scratch. "If you'll let Toothless lower his hands, Corrin, I'll staunch the bleeding with a bandage." He stepped beside her.

"Why should I trust you?" the thug snarled.

Kyle dropped his bag and stepped back. "I can't decide what's more amazing, Miranda shooting or you riding a horse."

"Technically, Red's a miraculous mule." Corrin kept the gun on the creep and reached her hand out to scratch Red. The mini bumped her knee. She dropped her fingers to her furry cheek and gently rubbed. "Both equines earned their oats."

"I'm thinking you're all pretty wonderful at this moment, after what could've been my crash ending."

Toothless waved his good arm. "Okay, okay! Help me before I bleed to death while you two chat."

"Anyone called the sheriff?" Kyle bandaged him.

"There's no cell signal," Corrin said.

"If you two can drive them down, I'll walk the horses home and make the call when I'm in range," Miranda offered.

Corrin faced off with the thugs. "Sure. I'm not afraid to fire this gun." The revolver wavered in her hands.

Kyle cut another piece of rope. "Hold out your hands, you don't want to make her angrier."

Terrified at the close call, her knees threatened to buckle. "These are the gutless wonders who threatened me with the chainsaw, and I'd bet the ones who torched the shop. If they sneeze crooked, they'll be sorry."

"Ms. Patten, care to pilot my Jeep?" Kyle tightened the rope on the guy's wrist. "I'll hold the gun and navigate."

"I'm happy to drive us out of here. Please bring the little horse with us." Corrin released a nervous giggle. "You know you're in Montana when . . . you're asked to chauffeur creeps by Jeep."

"Gads, I hope not." Miranda rubbed her back. "A leg up first please, Doctor?"

"Yes, ma'am." He helped her onto Red, then picked up the little horse and set her in the back of the Jeep. "Miranda, I'm prescribing you call your husband to fix dinner while you relax. Promise me you won't ride again. You're progressing faster than I anticipated."

"Sure thing. I'm picking up that you and Corrin are doing likewise." Miranda winked at Corrin.

Kyle's grin was infectious. "I'd have preferred less drama, but the words I've longed to hear from you about loving me were a result." He kissed Corrin's cheek and removed the gun from her hand.

"Get in the back and sit still." He told the thugs, then climbed in the passenger seat and faced backward, aiming the gun between the seats. "You threatened Corrin twice. I'm going to do everything in my power to see that you're locked up for good."

Corrin smiled. She'd found the right man to love. "Sorry it took so long to tell you what my heart knew." Joy filled Corrin while she navigated the Jeep around rocks on a dirt track. "Aren't prairies smooth? Why's it called Prairie Ridge?"

"Because of the poisonous prairie rattlesnakes, which are thankfully hibernating," Kyle said.

Toothless nudged his buddy. "Told you we wouldn't find one to use on the doc."

The other man kicked him. "Shut up moron, we're going to be charged with attempted murder."

~ ~ ~

Corrin hummed a holiday tune while Kyle raised a glass of sparkling cider. "Finished decorating a week before December 25. A new record."

"You two did a great job with the Christmas tree, dinner's ready, and we can thoroughly relax for Christmas," Roy said.

"On many accounts." Kyle flashed her his melt-an iceberg smile. "The crooks from Prairie Ridge are in jail, and Sam gassed up a black SUV and a gray sedan last week at his station, both with Washington plates. They headed to the highway."

"Miranda's relieved," Corrin said. "She knew if anything happened to her, Grant would be our first case defending a client charged with assault."

"I'd understand his motives." Kyle locked eyes with her, the fierceness in his voice peeling away her final layer of angst.

Roy held out her preferred dining room chair, the one facing the lake. "Grant's installed security cameras in a continuous circle covering his barn, shop, and house. I don't blame him though, the thugs are not willing to testify against their boss and he's got a child on the way."

The word 'child' slammed her. Corey hadn't responded well to the recent round of meds. She forced the last bite of Roy's pot roast. "Delicious as always. Thank you. I need to scoot home and get my bedroom ready for Aunt Iris's visit."

Roy's cheeks warmed to a flattering shade, emphasizing his blue eyes. "I hate to think of you sleeping on a couch, Corrin. Iris can stay here. The cleaning ladies freshened both guest rooms yesterday."

"I can handle a guest," Kyle said with another sexy smile.

He wasn't offering the spare room. Tempting as it felt, she stood and mimicked a curtsy to hide an impending blush. "I do appreciate the offers. Thoughtful gentlemen make a girl's heart dance to a pitty-pat." She fanned her face. "We ladies have much to discuss during our sleepover. Have ice ready when those ears of yours are a burnin'."

"You be ready at nine tomorrow to go fetch your delightful aunt. Afterward, say whatever you want." Roy began to clear the table.

Kyle grinned at her. "Hmm, I'd pay to be a fly on your wall."

He'd be the bright red one if he knew her indecent thoughts featuring him. Or would he?

~ ~ ~

Kyle sat back in his chair, admiring the women joining them for Christmas dinner.

They'd cut fresh holly for the mantle—his mom's tradition. He knew she'd consider Iris a blessing sent to care for her Roy-boy.

"This is the best dinner I've ever had prepared by a father and son team." Iris beamed at Roy. "And I can't believe I'm wearing an engagement ring made from your father's diamond tie tack." She held the sparkling stone to the candlelight.

"I can't believe you said yes." Roy squeezed her hand.

"If I hadn't promised I'd train my replacement, I'd have driven the moving truck over myself," Iris replied.

Kyle could picture either of the petite women in the driver's seat of an eighteen-wheeler. Corrin would be the one blasting a horn at anyone who cut in front of her. The two of them shared the same spunky attitude, same as his mom. "You women are amazing."

"So are you men," Corrin responded with a smile. "The fedora Roy gave me will keep my ears warm until spring. These birthstone teardrops to match my necklace are the most elegant Christmas gift I've ever gotten." She fingered her earlobe, holding one of the aquamarine earrings he'd commissioned from a jeweler in Three Falls.

"I treasure the sketches you did of my clients," Kyle said. "They must've taken you hours."

A horn beeped twice from the driveway.

"That's my signal." Kyle smiled and rose. His pulse quickened. "I've one more present for my special lady."

Corrin flicked her eyes to Iris's ring and went pale. "You'll embarrass me with another gift."

Kyle opened the front door and pulled in a wide, tall box secured by a thick red rope.

"A Christmas surprise," Iris said.

"Not entirely." Kyle set the box in front of Corrin and grabbed his camera. "This present chose her."

Corrin's eyebrows rose. "Chose me?" A distinct neigh sounded from the box.

She yanked off the rope and lifted a flap. "The tiny black filly!"

The horse's nose popped out first, and then she put her hooves on the top edge and let out a delicate wicker.

"She's got a sweet little whinny," Corrin said.

Kyle lifted her out, and she nuzzled Corrin. "She recognized your voice."

"How cute, when she neighs, her muzzle quivers," Iris said. "She's fascinated with you, honey."

"Nose itching?" Corrin scratched her. "She helped rescue Kyle." She leaned over her neck. "You're a brave girl, with a charming little whinny." The horse's head bobbed.

They made the perfect pair. Kyle snapped several photos. "You might want to consider Whinny for her name. She responded to it both times." He stood with his hands in his pockets. "Are you okay with adopting her?"

"I thought she was visiting again." Corrin's eyes widened. "You think I'm responsible enough to care for her?"

Her questioning, shy-girl's innocence melted his heart, ember by flaming ember. He put his hand on her shoulder. "Of course. She escaped multiple times from the Bells and always headed straight to you."

Childlike wonder brightened Corrin's eyes. "I've never had a pet, not even a fish. Too many mouths to feed in our family. I would love to add a furry buddy to my family. I can't wait to tell Willy and Corey about Whinny. If her next medicine works better, maybe they can visit her."

"I'll help with their tickets," Iris said. "Will Whinny get big enough to hold a small child?"

"If they weigh under sixty pounds," Kyle said. "She should reach twenty-eight inches at the withers, which is the tallest point on her back. The bonus is that she can graze on our lawns."

"How'd I raise such a clever boy, Whinny?" Roy petted her head. "Now I know what they mean by the old saying, 'A short horse is soon curried.'"

"Why would anyone relinquish such a treasure?" Corrin asked, while she finger combed Whinny's long, russet tipped mane.

Kyle pointed to the white hair on her shoulders and rump. "The first owners wanted her to pull a heavy cart when she was way too young. They beat her to get her to mind. She can't tolerate loud noise or metal banging. The physical damage remains as scars, so gaining her full trust will take patience. Understandably, she's been tough to rehome until you entered the picture. They've tried a couple of times."

"Oh my God. So little and asked to pull a cart." Corrin stroked Whinny's neck. "Humans can be such monsters."

"That's an awful thing to happen to a pretty pony," Roy said.

"The Bells left a supply of food on the back porch. They'll be delighted she has found a permanent family, as they want to keep fostering rescues. Bobby will walk her any time you ask."

"How perfect," Corrin said. "I'd be worried they'd miss each other."

"Bobby helped house train Whinny as part of their foster program. He slept in their back yard shed with the male pony they fostered first."

"Oh dear. I didn't think about her needing shelter or a barn."

"The McPhersons own the property and little barn next to my clinic. Their pygmy goats have met Whinny, and they get along. Mr. McPherson suggested you keep her there."

Whinny let out a loud nicker, as if in agreement.

Corrin cooed to the horse. "Thanks to Uncle Kyle, you and those dainty hooves will only be a house away from me. Should we shake on the fact that you won't try to escape?"

The horse placed her left front hoof into Corrin's outstretched hand.

An unadorned one. A diamond ring worn by Kyle's mother and grandmother sat in the safe. Kyle rubbed his chin. *Not yet.* A little more patience would cure her skittish reluctance to commit. "Those hooves will need a regular trim."

Corrin nodded. "I bet Ed Bell knows a farrier. He gave me free vet care for life." She lifted the red rope, which had a clasp on the end. "Want to take a walk, Whinny? With Kyle, if he's available."

He stood, smiling. "I'm always available to you."

Corrin's cheeks turned pink. "I'll wear my new fedora." She grabbed the dark blue hat and lifted their coats from the rack.

Kyle petted the horse. "I got her tack." He handed Corrin a body harness and showed her how to make adjustments.

"It's perfect!" She grabbed Kyle's collar and smooched his lips, in a teasing, playful way. "You are the best man ever!"

If his luck held, he'd rate groom someday. "Glad to hear."

Roy turned his back to them. "Come on Iris, let's sit where we can have a view of Whinny on her first neighborhood stroll with her forever family." They moved to the couch opposite the picture window.

"I never thought I'd live to see the day Corrin touched a horse," Iris announced. "You are a magician, Kyle."

"He's more than a magician, he's a woman whisperer." Corrin scratched Whinny's head.

"Only to one woman," Kyle stated as they headed outside with plans for the evening, and if his luck held an endless succession of tomorrows.

~ ~ ~

Corrin pumped her fist in the air. She'd done it, she'd taken Montana's February bar exam. She repeated the statement to herself again. Finished, confident, and returning to Emma Springs in time to create a surprise lunch for Kyle.

The drive flew by. She parked her car in her garage, then ran across the yard and secured Whinny in her harness. They jogged to town.

After grabbing the fixings for sandwiches, she exited Emma's Grocery Store toting a hefty bag. "Hey Whinny, good job on not leaving a horsey deposit to clean up. Let's get cracking." She untied her from the replica hitching post.

The filly nudged her thigh.

"I know, we're off schedule, but we'll get lunch ready in time." Being towed at a fast clip by an exuberant pony had advantages.

In the flick of a long, black horsetail, she'd packed the thick sandwich, chips, and cookies into a picnic hamper.

Wind whipped snow flurries onto her cheeks as she crossed the street. She used her spare key and turned the knob on Kyle's clinic door, hoping to spring a surprise.

His irritated voice stopped her in the doorway.

"I don't want to date you, Betsy!" he shouted. "I'm involved with Corrin, and that's final." He slammed the phone.

Bloody hell! The cougar hadn't given up on her prey. The basket slipped from her hand and thudded onto the floor.

Kyle emerged from behind the desk and pulled her into his arms. "I'm sorry if you didn't want our relationship made public."

"She must be the only resident who doesn't know. Enough about her. We're celebrating! I took the exam."

Kyle lifted her up and spun her around. "And I'll wager you passed!" He set her down, his hands resting on her waist.

Respond, her body demanded. "May I have a celebratory kiss?" She turned her eyes to him, her pulse pounding.

"I thought you'd never ask." His gaze dropped to her mouth. His fingers trailed down her neck, sending delightful spirals deep, deep down.

She wrapped her fingers around his neck and pressed her lips onto his, searching, exploring, and letting go of hesitation. He kissed back, igniting the rippling sensations coursing through her body. The strength of his muscled chest against hers brought wonderful, demanding surges of desire. She longed to explore his unclothed skin and much more. With trembling fingers, she unbuttoned his shirt and slid her palm over his beating heart. Her hand stopped.

He let out a long breath and smoothed a strand of hair away from her temple. "I'm flesh and blood, you ought to be able to feel my heart beating double time." He lifted her palm and brushed his lips against her quivering skin. "If we go further right now, I'll want to break my promise to patiently wait until you're ready."

She nodded, mentally unready for that step. "Can you hold me a little longer? You make me feel cherished, and I need that."

"Of course." He pulled her closer and massaged his fingers down her back. "A snowstorm may hit tonight." He slowly released his hold. "Gas up and be certain you have wood in case the power goes out. I'm on call, and I've got another expectant mom due before Miranda. My bet is she'll go into labor during the blizzard."

"Good distraction, doctor." He'd led their thoughts away from his nearby bedroom. "I should get an extra sack of feed for Whinny. If you have time after lunch, maybe we can go together."

"I can't today, I need to check on Julia. A nasty bug's going around Three Falls. Sorry."

She picked up the heavy basket. "Lunch then. I'm hungry."

"Me, too." He raised an eyebrow, then uncovered the food.

Warm ripples thrummed below her belly. "I brought Springs Root Beer." She held one out to Kyle.

Soon she'd be ready to share more than food.

~ ~ ~

Throughout the afternoon and evening, snowdrifts mounded under Corrin's window ledge. She stared out, watching the flakes land.

Her phone rang, and she jumped. She'd nodded off, dreaming of the kisses she and Kyle had shared at lunchtime.

"Miranda and Grant have a healthy baby girl." Kyle announced into her ear.

"No way! That's wonderful!" Corrin exclaimed. "She's not due for ten days. I was supposed to be there."

"Their little Annie Rose had other plans. Shortest labor I've ever seen with a newborn. Miranda sends her apologies. I barely got there in time."

"I'm thankful you did."

"Me too. There's nothing on earth like cradling a newborn in your arms, looking into their innocent eyes."

A baby to love and cherish. Corrin recalled quiet moments rocking her sisters and brother to sleep in her arms. They'd been trusting babies that needed her. "I can't wait to meet Annie Rose," she said. "Is Miranda okay?"

"She's fine and there's a new baby boy in Emma Springs. The bigger the snowstorm, the more babies. Lucky this time, both were uncomplicated births. We need a basic medical clinic closer than Three Falls. Someday I plan to build one."

Her pulse quickened. "That's a wonderful idea, Kyle."

"Dad and I are considering home equity loans for financing. It would give us a start." He yawned into the phone. "Sorry, I need to head home and grab a nap."

"Safe travels." She stretched, and then walked from the bedroom into her living room.

The fog lifted off the water. Ice shards had melted from the edges of the pond, same as the pool of warmth surrounding her once frozen heart.

Next time Kyle offered marriage, she'd have the right answer.

CHAPTER 18

Corrin blinked at her computer screen. A big grin spread across her face while she read the best email she'd ever received. Her dream, years of studying, Roy's mentoring, and Kyle's encouragement culminated in a single line posted on the State Bar of Montana website.

Kyle had driven to Three Falls, but she wouldn't wait another second to phone him.

"Hi. Got a minute?" she asked.

"For you? Countless hours." His smooth, rich voice held a sexy edge. "You sound happy."

"I passed the bar!"

"Congratulations! Wow! Have you told Dad yet?"

Corrin tucked her hair behind her ear. "I hoped we'd do it together. May I treat you both to dinner at the Springs Cafe tonight at six?"

"Sure. I'll tell Dad. I'm so proud of you, my shirt may bust open."

Corrin grinned. He meant it. "Thank you."

That evening, she pinned the scrimshaw brooch onto her blue angora sweater before walking to town with Kyle.

Roy proposed a toast after hearing her news. "To my new partner. The paperwork will be forthcoming." His smile radiated genuine enthusiasm.

Kyle clinked her glass, his blue eyes bright with pride.

She could list a dozen accolades for each man. "It's a privilege and an honor to work with you, Roy," she said.

Her grilled trout tasted better than any fancy sushi from Seattle. Locally sourced and well-seasoned, it suited her mood perfectly.

Conversation turned to their next hearing. "MFB's proficient at mitigating out wetlands," she said.

"You nailed their coffin with the Clean Water Act." Roy buttered a roll. "I have faith in our system to protect our slice of America's waterways."

"I have faith in Corrin," Kyle stated.

~ ~ ~

Corrin reviewed her bulleted points the morning of the hearing. Their evidence appeared sound, but more than once she'd seen downward spirals after unexpected sources presented in court.

In an hour, she'd be en route to the hearing with Kyle. By noon, they'd learn the future of Sunrise Lake.

She pulled her cherry red power suit from the closet, wishing to absorb every amp it generated.

They arrived to find Miranda seated and fidgeting with her phone in the examiner's chamber. "Grant's folks happily volunteered for baby duty today. And guess what Pat overheard Betsy saying to the butcher yesterday? She's selling her place."

"That's good news." Corrin said. "Maybe Piersall's giving up. Come to think of it, I haven't seen Betsy around lately,"

Fernley and Piersall entered the hearing room. Meyer, Brine, and the new guy flanked them.

Heavy artillery. Corrin gave a cursory nod to Mr. Meyer, who flicked his hand in return.

The hearing examiner entered the room with a three-inch thick file. He gave a brief overview of the case and surveyed the audience. "Upon consideration of the information presented and in accordance with the CWA NPDES Compliance Monitoring Strategy, it is in my jurisdiction to restrict development in the watershed surrounding Sunrise Lake to residential."

A rumble of relief from townspeople traveled through the room.

Expressions remained neutral on the faces of the three men seated in the front, dressed for court in Seattle or a funeral in Emma Springs.

Piersall flashed a sadistic smile at Corrin.

She tensed but met his steely eyes.

"We beat them." Miranda pulled her into a hug, her long arms wrapped around Corrin's stiff shoulders.

A horrible sense told her that they'd only kicked the proverbial hornets nest, and Piersall, the angriest hornet, had his stinger aimed at her. She forced elation and returned Miranda's hug. "Yes."

Kyle stood in front of her, arms extended. "I never doubted you two. Good job." He pulled her to her feet and kissed her. "I can see there's a problem. Tell me later," he whispered.

Roy patted Corrin's back and then Miranda's. "I knew we'd prevail."

"Excuse me for interrupting the celebration." Philip Meyer cleared his throat, his precursor to all MFB meetings. "Ms. Patten, might I have a private word with you?" The rest of his entourage had slithered out after the verdict.

"I guess," Corrin led him to the corridor outside. "Yes?"

"On behalf of MFB, compliments on winning this case. Very impressive work." He shook her hand. "Congratulations on passing the bar, a career milestone."

Bully for them, they'd checked the posted notice of successful examinees. Corrin crossed her arms, waiting. Meyer's arguments typically built to a crescendo in court, and he hadn't reached it yet. "Thank you."

"We want you back and will fast track you to partner. The offer includes a substantial signing bonus and key to our suite at the Seattle Club if you need lodging."

Serious tactics to woo her. "Your offer is flattering. I'm satisfied working with honest people in Emma Springs."

His eyes narrowed. "Situations often change," he warned, then pivoted and shoved open the lobby door.

"He left in a huff." Kyle placed his hand on her shoulder. "You look shaken. Whatever offer he made, remember mine."

"I do, I mean, I will," she stammered. "Piersall threw me a ruthless smile before he left the courtroom. Mr. Meyer implied we're not through dealing with them."

"My sense, too. Tonight's my meeting in Three Falls. I'm happy to chauffeur you to the library. It'll be interesting to see if Betsy shows her face."

"Ugh," she groaned. "I generally unwind after a trial by reading a good book. I don't have any books on hold, but I can ride along with you and sit in the library."

"I'll vote and leave. Put your feet up and flip pages. Make it a romance story with a happy ending."

"Deal. Drive safe. They're predicting another storm," Corrin said.

Kyle took her into his arms. "I'd bail if they didn't need a quorum for a vote. Shouldn't be gone long." He kissed his way to her lips.

"Safe travels." She held his coat and prolonged their goodbye kiss.

Silly, she'd see him later.

~ ~ ~

Someone pounded on Corrin's front door. She stuck the marker in her book.

Kyle didn't pound. She slid her new can of pepper spray off the counter and peered through the peephole. A tall man with dark blue eyes stood shivering on her porch.

She flung open the door. "Mitch, you're the last person I ever expected in Emma Springs."

"Hello to you, too, sis." He opened his arms and gave her a brotherly squeeze.

Corrin ushered him out of the wind. "What's happened?"

Whinny nickered softly at the newcomer and smelled his knee.

"Hey there, little thing." Mitch patted the mini's head "Bad news. Corey's at Tacoma Children's Hospital. She may have a rare lung disease. Her big wish is to see you."

"Oh my God!" The pepper spray dropped to the floor. "Why didn't you call?"

"Tried, the number we had doesn't work." Mitch picked up the spray and set it on the counter. "The letter you sent Corey had this return address."

"I'd swear I gave Grace my new number."

"Her life's been crazy. We're out of options, sis." He followed her into the living room. "They're pushing for treatments to start ASAP, to the tune of five thousand each week for the first month." He dragged his nails across his stubbly cheek. "We need proof we can pay."

"I'll help." Corrin dashed to her bedroom and started tugging clothes off hangers. "Grab the suitcase from under my bed and pack this stuff. We need to head out tonight to beat a snowstorm."

"Fine. I'll pilot. I slept most of the way on the bus, before I caught a ride here from your veterinarian. Nice guy."

"That's Ed Bell." A warm muzzle nudged Corrin's leg. "This is Whinny. Roy and Kyle are both at meetings and really busy this week. We'll drop Whinny off at Miranda's on the way out of town. They have grain and hay."

"Back in a minute." She trotted to the living room. "I'll grab Whinny's stuff and my laptop from across the street. Load the pile by the door."

She found the halter, then looked out the window. Lights blazed from Roy's house. He'd understand her need to leave.

~ ~ ~

A bank of dark snow clouds loomed in the eastern sky. Kyle frowned driving home from the foundation meeting. Dad might have a conflict of interest representing Betsy in her divorce after what she'd done. He needed to be warned, then he'd head to Corrin's.

Kyle parked the Jeep in his garage and slid across the road and onto Roy's driveway. *Damn ice!* Three locks later, he pushed open the door to his father's office. "The blizzard forecast must've shortened both our meetings. You won't believe what Betsy tried to do."

"What now?" Roy turned from his monitor screen.

"She resigned from the board and submitted a resignation for me. Faked my signature." Kyle tilted his head. "What's that noise?"

"My furnace needs a tune-up." Roy stated. "She might've been following orders from Piersall."

The gutless bastard. Anger rushed through him. "Enough already, Dad," Kyle exclaimed. "No more defending her. Quit your association with her now."

"There's an agreement," Roy bellowed back.

"Emma Springs might've lost the lawsuit because of her. You have to sever all ties for the good of the town." Kyle leaned over the desk. "Terminate your business agreement."

Roy's face reddened. "As I recall, you were interested in her."

"No. I never got involved." Kyle objected with his hand up. "Merely a random thought contemplating another Montana winter."

A door clicked shut. Kyle straightened. "That wasn't your furnace." He jogged to the front door, stepped from the porch to the sidewalk, and both feet flew out from under him.

~ ~ ~

Fluffy snowflakes surrounded Corrin. From across the street, Roy's door banged. She swiveled in her driveway and caught a flash of Kyle's blond head leaving

Roy's porch. She checked her watch. Soon as he got here, she'd clarify the things she'd just heard.

Mitch tapped on her window and pointed at the door.

He was right, they needed to go. She dashed inside. "Back the car out, Mitch. I'm almost done." She threw him the keys, then stuffed water bottles and her laptop into a duffel, shut off the lights, and locked the front door.

Kyle didn't show, and her mind replayed the fight she'd overheard retrieving her laptop. "No more defending her, could've lost the lawsuit," Kyle had yelled.

Bloody hell. Had they been discussing her? She should've interrupted him and his dad. She swallowed hard. Vanishing had been the strategy during her parents' ugly fights. Why hadn't she confronted them as an adult instead of running like a shocked kid?

Kyle had said more. "Business agreement, never involved," he'd argued with Roy.

Her brain returned to Kyle's last statement to his dad negating romantic interest. Her shoulders slumped. Kyle had stopped them from going further in the session before their indoor picnic lunch, and it didn't seem like that much of a struggle for him to do so. If he hadn't stopped it, she'd have been tempted to rip off his shirt and lead him to his bedroom.

Her garage door banged closed.

A biting wind whipped hair across her face while she looked across the street. She must've heard incorrectly, but where was he?

"Hey, space cadet. Your car's not built for ice or snow," Mitch said. "Get in."

"I carry spider spikes," she tossed him the duffel bag.

Mitch dropped her bag in the trunk and then steadied her with his hand while he led her to the passenger side of the Firebird. He pulled her into a hug. "Your presence means the world to Corey and the family."

"Corey's my fairy girl." She opened the passenger door and whistled.

Whinny bounded through the snow and hopped into the back seat.

"Snow's getting thicker, let's jet," Mitch ordered.

Kyle must've gone back inside. But why? She'd phone him. More than Corrin's fingers remained chilled while Mitch drove into a curtain of flurries.

She dialed Kyle's number and got voicemail. Why hadn't she walked back over, straightened things out, and gotten a goodbye hug?

Curse her old, damned insecurities.

~ ~ ~

Buildings outlining Bellevue, Washington, dotted the distant horizon, signaling their journey's completion. Morning sun cast bronze tones onto the top floors. Probably law offices, Corrin guessed.

"I promised we'd head to Mom and Dad's first," Mitch said.

Corrin stiffened in the Firebird's seat. "I won't stay there. Corey's my concern."

"You haven't asked, but I'm going to lay it out. Dad quit drinking after you left home. He's kept the family together doing handy work. He's a decent carpenter and a good painter."

"He used to insist he'd once painted a barn in a day," Corrin said.

"And you insisted we pay attention to details."

"That, I don't recall. I was too busy doling out band aids," she scoffed. "How's Grace managing to work?"

"Mom babysits Corey and Willy while Grace pulls shifts at Burger Town. It must be the twin thing—I swear I sensed her pain after Greg died."

"I wish she'd gone to community college."

"She's devoted to her kids. Can't help that you got the book genes, we got blue jeans."

"Not entirely true. We've all got talents." She rotated the bracelet on her wrist. A slice of Chinese jade sat between the Australian opal and turquoise from New Mexico.

Travel meant nothing when someone you loved needed the money. She rested her head against the seat. After her recent conversation with Grace, she inferred Corey's treatments costing upwards of sixty grand.

If only she could reach Kyle. Miranda had alerted her that he'd phoned her in frustration. Rounds of phone tag kept them from talking. Between all the miles they had no cell service and his work handling a town full of patients with the flu, they kept missing each other's calls. This was too important for an emotionless text.

She tried his number again, getting the out-of-range recording. She tossed the phone into her purse.

They'd reached the edge of King County. Not the designer side of Seattle's urban mecca, but rather the ragged hem filled with decaying rental houses in the threadbare outskirts of a forgotten coal town.

Mitch downshifted and turned onto a familiar, unkempt lane. Black dust trailed behind the car. "Not certain who'll be here. Everyone's doing stints at the hospital so Corey's never alone." He parked in front of a fenced yard fronting a rambler.

A man painting a shutter paused in mid stroke. His arms stuck out of a ragged sweatshirt. Splatters of paint dotted his overalls.

Corrin studied her father. No resentment or repulsion surfaced. She heaved open the car door.

"Hi there," he said. "Thank you for coming." He reached out a paint-spattered hand. "Corey will perk up seeing you." His eyes misted over.

Corrin looked away. Dad was a title you earned. "I can only cover the first treatment, until I find a higher paying job, Wayne."

He flinched. "There's more to this than the money. Corey needs to see a united family. I want to make up for not confronting my alcoholism earlier. I apologize, Corrin. I needed to do it in person."

He'd aged to a shadow of the imposing, angry man she remembered. "You had a problem, and Mitch told me you've gotten help." Corrin inhaled, expecting to detect the faint smell she detested.

She didn't.

He wiped his forehead with a cloth. "Tuesday nights I get the support I need at my AA meetings, there and from your mom."

"Good for you." She avoided eye contact. Words didn't prove anything. "I need to see Corey today, then Aunt Iris." She leaned against the front of her car.

"Iris is on my list of amends, too. I wanted to apologize to her in your presence."

Mitch passed off her car keys and kissed Corrin's forehead. "I'd hoped you'd give Dad one more chance after you saw him."

The keys warmed her hand. Family warmth.

~ ~ ~

Kyle redialed Corrin's number. He pounded the desk in his office when he heard a ring, then the second one.

Damn! Why didn't I yell from the ground, he chastised himself for the umpteenth time. So what, the guy was tall, had stroked Corrin's cheek, and hugged her. How was he supposed to know it was her brother? He should've gotten up from Dad's icy walkway and talked to her, smacked head or not. Stupid misunderstandings.

Corrin's real voice answered on the third ring.

His pulse spiked. "Thank God you answered. Please listen. The night you left, you overheard me discussing Betsy. You have to know it's the truth. I love you."

"I love you too, Kyle. Miranda told me what you mistakenly concluded about Mitch. I'm going to be stuck in Seattle for a while. MFB offered me a position that pays enough money for Corey's treatments."

The words hit with the force of a gut punch. *No!* MFB didn't deserve her. "How much money do you need? I'm almost through with paperwork to get a home equity loan on my house. I should have money in my account in a few weeks. You can have whatever you need."

"There are two problems. How soon and how much." Her voice held a tense edge. "Hey, we can have the long-distance relationship you proposed earlier," she used a teasing tone.

Her attempt at humor failed. He couldn't lose her again to Seattle, not now. Not when they both knew they belonged together. "I want to help."

"I know. They may need proof I have the first month's twenty thousand in an account. Time is my enemy and Emma Springs needs your new clinic."

"The clinic can wait. Please don't reach an impulsive verdict without examining all the facts."

"Clever turn of phrase, but Corey needs to start treatment ASAP. You made me aware of family responsibility, for knowing what matters," she choked on the last words.

"Let me help. I love you."

"I know," her voice trembled. "Love you too, gotta go."

Kyle cradled the phone. Miranda had been right, Corrin sounded desperate.

The Children's Research Foundation offered grants. He found the list of directors and typed in the chairman's number. He'd doled out plenty of favors, time to collect one.

After several hours of conversations, he finally took a long, calming breath. He'd requested assistance, rearranged his patients, and driven to Three Falls Airport to take his first commercial flight.

He passed through TSA, found his seat, and adjusted the buckle. In his mind, he pictured the pilot, going through the flight check. Next, they'd taxi the runway, gaining speed.

Then gracefully, they'd get the lift and be airborne. While the plane took off, in his head he ran through each maneuver the pilot made.

Out the window, clouds surrounded them. They'd taken off and he hadn't broken a sweat.

Once the plane reached altitude, he began jotting notes to ask Corey's physicians at the Tacoma Children's Hospital. He flipped to a new page and stopped. What if Corrin thought his coming to Seattle showed arrogance, or worse, interference in her family's personal affairs?

He tipped his head back and closed his eyes. Not everyone welcomed a second, unsolicited opinion. He wanted to help Corey, and relay that his motivation went well beyond getting Corrin back to Emma Springs.

"Flight attendants, prepare for landing," the pilot announced.

Kyle's brain methodically pictured the motion of the controls. The tires bumped twice on pavement, and the plane landed at SeaTac Airport.

He'd done it—flown with another pilot at the controls. Kyle thumped his thigh. Corrin's wanderlust had instigated a series of secret Friday flight lessons, and now he'd used this newfound ability to cut travel time to a fraction. Unfortunately, to assist sick little Corey.

In the airport arrival area, a familiar dark-haired man with a wide grin stood half a head above the crowd. His and Grant's former college roommate, John Fleckard, approached him. "Boy, she must be something. Kyle Werner, arriving by airplane."

Kyle gave him a Montana man-hug. "Wait until you get to know Corrin." He followed John between rows of cars in the parking garage.

"Can't wait." John pressed his key fob, and the trunk of a black Tesla opened.

"One of Corrin's goals is to travel the world," Kyle smiled. "I don't plan to cruise on ships until I'm eighty."

"I briefly met her at Grant's wedding reception, where I observed you two. Plenty of sparks," John said.

"Much more." Metallic city noises and exhaust fumes assailed Kyle's senses until he closed the car door. "Business must be good. Thanks for putting me up."

"Green building is finally becoming popular. Your family and Grant's welcomed me many times to Montana. Speaking of which, from the photos, our former agent enjoys the daddy badge."

"Come see for yourself. If this trip's successful, you can be a groomsman."

~ ~ ~

Corrin fought tears and strode into the hospital room. Her appointment with Social Security concerning experimental medical care for Corey had been depressingly unproductive.

She forced a cheerful smile and placed a stuffed black pony into Corey's thin arms.

"Aunt Corrin, I knew you'd come to visit again today." Corey waved a juice box. Her grin lacked a front tooth.

"I honor my promises. You're such a clever girl. Without that tooth it must be easier to suck from a straw," Corrin said.

Corey smoothed the russet mane on the new toy. "You're the first one to figure out my trick." She pulled the velvety animal to her chest. "Maybe I can ride a pony someday."

Corrin straightened the stiff skirt on her business suit. Her shoes pinched her feet. "I'll talk to Whinny, my miniature horse. I have an appointment, then I'll gallop back and tell more mini Whinny stories."

"Maybe the new doctor will be here," Grace smiled. "He made Corey and I laugh earlier." She stroked her daughter's cheek.

"You mean Doc Kyle, Mommy?"

Corrin started. No way Kyle drove faster than her leadfooted brother. She slid the chart from the wall holder and flipped to the second page.

'Kyle Werner, Consulting Physician,' stood out in bold print near the bottom. Her mind whirled while she stuck the chart back in place. "Wish me luck. I'm dining in the shark tank with the MFB partners."

Corey shook her finger at her. "You shouldn't eat near sharks. Said so in a book I read. They're nasty if they smell blood."

"Only kidding, we're meeting at Crown's, honey. Not much seafood on the menu."

"I'm sorry to burden you again," Grace said.

"Family is never a burden, sis."

"You started work for the lawyer in Emma Springs. Don't you have a contract with him?" Grace asked.

"We had a handshake. Neither of us had time to write up an official document. It wouldn't matter. Roy understands family coming first." Corrin kissed them both goodbye.

She dialed Kyle's number and got voicemail, making the walk from the hospital to the elegant restaurant seem painfully short.

Seattle's best steak house occupied a busy corner. Light-colored brick on the outside, dark and intimidating inside. A waiter led her to Mr. Meyer, who stood and indicated a chair. "Nice to see you, Corrin."

"And you." She slid into the padded leather, while she fought the acute sense of it closing in around her, choking life from her body.

Meyer swirled a glass filled with golden liquid. "Care for a drink?"

The scent of scotch made Corrin's stomach lurch. "No, thank you, sir. A club soda, please."

He signaled the waiter, gave her drink order, and leaned forward. "Let's conduct business first and then dine, shall we? I spoke with the partners. Your base will be six figures, which is generous considering the newness of your license."

Corrin settled a linen napkin on her lap. "You mentioned an additional signing bonus."

"Twenty-five thousand is what we can offer as soon as you're cleared and sworn in. We have a project waiting for you."

Corey needed at least six treatments, maybe more. Corrin squeezed the edge of the linen tablecloth brushing her lap. "I'll accept nothing under thirty thousand, sir."

Meyer sat back in his chair. "I'm not certain—"

The maître d' appeared at the edge of the table. "Mr. Meyer, another gentleman insisted he speak with your guest."

A red-faced, huffing Kyle stepped from behind him and smiled at Corrin. "I need a moment alone with Ms. Patten." He offered his hand to her.

She grasped his warm fingers, rose from the seat, and followed him into an unoccupied coat closet.

"I sprinted here from the hospital when I found out who you were meeting."

She couldn't take money planned for his clinic, not if she could earn enough. Steeling herself against Kyle's persuasive manner presented a problem. "I won't use money intended for the clinic. Emma Springs residents deserve nearby services."

Kyle stepped forward. She backed into a row of soft fur coats. "I've a different solution," he whispered

What did she need most? His arms wrapped around her, or to be relieved from shouldering all the problems alone. "Of course you do, you're my magician." She raised her eyes to meet his. "Hold me while you explain. Please."

Kyle's embrace settled her unease. "The board I sit on has contacts with pharmaceutical companies. We can get Corey into a trial of the newest medication for this type of lung disorder in children. It won't cost a dime, and her pediatrician agrees it's the best choice. He's willing to help expedite the paperwork."

"I thought I'd explored all options." Tears wet her eyes.

"Not mine."

"I'm sorry about the earlier mix up," Corrin said, "From your dad's porch you must have seen me pack my car. I thought you might be relieved I left with all my problems."

He kissed her brow. "From the ground, I watched a big, brawny guy hug you. You'd left before I managed to dust off my pride and stumble over with a gash on my head. No more assumptions, okay?"

"Deal. I'm glad you weren't hurt." She ran her fingers through his hair, massaging a bump on his scalp. "How'd you get here so quickly?"

He lifted her wrist and twirled her bracelet. "A commercial flight. What's more, I took flying lessons to surprise you."

She leaned into his muscled chest. "You learned to fly, for me? That's so romantic."

Kyle tipped her chin. "Yes. And I've drafted an ad to hire a PA to help with my practice. If you want to live in Seattle, I'll work it out for us to be together."

Warmth spread throughout her chest. "You'll never have to leave home. Emma Springs is where I want to live. With you."

"Even better." His kiss pushed heat deep into her core.

"Let's give our regards to your former boss and get something to eat in a sunnier place where we can discuss our future." He gently squeezed her hand. "I've missed the spark you give my life."

Hesitancy shattered into a dazzling pool of light around her heart. "You're my torch."

"I want you forever, Corrin. Forever and a day."

~ ~ ~

"I propose a toast to Doc Kyle." Wayne Patten lifted a glass filled with sparkling cider and made eye contact with each person at his dining room table. "Corey will get the treatment she needs, and I've never seen Corrin happier."

"Hear, hear," the family chimed.

Corrin raised her glass, struggling to keep her cider from sloshing. "I've never been prouder of my family or Kyle. How you've pulled together for Corey is amazing."

"Medicines need a binder or a delivery system. That's you, my love," Kyle responded.

The changes in her parents from when she'd left home were monumental. Vague childhood memories of a mother who sang lullabies and a sweet daddy who carried her on his shoulders began to resurface. "A fateful trip to Montana led me to Kyle and then back to my family. I'd love you to experience the peace and beauty of Emma Springs. Make the trip soon, Mom and Dad." She tipped her glass toward her father.

Corrin's mom raised her napkin and dabbed her eyes. "If Corey's able to travel, maybe Grace and the kids can join us," she said.

"Dad and I both have guest bedrooms." Kyle squeezed Corrin's hand under the table.

"God willing, our Corey will be fine." Her mom closed her eyes for a moment.

Corrin pictured her namesake, the fragile girl with skinny arms and a gap-toothed smile.

~ ~ ~

"Are you certain you're okay riding in a boat on Puget Sound, Corrin?" Kyle waved at John, who stood at the top of the stairs leading to yachts docked at Seattle's premier marina.

Thoughtful came second nature to Kyle. "As long as I'm with you," she said.

"Hey captain, how's things?" Kyle yelled.

John flashed another bright smile. "Boat's gassed, and noting your companion, your plan succeeded."

Kyle squeezed Corrin's hand. "Everything's positive. No cancer, and Corey's reacted favorably to the first treatment. We've delayed traveling back to Emma Springs for a few days, so I can consult with her pediatrician." He held the gate for her to pass through.

"I remember a few things from Grant's wedding." John's dark eyes met hers. "Let's see, Kyle's description of you contained the words charming, smart, beautiful, and with sisters. Did I mention sisters?"

Neither sister had dated boys with brains, and their high school had lacked John's version—tall, dark, and disarming. "Did Kyle mention one's a missionary in Kenya, and the other's a widow raising kids?" Corrin said.

"Positive attributes in my opinion," John said.

She put her finger to her lips and studied John while he loosened the bow line on his sleek, black boat. As an architect, he'd appear too successful for altruistic Leslie, but might be a good contact for Grace, who'd learned the consequences of marrying the high school chug-a-lug champion. John's strong ties to Seattle were a plus.

"Hop aboard, and we'll cast off." John coiled a rope.

Even standing on the dock with water splashing through the planks, he emanated a quiet confidence, similar to Kyle's, but not quite. She'd throw out a chance for him to meet Grace. "Thank you for offering to ferry me back and forth to the hospital," Corrin began. "If you'd like to meet my family, John, you're welcome to join us any time. I'll treat you to a swell lunch in the hospital cafeteria."

She made the short jump to the boat. What had Miranda told her? Something about John knowing wealthy clients through his green-building designs, but under the surface he wanted someone to share his life with: as his friends had found. She'd pay attention.

John threw the rope to Kyle. "I'll join you tomorrow, on the condition we pack sandwiches before we leave." A grin transformed him from reserved to mischievous.

"Deal," Corrin nodded, and winked at Kyle.

"Follow me to the bridge, kids." John stepped onto the boat and ducked into a door at the bow.

"Lunch is a great idea. Introducing Grace and John occurred to me, too." Kyle said. "They'd balance each other well. Good job, counselor."

"Heaven knows she could use stability in her life," Corrin said.

He took her hand and led her to where John stood at the control panel.

Swells of water lapped against the wooden piers while they motored away from the docks. In front of them, Puget Sound buzzed with activity. A ferry crossed to Bainbridge Island and a sailboat heeled on her side, its blue spin drifter unfurled.

John's boat barely wavered while it sliced through dark water, but Corrin couldn't keep her eyes from darting between Kyle and the shore. "I'm moving to the back deck."

Kyle took her arm. "I'm right here." He pulled her to his side. "Tell me what you need."

Corrin rested against a seat while she watched Seattle skyscrapers fade from view. "Keep holding me tight."

Kyle pulled her close. "Forever and a day."

~ ~ ~

Kyle and John's bantering had entertained her during the two-night stay in the guest rooms at his island home. A picturesque canopy of shade trees slanted to the water's edge of his property, but she missed the ponderosa pines of Montana.

"Your place is fabulous, John." Kyle draped his arm across Corrin's shoulder while they motored back to Seattle. "It's totally hidden from view."

"Designed for privacy." John eased his boat through choppy water. "Maybe bordering on isolation. It's time for a change in scenery."

"Or additional companionship," Kyle teased. "Grace speaks highly of you. Two visits and you won her and the kids over."

Kyle was spot on. Her sister had perked up when John walked into the hospital room with them. "You were thoughtful to bring Corey drawing supplies and the transformer truck for Willy," she said. "The healthy child is often forgotten. Kindness always impressed Grace."

"Your sister is a special woman." John paused with his hand gripped tightly on the steering wheel. "Do you think Grace would have dinner here with me? I'd insist on Corey and Willy joining us."

"If I describe the fettuccini alfredo you made." Corrin squeezed Kyle's hand.

A slow, genuine smile crossed John's face. "I can cook most anything. I miss being around a family." His head swung from left to right before he sped up. "Let's get back to the hospital and check on Corey's latest tests."

"Good plan. The lab promised the results of the treatment by five today," Kyle said.

Worry wrinkled Kyle's blond eyebrows.

Her stomach pitched, not from the waves. Nothing better prevent Corey's recovery. Nothing.

~ ~ ~

Kyle reread the paragraph. Figuring out how to tell Grace and her family that Corey's lung infection resulted from environmental toxins wouldn't be easy. His jaw clenched. All because of Piersall's negligence to properly clean up after years of mining in Ebony Cove. The scumbag Piersall family had evaded that law.

"Something's wrong." Corrin leaned close.

She knew him too well. "Not what you think. Stay calm." Corey rested against a stack of pillows. John stood on one side, holding Willy. The little boy showed his sister shells, one by one.

Grace stood on the other side. She balanced a sippy cup of juice for her daughter in one hand and smoothed golden curls off the impish face with the other. Corrin's parents sat next to her.

"The great news is how well Corey's responding to the treatment," Kyle said. "So well, they're scheduling the next dose tomorrow."

"That's a huge relief. Do they know what triggered it?" Grace asked. Her eyes flicked to Willy. "Could it be hereditary?"

"Not likely." Kyle squared his shoulders, preparing for a backlash. "Preliminary reports show there may be a link with outdoor air quality."

"Residual coal dust." Corrin clenched the metal bar at the foot of the bed. "My car's covered in tiny black specs."

Kyle met Corrin's steely eyes, then shifted his gaze to Corey and smiled. "More good news is that the condition should recede by eliminating exposure to potential irritants."

All color drained from Grace's face. "We can't move. I walk to Burger Town and Mom watches the kids while I work."

"Am I gonna get better, Mommy?" Corey asked.

"Yes, honey," Grace said in a soothing voice.

"I doubt there's legal recourse." Corrin said to her sister. "Together, we'll devise a solution."

Beeps from Corey's monitor invaded a panicky silence.

"Can you type, Grace?" John asked casually.

"I worked on yearbook and the weekly newsletter in high school." Grace's shoulders drooped. "Years ago."

"Like riding a bike, I'd imagine." John winked at Corey. "I'm researching the advantages to my style of eco-building for a book. I need my notes transposed into a manuscript before it goes to an editor." He shifted Willy from one hip to the other. "I can offer room and board with a salary. My home has four bedrooms, and the air is pure."

All the energy in the room paused. "Would you help me find more shells?" Willy tugged on John's collar.

Grace looked from Corey to Willy to John. "I'll accept your offer, on one condition."

"Name it."

"If we bother you or my work doesn't help, you'll say so." Grace's voice held a firm edge. "I won't accept charity from anyone."

"Deal." John high-fived Willy. "If your mom says it's okay, we'll hunt shells every day."

Corrin silently blessed caring, handsome John. Tears pooled in her eyes. She squeezed them shut.

"The women in this family hold themselves to high standards, John. For the right reasons." Kyle slipped his arm around Corrin's waist and kissed her cheek.

"The kids had to be determined," Wayne said, and took his wife's hand. "Their mother and I dealt with our own demons while our children grew. We're here for them now. I bet we can borrow Mitch and his truck."

"If Corrin agrees, we can stay through the weekend to help move things," Kyle said.

"Are you ready for us, John?" Worry creased Grace's heart-shaped face.

John ruffled Willy's tawny hair. "Never been more ready in my life."

~ ~ ~

Corrin leaned against the rail to view Grace, Corey, and Willy waving from the stern of John's boat.

The move had gone well, and Grace showed genuine excitement for the first time in years.

Wind whipped across the dock and chilled Corrin's damp cheek. Her arm automatically waved back and forth. Soon the family would be a speck in the vast, inky pool of Puget Sound. "Thank goodness they're headed to a healthy home."

"The setup's perfect for Corey," Kyle said. "John, too. His ex-wife had lied about wanting kids."

Corrin's smile wavered. "They both need to put aside past history."

"Agreed." Kyle pulled her close. "I thought he'd burst yesterday when Corey asked if wood fairies built his house."

"She reads the books I send her." She wiped her sleeve across her face. "Time for us to hit the freeway before the rush hour commuters clog the freeway."

"I see tears." Kyle gently cradled her face. "Corey is going to be fine, I read the report."

"My tears are joyful. I'm relieved treatments are working."

"Me, too. I want you to be certain you're ready to leave Seattle. Your happiness is my first concern."

"Our love makes me happy. I realize the person who shares your life journey is more important than what lies at the end."

Kyle brushed his lips against hers. "I'd be honored to travel beside you."

She inhaled pure Kyle. Leaning into him and savoring all he offered came naturally. Her lips sought his, her passion demanding action. Her fingers massaged his lower back and then travelled to his firm rear. His warm lips caressed her neck, sending delicious sparks to her core. She tilted her head back, "Oh, you have the best—"

A ferry horn blasted, announcing the boat docking nearby.

"The best what?" He caressed her cheek.

"Assets, hands down." Corrin patted his butt, wanting all the things she'd been afraid of for too many years.

"Then marry me." He dropped to one knee and grabbed her left hand. "Marry me, Corrin Lynette Patten, and make me the happiest man alive."

CHAPTER 19

Kyle's proposal echoed in Corrin's brain. His eyes held the promise of love, passion, and loyalty.

Seagulls circled overhead squawking. Waves crashed into the breakwater.

Her breath came in short gasps. She never wanted to disappoint him. "I want to marry you, believe me."

"Trust in us. Say yes." His knee shoved a pebble from the wooden dock.

"Yes, yes, yes." She lifted him to his feet. "I'll need guidance in certain, ah, things." Warmth crept to her cheeks.

He stroked her rear. "I'm not worried in the least. You have a natural touch."

She grabbed him by the collar of his coat. "And I want to explore all of you, Kyle Werner."

"Deal. Now, onto another serious question. Dad gave me Mom's engagement diamond. If you prefer, we'll buy a different one." He pulled out a small case.

Her hand flew to her heart. "I want your mom to be a part of our marriage. She raised a fine son."

He opened the box and slipped the ring on her finger.

"It's beautiful. I will cherish it forever."

"I'd hoped you'd think so. Are you ready to aim your Firebird to I-90 and head home?"

Home. She'd return to a welcoming place, where her future included a man worth the wait. "With you, of course." She turned to face east, toward Montana.

A band of dark, ominous clouds stretched across the sky.

~ ~ ~

H.P. scratched his signature onto the paperwork transferring the bulk of his trust fund to the offshore account, set up as a fake charity. A few lawyers earned their pay. He'd send it out tomorrow with the Three Falls pony express.

The neon tomahawk below his hotel window flashed red light, a blinking beacon, matching his urge to chop apart every aspect of the bitch's life. One stroke, her career. The next, her happy life with the good ol' doc.

The hicks in Emma Springs would hate her. Researching the cheapest manufactured houses and advertising no background checks should catch the eye of degenerates to inhabit them. And the right property manager could offer first dibs to known drug dealers. Might even be a positive return on investment numbers for the initial report to the Piersall Enterprises board members. Using his private funds would be a brilliant way to facilitate the project filing for bankruptcy a few months down the road.

He redialed Mikey's number and smiled when the moron answered. "Did you get the gun and the silencer?"

"Yup. Give the word and they're dead ducks," Mikey replied.

~ ~ ~

"Thirty miles and we'll glimpse Mt. Hanlen. I made this trip often in college." Kyle drew Corrin's hand to his lips, making flutters in her belly. "And I'm returning with a fiancée."

His kiss on her fingers caressed with the soft touch of velvet. "Fiancée sounds utterly romantic when you say it."

"I'll keep up the effort."

"Please do." She touched the scrimshaw pin on her lapel. "I've never belonged to a community before. With Dad and Mom driving Aunt Iris over the pass this spring, maybe more of my family will join us."

"Hope we don't have to go through the same welcoming pitch. You were a tough sell."

"Leaving Seattle, I couldn't imagine life without buses, espresso shops, and demanding clients. Now it's the opposite."

"Speaking of which, Dad mentioned that Betsy's divorce has advanced to the final stage. On another bright note, he bought a bottle of sparkling cider to toast our engagement. I hope it's alright, he's waiting to greet us tonight, no matter how late."

"I'm touched."

They'd reached the turn to Bobby's house. "No marauding horses tonight." Corrin's gaze wandered to the hillside. "Bloody hell! There's another county signboard. Visible this time."

"I'd bet you'll want to investigate." Kyle turned onto the road and parked beside the farmhouse.

"Correct diagnosis, doctor." Corrin jumped out, took photos with her phone, and returned scowling. "Now Piersall's applying for a residential development." Her finger scanned her phone screen. "Good grief, if I remember correctly, NX2 zoning allows for up to eight homes per acre. They'll be able to lean out and wash each other's windows."

"Wow, that's tightly spaced. Your homecoming includes job security."

Corrin pocketed her cell. "Let's not spoil Roy's reception until I check the legalities."

"Agreed." Kyle drove to his dad's home and honked. Roy trotted out to the car after they swung into his driveway.

"The sight of you two makes me feel forty years younger." He opened Corrin's door, helped her out, and pulled her into a hug. "I wanted you in the family the first night we met. Kyle needed a woman unafraid to challenge him, like his mom." He held her hand to the light, and the diamond sparkled. "He's prone to a stubborn streak, you know."

"Kyle employed devoted persistence," Corrin jested, then touched Roy's forearm. "Thank you for Flor's diamond. Wearing it means the world to me." She kissed a beaming Kyle. "I'm ready for a celebration tonight and a workload tomorrow."

"Any time I'm with you, Cupcake," he whispered, "it's my own personal celebration." Kyle took her hand and led her inside.

Life had turned, and she'd floated with the tide.

She glanced at the hillside stream and buttoned her coat, fighting the image of paddling against a strong current.

~ ~ ~

Betsy tapped the circled photo on the page copied from a ten-year-old high school yearbook. H.P. gritted his teeth. Even her spikey nails irritated him.

"What do you know, H.P." She pursed her botoxed lips. "Corrin might be a natural strawberry blonde. Why do you hate her?"

He surveyed Betsy's idea of a cabin—outfitted with chrome furniture and modern art. God, he'd be glad to be done with her and the bitch. "Her family worked for my old man before he closed the mining operation in Ebony Cove, another hick town." He took the yearbook page and crumpled it. "I'd gotten a speedboat for my twenty-first birthday. Mikey and I invited her and her friend for the first ride. Didn't catch they were jailbait. They decided not to party with us. Patten threatened to squeal to the cops and got hush money."

"Born to be a lawyer," Betsy crossed one leg over the other, hitching her skirt higher up her bare thigh. "You paid instead of fighting the charges?"

By what she was offering, his family money continued to attract opportunists. He scowled. "Paid her and left the University of Washington to ensure the company's sterling reputation in case I screwed up again. Forced to move two thousand miles from my girlfriend. As if graduating from a corn-husker college wasn't bad enough." He took a long draught of cognac. "After graduating, my old man wanted me to oversee his pipe dreams of opening an exclusive ski resort for Mother. Not why I got an MBA."

"Your mother's a snow bunny?"

"Hardly. More of a spend bunny who happens to ski. My parents visited this hick town decades ago. My father envisioned creating the next Vail-type resort in Emma Springs or on one of the other hillsides where he carelessly invested. The laws changed and so will the plan for this land I'm stuck with. I'll cram over a hundred houses on this side of their pristine mountain."

Betsy smirked. "Glorious Mt. Hanlen's view. Touted enough around town to make a sane person gag." She leaned forward, showing cleavage. "Just remember our deal. You purchase my property after my divorce papers are signed."

"I don't ever forget a deal." H.P. lit a match to the yearbook page and threw it in the fireplace.

He owned two council members, and he'd persuade more. Two weeks until the directors of Piersall Enterprises met, and he needed the initial housing plans approved.

It didn't matter how much of his trust fund he spent, Corrin Patten would feel the life squeezed out of her, breath by breath.

~ ~ ~

"Will they discuss Piersall's proposed houses at your Lions Club meeting today?" Corrin stood at the edge of Roy's desk.

He shuffled papers and produced an agenda. "That's listed, and some for-profit prison Sharlene Underson endorses. It's her brilliant idea to provide local jobs. The Lions Club members volunteer to meet humanitarian needs and promote peace. Not certain how a prison fits in."

"A prison nearby?"

"Don Underson listed the land adjacent to Rane Calderon's property. No land survey for decades, and Rane's worried the perimeter markers encroach on his property, which contains burial grounds of his Native American ancestors. He's put in an offer and is prepared for a legal fight."

Corrin pursed her lips. "Federal laws supposedly conserve sacred sites. Historically, though, lawsuits have failed to protect the rights of Indigenous people, but I haven't researched the outcomes recently."

"No *SOLD* sign yet." Roy rubbed his temple. "Let's not get worried until we see the county documents."

"Understood. I heard you dictate into an oversized pen yesterday. Need me to transcribe?"

"I recorded a couple of ideas to fight potential hillside development. Please evaluate if they're worth researching." He handed her the pen-like gizmo with the instruction book and then lifted his coat from the back of the chair.

"Have pen, will persevere," Corrin teased.

"Oh, nearly forgot. Betsy's scheduled to stop by to sign the last papers. We're at a deadline." He pointed to a file on his desk. "I'd appreciate your extracting four signatures from her."

"Good planning, Roy. You get lunch with friends, and I must play nauseatingly nice with the enemy."

He chuckled. "Tums are on the shelf in the kitchen. Betsy's fees refurbished the cottage and will pay for your honeymoon, if you two ever set a date."

"I'll picture dollar signs while I'm biting my tongue to shreds." She followed Roy to the front door. "Don't worry, I can be professional with anything, I mean anyone."

"And I'm glad," Roy said. "I'll untether Whinny and bring her inside for moral support."

"And a nap on the dog bed. Kyle thinks I'm trying to give her a canine complex."

"Whinny will grow out of her puppy-sized accommodations someday. Then we'll have to adjust," Roy teased, leaving the room.

Whinny trotted in and bumped her knee. "Need a treat? Shake my hand."

The horse raised a tiny hoof.

"Good girl." She gave her a baby carrot. "Please find your bed."

The little horse darted to the padded cushion and flopped down, folding in her legs.

She couldn't help grinning while she pulled on headphones, and adjusted Roy's pen device. His calm voice presented concerns of why Piersall seemed hell bent on a development in Emma Springs.

She jotted notes on a legal pad until Whinny nosed her skirt. "Yes?" She lifted the headphones.

Rapping sounded from the front door.

She slipped the fat pen into her jacket pocket and checked the peephole. A manicured hand flipped a strand of shiny brown hair.

Zero minus tongue-biting time. "Hi Betsy. Paperwork's ready."

Betsy cased Roy's office, her gaze landing on his calendar. "Your boss attends one of those altruistic animal meetings today, doesn't he?"

Narcissists never understood philanthropy. Corrin tried her best to peel her lips into a smile. "Correct. Please sign at the four pink tabs." What she'd give to ink a permanent scarlet tattoo on the scheming woman's forehead, and the B wouldn't denote her first name.

Betsy flipped through the pages and signed, then leaned her butt on the edge of Roy's desk. "How's it feel being officially a local?" One of her toes tapped on the carpet.

"Just fine." Corrin straightened the edge of the pile of papers. "Thanks for stopping—"

The doorbell rang three times. "I wasn't expecting another client." She motioned to the door, but Betsy didn't budge. Would she need a crane to haul her out? "You're finished."

"Not quite. I invited a couple of prospects to meet you."

A pack of cougars invading town? Irritating women presented a nuisance, nothing more. And they had money.

She yanked open the door and gasped.

Piersall and Fernley stood on the porch.

Fernley thrust his arm against the door. "If it isn't Blondie." He pushed past her into the entry, carrying a covered birdcage.

Whinny sniffed his trouser leg, snorted, and dashed outside.

"Whinny!" Corrin called.

Piersall shoved his way in, reached around her, and slammed the door.

Their demeanors radiated ugly. "You're not welcome here." His musky cologne made her stomach lurch.

"This won't take long," Piersall sneered. "I've been waiting for the perfect time."

He wouldn't dare try anything. Just in case. . . Corrin dropped her hand into her pocket and fingered Roy's gadget. Had she hit record? "We don't want your business. Get out. Right now. All of you."

Fernley ducked into Roy's office, set the cage on the desk, and plopped into Roy's chair. "You need to listen for a change." His gaze flicked from the gilded clock to the leather-topped desk. "By the looks of this archaic place, there's probably a reel-to-reel deck buried in here. You'd get an earful hitting record."

"Good point," Piersall said, and laughed.

Had they given permission to record? She pointed at Fernley. "Get out of Roy's chair."

"He can sit where he wants." Piersall pushed her toward one of the armchairs for clients. "You'd better sit down."

"I'm calling the police." She reached for Roy's desk phone.

Fernley pulled out the cord.

"Get out," she ordered. "Now!"

"We understand your niece needs a final round of treatment in Tacoma." At her gasp, Piersall's eyes shone with satisfaction. "Sad thing, the foundation board might curtail grants if I can't donate."

"You'd put an innocent child's life in danger? What kind of monsters are you?" Her stomach clenched into a knot. "The hearing examiner ruled against the resort, and he'll deny your packed houses."

Betsy stood up. "What—?"

"Shut up," Piersall commanded, then turned to Corrin, his teeth bared. "I've waited to pay you back after you tried to nail a rape charge on me and extorted money from my family."

"You immoral pedophile! You tried to intoxicate and then sexually molest fourteen-year-old girls in the middle of the Sound. We fought back, and you left us in the freezing water to die."

Betsy pointed at H.P. "You lied to me."

"We would've gone back but saw the other boat." H.P. shouted at Betsy. "This conniving bitch got plenty of blackmail money."

"I never received money!" Corrin exploded. "We were stupidly naive and too embarrassed to tell anyone. Someone swindled you."

H.P.'s eyes narrowed. "If not her," he pointed at Fernley, "you fleeced my family. I wondered how you swung the new Charger and a trip to Europe."

"Poor H.P., forced to go to an out-of-state college," Fernley said. "I felt so, so sorry for you. You've blown through money all your life. Hanging with you earned me a share."

"You're a mercenary bloodsucker!" H.P. ranted.

"Exactly what you deserve." Fernley lifted the birdcage and uncovered it. "No more screwing around. Here's the deal, Blondie."

A duck flapped against the wire enclosure.

"You captured the wood duck!" Corrin stepped toward the frightened bird.

"Look closer, Blondie. It's amazing what a taxidermist and a paintbrush can do with a live specimen," Fernley bragged.

Corrin peered into the cage. Painted on markings colored the bird's feathers. "You faked a wood duck?"

"You're going to sign an affidavit stating you engineered the entire duck story," Piersall said. "No building restrictions, and the kid gets her shots."

Idiots! Connecting waters protected the lake, not the wood duck's habitat, and half the town watched that nest. Corrin kept her face neutral, while her knees shook.

H.P. pulled an envelope from his chest pocket. "Mikey's going to eliminate the real wood ducks. Then this bird's going to be found lying in the weeds. Guess who'll be disbarred? You're lucky your boyfriend didn't end up dead, too."

Ohmygod. She wanted to yell at the murderous degenerate, but bit back the words. What if she'd hit the wrong button on the pen? If she'd failed to record him, and signing his document saved Corey, she'd risk disbarment. "You'll still build on the site?"

"We've found the cheapest manufactured homes on the market. Seeing as all of this happened after you hit town, the local yokels will blame you when I move in lowlifes, then declare bankruptcy and leave the hillside squatters." Piersall's eyes blazed with anger while he opened the envelope.

The Special Zoning District protected the lake. Now she'd have to fake resignation to keep him from blowing a gasket. She slumped her shoulders. "I'll sign your paperwork."

Fernley jabbed a pen at her.

"Wait." Betsy faced Piersall, with her hands on her hips. "You never told me you took her out in a boat and molested her. I don't want any part of this. Come on, Corrin." She reached her hand out.

Piersall shoved Betsy into a chair. "None of your business."

"Get Blondie to sign and let's get the hell out of here!" shouted Fernley.

The front door burst open.

"Corrin?" Kyle called. "Are you okay?"

Whinny galloped into the room and slid against Corrin. "I am now." She let her shaky hand rest on the horse's head. "They're trying to blackmail me. Call the police."

"Already did," Kyle replied. "Whinny bolted into my examining room." He strode to her side and put his arm around her waist. "I recognized Piersall's license plate."

Piersall pulled out a lighter and held it to the papers. "You don't have anything on us. Her word against ours." He dropped the burning pile into Roy's metal trash can. "Now you see it, now you don't."

Betsy stood up and moved to Corrin's other side. "Not so. I'll defend Corrin."

Sirens blared from the street.

"You bought speculation property, you dumb broad," Fernley said. "And your reputation's in the crapper."

Someone knocked on the open front door, then two officers hustled inside.

Corrin recognized Sheriff Riley.

"Dr. Werner, we got a call you needed assistance."

"Might as well grab another donut, boys, you trotted in a little too late." H.P. fanned the smoke from the waste basket.

"Not exactly." Corrin slipped the recorder from her pocket and took a breath. "I have everything on tape. These two suggested I start a recorder, and I obliged." She pressed the replay button. Her heart skipped a beat.

Piersall's voice blasted out, loud and clear.

Fernley rose from Roy's chair, slid around the other side of the desk, and grabbed for the pen. Whinny reared and thrust her hooves toward Fernley's crotch.

"Get that animal away," Fernley yelled and then bolted toward the door.

The second officer grabbed Fernley's arm. "Not so fast."

"It's okay, Whinny." Corrin stroked the horse and turned to Sheriff Riley. "I have a verbal confession of attempted rape of a minor and attempted murder of Kyle."

"All right, you two, hands behind your backs," the sheriff said.

Kyle kissed her cheek. "Nicely done."

Roy stood in the doorway of his crowded office. "What's—"

"You'll never be more than white trash!" H.P. shouted at Corrin. "I helped write the MFB ad to hire you. Brine's my frat bro."

White trash, an ugly term she hadn't heard for a decade. Corrin shrank into Kyle.

Piersall smirked. "You know, doc, I can picture your bitch with her arms restrained behind her back, pretending to be a sweet little teenager."

A low growl erupted from Kyle, and he raised his fists to fighting position.

Roy sprang forward. "Not worth it, son, you'd lose your license."

"Put your hands behind your back, Mr. Piersall." Sheriff Riley cuffed Piersall. "Secure Mr. Fernley in the patrol car please," he said to the other officer. "I'll follow with this one. Roy, take Betsy outside please, we'll need statements."

"Sure thing," Roy said. He escorted her out.

Kyle stood by Corrin's side.

She lifted her chin. Piersall would walk past them to leave Roy's office, and she'd enjoy the moment.

Sheriff Riley turned to face her and Kyle. "I appreciate your patience while we worked this case. Someone may finally be called on the carpet." He moved H.P. in front of him, holding on to the handcuffs. "Watch your step, Mr. Piersall, it's easy to fall in cuffs."

The officer's gaze shifted to Kyle's shoe. "We'll be out of here in a minute, Dr. Werner," he said, and then pulled out a handkerchief and sneezed into it. "The allergy medicine you prescribed helps if I remember to use it."

Kyle nodded. "Glad to hear."

Corrin tapped her foot and squeezed his hand.

"All yours if an opportunity arises," he whispered. In a swift movement, he propelled her in front of him, keeping his hands on her upper arms.

Corrin's heart pounded.

Two steps, and Piersall would pass in front of her.

"Start walking, Mr. Piersall." The sheriff covered his mouth, let go of the handcuffs, and coughed into the handkerchief again.

Fourteen years of hell due to this creep. Corrin stuck out her foot. Piersall's shin pushed hard against her leg. She held her stance, anchored by Kyle's firm grip.

"Shit," Piersall pitched forward onto his knees, and then his chin hit the floor. He moaned.

A giant ball of ugly released from the pit of Corrin's stomach and left her body.

"Warned you about walking, sir. No need to rush." Sheriff Riley stated.

Piersall turned an angry red face to them. "I didn't trip on my own you idiot, the doctor kicked me."

"Nope." The sheriff stated. "The doctor's unable to reach you from where he's standing.

Piersall sat back on his haunches. "Then the bitch attacked me!" he yelled. "Press charges."

Sheriff Riley yanked him to his feet. "I didn't see what happened, sir. You think petite Ms. Patten knocked you down? Well, my advice is to keep that rumor to yourself where you're going." He turned a serious face to them. "He'll be locked up soon, folks."

H.P.'s mouth dropped open, as if he'd just thought of a shared jail cell. The sheriff maneuvered him toward the door.

Corrin pivoted and hugged Kyle. "Thank you, thank you." She nuzzled his neck.

"At least you got a token payback," Kyle said. "I wanted to pummel the bastard to a pulp."

"But you didn't." She put his hand to her heart. "The black, ugly memory of Piersall will be replaced with the image of his panicked face at the thought of jail."

Kyle pulled her into a long, slow kiss before he released her. He tilted her chin. "Your eyes are brighter. Seriously, there's a difference."

Corrin cradled his chin. "Piersall assumed he twisted the knife telling me he'd orchestrated my hiring. All these years I assumed my appearance got me hired. Mr. Meyer is the one who dangled partnership, because of my work. Best of all, I found you, the man who guided my escape after I was being torn by vengeance."

"I see confidence in your eyes." Kyle dipped his head the remaining inch and his lips caressed hers.

"Piersall and Fernley didn't appear cocky while being loaded into the patrol car," Roy declared from the doorway. "Oh, sorry to interrupt."

"Thank you for restraining me from decking him, Dad."

"Had to. I wanted to club him, too," Roy said. He stepped into the office and picked up the caged duck. "Julia Bell keeps ducks as pets, I'll see if she'll keep him." He headed toward the door. "Betsy's giving a statement, and she sent Corrin her apology."

"Maybe she'll wise up after being used by the rich degenerate," Corrin said.

Kyle squeezed her hand. "They must've thought Betsy could get intel while we were on the foundation board together. I'll alert the chairman to Piersall's threat. Don't worry, the town would do a fundraiser for Corey."

No one had extra thousands to spare. She wouldn't jeopardize the last round of treatments, and wouldn't work for MFB, no matter what. Think lawyer, she told herself and thumped her temple. "I appreciate your ideas. Here's mine. We'll offer Piersall a deal."

A deal with the devil.

~ ~ ~

Corrin's insides twisted into more strands than were in Whinny's lead rope. She shifted on the metal chair in the prison's visitation room. Cold reality hit. She needed her plan to work.

Roy sat with his customary composure, studying the documents provided by Piersall's lawyer, who faced him from across the metal table. Kyle sat on her right, his arm draped protectively across the back of her chair.

A buzzer jarred them both.

The prisoners' door opened, and Piersall stumbled out, sporting a purple bulge under one eye. A burly guard pushed him into the chair next to his lawyer.

Roy sat back and folded his arms across his chest. "We've met with Deputy Prosecuting Attorney Adams." He nodded to a man seated at the end of the table. "Your client is charged with being an accessory to Kyle's attempted murder. Your proposal indicates you want that charge dropped and your client disassociated with both the evidence-tampering duck affair, and his bribing of a government official and a realtor. All you are willing to offer is a recommendation to the foundation to continue current drug trials."

"Correct," said his lawyer.

Corrin placed her hands on the edge of the table. "I contacted the other woman from the boat. The statutes may be up, but we can bring it all forward in the press. The timing is perfect with continuous resurgences of the #Me-Too movement. Here's our offer." She pushed papers with bulleted sections to each of them.

Corrin's childhood friend had agreed that additional jail time lost out to Corey's health. She read aloud from her copy. "The attempted murder charge will be downgraded to a lesser charge. Your family will continue funding the drug trials for a minimum of five more years. You'll offer the land fronting Sunrise Lake back to the original owners at a thirty percent discount. If they decline, the same purchase price is offered to Stan Johnson, who owns the property where the mineshaft sits. Refuse, and Emma Springs residents are determined you'll rot for the longest time possible."

Piersall's lawyer stared at the page.

She sat back. "If prior to pleading, you have a problem with paying the $500,000 restitution to me and also the other victim from the boat, I suggest you consult with MFB. They were aware of my concerns from the onset, in print."

Roy's head jerked, and Kyle cleared his throat. Neither were aware of the amount she'd requested.

Kyle put his hand under the table and gave her knee a quick squeeze.

"This offer lasts until 5 p.m. Friday," Corrin stated. "On Monday we meet with the DA."

Roy stood. "You can reach us at our office." He shoved a card across the table. Both their names boldly stood out atop a muted photo of Sunrise Lake.

Kyle grasped Corrin's hand, supporting her as if he knew her muscles felt as brittle as thin ice.

Section doors clanked shut behind them. Corrin squinted in daylight.

"Good job, partner." Roy stopped at the Jeep. "They'd be fools not to take your offer."

"Our offer." Corrin's brain whirled. Seeing Piersall behind bars produced emotions she'd need to process. Later. She hopped into the back seat of the Jeep. "One thing troubles me, though. You're certain the mountain man, Stan, has enough money to buy the rest of his hillside reaching to the lake?"

"Stan bought stocks before he bid goodbye to civilization in the early 1980s." Kyle said. "His favorite food's an apple, and that logo caught his eye."

"Another benefit of eating fruit," she tried to sound less nervous than she felt.

Kyle nodded. "Tom Morley contacted Stan when the zoning issues started, and he's willing to pay any amount to protect his privacy." He aimed the Jeep onto the familiar highway home.

One last hurdle and she'd truly relax. "What will we do if Piersall refuses?"

"I have faith he won't," Roy stated. "You deserve millions in compensation."

"I wouldn't turn it down."

If they won, hopefully they'd approve her plan to use any money that Corey didn't need to benefit the community. If they lost . . .

CHAPTER 20

Two days had passed since they'd met Piersall in jail.

When would they decide? Corrin fretted while she washed her soup bowl.

Whinny ran to the door and nickered.

Kyle's familiar knock sounded.

She pulled it open. His shoulders drooped, and a letter dangled from his hand.

"Is that a response from the foundation about Corey?" She tugged him inside.

"No, thank God. They've denied my home equity loan. My house is too old."

Corrin swallowed. "If Piersall doesn't take our offer, I could sell my car to raise cash for Corey."

He lifted her chin. "I can't believe they'd discontinue Corey's medicine. I've been playing phone tag with the person who can verify the duration of her treatment. I left Dad's number as an alternate."

She leaned her head on his shoulder. "I should've asked for less compensation."

"No. You deserve every penny. Promise me you won't dwell on things you view as past mistakes. I'll do the same." He swiveled her bracelet to the opal. "Mom loved opals. A rock matrix once surrounded your richly hued stone, kind of how you protected yourself on your own. That's not true anymore."

"I know, but it's hard for me to ask for help."

He ran his fingertips along her chin and cradled her face. "The town's willing to step forward with support and polish off those last grains to let your full opalescent radiance shine."

She pulled his body against hers. "Where would I be without you?"

"A question I never want you to answer." His kisses pressed softly at first, then demanded.

She untucked his shirt and ran her fingers across his muscled chest.

Whinny grabbed Kyle's cuff, then let go, and bumped his hip pocket.

"Hey, you can wait a second for a treat," Corrin scolded.

Kyle shook his head. "My fault, I created a little carrot addict."

"I'm developing other addictions. I couldn't help myself just now," Corrin shyly smiled up at him. "Sorry."

He pressed his forehead to hers, then gently bumped noses with her. "Don't ever be sorry. I want to marry you and be together."

Do it, her heart sang out. "Let's pick a date." She grasped his hand.

His smile could brighten a cave. "Really?" He lifted her off her feet and let her slide down his chest. "Pick a date. Three wonderful words! I can't wait to tell Dad."

~ ~ ~

Corrin smoothed her hair while they entered Roy's house. The hall mirror showed a blush on her cheeks.

Iris stepped out of the kitchen "Surprise! The mountain pass has been closed to travelers. Neither of us wanted to be alone all winter, so I caught a flight."

"Wow!" Corrin hugged her aunt. "I'm excited."

"Me, too," Roy proclaimed. He kissed Iris on the cheek. "We're going to get married at the end of next month. By then the weather should allow the Patten family to make the journey with a moving truck full of my soon-to-be wife's things."

Corrin looked into Kyle's hopeful eyes and grabbed his hand. She squeezed, and he squeezed back.

Kyle leaned close to her ear. "Being married next month would be another wish come true."

"Wishes and hopes, ponies and ropes, all tied in a neat little bundle for my love." Corrin kissed his cheek and turned to face Iris and Roy. "Are you okay with a double ceremony?"

"Yes!" Roy and Iris exclaimed at the same time.

Kyle gave his dad a bear hug. "You two planned this, didn't you?"

"We'll never tell." Iris hugged Corrin. "Your smile is back and soon everyone else's will be too. It'll be a family reunion."

"Family," Roy pressed his palm onto his forehead. "In all the excitement, I forgot. A man called for Kyle this morning. Assured me that Corey's treatments will continue on an as-needed basis."

"That's wonderful news!" Corrin declared.

"If Corey keeps progressing, John will help Grace get her kids here," Kyle said. "From what he's told me during phone calls, he doesn't stray far from them."

"You girls start planning and send me the bills." Roy put his arms around Iris and Corrin.

"Aunt Iris, we're B2Bs! I'm excited to bursting." Corrin declared.

"Me too, honey. Me, too," Iris agreed.

Corrin let out a deep breath. She'd seen more of her family in the last two months than in the prior ten years. Their future included sharing holidays and birthdays.

One more round of good luck and Kyle would get another wish.

~ ~ ~

Hiking on a Friday. No one would've believed Corrin Patten would own a pair of waffle stompers or a packsaddle for her mini horse. The wonderful additions sat in her kitchen, ready for her to enjoy a day off.

Her doorbell rang.

She smiled and opened the door.

Her black pony bounced free of Bobby's grip and snuggled her furry cheek against Corrin's knee. She automatically scratched between the soft ears.

"Thanks, Bobby," she handed two dollars to the little boy who'd become her favorite horse handler. "Whinny and I appreciate you providing daily exercise. She's gaining muscle."

Bobby flexed the bump in his thin arm. "See mine?"

"Nice guns, warrior. You'll need them when she sees something of interest."

"Yup. She's almost ready," Bobby grinned.

She unclipped Whinny's lead line. "Ready for what?"

"Whoops. I mean. always ready." Bobby's face reddened. "Gotta go, Commander." He flicked a salute and skipped out of her driveway.

"Bye," she called, then pursed her lips. He'd reddened as if he'd spilled a secret.

Kids always had secrets. She opened the refrigerator. Food mattered on her first picnic as an engaged woman.

She slipped two bottles of root beer into pockets on the end of the soft-sided hamper, loaded in a stack of thick turkey sandwiches, and slid in her sketch pad.

Kyle's promised cupcakes would take up the remaining space. "Don't worry, Whinny, I have plenty of baby carrots and water for you." She laced up her boots.

Whinny brushed her head against Corrin.

"Kyle must be running late. Let's go find him." She strapped the packsaddle to the colt's back and secured the hamper. The mini horse had grown several inches since they'd first met and now Dr. Bell had approved of very light loads on her broader back.

She checked her phone, then stuck it in her pocket. Piersall's lawyer had three hours to call and accept the offer. At MFB, it would've been finalized by noon.

She couldn't match Whinny's enthusiastic trot while they crossed the yard to Kyle's back door. She knocked once, waited, and knocked louder.

The door opened. "Hi," Kyle rubbed his eyes, then gave Whinny a pat on the head. "Sorry, I sat for a moment and lost track of the time. The short shift at the hospital last night turned into an all-nighter."

He yawned and pointed to her hiking boots. "You're ready for your first foray into the forest." He attached a rolled-up blanket to Whinny's pack.

"We can do it another time. You look beat," she offered.

He pulled a package from the counter. "Nope, I've got the requisite cupcakes, and I'm ready to go."

Kyle perked up while he described the patients he'd met during his shift. At the crest of the first real slope separating the meadow from the foothills, he pulled Whinny to a stop. "If you don't mind a shorter hike today, I'd settle for this view."

Corrin studied the woods behind them, the meandering stream below, and the lake where her cottage and his home sat. She took a deep breath of crisp, pine-scented air. "This is a perfect spot. I brought my sketch pad. Maybe after lunch I can do a quick drawing?"

"And I can grab a nap." Kyle kissed her cheek. "Sorry I'm not in full form." He removed Whinny's packsaddle and unfurled the blanket.

"We've got the rest of our lives to be in full whatever you please." She laid out lunch and enjoyed every bite of her first official picnic.

Whinny grazed nearby.

Kyle raised a pink frosted cupcake. "Here's to my beautiful fiancée." His lips brushed hers in the sweetest, most endearing kiss to date. "Mind if I recharge with twenty winks while you draw?"

"Not at all." While he reclined on the blanket, she pulled out her pad and pencils. She outlined a heart on the corners of the paper and filled in the edges with the lake, the old snag where real, unpainted wood ducks lived, and his house. Soon it would be her home, too. She drew short strokes for grass.

Kyle rolled toward her, propped on one elbow. "Snoozing helped."

She pointed skyward. "I enjoy watching the eagles catching downdrafts to the lake at dusk."

"Dusk!" He checked his watch. "Egad, I slept longer than I'd planned."

"What's the rush?"

"Dad's taking Iris for dinner at the Springs Cafe, and he hoped we'd join them. I forgot to mention it earlier."

Odd for social butterfly, Kyle, to forget. He must be tired. "You bet. It's the Friday night fish fry, isn't it?"

"Yup. Dad wants to get a good seat. We need to trot downhill and change our clothes. I don't suppose you'd wear my favorite angora sweater?"

"I honor requests," she said.

They packed up and headed to her cottage.

Kyle left her at the door with a brief kiss. "I'll put Whinny back in her paddock. See you in five?"

Roy wouldn't care if they were a little late. "I'll do my best." She closed the door and walked to her bedroom.

Her phone rang. The screen showed a Seattle area code and an unfamiliar number. Nervous energy pulsed in her belly. Had Piersall accepted the deal? "Hello."

~ ~ ~

Corrin had barely brushed out her hair when Kyle reappeared. Containing her excitement to announce the great news in Roy's presence took extra vigilance.

Hand in hand, she and Kyle entered the cafe. A huge *HAPPY ENGAGEMENT X 2* banner hung across the sidewall.

Corrin stopped and scanned the room. Every table contained smiling residents of Emma Springs. Outside the kitchen, they'd set up a buffet with assorted covered dishes and crockpots. Aromas of baked beans, beef, and apple pie scented the air.

Iris stepped beside her. "You're as surprised by our shared celebration as I am."

"Piersall accepted, Iris," she whispered. "I can't wait to tell Roy and Kyle."

Clapping erupted from the room.

"These folks cooked up something special for you two ladies," Roy proposed, and led Iris to a table with a bouquet of flowers and four place settings.

"Shall we join them?" Kyle asked.

Bobby ran to Corrin. "Please can you open the big gift first?"

"Ahh, if it's okay with your folks," Corrin stammered. "This party's a wonderful gift."

Bobby rushed to his mom, and then dashed to the corner, and stopped at a five-foot covered mound the size of a dining room table.

"Every person in this room contributed to these presents. That's how special you and Iris are to us," Kyle whispered in her ear.

Bobby approached, pulling the big bundle. Corrin spotted a wheel larger than a bicycle tire. Was he towing a tall wheelbarrow underneath the intricate patchwork quilt?

"Just a moment, Commander." Bobby set a long metal bar down, picked up a ribbon-bound book from atop the quilt, handed it to Iris, and then returned to Corrin.

His grin brought goosebumps to her arms. "I can help you get it uncovered." His eyes shone with excitement.

"Please do." They lifted the quilt together.

"A mini pony-sized trailer," she murmured. Carved finials adorned the front, and a covered box tall enough to accommodate Whinny had her name painted on the side. A rubber mat covered the floor. Tears wet her eyes. She placed her hand on her brooch and turned to the crowd. "I'm a speechless lawyer."

Bobby grinned. "It's the perfect size for your Firebird to pull."

Corrin pulled him into a hug. "You've been training Whinny to go in and out, haven't you?"

"Yes, ma'am. And she's smart enough to know there are adventures ahead with you. We didn't force her inside. Mom took things slowly and bought a hay bag for the front to keep her busy." Bobby slipped her a greeting card.

She kissed his cheek. "What a thoughtful gift."

Iris stepped to her side and opened the handmade book and flipped through the pages. "Thank you all. I'll be cashing in on these coupons and truly look forward to coffee and apple cake with Julia Bell, the load of mulched manure from Mase, the hour of rototilling from Mr. McPherson, and all the other wonderful gifts you've welcomed me with." She held the book to her chest. "Thank you."

"Now it's my turn." Corrin opened her card. "Stan, thank you for the wonderful decorative carving on the front. Sam, the offer to install a trailer hitch is appreciated. Kat, your heirloom quilt will keep me warm on future chilly days at the barn or if we go on an outing. Julia, writing Whinny's name for all to see was a great idea. And Grant, I'll thank the students who constructed the trailer in person. There's a long list of folks who contributed, so I'll walk around and thank you individually. Whinny and I thank you for your thoughtfulness."

Kyle took her hand. "It took a village to convince these fabulous women to move to Emma Springs. Dad and I want to express our gratitude." He clapped and Roy moved alongside Iris.

"Ditto, son. I've been told to announce dinner," Roy beamed. "Join me?" he asked Iris.

"In a second, Roy. Hold on, folks." Iris waved her hand and then leaned in close to Corrin. "Don't wait. Tell them now, honey." The room quieted.

Corrin's throat went dry. She swallowed. "I have another announcement. I requested money as part of the settlement against Piersall."

"You may want to purchase a double pony trailer," Mase teased.

"No, Mase," Corrin said seriously. "A good community requires a great attending physician, and we're blessed with Kyle." She kissed his cheek. "Wise people looking for a home for their family want nearby medical care. The Rural Health Information Hub of Montana lists grants and monies available to fund rural clinics."

Kyle's head swiveled toward her.

"Roy, if you agree, the half million dollars from Piersall will be seed money to upgrade Kyle's space. Iris suggested we name it after one of the most beloved residents, the Flor Werner Memorial Clinic."

Cheers and whoops surrounded them.

Roy swiped a tear from his eye and pulled Iris into a hug. "Thank you. Thank you." He threw out a thumbs up.

Kyle clutched Corrin to his chest, gently kissed her lips, and then released her. "You, my love, have made all my dreams come true."

"As have you, Kyle." She placed her palm on her brooch and gazed at the room filled with smiling faces, then out the café windows to Sunrise Lake.

Kyle lovingly stood beside her, ducks swam in pristine water, and she'd made the best decision ever— to let go of the past and welcome the many facets of love into her life.

You know you're in Montana when . . . you're home.

I hope you enjoyed my story, and I'd appreciate it if you'd write an honest review on Goodreads or Amazon. Celebrate Corrin and Kyle's wedding in Emma Springs with a copy of the free epilogue to *Torn by Vengeance*, at www. sallybrandle.com. If you'd like to know how Elon and Rane meet in Emma Springs, keep reading for an excerpt from *The Targeted Pawn*.

Happy trails,
Sally

From *The Targeted Pawn*

By Sally Brandle

Some games are played to a deadly end.

… Four hundred miles and twenty-four hours between her and Tim wasn't enough. Elon checked her rearview mirror. Not good she'd overslept at the motel in Eastern Idaho, but she'd be safely in Montana for a late breakfast.

She lifted the travel mug of tea she'd brewed in the motel room, inhaling the scent from her stash of Mom's recipe for a mind-clearing herbal remedy. Eighty-mile gusts couldn't blow through her brain and dispel today's double shot of doubt.

The spicy aroma intensified while her mouth drew in the warm liquid, then bitterness assaulted her taste buds. Her eyes shot around the interior of the old car, not locating a place to spit. She forced a swallow and returned the mug to the cup holder. One of the kids must've used it for chocolate milk or a smoothie and put it away dirty. Cleanliness wasn't imperative to nineteen-year-old boys. The foul aftertaste coated her tongue. Breath mints, next stop, she decided, and drove another half hour through farmland backed by stands of trees.

A tricycle bell dinged from her phone in the dash holder. She grinned. Jeremy's tone, technically her first born. "Hey kiddo, what's up?"

"Wanted to see how you're doing. Hope Old Gold's not tarnished," he teased.

"Car's running great, thanks to Hans and Mastercard. Anything else?"

"Yeah. I need to buy another textbook. As of an hour ago, Dr. Deceitful cut off our credit card."

The jerk. Tim deserved the neighbor's nickname, but she shouldn't have told the kids. "Did you speak to your father directly?"

"He didn't answer his phone, so I biked to our house. I mean his house. A new Beemer sat in the drive. His latest ho' answered the door with a smirk on her scrawny face and a key fob in her hands. She looks like the poster child for a feed the starving children campaign."

Elon squeezed the worn shifter knob. The ink hadn't dried on the petition for divorce papers and the latest fling occupied the only home her boys ever lived in. "Jeremy, don't call her names."

"Call 'em as I see 'em," he snapped. "You should be driving the Beemer."

Tim's newest toothpick could have him, the car, and the house. She would have been the kids' roommate if they had chosen their family home and not to live in her folks' old condo, cheaper and closer to the University of Washington campus. Her arms felt like lead weights. "We don't know what your father told the young woman, so don't judge her."

"Regardless of scrawny's, ah, profession, you need to quit overlooking our paternal unit's dark side. Brandon told me you fell. We're betting he messed up the basement stairs, that's why you crash-landed. You could've broken your neck. The last few months, he's grown colder, if that's possible. Did he know you planned to grab stuff at the house before you left town yesterday?"

Her pulse spiked. *Tim weakened the boards. No. Jeremy was the dramatic twin.* "He'd left paperwork for me." She took deep breaths. "I'm not going to jump to conclusions. You shouldn't either, he's your father. Doctors swear an oath to save people, not commit murder."

"Wake up, Mom. He must've figured you'd go downstairs."

Not the time to mention Tim's note inviting her to grab a suitcase in the basement. In an emergency, they might need to contact him. "It's an old house with rotted stairs. I should've noticed them." She grabbed the tea and took a slug without thinking, winced at the flavor, and wedged the mug out of sight between two bags on the floorboard. "Brandon and I took those stairs multiple times before we moved out to start at the UW. No creaks or issues. We think he'll track you to your new job out of spite. Try to hamstring you."

What a screwed-up life, when her own children thought their father capable of harming her, no matter how crappy a parent he'd been. Besides, greed seemed a more plausible reason for Tim to want her to remain in Seattle, broken limbs or not. She'd tell Corrin, to add potential ammo to her lawyer arsenal. *Wait, what had Jeremy just said? Tim might track her?* "I didn't leave a forwarding address, so he can't find me."

"Your cell can. Soon as you're able, stick a paperclip in the little drawer on the side of your phone to remove the SIM card holding your contacts, then smash it. Promise?"

Of course, she hadn't thought of a tracking app. She slumped into the seat. "I promise. He'll drop us from his calling plan anyway. If you need me, check the emergency list on the refrigerator door. I left the ranch's phone number. Should arrive there this afternoon. Wish me luck."

"You'll do fine melting iron. When we've screwed up, your mom-glower burned us a few times," Jeremy joked. "Seriously. You can do anything you put your mind to. Words you taught us. And we'll work part-time."

Warmth filled her. Confident young men had replaced her dyslexic and bullied little boys. "Taking a job on campus may be in your future. Not yet though. You guys are my pride and joy. Don't ever forget."

"We won't. I better finish the paper for my three o'clock Freshman English torture session. Jeeze, I hate that class."

Damn Tim for dragging the twins into his ugly exodus from their marriage when they needed to concentrate on college. "You're a born storyteller. Now you'll learn how to craft your tales into print. Don't worry about me. Love—" The cell signal died. "You both," she whispered, and pressed her fingers onto the etched grooves in the locket.

The challenges of raising children flowed in and out like tides. How much did Jeremy's book cost? Regardless, she needed the job to pay these kinds of expenses and bank money for their winter quarter. Just in case.

Her jaw clenched. A new BMW cost enough for two years expenses at the UW. If Tim really bought the car for his latest mistress, she'd love to roll it over his feet. The pounding in her chest intensified. Boxes in the back seat rattled when the tires hit the centerline rumble strip.

She corrected the steering and slowed the car, preparing to pull over. *Don't let anger at Tim cause an accident.* Deep breaths cleared her head and steadied her hands again. Her brain kept mulling over Jeremy's assumptions about their dad's capabilities.

History didn't lie. Twenty years ago, Tim persuaded her father into purchasing the house as a surprise to her to celebrate their engagement, then duped the closing agent to list only his name on the title. And she'd been clueless until last week.

The bad taste from the tea lingered in her mouth, intensifying the urge to vomit. Or Tim's deceit made her physically sick. How naïve she'd been—letting her high school's prom king trick her from the start. He'd preyed on an insecure sophomore, and she'd fallen for his fake lines as he weaseled his way into her life.

Her spine stiffened. No more lying down for Dr. Tim Hardy to stomp on her, in his custom-made, Italian loafers, on his way out the door to a hotel rendezvous. She'd shielded young Jeremy and Brandon from Tim's indifference to them, now she'd fight him for every nickel.

But first, she needed gas. Thank goodness Corrin had also suggested carrying cash.

She filled the tank, bought munchies, and walked out into sunny fall weather, biting into a sweet snack cake. Eggs and bacon took too long, and fake frosting and the orange juice diminished the icky feeling of sandpaper in her throat.

Her eyes dropped to her worn tires—even after the scolding by her mechanic, buying replacements came after Jeremy's book and a burner phone.

Getting a job in order to hold out for half the value of Tim's medical practice in the divorce had seemed a great idea a few days ago, before the stairs mishap and the ticket. How dirty would Tim play?

Give it a rest. Jeremy's worries equaled nothing more than teenage dramatics. Tim possessed no interest in tracking her, she reasoned, and got in her car. She adjusted the rearview mirror, and her sleeve fell to her elbow, exposing the ugly bruise from the fall.

~ ~ ~

Fractured plans grated on Tim worse than an office full of babies needing surgery with no available hospital space. He stuck his phone in his pocket, locked his clinic office, and left through the back door.

Elon's spotty cell signal hadn't returned for an hour since she'd driven farther east this morning, and now he'd delayed two scheduled patient checks. No leisurely lunch today.

Only a stupid, stubborn, lard brain would've fled the state.

Getting rid of her should've been easy. He walked to his parking space. Sliding into his Porsche, he drove the familiar route to Tacoma Children's Hospital.

The faint scent of Jasmine's flowery perfume on the scarf she'd left on the seat made him smile. He'd soon share his life beside the right woman. Years of sacrifice wouldn't be derailed by an old car piloted by a worthless haus frau.

He patted his blazer's chest pocket holding the Hawaiian vacation brochure, picturing in his mind the lithe figure of a bikini-clad Jasmine. They'd be celebrating by this time next month.

Tapping the gas pedal, he flew through a yellow light and turned into the familiar lot. The hospital cast a shadow onto parking spaces reserved for doctors. He wheeled into the last empty one and climbed out.

Thoughts of desperate mothers expecting immediate help increased his steps. Once his new building went up, he'd oversee a team of surgeons ready to help kids in a state-of-the-art facility. After clipping on his hospital ID badge, he refreshed his phone screen.

No blasted tracer signal meant the time had arrived to initiate procedure mode. He clicked on his phone's note app and quickly tapped a plan. *Check if the stolen car report went out of state. Reschedule appointments for potential Montana trip.* He stopped when the screen became blurry and closed his eyes, anticipating his impaired retinas to flash the awful shimmering lights.

The kaleidoscope began. *Fate be damned.* He'd worked hard to provide for Elon and the offspring she'd wanted— and he'd sure as hell earned his dream life without her dead weight dragging him under.

~ ~ ~

Elon's Mercedes crested another rise in lord-only-knew where Montana. She adjusted the sun visor to view the first sign of human existence in over an hour. The shiny red pickup ahead slowed to a crawl in the valley below.

A silver silhouette of a reclining nude woman decorated one black mud flap; the other side advertised BABE TRADER written in shiny chrome. The truck's passenger door opened. A bald guy leaned out and tossed a live animal as if it were trash.

Elon gasped. A dog with its legs braced for impact landed on scraggly tufts of grass.

Tires squealed, and the truck sped off.

"Scumbags!" Her pulse spiked, every impulse screaming to give chase and ram decency into the creeps. Instead, she stomped on the clutch and brake while her hand shifted.

Her focus moved to the poor dog. The hollow place in her heart knew exactly how the animal felt—chucked out after tolerating disrespect for too long.

The black and white ball of matted fur hunkered near the ragged edge of the road.

Border collie? She steered to the shoulder and parked. Her fingers shook while she shifted her suitcase in the trunk to locate the emergency blanket and a granola bar.

Sweet aromas wafted in the clean air from the unwrapped peanut butter snack.

The cringing dog raised its nose. A silver choke chain jingled on its shaking body.

"It's going to be all right," Elon whispered. "I got thrown out, too." She scowled, picturing Tim waving his single owner deed to the house in her face. "Come on, pup."

The dog took a tentative step, stopped, and tucked her tail, as if expecting a kick.

"You're safe with me." She pitched the snack bar between the dog's front paws. "The way you flew out of that truck brought to mind a furry, fallen angel."

Chocolatey brown eyes studied Elon's face before it snatched the granola bar and swallowed it in a single gulp.

She took slow steps to within a couple feet of the quivering animal. "If you're hurt, I'll find a vet." Beyond the dog stretched a horizon dotted by pine trees and sloping foothills shaded by fluffy, cotton shaped clouds. Brown fall grassland stretched endlessly ahead, blemished only by snaking blacktop. Too bad life's circumstances wouldn't allow pooch or savior to enjoy the beauty right now.

"I'm going to carry you to the car and pray you're not injured." Elon gradually approached the dog, draped the blanket over it's back, and lifted. "Easy now, little Angel." The animal quieted in her arms. "You don't weigh much for your size. Didn't those thugs feed you?"

Inside the car, the dog slunk against the bucket seat, one speckled paw gripping the leather cushion.

"May I call you Angel?" she asked quietly and patted the seat. "You can lie down, Angel."

The dog dropped to a tense crouch.

Curses on the men who'd do this to an innocent animal, and curses on Tim! She grabbed her phone from the console, bent a paperclip, and removed the tiny SIM card, as Jeremy had instructed. Her pulse quickened as she gently shut the door and stepped to the back bumper. She raised her hand over her head and chucked the cell to the ground.

The case crashed against gravel. Field crickets stopped chirping.

"Trace that, Tim Hardy," she announced, and stomped her heel onto the screen, cracking the glass. Sun glared off the shiny pieces. She pulled a tissue from her pocket, collected the shards, and dropped it in the corner of the trunk. Her eyes caught sight of her wedding band. Should she pitch the meaningless symbol?

She slid the plain silver ring to her knuckle, then stopped and moved it back in place. As much as she despised Tim, she'd decided to keep it on to prove to the boys she took vows seriously, even though his view of marriage equaled access to her parents' money. Also, wearing it might continue to ward off unwanted advances. Once burned, twice wary.

Angel raised her head when she climbed inside. "Probably should've waited until we found the ranch. Ah well, service is spotty here, and severing another connection to Tim felt great. Not like he'd ever care where I went." A niggling suspicion told her he did.

She placed her hand next to the dog's grubby outstretched foot and stroked until no toenails dug into the seat. "We'll be at our new home soon."

Angel's warm doggy tongue licked the top of Elon's hand, easing nerves rattled to brittle by events of the last weeks. Her teary eyes met the pup's timid dark ones, and a bond of undeserved humiliation passed between them.

"We're both due for a fresh start on a farm." The Mercedes' engine hummed to life after she twisted her key.

Not a pickup or hay-hauler appeared on the two-lane highway.

Quick glances in the review mirror helped her fight the creepy sensation she wasn't alone while the car covered the last fifty miles. Still, fine hairs rose on her forearms.

"I see our landmark," her hand trembled, down shifting.

Angel tilted her head, one black ear cocked and the other flopped at an angle.

"It's an old stove my employer described in his letter. Those two 'Cs' welded side by side on the warming shelf stand for Calderon Cattle."

The skills she'd learned to create metal sculptures in high school were rusty at best. And basic. And lifting broken machinery took strength. "Saints preserve us."

Her hands stuck to the wheel as she turned onto the dusty lane, passing a mailbox welded to one end of the boxy cast iron antique.

Baking and cooking might save her. Years ago, her grandma used a similar wood burning stove at their cabin to bake the best bread on earth. Elon had first learned cooking secrets at her side. Memories of her loving parents and grandparents had forged to steel in her brain. Thoughts of their harmonious marriages had kept her trying to please Tim after she'd discovered his infidelity.

Nothing had dazzled him, but fresh makeup never hurt during a first impression. Throwing the car in neutral, and stepping on the brake, she fished out blush and lipstick and applied a liberal dose.

Her hand hesitated before she shifted into first. Quit stalling, she scolded herself and stepped on the gas. At a curve, she veered left in time to dodge a branch hanging from the last tree on the hill.

Below sat a rambling log house, a sizable barn, and a square building attached to a carport capable of holding a couple of tall RVs. The structures sat adjacent to an open field. Cattle grazed in the background.

Her decades old car, engineered for the autobahn, bumped on rutted gravel leading down a gentle slope. She parked at the edge of a large corral, beside a shiny white truck. Edward Bell, DVM stood out in black letters on the cab door. Her fingers relaxed.

"Stay here, Angel." She patted the dog and lowered the windows. Dust surrounded her feet as she approached an assortment of men outside a wooden corral, standing with their backs to her. Not a Stetson or baseball cap swiveled her way. All heads faced the activity in the corral.

She stood on tip toes. On the other side of the split rail fence, a mountain-sized bull lay flopped on the ground, a wide canvas sling around his belly. Its dusty head was cradled by a broad-shouldered man. His cowboy hat topped jet-black hair and a rugged, handsome face, right down to the square jaw and chiseled cheeks.

It was a scene straight out of a Levi's ad—the boot cut style. She blinked and noticed a gray-haired man wearing a dark blue jumpsuit, crouched over the animal's hind leg. A stethoscope dangled from his chest pocket. He held a needled syringe in one hand, balanced a probe in the other, and used his pinky to adjust settings on a portable machine sitting near his feet.

Elon glanced at the blurry screen image, wiped her palms on her jeans, and stepped closer to the onlookers. "I may be able to help adjust the image for clarity," she offered quietly.

The guy ahead of her flinched and turned to face her. "Hey, there's a gal here who says she can help," he shouted.

Grubby male faces jerked around. A ruddy-faced younger man looked owl-eyed surprised.

"Might be able to help," she corrected in a shaky voice. "I've only assisted with ultrasound images of babies."

The man in the jumpsuit raised his head. "Bones are bones, Miss. To a doctor or a veterinarian." He waved the probe and threw her a relieved smile. "Come on in. I'd appreciate an extra pair of experienced hands."

Pungent diesel and manure scents radiated from nearby blue jeans and Carhartt's.

"Excuse me," she said, then turned sideways and shuffled between two men.

A stocky guy in greasy, blue-striped bib overalls swiveled his barrel chest and gave her the once over. A low wolf-whistle pierced the air. "Nice ass . . . istant, doc."

Snickers came from the group until the cowboy holding the bull's head shot them a glare fierce enough to send a sane person running for cover.

The foul-mouthed brute in bibs kept staring. Heat rose to her face. She'd had it up to her hairline with men—doctors, lawyers, and creeps in red pickups.

"Clear a path, boys." Beads of perspiration lined the vet's wrinkled brow. "A doctor's office you say?"

"Correct. I know an ultrasound from ultra-crude." She tugged the back of her wrinkled, crimson-colored blouse over her butt and wiggled through the gap in the wooden fence rails. Barely.

"I appreciate you already." The vet raised the syringe. "Serum I'm injecting needs to flow precisely into the fracture above the bull's fetlock."

"Not familiar with a fetlock. Let's see if we can clarify the picture." She bent over the machine and adjusted two dials until a clear image appeared.

"Yes, that's it. Perfect." The vet nodded. His eyes remained on the monitor while he moved the probe. "Now, I can administer the BoneGlu." He poked into the cow's hide and pushed the plunger of the fist-sized syringe. The screen displayed liquid oozing into a bone break.

The doctor removed the long needle and wiped the patch of shaved hide. "You had excellent timing, Miss. Next, I'll splint and wrap the area." He threw a two-fingered salute to the cowboy kneeling at the front end of the animal. "Rane, you can relax."

Rane, as in Rane Calderon? No way! Elon swallowed a groan. Tall, dark, and deadly described her new boss. And he had to be within a couple years of her age.

Rane gently patted the sleeping bull's head. "Thanks, Ed. Tomo deserves a fighting chance. Glad the BoneGlu inventor sourced and overnighted enough. I'll tell him how it works on a two-thousand-pound patient."

The veterinarian tipped the control pad of the machine and snapped it shut. "Good idea. And a huge thanks to your guest. Watch for signs Tomo's waking from the sedative in thirty minutes."

"Got it." Rane's attention shifted to Elon. "To whom do I owe gratitude?" Narrowed eyes pierced into her—cold, confident, and demanding an answer.

She'd saved the day, so why'd his glare mimic Tim's perennial disdain? "I'm Elon, the welder and cook you hired last week."

A chorus of chuckles and guffaws erupted from the men. "And I bet she isn't kidding, boss," one of them spouted.

Not hardly. Elon wiggled back between the boards and spanked dust from her new pair of stretchy jeans, doing their best to chafe her legs.

Rane stood up, towering at least six foot three. He pressed his lips into a sour line and let his gaze rest momentarily on her bust. "Elon isn't a woman's name," he stated.

Murmurs stopped. Men leaning on the fence backed away, creating clouds of sifted earth.

Elon brushed off the front of her loose shirt. Not enough miles on the map to drive away from nasty confrontations. Wasn't the first time she'd defended her name, wouldn't be the last. "I guess my great-grandmother didn't abide by that rule." She met his dark, russet-colored eyes. "This Elon isn't related to any muskrats or electric cars."

Rane issued a snort, put his hands on the top rail, and vaulted to her side. He threw off an intimidating shadow. "I'm Rane Calderon, owner of this spread," he announced, as if she hadn't realized that disturbing fact. "We'll settle this in the kitchen." He stood straight backed—the teacher pointing to the dunce chair and indicated the house with his thumb. "Thanks for assisting Ed," he murmured.

How gracious of him. Well, Angel rated higher than an irritated bull coddler. "You're welcome." She flashed her brightest smile. "I'd appreciate a moment with the veterinarian before we meet, Mr. Calderon."

"Make it quick." Rane's stomping broke the pin-drop quiet as he headed toward a wraparound porch.

About the Author

Sally Brandle is an award winning author of edgy, sweetly intimate love stories, providing a heartwarming, page-turning escape. Sally left a career as an industrial baking instructor to bring to life stories motivating readers to trust their instincts. Her rescue pets are her companions during long spells of writing. Afternoon thought sessions are spent riding on the wind with her thirty-four-year-old Quarter Horse.

Sign up for her newsletter at www.sallybrandle.com

www.ingramcontent.com/pod-product-compliance
Lightning Source LLC
Chambersburg PA
CBHW070734190726
48292CB00002B/261